TO SAVE A WORLD

A WORLD

THE PLANET SAVERS
THE WORLD WRECKERS
THE WATERFALL

Marion Zimmer Bradley

DAW BOOKS, INC.

DONALD A. WOLLHEIM, FOUNDER

375 Hudson Street, New York, NY 10014

ELIZABETH R. WOLLHEIM
SHEILA E. GILBERT
PUBLISHERS

http://www.dawbooks.com

First Printing, December 2004
1   2   3   4   5   6   7   8   9

DAW TRADEMARK REGISTERED
U.S. PAT. OFF. AND FOREIGN COUNTRIES
—MARCA REGISTRADA.
HECHO EN U.S.A.
PRINTED IN THE U.S.A.

CONTENTS

AUTHOR'S NOTE

There is a momentum to every operation of growth. The Terran Empire, like every process of human endeavor, was geometric rather than linear in this progression. It began with a few isolated star systems and planets; they in turn developed, put forth colonies, and then began to burgeon, effloresce, grow in wild and unrestrained proliferation. Within a thousand years a detached scientist might compare their growth—from a perspective of millennia—to that of the spread of the water hyacinth on Earth in the pre-space days; first an isolated phenomenon, then a study in wild growth, finally a menace that threatened to encompass and crowd out everything else.

Something of the same momentum can be seen in the isolated progress of the Terran Empire on a single planet. First a small scientific outpost, then a colony, a Trade City—

Darkover, isolated at the edge of a galaxy, with a sun so dim that its name was known only in star catalogs, had halted in the first stages of this isolation for a hundred years.

But now—look out, Darkover! For the worldwreckers are coming.

—M.Z.B.

THE PLANET SAVERS

CHAPTER ONE

By the time I got myself all the way awake I thought I was alone. I was lying on a leather couch in a bare white room with huge windows, alternate glass-brick and clear glass. Beyond the clear windows was a view of snow-peaked mountains which turned to pale shadows in the glass-brick.

Habit and memory fitted names to all these. The large office, the orange flare of the great sun, the names of the dimming mountains. But beyond a polished glass desk, a man sat watching me. And I had never seen the man before.

He was chubby, and not young, and had ginger-colored eyebrows and a fringe of ginger-colored hair around the edges of a forehead which was otherwise quite pink and bald. He was wearing a white uniform coat, and the intertwined caduceus on the pocket and on the sleeve proclaimed him a member of the Medical Service attached to the Civilian HQ of the Terran Trade City.

I didn't stop to make all these evaluations

consciously, of course. They were just part of my world when I woke up and found it taking shape around me. The familiar mountains, the familiar sun, the strange man. But he spoke to me in a friendly way, as if it were an ordinary thing to find a perfect stranger sprawled out taking a siesta in here.

"Could I trouble you to tell me your name?"

That was reasonable enough. If I found somebody making himself at home in my office—if I had an office—I'd ask him his name, too. I started to swing my legs to the floor, and had to stop and steady myself with one hand while the room drifted in giddy circles around me.

"I wouldn't try to sit up just yet," he remarked, while the floor calmed down again. Then he repeated, politely but insistently, "Your name?"

"Oh, yes. My name." It was—I fumbled through layers of what felt like gray fuzz, trying to lay my tongue on the most familiar of all sounds, my own name. It was—why, it was—I said, on a high rising note, "This is damn silly," and swallowed. And swallowed again. Hard.

"Calm down," the chubby man said soothingly. That was easier said than done. I stared at him in growing panic and demanded, "But, but, have I had amnesia or something?"

"Or something."

"What's my *name*?"

"Now, now, take it easy! I'm sure you'll remember

it soon enough. You can answer other questions, I'm sure. How old are you?"

I answered eagerly and quickly, "Twenty-two."

The chubby man scribbled something on a card. "Interesting. In-ter-est-ing. Do you know where we are?"

I looked around the office. "In the Terran Headquarters. From your uniform, I'd say we were on Floor 8—Medical."

He nodded and scribbled again, pursing his lips. "Can you—uh—tell me what planet we are on?"

I had to laugh. "Darkover," I chuckled, "I hope! And if you want the names of the moons, or the date of the founding of the Trade City, or something—"

He gave in, laughing with me. "Remember where you were born?"

"On Samarra. I came here when I was three years old—my father was in Mapping and Exploring—" I stopped short, in shock. "He's dead!"

"Can you tell me your father's name?"

"Same as mine. Jay—Jason—" the flash of memory closed down in the middle of a word. It had been a good try, but it hadn't quite worked. The doctor said soothingly, "We're doing very well."

"You haven't told me anything," I accused. "Who are you? Why are you asking me all these questions?"

He pointed to a sign on his desk. I scowled and spelled out the letters. "Randall—Forth—Director—Department—" and Dr. Forth made a note. I said aloud, "It is—Doctor Forth, isn't it?"

"Don't you know?"

I looked down at myself, and shook my head. "Maybe *I'm* Doctor Forth," I said, noticing for the first time that I was also wearing a white coat with the caduceus emblem of Medical. But it had the wrong feel, as if I were dressed in somebody else's clothes. I was no doctor, was I? I pushed back one sleeve slightly, exposing a long, triangular scar under the cuff. Dr. Forth—by now I was sure *he* was Dr. Forth—followed the direction of my eyes.

"Where did you get the scar?"

"Knife fight. One of the bands of those-who-may-not-enter-cities caught us on the slopes, and we—" the memory thinned out again, and I said despairingly, "It's all confused! What's the matter? Why am I up on Medical? Have I had an accident? Amnesia?"

"Not exactly, I'll explain."

I got up and walked to the window, unsteadily because my feet wanted to walk slowly while I felt like bursting through some invisible net and striding there at one bound. Once I got to the window the room stayed put while I gulped down great breaths of warm sweetish air. I said, "I could use a drink."

"Good idea. Though I don't usually recommend it." Forth reached into a drawer for a flat bottle; poured tea-colored liquid into a throwaway cup. After a minute he poured more for himself. "Here. And sit down, man. You make me nervous, hovering like that."

I didn't sit down. I strode to the door and flung it open. Forth's voice was low and unhurried.

"What's the matter? You can go out, if you want to, but won't you sit down and talk to me for a minute? Anyway, where do you want to go?"

The question made me uncomfortable. I took a couple of long breaths and came back into the room. Forth said, "Drink this," and I poured it down. He refilled the cup unasked, and I swallowed that too and felt the hard lump in my middle began to loosen up and dissolve.

Forth said, "Claustrophobia too. Typical," and scribbled on the card some more. I was getting tired of that performance. I turned on him to tell him so, then suddenly felt amused—or maybe it was the liquor working in me. He seemed such a funny little man, shutting himself up inside an office like this and talking about claustrophobia and watching me as if I were a big bug. I tossed the cup into a disposal.

"Isn't it about time for a few of those explanations?"

"If you think you can take it. How do you feel now?"

"Fine." I sat down on the couch again, leaning back and stretching out my long legs comfortably. "What did you put in that drink?"

He chuckled. "Trade secret. Now, the easiest way to explain would be to let you watch a film we made yesterday."

"To watch—" I stopped. "It's your time we're wasting."

He punched a button on the desk, spoke into a mouthpiece. "Surveillance? Give us a monitor on—" he spoke a string of incomprehensible numbers, while I lounged at ease on the couch. Forth waited for an answer, then touched another button and steel louvers closed noiselessly over the windows, blacking them out. The darkness felt oddly more normal than the light, and I leaned back and watched the flickers clear as one wall of the office became a large vision-screen. Forth came and sat beside me on the leather couch, but in the picture Forth was there, sitting at his desk, watching another man, a stranger, walk into the office.

Like Forth, the newcomer wore a white coat with the caduceus emblems. I disliked the man on sight. He was tall and lean and composed, with a dour face set in thin lines. I guessed that he was somewhere in his thirties. Dr. Forth-in-the-film said, "Sit back, doctor," and I drew a long breath, overwhelmed by a curious sensation.

I have been here before. I have seen this happen before.

(And curiously formless I felt. I sat and watched, and I knew I was watching, and sitting. But it was in that dreamlike fashion, where the dreamer at once watches his visions and participates in them . . .)

"Sit down, doctor," Forth said. "Did you bring in the reports?"

Jay Allison carefully took the indicated seat, poised nervously on the edge of the chair. He sat very straight, leaning forward only a little to hand a thick folder of papers across the desk. Forth took it, but didn't open it. "What do you think, Dr. Allison?"

"There is no possible room for doubt." Jay Allison spoke precisely, in a rather high-pitched and emphatic tone. "It follows the statistical pattern for all recorded attacks of forty-eight-year fever—by the way, sir, haven't we any better name than that for this particular disease? The term 'forty-eight-year fever' connotes a fever of forty-eight years' duration, rather than a pandemic recurring every forty-eight years."

"A fever that lasted forty-eight years would be quite a fever," Dr. Forth said with a grim smile. "Nevertheless that's the only name we have so far. Name it and you can have it. Allison's disease?"

Jay Allison greeted this pleasantry with a repressive frown. "As I understand it, the disease cycle seems to be connected somehow with the once-every-forty-eight-years' conjunction of the four moons, which explains why the Darkovans are so superstitious about it. The moons have remarkably eccentric orbits—I don't know anything about that part, I'm quoting Dr. Moore. If there's an animal vector to the disease, we've never discovered it. The pattern runs like this; a few cases in the mountain districts, the next month a hundred-odd cases all over this part of the planet. Then it skips exactly three months without increase. The next upswing puts the number of the reported case in the thousands, and three months after *that*, it reaches real pandemic proportions and decimates the entire human population of Darkover."

"That's about it," Forth admitted. They bent together over the folder, Jay Allison drawing back slightly to avoid touching the other man.

Forth said, "We Terrans have had a Trade compact on Darkover for a hundred and fifty-two years. The first outbreak of this forty-eight-year fever killed all but a dozen men out of three hundred. The Darkovans were worse off than we were. The last outbreak wasn't as bad, but it was bad enough, I've heard. It had an eighty-seven percent mortality—for humans, that is. I understand the trailmen don't die of it."

"The Darkovans call it the trailmen's fever, Dr. Forth, because the trailmen are virtually immune to it. It remains in their midst as a mild ailment taken by children. When it breaks out into a virulent form every forty-eight years, most of the trailmen are already immune. I took the disease myself as a child—maybe you heard?"

Forth nodded. "You may be the only Terran ever to contract the disease and survive."

"The trailmen incubate the disease," Jay Allison said. "I should think the logical thing would be to drop a couple of hydrogen bombs on the trail cities—and wipe it out for good and all."

(Sitting on the sofa in Forth's dark office, I stiffened with such fury that he shook my shoulder and muttered "Easy, there, man!")

Dr. Forth, on the screen, looked annoyed, and Jay Allison said, with a grimace of distaste, "I didn't mean that literally. But the Trailmen are not human. It wouldn't be genocide, just an exterminator's job. A public health measure."

Forth looked shocked as he realized that the younger man meant what he was saying. He said, "Galactic Center would have to rule on whether they're dumb animals or intelligent nonhumans, and whether they're entitled to the status of a civilization. All precedent on Darkover is toward recognizing them as men—and good God, Jay, you'd probably be called as a witness for the defense! How can you say they're not human after your experience with them? Anyway, by the time their status was finally decided, half of the recognizable humans on Darkover would be dead. We need a better solution than that."

He pushed his chair back and looked out the window.

"I won't go into this political situation," he said. "You aren't interested in Terran Empire politics, and I'm no expert either. But you'd have to be deaf, dumb, and blind not to know that Darkover's been playing the immovable object to the irresistible force. The Darkovans are more advanced in some of the non-causative sciences than we are and, until now, they wouldn't admit that Terra had a thing to contribute. However—and this is the big however—they do know, and they're willing to admit, that our medical sciences are better than theirs."

"Theirs being practically nonexistent."

"Exactly—and this could be the first crack in the barrier. You may not realize the significance of this, but the Legate received an offer from the Hasturs themselves."

Jay Allison murmured, "I'm to be impressed?"

"On Darkover you'd be damn well better be impressed when the Hasturs sit up and take notice."

"I understand they're telepaths or something—"

"Telepaths, psychokinetics, parapsychs, just about anything else. For all practical purposes they're the Gods of Darkover. And one of the Hasturs—a rather young and unimportant one, I'll admit, the old man's grandson—came to the Legate's office, in person, mind you. He offered, if the Terran Medical would help Darkover lick the trailmen's fever, to coach selected Terran men in matrix mechanics."

"Good God," Jay said. It was a concession beyond Terra's wildest dreams; for a hundred years they had tried to beg, buy, or steal some knowledge of the mysterious science of matrix mechanics—that curious discipline which could turn matter into raw energy, and vice versa, without any intermediate stages and without fission by-products. Matrix mechanics had made the Darkovans virtually immune to the lure of Terra's advanced technologies.

Jay said, "Personally I think Darkovan science is overrated. But I can see the propaganda angle—"

"Not to mention the humanitarian angle of healing."

Jay Allison gave one of his cold shrugs. "The real angle seems to be this: *can* we cure the forty-eight-year fever?"

"Not yet. But we have a lead. During the last epidemic, a Terran scientist discovered a blood fraction containing antibodies against the fever—in the trailmen. Isolated to a serum, it might reduce the virulent forty-eight-year epidemic form to the mild form again. Unfortunately, he died himself in the epidemic, without finishing his work, and his notebooks were overlooked until this year. We have 18,000 men, and their families, on Darkover now, Jay. Frankly, if we lose too many of them, we're going to have to pull out of Darkover—the big brass on Terra will write off the loss of a garrison of professional traders, but not of a whole Trade City colony. That's not even mentioning the prestige we'll lose if our much vaunted Terran medical sciences can't save Darkover from an epidemic. We've got exactly five months. We can't synthesize a serum in that time. We've got to appeal to the trailmen. And that's why I called you up here. You know more about the trailmen than any living Terran. You ought to. You spent eight years in a Nest."

(In Forth's darkened office I sat up straighter, with a flash of returning memory. Jay Allison, I judged, was several years older than I, but we had one thing in common; this cold fish of a man shared with myself that experience of marvelous years spent in an alien world!)

Jay Allison scowled, displeased. "That was years ago. I was hardly more than a baby. My father crashed on a Mapping expedition over the Hellers—God only knows what possessed him to try and take a light plane over those crosswinds. I survived the crash by the merest chance, and lived with the trailmen—so I'm told—until I was thirteen or fourteen. I don't remember much about it. Children aren't particularly observant."

Forth leaned over the desk, staring. "You speak their language, don't you?"

"I used to. I might remember it under hypnosis, I suppose. Why? Do you want me to translate something?"

"Not exactly. We were thinking of sending you on an expedition to the trailmen themselves."

(In the darkened office, watching Jay's startled face, I thought, God, what an adventure! I wonder—I wonder if they want me to go with him?)

Forth was explaining. "It would be a difficult trek. You know what the Hellers are like. Still, you used to climb mountains, as a hobby, before you went into Medical—"

"I outgrew the childishness of hobbies many years ago, sir," Jay said stiffly.

"We'd get you the best guides we could, Terran and Darkovan. But they couldn't do the one thing you can do. You *know* the trailmen, Jay. You might be able to persuade them to do the one thing they've never done before."

"What's that?" Jay Allison sounded suspicious.

"Come out of the mountains. Send us volunteers— blood donors—we might, if we had enough blood to work on, be able to isolate the right fraction, and synthesize it, in time to prevent the epidemic from really taking hold, Jay. It's a tough mission and it's dangerous as all hell, but somebody's got to do it, and I'm afraid you're the only qualified man."

"I like my first suggestion better. Bomb the trailmen—and the Hellers—right off the planet." Jay's face was set in lines of loathing, which he controlled after a minute, and said, "I—I didn't mean that. Theoretically I can see the necessity, only—" he stopped and swallowed.

"Please say what you were going to say."

"I wonder if I am as well qualified as you think? No—don't interrupt—I find the natives of Darkover distasteful, even the humans. As for the trailmen—"

(I was getting mad and impatient. I whispered to Forth in the darkness "Shut the goddam film off! You couldn't send *that* guy on an errand like *that!* I'd rather—"

Forth snapped, "Shut up and listen!"

I shut up.)

Jay Allison was not acting. He was pained and disgusted. Forth wouldn't let him finish his explanation of why he had refused even to teach in the Medical College established for Darkovans by the Terran empire. He interrupted, and he sounded irritated,

"We know all that. It evidently never occurred to you, Jay, that it's an inconvenience to us—that all this vital knowledge should lie, purely by accident, in the hands of the one man who's too damned stubborn to use it?"

Jay didn't move an eyelash, where I would have squirmed. "I have always been aware of that, doctor."

Forth drew a long breath. "I'll concede you're not suitable at the moment, Jay. But what do you know of applied psychodynamics?"

"Very little I'm sorry to say." Allison didn't sound sorry, though. He sounded bored to death with the whole conversation.

"May I be blunt—and personal?"

"Please do. I'm not at all sensitive."

"Basically, then, Doctor Allison, a person as contained and repressed as yourself usually has a clearly defined subsidiary personality. In neurotic individuals this complex of personality traits sometimes splits off, and we get a syndrome known as multiple, or alternate, personality."

"I've scanned a few of the classic cases. Wasn't there a woman with four separate personalities?"

"Exactly. However, you aren't neurotic, and ordinarily there would not be the slightest chance of your repressed alternate taking over your personality."

"Thank you," Jay murmured ironically, "I'd be losing sleep over that."

"Nevertheless I presume you *do* have such a subsidiary personality, although he would not normally manifest. This subsidiary—let's call him Jay—would embody all the characteristics which you repress. He would be gregarious, where you are retiring and studious; adventurous where you are cautious; talkative while you are taciturn; he would perhaps enjoy action for its own sake, while you exercise faithfully in the gymnasium only for your health's sake; and he might even remember the trailmen with pleasure rather than dislike."

"In short—a blend of all the undesirable characteristics?"

"One could put it that way. Certainly, he would be a blend of all the characteristics which you, Jay, *consider* undesirable. But—if released by hypnotism and suggestion, he might be suitable for the job in hand."

"But how do you know I actually have such an—alternate?"

"I don't. But it's a good guess. Most repressed—" Forth coughed and amended, "most *disciplined* personalities possess such a suppressed secondary personality. Don't you occasionally—rather rarely—find yourself doing things which are entirely out of character for you?"

I could almost feel Allison taking it in, as he confessed, "Well—yes. For instance, the other day, although I dress conservatively at all times—" he glanced at his uniform coat, "I found myself buying—" he stopped again and his face went an unlovely terra-cotta color as he finally mumbled, "a flowered red sport shirt."

Sitting in the dark I felt vaguely sorry for the poor gawk, disturbed by, ashamed of the only human impulses he ever had. On the screen Allison frowned fiercely. "A—crazy impulse."

"You could say that, or say it was an action of the suppressed Jay. How about it, Allison? You may be the only Terran on Darkover, maybe the only human, who could get into a trailman's Nest without being murdered."

"Sir—as a citizen of the Empire, I don't have any choice, do I?"

"Jay, look," Forth said, and I felt him trying to reach through the barricade and touch, really touch, that cold, contained young man. "We couldn't *order* any man to do anything like this. Aside from the ordinary dangers, it could destroy your personal balance, maybe permanently. I'm asking you to volunteer something above and beyond the call of duty. Man to man—what do you say?"

I would have been moved by his words. Even at second hand I was moved by them. Jay Allison looked at the floor and I saw him twist his long well-kept surgeon's hands and crack the knuckles with an odd gesture. Finally he said, "I haven't any choice either way, doctor. I'll take the chance. I'll go to the trailmen."

CHAPTER TWO

The screen went dark again and Forth flicked the light on. He said "Well?"

I gave it back, in his own intonation, "Well?" and was exasperated to find that I was twisting my own knuckles in the nervous gesture of Allison's painful decision. I jerked them apart and got up.

"I suppose it didn't work, with that cold fish, and you decided to come to me instead? Sure, *I'll* go to the trailmen for you. Not with that Allison bastard—I wouldn't go anywhere with that guy—but I speak the trailmen's language, and without hypnosis, either."

Forth was staring at me. "So you've remembered that?"

"Hell yes," I said. "My Dad crashed in the Hellers, and a band of trailmen found me, half dead. I lived there until I was about fifteen, then their Old-One decided I was too human for 'em, and they took me out through Dammerung Pass and arranged to have me brought here. Sure, it's all coming back now. I spent five years in the Spacemen's Orphanage, then I went to work taking Terran tourists on hunting parties and so on, because I liked being around the mountains. I—" I stopped. Forth was staring at me.

"Sit down again, won't you? Can't you keep still a minute?" Reluctantly, I sat down. "You think you'd like this job?"

"It would be tough," I said, considering. "The People of the Sky—" (using the trailmen's name for themselves) "—don't like outsiders, but they might be persuaded. The worst part would be getting there. The plane, or the 'copter, isn't built that can get through the crosswinds around the Hellers, and land inside them. We'd have to go on foot, all the way from Carthon. I'd need professional climbers— mountaineers."

"Then you don't share Allison's attitude?"

"Dammit, don't insult me!" I discovered that I was on my feet again, pacing the office restlessly. Forth stared and mused aloud, "What's personality anyway? A mask of emotions, superimposed on the body and the intellect. Change the point of view, change the emotions and desires, and even with the same body and the same past experiences, you have a new man."

I swung around in mid-step. A new and terrible suspicion, too monstrous to name, was creeping up on me. Forth touched a button and the face of Jay Allison, immobile, appeared on the vision-screen. Forth put a mirror in my hand. He said, "Jason Allison, look at yourself."

I looked.

"No," I said. And again. "No. No. No."

Forth didn't argue. He pointed, with a stubby finger. "Look—" he moved the finger as he spoke. "Height of forehead. Set of cheekbones. Your eyebrows look different, and your mouth, because the expression is different. But bone structure—the nose, the chin—"

I heard myself make a queer sound; dashed the mirror to the floor. He grabbed my forearm. "Steady, man!"

I found a scrap of my voice. It didn't sound like Allison's. "Then I'm—Jay? Jay Allison with amnesia?"

"Not exactly." Forth mopped his forehead with an immaculate sleeve and it came away damp with sweat, "God, no, *not* Jay Allison as I know him!" He drew a long breath. "And sit down. Whoever you are, sit *down!*"

I sat. Gingerly. Not sure.

"But the man Jay might have been, given a different temperamental bias. I'd say—the man Jay Allison started out to be. The man he *refused* to be. Within his subconscious, he built up barriers against a whole series of memories, and the subliminal threshold—"

"Doc, I don't understand the psycho talk."

Forth stared. "And you do remember the trailmen's language. I thought so. Allison's personality is suppressed in you, as yours was in him."

"One thing, Doc. I don't know a thing about blood fractions or epidemics. My half of the personality didn't study medicine." I took up the mirror again and broodingly studied the face there. The high thin cheeks, high forehead shaded by coarse, dark hair which Jay Allison had slicked down, now heavily rumpled. I still didn't think I looked anything like the doctor. Our voices were nothing alike either. His had been pitched rather high. My own, as nearly as I could judge, was a full octave deeper, and more resonant. Yet they issued from the same vocal chords, unless Forth were having a reasonless, macabre joke.

"Did I honest-to-God study medicine? It's the last thing I'd think about. It's an honest trade, I guess, but I've never been that intellectual."

"You—or rather, Jay Allison is a specialist in Dark-ovan parasitology, as well as a very competent surgeon." Forth was sitting with his chin in his hands, watching me intently. He scowled and said, "If anything, the physical change is more startling than the other. I wouldn't have recognized you."

"That tallies with me. I don't recognize myself," I added, "—and the queer thing is, I didn't even *like* Jay Allison, to put it mildly. If he—I can't say *he*, can I?"

"I don't know why not. You're no more Jay Allison than I am. For one thing, you're younger. Ten years younger. I doubt if any of his friends—if he had any—would recognize you. You—it's ridiculous to go on calling you Jay. What should I call you?"

"Why should I care? Call me Jason."

"Suits you," Forth said enigmatically. "Look, then, Jason. I'd like to give you a few days to readjust to your new personality, but we are really pressed for time. Can you fly to Carthon tonight? I've hand-picked a good crew for you, and sent them on ahead. You'll meet them there."

I stared at him. Suddenly the room oppressed me and I found it hard to breathe. I said in wonder, "You were pretty sure of yourself, weren't you?"

Forth just looked at me, for what seemed a long time. Then he said, in a very quiet voice, "No. I wasn't sure at all. But if you didn't turn up, and I couldn't talk Jay into it, I'd have had to try it myself."

Jason Allison, Junior, was listed on the directory of the Terran HQ as "Suite 1214, Medical Residence Corridor." I found the rooms without any trouble, though an elderly doctor stared at me rather curiously as I barged along the quiet hallway. The suite—bedroom, minuscule sitting-room, compact bath—depressed me: clean, closed-in, and neutral as the man who owned them. I rummaged through them restlessly, trying to find some scrap of familiarity to indicate that I had lived here for the past eleven years.

Jay Allison was thirty-four years old. I had given my age, without hesitation, as twenty-two. There were no obvious blanks in my memory; from the moment Jay Allison had spoken of the trailmen, my past had rushed back and stood, complete to yesterday's supper (only had I eaten that supper twelve years ago?). I remembered my father, a lined, silent man who had liked to fly often, taking photograph after photograph from his plane for the meticulous work of

Mapping and Exploration. He'd liked to have me fly with him and I'd flown over virtually every inch of the planet. No one else had ever dared fly over the Hellers, except the big commercial space craft that kept to a safe altitude. I vaguely remembered the crash and the strange hands pulling me out of the wreckage and the weeks I'd spent, broken-bodied and delirious, gently tended by one of the red-eyed, twittering women of the trailmen. In all, I had spent eight years in the Nest, which was not a nest at all, but a vast sprawling city built in the branches of enormous trees. With the small and delicate humanoids who had been my playfellows, I had gathered the nuts and buds and trapped the small arboreal animals they used for food, taken my share at weaving clothing from the fibers of parasite plants cultivated on the stems, and in all those eight years I had set foot on the ground less than a dozen times, even though I had traveled for miles through the tree-roads high above the forest floor.

Then the Old-One's painful decision that I was too alien for them, and the difficult and dangerous journey my trailmen foster-parents and foster-brothers had undertaken, to help me out of the Hellers and arrange for me to be taken to the Trade City. After two years of physically painful and mentally rebellious readjustment to daytime living (the owl-eyed trailmen saw best, and lived largely, by moonlight) I had found a niche for myself, and settled down. But all of the later years (after Jay Allison had taken over,

I supposed, from a basic pattern of memory common to both of us) had vanished into the limbo of the subconscious.

A bookrack was crammed with large microcards; I slipped one into the viewer, with a queer sense of spying, and found myself listening apprehensively to hear that measured step and Jay Allison's shrill voice demanding what the hell I was doing, meddling with his possessions. Eye to the viewer, I read briefly at random, something about the management of compound fracture, then realized I had understood exactly three words in a paragraph. I put my fist against my forehead and heard the words echoing there emptily; "laceration . . . primary efflusion . . . serum and lymph . . . granulation tissue . . ." I presumed that the words meant something and that I once had known what. But if I had a medical education, I didn't recall a syllable of it. I didn't know a fracture from a fraction.

In a sudden frenzy of impatience I stripped off the white coat and put on the first shirt I came to, a crimson thing that hung in the line of white coats like an exotic bird in snow country. I went back to rummaging through the drawers and bureaus. Carelessly shoved in a pigeonhole I found another microcard that looked familiar, and when I slipped it mechanically into the viewer it turned out to be a book on mountaineering which, oddly enough, I remembered buying as a youngster. It dispelled my last, lingering doubts. Evidently I had bought it before the personalities had forked so sharply apart and separated, Jason from Jay. I was beginning to believe. Not to accept. Just to believe it had happened. The book looked well-thumbed, and had been handled so much I had to baby it into the slot of the viewer.

Under a folded pile of clean underwear I found a flat half-empty bottle of whisky. I remembered Forth's words that he'd never seen Jay Allison drink, and suddenly I thought, "The poor fool!" I fixed myself a drink and sat down, idly scanning the mountaineering book.

Not till I'd entered medical school, I suspected, did the two halves of me fork so strongly apart—so strongly that there had been days and weeks and, I suspected, years when Jay Allison had kept me prisoner. I tried to juggle dates in my mind, looked at a calendar, and got such a mental jolt that I put it face-down to think about when I was a little drunker.

I wondered if my detailed memories of my teens and early twenties were the same memories Jay Allison looked back on. I didn't think so. People forget and remember selectively. Week by week, then, and year by year, the dominant personality of Jay had crowded me out; so that the young rowdy, more than half Darkovan, loving the mountains, half homesick for a nonhuman world, had been drowned in the chilly, austere young medical student who lost himself in his work. But I, Jason—had I always been the watcher behind, the person Jay Allison dared not be? Why was he past thirty—and I just twenty-two?

A ringing shattered the silence; I had to hunt for the

intercom on the bedroom wall. I said, "Who is it?" and an unfamiliar voice demanded, "Dr. Allison?"

I said automatically, "Nobody here by that name," and started to put back the mouthpiece. Then I stopped and gulped and asked, "Is that you, Dr. Forth?"

It was, and I breathed again. I didn't even want to think about what I'd say if somebody else demanded to know why the devil I was answering Dr. Allison's private telephone. When Forth had finished, I went to the mirror, and stared, trying to see behind my face the sharp features of that stranger, *Doctor* Jason Allison. I delayed, even while I was wondering what few things I should pack for a trip into the mountains, and the habit of hunting parties was making mental lists about heat-socks and windbreakers. The face that looked at me was a young face, unlined and faintly freckled, the same face as always except that I'd lost my suntan; Jay Allison had kept me indoors too long. Suddenly I struck the mirror lightly with my fist.

"The hell with you, Dr. Allison," I said, and went to see if he had kept any clothes fit to pack.

CHAPTER THREE

Dr. Forth was waiting for me in the small skyport on the roof, and so was a small 'copter, one of the fairly old ones assigned to Medical Service when they were too beat up for services with higher priority. Forth took one startled look at my crimson shirt, but all he said was, "Hello, Jason. Here's something we've got to decide right away; do we tell the crew who you really are?"

I shook my head emphatically. "I'm not Jay Allison; I don't want his name or his reputation. Unless there are men on the crew who know Allison by sight—"

"Some of them do, but I don't think they'd recognize you."

"Tell them I'm his twin brother," I said humorlessly.

"That wouldn't be necessary. There's not enough resemblance." Forth raised his head and beckoned to a man who was doing something near the 'copter. He said under his breath, "You'll see what I mean," as the man approached.

He wore the uniform of Spaceforce—black leather with a little rainbow of stars on his sleeve meaning he'd seen service on a dozen different planets, a different colored star for each one. He wasn't a young man, but on the wrong side of fifty, seamed and burly and huge, with a split lip and weathered face. I liked his looks. We shook hands and Forth said, "This is our man, Kendricks. He's called Jason, and he's an expert on the trailmen. Jason, this is Buck Kendricks."

"Glad to know you, Jason." I thought Kendricks looked at me half a second more than necessary. "The 'copter's ready. Climb in, Doc—you're going as far as Carthon, aren't you?"

We put on zippered windbreakers and the 'copter soared noiselessly into the pale crimson sky. I sat beside Forth, looking down through pale lilac clouds at the pattern of Darkover spread below me.

"Kendricks was giving me a funny cye, Doc. What's biting him?"

"He has known Jay Allison for eight years," Forth said quietly, "and he hasn't recognized you yet."

But we let it ride at that, to my great relief, and didn't talk any more about me at all. As we flew under silent whirring blades, turning our backs on the settled country which lay near the Trade City, we talked about Darkover itself. Forth told me about the trailmen's fever and managed to give me some idea about what the blood fraction was, and why it was necessary to persuade fifty or sixty of the humanoids to return with me, to donate blood from which the antibody could be first isolated, then synthesized.

It would be a totally unheard-of thing, if I could accomplish it. Most of the trailmen never touched ground in their entire lives, except when crossing the passes above the snow line. Not a dozen of them, including my foster parents, who had so painfully brought me out across Dammerung, had ever crossed the ring of encircling mountains that walled them away from the rest of the planet. Humans sometimes penetrated the lower forests in search of the trailmen. It was one-way traffic. The trailmen never came in search of *them*.

We talked, too, about some of those humans who had crossed the mountains into trailmen country—those mountains profanely dubbed the Hellers by the first Terrans who had tried to fly over them in anything lower or slower than a spaceship.

"What about this crew you picked? They're not Terrans?"

Forth shook his head. "It would be murder to send anyone recognizably Terran into the Hellers. You know how the trailmen feel about outsiders getting into their country." I knew. Forth continued, "Just the same, there will be two Terrans with you."

"They don't know Jay Allison?" I didn't want to be burdened with anyone—not anyone—who would know me, or expect me to behave like my forgotten other self.

"Kendricks knows you," Forth said, "but I'm going

to be perfectly truthful. I never knew Jay Allison well, except in line of work. I know a lot of things—from the past couple of days—which came out during the hypnotic sessions, which he'd never have dreamed of telling me, or anyone else, consciously. And that comes under the heading of a professional confidence—even from you. And for that reason, I'm sending Kendricks along—and you're going to have to take the chance he'll recognize you. Isn't that Carthon down there?"

Carthon lay nestled under the outlying foothills of the Hellers, ancient and sprawling and squatty, and burned brown with the dust of five thousand years. Children ran out to stare at the 'copter as we landed near the city; few planes ever flew low enough to be seen, this near the Hellers.

Forth had sent his crew ahead and parked them in an abandoned huge place at the edge of the city which might once have been a warehouse or a ruined palace. Inside there were a couple of trucks, stripped down to framework and flatbed, like all machinery shipped through space from Terra. There were pack animals, dark shapes in the gloom. Crates were stacked up in an orderly untidiness, and at the far end a fire was burning and five or six men in Darkovan clothing— loose-sleeved shirts, tight-wrapped breeches, low boots—were squatting around it, talking. They got up as Forth and Kendricks and I walked toward them, and Forth greeted them clumsily in badly accented

Darkovan, then switched to Terran Standard, letting one of the men translate for him.

Forth introduced me simply as "Jason," after the Darkovan custom, and I looked the men over, one by one. Back when I'd climbed for fun, I'd liked to pick my own men; but whoever had picked this crew must have known his business.

Three were mountain Darkovans, lean swart men enough alike to be brothers; I learned after a while that they actually were brothers, Hjalmar, Garin, and Vardo. All three were well over six feet, and Hjalmar stood head and shoulders over his brothers, whom I never learned to tell apart. The fourth man, a redhead, was dressed rather better than the others and introduced as Lerrys Ridenow—the double name indicating high Darkovan aristocracy. He looked muscular and agile enough, but his hands were suspiciously well-kept for a mountain man, and I wondered how much experience he'd had.

The fifth man shook hands with me, speaking to Kendricks and Forth as if they were old friends. "Don't I know you from someplace, Jason?"

He looked Darkovan, and wore Darkovan clothes, but Forth had forewarned me, and attack seemed the best defense. "Aren't you Terran?"

"My father was," he said, and I understood; a situation not exactly uncommon, but ticklish on a planet like Darkover. I said carelessly, "I may have seen you around the HQ. I can't place you, though."

"My name's Rafe Scott. I thought I knew most of

the professional guides on Darkover, but I admit I don't get into the Hellers much," he confessed. "Which route are we going to take?"

I found myself drawn into the middle of the group of men, accepting one of the small, sweetish Darkovan cigarettes, looking over the plan somebody had scribbled down on the top of a packing case. I borrowed a pencil from Rafe and bent over the case, sketching out a rough map of the terrain I remembered so well from boyhood. I might be bewildered about blood fractions, but when it came to climbing I knew what I was doing. Rafe and Lerrys and the Darkovan brothers crowded behind me to look over the sketch, and Lerrys put a long fingernail on the route I'd indicated.

"Your elevation's pretty bad here," he said diffidently, "and on the 'Narr campaign the trailmen attacked us here, and it was bad fighting along those ledges."

I looked at him with new respect; dainty hands or not, he evidently knew the country. Kendricks patted the blaster on his hip and said grimly, "But this isn't the 'Narr campaign. I'd like to see any trailmen attack us while I have this."

"But you're not going to have it," said a voice behind us, a crisp authoritative voice. "Take off that gun, man!"

Kendricks and I whirled together to see the speaker, a tall young Darkovan, still standing in the shadows. The newcomer spoke to me directly.

"I'm told you are Terran, but that you understand the trailmen. Surely you don't intend to carry fission or fusion weapons against them?"

And I suddenly realized that we were in Darkovan territory now, and that we must reckon with the Darkovan horror of guns or of any weapon which reaches beyond the arm's length of the man who wields it. A simple heat-gun, to the Darkovan ethical code, is as reprehensible as a super-cobalt planetbuster.

Kendricks protested, "We can't travel unarmed through trailmen country! We're apt to meet hostile bands of the creatures—and they're nasty with those long knives they carry!"

The stranger said calmly, "I've no objection to you, or anyone else, carrying a knife for self-defense."

"A *knife?*" Kendricks drew breath to roar. "Listen, you bug-eyed son of a—who do you think you are, anyway?"

The Darkovans muttered. The man in the shadows said, "Regis Hastur."

Kendricks stared pop-eyed. My own eyes could have popped, but I decided it was time for me to take charge, if I were ever going to. I rapped, "All right, this is my show. Buck, give me the gun."

He looked wrathfully at me for the space of seconds, while I wondered what I'd do if he didn't. Then, slowly, he unbuckled the straps and handed it to me, butt first.

I'd never realized how undressed a Spaceforce man looked without his blaster. I balanced it on my palm for a minute while Regis Hastur came out of the shadows. He was tall, and had the reddish hair and fair skin of Darkovan aristocracy, and on his face was some indefinable stamp—arrogance, perhaps, or the consciousness that the Hasturs had ruled this world for centuries long before the Terrans brought ships and trade and the universe to their doors. He was looking at me as if he approved of me, and that was one step worse than the former situation.

So, using the respectful Darkovan idiom of speaking to a superior (which he was) but keeping my voice hard, I said, "There's just one leader on my trek, Lord Hastur. On this one, I'm it. If you want to discuss whether or not we carry guns, I suggest you discuss it with me in private—and let me give the orders."

One of the Darkovans gasped. I knew I could have been mobbed. But with a mixed bag of men, I had to grab leadership quickly or be relegated to nowhere. I didn't give Regis Hastur a chance to answer that, either; I said, "Come back here. I want to talk to you anyway."

He came, and I remembered to breathe. I led the way to a fairly deserted corner of the immense place, faced him and demanded, "As for you—what are you doing here? You're not intending to cross the mountains with us?"

He met my scowl levelly. "I certainly am."

I groaned. "Why? You're the Regent's grandson. Important people don't take on this kind of dangerous work. If anything happens to you, it will be my responsibility!" I was going to have enough trouble, I was thinking, without shepherding along one of the most revered personages on the whole damned planet! I didn't want anyone around who had to be fawned on, or deferred to, or even listened to.

He frowned slightly, and I had the unpleasant impression that he knew what I was thinking. "In the first place, it will mean something to the trailmen, won't it, to have a Hastur with you, suing for this favor?"

It certainly would. The trailmen paid little enough heed to the ordinary humans, except for considering them fair game for plundering when they came uninvited into trailmen country. But they, with all Darkover, revered the Hasturs, and it was a fine point of diplomacy. If the Darkovans sent their most important leader, they might listen to him.

"In the second place," Regis Hastur continued, "the Darkovans are my people, and it's my business to negotiate for them. In the third place, I know the trailmen's dialect—not well, but I can speak it a little. And in the fourth, I've climbed mountains all my life. Purely as an amateur, but I can assure you I won't be in the way."

There was little enough I could say to that. He seemed to have covered every point—or every point but one, and he added, shrewdly, after a minute, "Don't worry; I'm perfectly willing to have you take charge. I won't claim—privilege."

I had to be satisfied with that.

* * *

Darkover is a civilized planet with a fairly high standard of living, but it is not a mechanized or a technological culture. The people don't do much mining, or build factories, and the few which were founded by Terran enterprise never were very successful; outside the Terran Trade City, machinery or modern transportation is almost unknown.

While the other men checked and loaded supplies and Rafe Scott went out to contact some friends of his and arrange for last-minute details, I sat down with Forth to memorize the medical details I must put so clearly to the trailmen.

"If we could only have kept your medical knowledge!"

"Trouble is, being a doctor doesn't suit my personality," I said. I felt absurdly light-hearted. Where I sat, I could raise my head and study the panorama of blackish-green foothills which lay beyond Carthon, and search out the stone roadway, like a tiny white ribbon, which we could follow for the first stage of the trip. Forth evidently did not share my enthusiasm.

"You know, Jason, there is one real danger—"

"Do you think I care about danger? Or are you afraid I'll turn—foolhardy?"

"Not exactly. It's not a physical danger, Jason. It's an emotional—or rather an intellectual danger."

"Hell, don't you know any language but that psycho doubletalk?"

"Let me finish, Jason. Jay Allison may have been repressed, overcontrolled, but you are seriously impulsive. You lack a balance-wheel, if I could put it that way. And if you run too many risks, your buried alter-ego may come to the surface and take over in sheer self-preservation."

"In other words," I said, laughing loudly, "if I scare that Allison stuffed-shirt, he may start stirring in his grave?"

Forth coughed and smothered a laugh and said that was one way of putting it. I clapped him reassuringly on the shoulder and said, "Forget it, sir. I promise to be godly, sober, and industrious—but is there any law against enjoying what I'm doing?"

Somebody burst out of the warehouse-palace place, and shouted at me. "Jason? The guide is here," and I stood up, giving Forth a final grin. "Don't you worry. Jay Allison's good riddance," I said, and went back to meet the other guide they had chosen.

And I almost backed out when I saw the guide. For the guide was a woman.

She was small for a Darkovan girl, and narrowly built, the sort of body that could have been called boyish or coltish but certainly not, at first glance, feminine. Close-cut curls, blue-black and wispy, cast the faintest of shadows over a squarish sunburnt face, and her eyes were so thickly rimmed with heavy dark lashes that I could not guess their color. Her nose was snubbed and might have looked whimsical but was instead oddly arrogant. Her mouth was wide, and her chin round.

She held up her palm and said rather sullenly, "Kyla Rainéach, Free Amazon, licensed guide."

I acknowledged the gesture with a nod, scowling. The guild of Free Amazons entered virtually every field, but that of mountain guide seemed somewhat bizarre even for an Amazon. She seemed wiry and agile enough, her body, under the heavy blanketlike clothing, almost as lean of hip and flat of breast as my own; only the slender long legs were unequivocally feminine.

The other men were checking and loading supplies; I noted from the corner of my eye that Regis Hastur was taking his turn heaving bundles with the rest. I sat down on some still-undisturbed sacks, and motioned her to sit.

"You've had trail experience? We're going into the Hellers through Dammerung, and that's rough going even for professionals."

She said in a flat expressionless voice, "I was with the Terran Mapping expedition to the South Polar ridge last year."

"Ever been in the Hellers? If anything happened to me, could you lead the expedition safely back to Carthon?"

She looked down at her stubby fingers. "I'm sure I could," she said finally, and started to rise. "Is that all?"

"One more thing—" I gestured to her to stay put. "Kyla, you'll be one woman among eight men—"

The snubbed nose wrinkled up. "I don't expect you

to crawl into my blankets, if that's what you mean. It's not in my contract—I hope!"

I felt my face burning. Damn the girl! "It's not in mine, anyway," I snapped, "but I can't answer for seven other men, most of them mountain rough-necks." Even as I said it I wondered why I bothered; certainly a Free Amazon could defend her own virtue, or not, if she wanted to, without any help from me. I had to excuse myself by adding, "In either case you'll be a disturbing element—I don't want fights either!"

She made a little low-pitched sound of amusement. "There's safety in numbers, and—are you familiar with the physiological effect of high altitudes on men acclimated to low ones?" Suddenly she threw back her head and the hidden sound became free and merry laughter. "Jason, I'm a Free Amazon, and that means—no, I'm not neutered, though some of us are. But you have my word, I won't create any trouble of any recognizably female variety." She stood up. "Now, if you don't mind, I'd like to check the mountain equipment."

Her eyes were still laughing at me, but curiously I didn't mind at all.

CHAPTER FOUR

We started that night, a curiously lopsided little caravan. The pack animals were loaded into one truck and
didn't like it. We had another stripped-down truck
which carried supplies. The ancient stone roads, rutted and gullied here and there with the flood-waters
and silt of decades, had not been planned for any
travel other than the feet of men or beasts. We passed
tiny villages and isolated country estates, and a few of
the solitary towers where the matrix mechanics
worked alone with the secret sciences of Darkover,
towers of unpolished stone which sometimes shone
like blue beacons in the dark.

Kendricks drove the truck which carried the animals, and was amused by it. Rafe and I took turns
driving the other truck, sharing the wide front seat
with Regis Hastur and Kyla, while the other men
found seats between crates and sacks in the back.
Once, while Rafe was at the wheel, and the girl was
dozing with her coat over her face to shut out the

fierce sun, Regis asked me, "What are the trailcities like?"

I tried to tell him, but I've never been good at boiling things down into descriptions, and when he found I was not disposed to talk, he fell silent and I was free to drowse over what I knew of the trailmen and their world.

Nature seems to have a sameness on all inhabited worlds, tending toward the economy and simplicity of the human form. The upright carriage, freeing the hands, the opposable thumb, the color-sensitivity of retinal rods and cones, the development of language and of lengthy parental nurture—these things seem to be indispensable to the growth of civilization, and in the end they spell *human*. Except for minor variations depending on climate or footstuffs, the inhabitant of Megaera or Darkover is indistinguishable from the Terran or Sirian; differences are mainly cultural, and sometimes an isolated culture will mutate in a strange direction or remain atavists, somewhere halfway to the summit of the ladder of evolution—which, at least on the known planets, still reckons *homo sapiens* as the most complex of nature's forms.

The trailmen were a pausing-place which had proved tenacious. When the mainstream of evolution on Darkover left the trees to struggle for existence on the ground, a few remained behind. Evolution did not cease for them, but evolved *homo arborens:* nocturnal, nyetalopic humanoids who live out their lives in the extensive forests.

The truck bumped over the bad, rutted roads. The wind was chilly. The truck, a mere conveyance for hauling, had no such refinements of luxury as windows. I jolted awake—what nonsense had I been thinking? Vague ideas about evolution swirled in my brain like burst bubbles—the trailmen? They were just the trailmen, who could explain them? Jay Allison, maybe? Rafe turned his head and asked, "Where do we pull up for the night? It's getting dark, and we have all this gear to sort!" I roused myself, and took over the business of the expedition again.

But when the trucks had been parked and a tent pitched and the pack animals unloaded and hobbled, and a start made at getting the gear together—when all this had been done I lay awake, listening to Kendricks' heavy snoring, but myself afraid to sleep. Dozing in the truck, an odd lapse of consciousness had come over me—myself yet not myself, drowsing over thoughts I did not recognize as my own. If I slept, who would I be when I woke?

We had made our camp in the bend of an enormous river, wide and shallow and unbridged—the river Kadarin, traditionally a point of no return for humans on Darkover. Beyond the river lay thick forests, and beyond the forests the slopes of the Hellers, rising upward and upward; and their every fold and every valley was filled to the brim with forest, and in the forests lived the trailmen.

But though all this country was thickly populated with outlying colonies and nests, it would be no use to bargain with any of them; we must deal with the Old-One of the North Nest, where I had spent so many of my boyhood years.

From time immemorial, the trailmen—usually inoffensive—had kept strict boundaries marked between their lands and the lands of ground-dwelling men. They never came beyond the Kadarin. On the other hand, any human who ventured into their territory became, by that act, fair game for attack.

A few of the Darkovan mountain people had trade treaties with the trailmen; they traded clothing, forged metals, small implements, in return for nuts, bark for dyestuffs, and certain leaves and mosses for drugs. In return, the trailmen permitted them to hunt in the forest lands without being molested. But other humans venturing into trailmen territory ran the risk of merciless raiding; the trailmen were not bloodthirsty, and did not kill for the sake of killing, but they attacked in packs of two or three dozen, and their prey would be stripped and plundered of everything portable.

Traveling through their country would be dangerous.

I sat in front of the tent, staring at the expanse of water, rippling pink in the sunrise. The pack animals cropped short grass behind the tent. The trucks were vast sphinxes, shrouded under tarpaulins glistening with early dew. Regis Hastur came out of the tent, rubbed his eyes, and joined me at the water's edge.

"What do you think? Is it going to be a bad trip?"

"I wouldn't think so. I know the main trails and I can keep clear of them. It's only—" I hesitated, and Regis demanded, "What else?"

I said it, after a minute. "It's—well, it's you. If anything happens to you, we'll be held responsible to all Darkover."

He grinned. In the red sunlight he looked like a painting from some old legend. "Responsibility? You didn't strike me as the worrying type, Jason. What sort of dutter do you take me for? I know how to handle myself in the mountains, and I'm not afraid of the trailmen, even if I don't know them as you do. Come on—shall I get breakfast or will you?"

I shrugged, busying myself near the fire. Somewhat to the surprise of the other Terrans—Kendricks and Rafe—Regis had done his share of the camp work at every halt; not ostentatiously either, but cheerfully and matter-of-factly. This surprised Rafe and Kendricks, who accepted the Terran custom of the higher echelons leaving such things to the buck privates. But in spite of their rigid caste distinctions, social differences of the Terran type simply don't exist on Darkover. Neither does gallantry, and only Kendricks objected when Kyla took on the job of seeing to the packloading and did her share of heaving boxes and crates.

After a while Regis joined me at the fire again. The three roughneck brothers had come out and were splashing noisily in the ford of the river. The rest were still sleeping. Regis asked, "Shall I roust them out?"

"No need. The Kadarin's fed by ocean tides and we'll have to wait for low water to cross. Nearly noon before we could get across without ruining half our gear."

Regis sniffed at the kettle. "Sounds good," he decided, and dunked his bowl in; he sat down, balancing the food on his knee. I followed suit, and Regis demanded, "Tell me something about yourself, Jason. Where did you learn so much about the Hellers? Lerrys was on the 'Narr campaign, but you don't seem old enough for that."

"I'm older than I look," I said, "but I wasn't old enough for that." (During the brief civil war when Darkovans fought trailmen in the passes of 'Narr, I had—as a boy of eleven—spied on the human invaders; but I didn't tell Regis that.) "I lived with them for eight years."

"*Sharra!* Was that you?" The Darkovan prince looked genuinely impressed. "No wonder you got this assignment! Jason, I envy you!"

I gave a short bark of laughter.

"No, I'm serious, Jason. As a boy I tried to get into the Terran space service. But my family finally convinced me that as a Hastur I had my work already cut out for me—that we Hasturs were committed to trying to keep Terra and Darkover on a peaceful basis. It puts me at a terrific disadvantage, you know. They all think I ought to be wearing cushions around my head in case I take a tumble."

I snapped, "Then why in hell did they let you come on a dangerous mission like this?"

The Hastur's eyes twinkled, but his face was completely deadpan and his voice grave. "I pointed out to my grandsire that I have been assiduous in my duty to the Hasturs. I have five sons, three legitimate, born in the past two years."

I choked, spluttered, and exploded into laughter as Regis got to his feet and went to rinse his bowl in the river.

The sun was high before we left the camp. While the others were packing up the last oddments, ready for the saddle, I gave Kyla the task of readying the rucksacks we'd carry after the trails got too bad even for the pack animals, and went to stand at the water's edge, checking the depth of the ford and glancing up at the smoke-hazed rifts between peak and peak.

The men were packing up the small tent we'd use in the forests, moving around with a good deal of horseplay and a certain brisk bustle. They were a good crew, I'd already discovered. Rafe and Lerrys and the three Darkovan brothers were tireless, cheerful, and mountain-hardened. Kendricks, obviously out of his element, could be implicitly relied on to follow orders, and I felt that I could fall back on him. Strange as it seemed, the very fact that he was a Terran was vaguely comforting, where I'd anticipated it would be a nuisance.

The girl Kyla was still something of an unknown

quantity. She was too taut and quiet, working her share but seldom contributing a word—we were not yet in mountain country. So far she was quiet and touchy with me, although she seemed natural enough with the Darkovans, and I let her alone.

"Hi, Jason, get a move on," someone shouted, and I walked back toward the clearing, squinting in the sun. It hurt, and I touched my face gingerly, suddenly realizing what had happened. Yesterday, riding in the uncovered truck, and this morning, unused to the fierce sun of these latitudes, I had neglected to take the proper precautions against exposure and my face was reddening with sunburn. I walked toward Kyla, who was cinching a final load on one of the pack animals, which she did efficiently enough.

She didn't wait for me to ask, but sized up the situation with one amused glance at my face. "Sunburn? Put some of this on it." She produced a tube of white stuff; I twisted at the top inexpertly, and she took it from me, squeezed the stuff out in her palm, and said, "Stand still and bend down your head."

She smeared the mixture across my forehead and cheeks. It felt cold and good. I started to thank her, then broke off as she burst out laughing. "What's the matter?"

"You should see yourself!" she gurgled.

I wasn't amused. No doubt I presented a grotesque appearance, and no doubt she had the right to laugh at it, but I scowled. It hurt. Intending to put things back on the proper footing, I demanded, "Did you make up the climbing loads?"

"All except bedding. I wasn't sure how much to allow," she said. "Jason, have you eyeshades for when you get on snow?" I nodded, and she instructed severely, "Don't forget them. Snowblindness—I give you my word—is even more unpleasant than sunburn—and *very* painful!"

"Damn it, girl, I'm not stupid!" I exploded.

She said, in her expressionless monotone again, "Then you *ought* to have known better than to get sunburnt. Here, put this in your pocket." She handed me the tube of sunburn cream. "Maybe I'd better check up on some of the others and make sure they haven't forgotten." She went off without a word, leaving me with an unpleasant feeling that she'd come off best, that she considered me an irresponsible scamp.

Forth had said almost the same thing.

I told the Darkovan brothers to urge the pack animals across the narrowest part of the ford, and gestured to Lerrys and Kyla to ride one on either side of Kendricks, who might not be aware of the swirling, treacherous currents of a mountain river. Rafe could not urge his edgy horse into the water; he finally dismounted, took off his boots, and led the creature across the slippery rocks. I crossed last, riding close to Regis Hastur, alert for dangers and thinking resentfully that anyone so important to Darkover's policies should not be risked on such a mission. Why, if the Terran Legate had (unthinkably!) come with us, he would be surrounded by bodyguards, Secret Service men, and dozens of precautions against accident, assassination, or misadventure.

All that day we rode upward, encamping at the farthest point we could travel with pack animals or mounted. The next day's climb would enter the dangerous trails we must travel afoot. We pitched a comfortable camp, but I admit I slept badly. Kendricks and Lerrys and Rafe had blinding headaches from the sun and the thinness of the air; I was more used to these conditions, but I felt a sense of unpleasant pressure, and my ears rang. Regis arrogantly denied any discomfort, but he moaned and cried out continuously in his sleep until Lerrys kicked him, after which he was silent and, I feared, sleepless. Kyla seemed the least affected of any; probably she had been at higher altitudes more continuously than any of us. But there were dark circles beneath her eyes.

However, no one complained as we readied ourselves for the last long climb upward. If we were fortunate, we could cross Dammerung before nightfall; at the very least, we should bivouac tonight very near the pass. Our camp had been made at the last level spot; we partially hobbled the pack animals so they would not stray too far, and left ample food for them, and cached all but the most necessary of light trail gear. As we prepared to start upward on the steep, narrow track—hardly more than a rabbit-run—I glanced at Kyla and stated, "We'll work on rope from the first stretch. Starting now."

One of the Darkovan brothers stared at me with contempt. "Call yourself a mountain man, Jason? Why, my little daughter could scramble up *that* track without so much as a push on her behind!"

I set my chin and glared at him. "The rocks aren't easy, and some of these men aren't used to working on rope at all. We might as well get used to it, because when we start working along the ledges, I don't want anybody who doesn't know how."

They still didn't like it, but nobody protested further until I directed the huge Kendricks to the center of the second rope. He glared viciously at the light nylon line and demanded with some apprehension, "Hadn't I better go last until I know what I'm doing? Hemmed in between the two of you, I'm apt to do something damned dumb!"

Hjalmar roared with laughter and informed him that the center place on a three-man rope was always reserved for weaklings, novices, and amateurs.

I expected Kendricks' temper to flare up; the burly Spaceforce man and the Darkovan giant glared at one another, then Kendricks only shrugged and knotted the line through his belt. Kyla warned Kendricks and Lerrys about looking down from ledges, and we started.

The first stretch was almost too simple, a clear track winding higher and higher for a couple of miles. Pausing to rest for a moment, we could turn and see the entire valley outspread below us. Gradually the trail grew steeper, in spots pitched almost at a fifty-degree angle, and was scattered with gravel, loose rock, and shale, so that we placed our feet carefully, leaning forward to catch at handholds and steady ourselves against rocks. I tested each boulder carefully, since any weight placed against an unsteady rock might dislodge it on somebody below. One of the Darkovan brothers—Vardo, I thought—was behind me, separated by ten or twelve feet of slack rope, and twice when his feet slipped on gravel he stumbled and gave me an unpleasant jerk. What he muttered was perfectly true; on slopes like this, where a fall wasn't dangerous anyhow, it was better to work unroped; then a slip bothered no one but the slipper. But I was finding out what I wanted to know—what kind of climbers I had to lead through the Hellers.

Along a cliff face the trail narrowed horizontally, leading across a foot-wide ledge overhanging a sheer drop of fifty feet and covered with loose shale and scrub plants. Nothing, of course, to an experienced climber—a foot-wide ledge might as well be a four-lane superhighway. Kendricks made a nervous joke about a tightrope walker, but when his turn came he picked his way securely, without losing balance. The amateurs—Lerrys Ridenow, Regis, Rafe—came across without hesitation, but I wondered how well they would have done at a less secure altitude; to a real mountaineer, a footpath is a footpath, whether in a meadow, above a two-foot drop, a thirty-foot ledge, or a sheer mountain face three miles above the first level spot.

After crossing the ledge, the going was harder. A steeper trail, in places nearly imperceptible, led between thick scrub and overhanging trees, closely clustered. In spots their twisted roots obscured the trail; in others the persistent growth had thrust aside rocks and dirt. We had to make our way through tangles of underbrush which would have been nothing to a trailman, but which made our ground-accustomed bodies ache with the effort of getting over or through them; and once the track was totally blocked by a barricade of tangled dead brushwood, borne down on floodwater after a sudden thaw or cloudburst. We had to work painfully around it over a three-hundred-foot rockslide, which we could cross only one at a time, crabfashion, leaning double to balance ourselves; and no one complained now about the rope.

Toward noon I had the first intimation that we were not alone on the slope.

At first it was no more than a glimpse of motion out of the corner of my eyes, the shadow of a shadow. The fourth time I saw it, I called softly to Kyla, "See anything?"

"I was beginning to think it was my eyes, or the altitude. I saw, Jason."

"Look for a spot where we can take a break," I directed. We climbed along a shallow ledge, the faint imperceptible flutters in the brushwood climbing with us on either side. I muttered to the girl, "I'll be glad when we get clear of this. At least we'll be able to see what's coming after us!"

"If it comes to a fight," she said surprisingly, "I'd rather fight on gravel than ice."

Over a rise, there was a roaring sound. Kyla swung up and balanced on a rock-wedged tree root, cupped her mouth to her hands, and called, "Rapids!"

I pulled myself up to the edge of the drop and stood looking down into the narrow gully. Here the track we had been following was crossed and obscured by the deep, roaring rapids of a mountain stream.

Less than twenty feet across, it tumbled in an icy flood, almost a waterfall, pitching over the lip of a crag above us. It had sliced a ravine five feet deep in the mountainside, and came roaring down with a rushing noise that made my head vibrate. It looked formidable; anyone stepping into it would be knocked off his feet in seconds, and swept a thousand feet down the mountainside by the force of the current.

Rafe scrambled gingerly over the gullied lip of the channel it had cut, and bent carefully to scoop up water in his palm and drink. "Phew, it's colder than Zandru's ninth hell. Must come straight down from a glacier!"

It did. I remembered the trail and remembered the spot. Kendricks joined me at the water's edge, and asked, "How do we get across?"

"I'm not sure," I said, studying the racing white torrent. Overhead, about twenty feet from where we clustered on the slope, the thick branches of enormous trees overhung the rapids, their long roots partially bared, gnarled and twisted by recurrent floods; and between these trees swayed one of the queer swing-bridges of the trailmen, hanging only about ten feet above the water.

Even I had never learned to navigate one of these swinging bridges without assistance; human arms are no longer suited to brachiation. I might have managed it once; but at present, except as a desperate final expedient, it was out of the question. Rafe or Lerrys, who were lightly built and acrobatic, could probably do it as a simple stunt on the level, in a field; on a steep and rocky mountainside, where a fall might mean being dashed a thousand feet down the torrent, I doubted it. The trailmen's bridge was out—but what other choice was there?

I beckoned to Kendricks, he being the man I was the most inclined to trust with my life at the moment, and said, "It looks uncrossable, but I think two men could get across, if they were steady on their feet. The others can hold us on ropes, in case we do get knocked down. If we can get to the opposite bank, we can stretch a fixed rope from that snub of rock—" I pointed, "and the others can cross with that. The first men over will be the only ones to run any risk. Want to try?"

I liked it better that he didn't answer right away, but went to the edge of the gully and peered down the rocky chasm. Doubtless, if we were knocked down, all seven of the others could haul us up again; but not before we'd been badly smashed on the rocks. And once

again I caught that elusive shadow of movement in
the brushwood; if the trailmen chose a moment when
we were half-in, half-out of the rapids, we'd be ridicu-
lously vulnerable to attack.

"We ought to be able to get a fixed rope easier than
that," Hjalmar said, and took one of the spares from
his rucksack. He coiled it, making a running loop on
one end, and, standing precariously on the lip of the
rapids, sent it spinning toward the outcrop of rock we
had chosen as a fixed point. "If I can get it over—"

The rope fell short, and Hjalmar reeled it in and
cast the loop again. He made three more unsuccessful
tries before finally, with held breath, we watched the
noose settle over the rocky snub. Gently, pulling the
line taut, we watched it stretch above the rapids.
The knot tightened, fastened. Hjalmar grinned and let
out his breath.

"There," he said, and jerked hard on the rope, testing it with a long hard pull. The rocky outcrop broke,
with a sharp *crack*, split, and toppled entire into the
rapids, the sudden jerk almost pulling Hjalmar off his
feet. The boulder rolled, with a great bouncing splash,
faster and faster down the mountain, taking the rope
with it.

We just stood and stared for a minute. Hjalmar
swore horribly, in the unprintable filth of the mountain tongue, and his brothers joined in. "How the
devil was I to know the *rock* would split off?"

"Better for it to split now than when we were depending on it," Kyla said stolidly. "I have a better

idea." She was untying herself from the rope as she spoke, and knotting one of the spares through her belt. She handed the other end of the rope to Lerrys. "Hold on to this," she said, and slipped out of her blanket windbreak, standing shivering in a thin sweater. She unstrapped her boots and tossed them to me. "Now boost me on your shoulders, Hjalmar."

Too late, I guessed her intention and shouted, "No, don't try—" But she had already clambered to an unsteady perch on the big Darkovan's shoulders and made a flying grab for the lowest loop of the trailmen's bridge. She hung there, swaying slightly and sickeningly, as the loose llanas gave to her weight.

"Hjalmar—Lerrys—haul her down!"

"I'm lighter than any of you," Kyla called shrilly, "and not hefty enough to be any use on the ropes!" Her voice quavered somewhat as she added, "—and hang on to that rope, Lerrys! If you lose it, I'll have done this for nothing!"

She gripped the loop of vine and reached, with her free hand, for the next loop. Now she was swinging out over the edge of the boiling rapids. Tight-mouthed, I gestured to the others to spread out slightly below—not that anything would help her if she fell.

Hjalmar, watching as the woman gained the third loop, which joggled horribly to her slight weight, shouted suddenly, "Kyla, quick! The loop *beyond*— don't touch the next one! It's frayed—rotted through!"

Kyla brought her left hand up to her right on the third loop. She made a long reach, missed her grab, swung again, and clung, breathing hard, to the safe fifth loop. I watched, sick with dread. The damned girl should have told me what she intended.

Kyla glanced down and we got a glimpse of her face, glistening with the mixture of sunburn cream and sweat, drawn with effort. Her tiny swaying figure hung twelve feet above the white tumbling water, and if she lost her grip, only a miracle could bring her out alive. She hung there for a minute, jiggling slightly, then started a long back-and-forward swing. On the third forward swing she made a long leap and grabbed at the final loop.

It slipped through her fingers; she made a wild grab with the other hand, and the liana dipped sharply under her weight, raced through her fingers, and, with a sharp snap, broke in two. She gave a wild shriek as it parted, and twisted her body frantically in mid-air, landing asprawl half-in, half-out of the rapids, but on the further bank. She hauled her legs up on dry land and crouched there, drenched to the waist but safe.

The Darkovans were yelling in delight. I motioned to Lerrys to make his end of the rope fast around a hefty tree-root, and shouted, "Are you hurt?" She indicated in pantomime that the thundering of the water drowned words, and bent to secure her end of the rope. In sign language I gestured to her to make very sure of the knots; if anyone slipped, she hadn't the weight to hold us.

I hauled on the rope myself to test it, and it held fast. I slung her boots around my neck by their cords, then, gripping the fixed rope, Kendricks and I stepped into the water.

It was even icier than I expected, and my first step was nearly the last; the rush of the white water knocked me to my knees, and I floundered and would have measured my length except for my hands on the fixed rope. Buck Kendricks grabbed at me, letting go the rope to do it, and I swore at him, raging, while we got on our feet again and braced ourselves against the onrushing current. While we struggled in the pounding waters, I admitted to myself that we could never have crossed without the rope Kyla had risked her life to fix.

Shivering, we got across and hauled ourselves out. I signaled to the others to cross two at a time, and Kyla seized my elbow. "Jason—"

"Later, dammit!" I had to shout to make myself heard over the roaring water, as I held out a hand to help Rafe get his footing in the ledge.

"This—can't—wait," she yelled, cupping her hands and shouting into my ear. I turned on her. "*What!*"

"There are—*trailmen*—on the top level—of that bridge! I saw them! They cut the loop!"

Regis and Hjalmar came struggling across last; Regis, lightly-built, was swept off his feet and Hjalmar turned to grab him, but I shouted to him to keep clear—they were still roped together and if the ropes fouled we might drown someone. Lerrys and I leaped down and hauled Regis clear; he coughed, spitting icy water, drenched to the skin.

I motioned to Lerrys to leave the fixed rope, though I had little hope that it would be there when we returned, and looked quickly around, debating what to do. Regis and Rafe and I were wet clear through; the others were wet to well above the knee. At this altitude, this was dangerous, although we were not yet high enough to worry about frostbite. Trailmen or no trailmen, we must run the lesser risk of finding a place where we could kindle a fire and dry out.

"Up there—there's a clearing," I said briefly, and hurried them along.

It was hard climbing now, on rock, and there were places where we had to scrabble for handholds, and flatten ourselves out against an almost sheer wall. The keen wind rose as we climbed higher, whining through the thick forest, soughing in the rocky outcrops, and biting through our soaked clothing with icy teeth. Kendricks was having hard going now, and I helped him as much as I could, but I was aching with cold. We gained the clearing, a small bare spot on a lesser peak, and I directed the two Darkovan brothers, who were the driest, to gather dry brushwood and get a fire going. It was hardly near enough to sunset to camp, but by the time we were dry enough to go on safely, it would be, so I gave orders to get the tent up, then rounded angrily on Kyla:

"See here, another time don't try any dangerous tricks unless you're ordered to!

"Go easy on her," Regis Hastur interceded, "we'd never have crossed without the fixed rope. Good work, girl."

"You keep out of this!" I snapped. It was true, yet resentment boiled in me as Kyla's plain sullen face glowed under the praise from Hastur.

The fact was—I admitted it grudgingly—a light-weight like Kyla ran less risk on an acrobat's bridge than in that kind of roaring current. That did not lessen my annoyance; and Regis Hastur's interference, and the foolish grin on the girl's face, made me boil over.

I wanted to question her further about the sight of trailmen on the bridge, but decided against it. We had been spared attack on the rapids, so it wasn't impossible that a group, not hostile, was simply watching our progress—maybe even aware that we were on a peaceful mission.

But I didn't believe it for a minute. If I knew anything about the trailmen, it was this—one could not judge them by human standards at all. I tried to decide what I would have done, as a trailman, but my brain wouldn't run that way at the moment.

The Darkovan brothers had built up the fire with a thoroughly reckless disregard of watching eyes. It seemed to me that the morale and fitness of the shivering crew was of more value at the moment than caution; and around the roaring fire, feeling my soaked clothes warming to the blaze and drinking boiling hot tea from a mug, it seemed that we were right. Optimism reappeared. Kyla, letting Hjalmar dress her hands which had been rubbed raw by the slipping lianas, made jokes with the men about her feat of acrobatics.

We had made camp on the summit of an outlying arm of the main ridge of the Hellers, and the whole massive range lay before our eyes, turned to a million colors in the declining sun. Green and turquoise and rose, the mountains were even more beautiful than I remembered. The shoulder of the high slope we had just climbed had obscured the real mountain *massif* from our sight, and I saw Kendricks' eyes widen as he realized that this high summit we had just mastered was only the first step of the task which lay before us. The real ridge rose ahead, thickly forested on the lower slopes, then strewn with rock and granite like the landscape of an airless, deserted moon. And above the rock, there were straight walls capped with blinding snow and ice. Down one peak a glacier flowed, a waterfall, a cascade shockingly arrested in motion. I murmured the trailmen's name for the mountain, aloud, and translated it for the others.

"The Wall Around the World."

"Good name for it," Lerrys murmured, coming with his mug in his hand to look at the mountain.

"Jason, the big peak there has never been climbed, has it?"

"I can't remember." My teeth were chattering and I went back toward the fire. Regis surveyed the distant glacier and murmured, "It doesn't look too bad. There could be a route along that western *arête*—Hjalmar, weren't you with the expedition that climbed and mapped High Kimbi?"

The giant nodded, rather proudly. "We got within a hundred feet of the top, then a snowstorm came up and we had to turn back. Some day we'll tackle the Wall Around the World—it's been tried, but no one ever climbed the peak."

"No one ever will," Lerrys stated positively. "There's two hundred feet of sheer rock cliff. Prince Regis, you'd need wings to get up. And there's the avalanche ledge they call Hell's Alley—"

Kendricks broke in irritably, "I don't care whether it's ever been climbed or ever will be climbed, we're not going to climb it now!" He stared at me and added, "I hope!"

"We're not." I was glad of the interruption. If the youngsters and amateurs wanted to amuse themselves plotting hypothetical attacks on unclimbable sierras, that was all very well, but it was, if nothing worse, a great waste of time. I showed Kendricks a notch in the ridge, thousands of feet lower than the peaks, and well sheltered from the ice falls on either side.

"That's Dammerung; we're going through there.

We won't be on the mountain at all, and it's less than 22,000 feet high in the pass—although there are some bad ledges and washes. We'll keep clear of the main tree-roads if we can, and all the mapped trailmen's villages, but we may run into wandering bands—" abruptly I made my decision and gestured them around me.

"From this point," I broke the news, "we're liable to be attacked. Kyla, tell them what you saw."

She put down her mug. Her face was serious again, as she related what she had seen on the bridge. "We're on a peaceful mission, but they don't know that yet. The thing to remember is that they do not wish to kill, only to wound and rob. If we show fight—" she displayed a short ugly knife, which she tucked matter-of-factly into her shirt-front, "they will run away again."

Lerrys loosened a narrow dagger which, until this moment, I had thought purely ornamental. He said, "Mind if I say something more, Jason? I remember from the 'Narr campaign—the trailmen fight at close quarters, and by human standards they fight dirty." He looked around fiercely, his unshaven face glinting as he grinned. "One more thing. I like elbow room. Do we have to stay roped together when we start out again?"

I thought it over. His enthusiasm for a fight made me feel both annoyed and curiously delighted. "I won't make anyone stay roped who thinks he'd be safer without it," I said. "We'll decide that when the time comes, anyway. But personally—the trailmen are used to running along narrow ledges, and we're not. Their first tactic would probably be to push us off, one by one. If we're roped, we can fend them off better." I dismissed the subject, adding, "Just now, the important thing is to dry out."

Kendricks remained at my side after the others had gathered around the fire, looking into the thick forest which sloped up to our campsite. He said, "This place looks as if it had been used for a camp before. Aren't we just as vulnerable to attack here as we would be anywhere else?"

He had hit on the one thing I hadn't wanted to talk about. This clearing was altogether too convenient. I only said, "At least there aren't so many ledges to push us off."

Kendricks muttered, "You've got the only blaster!"

"I left it at Carthon," I said truthfully. Then I laid down the law:

"Listen, Buck. If we kill a single trailman, except in hand-to-hand fight in self-defense, we might as well pack up and go home. We're on a peaceful mission, and we're begging a favor. Even if we're attacked— we kill only as a last resort, and in hand-to-hand combat!"

"Damned primitive frontier planet—"

"Would you rather die of the trailmen's disease?"

He said savagely, "We're apt to catch it anyway— here. You're immune, you don't care, you're safe! The rest of us are on a suicide mission—and damn it, when I die I want to take a few of those goddamn monkeys with me!"

I bent my head, bit my lip, and said nothing. Buck couldn't be blamed for the way he felt. After a moment, I pointed to the notch in the ridge again. "It's not so far. Once we get through Dammerung, it's easy going into the trailmen's city. Beyond there, it's all civilized."

"Maybe *you* call it civilization," Kendricks said, and turned away.

"Come on, let's finish drying our feet."

And at that moment they hit us.

CHAPTER FIVE

Kendricks' yell was the only warning I had before I was fighting away something scrabbling up my back. I whirled and ripped the creature away, and saw dimly that the clearing was filled to the rim with an explosion of furry white bodies. I cupped my hands and yelled, in the only trailman dialect I knew, "Hold off! We come in peace!"

One of them yelled something unintelligible and plunged at me—another tribe! I saw a white-furred, chinless face, contorted in rage, a small ugly knife—a female! I ripped out my own knife, fending away a savage slash. Something tore white-hot across the knuckles of my hand; the fingers went limp and my knife fell, and the trailman woman snatched it up and made off with her prize, swinging lithely upward into the treetops.

I searched quickly, gripped with my good hand at the bleeding knuckles, and found Regis Hastur struggling at the edge of a ledge with a pair of the creatures. The crazy thought ran through my mind that if they killed him all Darkover would rise and exterminate the trailmen and it would all be my fault. Then Regis tore one hand free, and made a curious motion with his fingers.

It looked like an immense green spark a foot long, or like a fireball. It exploded in one creature's white face and she gave a wild howl of terror and anguish, scrabbled blindly at her eyes, and with a despairing shriek, ran for the shelter of the trees. The pack of trailmen gave a long formless wail, and then they were gathering, flying, retreating into the shadows. Rafe yelled something obscene and then a bolt of bluish flame lanced toward the retreating pack. One of the humanoids fell without a cry, pitching senseless over the ledge.

I ran toward Rafe, struggling with him for the shocker he had drawn from its hiding place inside his shirt. "You blind damned fool!" I cursed him. "You may have ruined everything—"

"They'd have killed him without it," he retorted wrathfully. He had evidently failed to see how efficiently Regis defended himself. Rafe motioned toward the fleeing pack and sneered, "Why don't you go with your friends?"

With a grip I thought I had forgotten, I got my hand around Rafe's knuckles and squeezed. His hand went limp and I snatched the shocker and pitched it over the ledge.

"One word and I'll pitch you after it," I warned. "Who's hurt?"

Garin was blinking senselessly, half dazed by a blow; Regis' forehead had been gashed and dripped blood, and Hjalmar's thigh sliced in a clean cut. My own knuckles were laid bare and the hand was getting numb. It was a little while before anybody noticed Kyla, crouched over speechless with pain. She reeled and turned deathly white when we touched her; we stretched her out where she was, and got her shirt off, and Kendricks crowded up beside us to examine the wound.

"A clean cut," he said, but I didn't hear. Something had turned over inside me, like a hand stirring up my brain, and . . .

Jay Allison looked around with a gasp of sudden vertigo. He was not in Forth's office, but standing precariously near the edge of a cliff. He shut his eyes briefly, wondering if he were having one of his worst nightmares, and opened them on a familiar face.

Buck Kendricks was bone-white, his mouth widening as he said hoarsely, "Jay! Doctor Allison—for God's sake—"

A doctor's training creates reactions that are almost reflexes; Jay Allison recovered some degree of sanity as he became aware that someone was stretched out in front of him, half naked, and bleeding profusely. He motioned away the crowding strangers and said in his bad Darkovan, "Let her alone, this is my work." He didn't know enough words to curse them away, so he switched to Terran, speaking to Kendricks:

"Buck, get these people away, give the patient some air. Where's my surgical case?" He bent and probed briefly, realizing only now that the injured was a woman, and young.

The wound was only a superficial laceration; whatever sharp instrument had inflicted it had turned on the costal bone without penetrating lung tissue. It could have been sutured, but Kendricks handed him only a badly filled first-aid kit; so Dr. Allison covered it tightly with a plastic clipshield which would seal it from further bleeding, and let it alone. By the time he had finished, the strange girl had begun to stir. She said haltingly, "Jason—?"

"Dr. Allison," he corrected tersely, surprised in a minor way—the major surprise had blurred lesser ones—that she knew his name. Kendricks spoke swiftly to the girl, in one of the Darkovan languages Jay didn't understand, and then drew Jay aside, out of earshot. He said in a shaken voice, "Jay, I didn't know—I wouldn't have believed—you're *Doctor Allison*? Good God—Jason!"

And then he moved fast. "What's the matter? Oh, Christ, Jay, don't faint on me!"

Jay was aware that he didn't come out of it too bravely, but anyone who blamed him (he thought resentfully) should try it on for size; going to sleep in a comfortably closed-in office and waking up on a cliff at the outer edges of nowhere. His hand hurt; he saw that it was bleeding and flexed it experimentally, trying to determine that no tendons had been injured. He rapped, "How did this happen?"

"Sir, keep your voice down—or speak Darkovan!"

Jay blinked again. Kendricks was still the only familiar thing in a strangely vertiginous universe. The Spaceforce man said huskily, "Before God, Jay, I hadn't any idea—and I've known you how long? Eight, nine years?"

Jay said, "That idiot Forth!" and swore, the colorless profanity of an indoor man.

Somebody shouted, "Jason!" in an imperative voice, and Kendricks said shakily, "Jay, if they see you—you literally are not the same man!"

"Obviously not." Jay looked at the tent, one pole still unpitched. "Anyone in there?"

"Not yet." Kendricks almost shoved him inside. "I'll tell them—I'll tell them something." He took a radiant from his pocket, set it down and stared at Allison in the flickering light, and said something profane. "You'll—you'll be all right here?"

Jay nodded. It was all he could manage. He was keeping a tight hold on his nerve; if it went, he'd start to rave like a madman. A little time passed, there were strange noises outside, and then there was a polite cough and a man walked into the tent.

He was obviously a Darkovan aristocrat and looked vaguely familiar, though Jay had no conscious memory of seeing him before. Tall and slender, he possessed that perfect and exquisite masculine beauty

sometimes seen among Darkovans, and he spoke to
Jay familiarly but with surprising courtesy:

"I have told them you are not to be disturbed for a
moment, that your hand is worse than we believed. A
surgeon's hands are delicate things, Doctor Allison,
and I hope that yours are not badly injured. Will you
let me look?"

Jay Allison drew back his hand automatically, then,
conscious of the churlishness of the gesture, let the
stranger take it in his and look at the fingers. The man
said, "It does not seem serious. I was sure it was
something more than that." He raised grave eyes.
"You don't even remember my name, do you, Dr.
Allison?"

"You know who I am?"

"Dr. Forth didn't tell me. But we Hasturs are partly
telepathic, Jason—forgive me—Doctor Allison. I have
known from the first that you were possessed by a
god or daemon."

"Superstitious rubbish," Jay snapped. "Typical of a
Darkovan!"

"It is a convenient manner of speaking, no more,"
said the young Hastur, overlooking the rudeness. "I
suppose I could learn your terminology, if I considered it worth the effort. I have had psi training, and I
can tell the difference when half of a man's soul has
driven out the other half. Perhaps I can restore you to
yourself—"

"If you think I'd have some Darkovan freak meddling with my mind—" Jay began hotly, then stopped.

Under Regis' grave eyes, he felt a surge of unfamiliar humility. This crew of men needed their leader, and obviously he, Jay Allison, wasn't the leader they needed. He covered his eyes with one hand.

Regis bent and put a hand on his shoulder, compassionately, but Jay twitched it off, and his voice, when he found it, was bitter and defensive and cold.

"All right. The work's the thing. I can't do it, Jason can. You're a parapsych. If you can switch me off—go right ahead!"

I stared at Regis, passing a hand across my forehead. "What happened?" I demanded, and in even swifter apprehension. "Where's Kyla? She was hurt—"

"Kyla's all right," Regis said, but I got up quickly to make sure. Kyla was outside, lying quite comfortably on a roll of blankets. She was propped up on her elbow drinking something hot, and there was a good smell of hot food in the air. I stared at Regis and demanded, "I didn't conk out, did I, from a little scratch like this?" I looked carelessly at my gashed hand.

"Wait—" Regis held me back, "don't go out just yet. Do you remember what happened, Doctor Allison?"

I stared in growing horror, my worst fear confirmed. Regis said quietly, "You—changed. Probably from the shock of seeing—" he stopped in midsentence, and I said, "The last thing I remember is seeing that Kyla was bleeding, when we got her clothes off. But—good Gods, a little blood wouldn't scare *me*, and Jay Allison's a surgeon, would it bring him roaring up like that?"

"I couldn't say." Regis looked as if he knew more than he was telling. "I don't believe that Dr. Allison—he's not much like you—was very concerned with Kyla. Are you?"

"Damn right I am. I want to make sure she's all right—" I stopped abruptly. "Regis—did they all see it?"

"Only Kendricks and I," Regis said, "and we will not speak of it."

I said, "Thanks," and felt his reassuring handclap. Damn it, demigod or prince, I *liked* Regis.

I went out and accepted some food from the kettle and sat down between Kyla and Kendricks to eat. I was shaken, weak with reaction. Furthermore, I realized that we couldn't stay here. It was too vulnerable to attack. So, in our present condition, were we. If we could push on hard enough to get near Dammerung Pass tonight, then tomorrow we could cross it early, before the sun warmed the snow and we had snow-slides and slush to deal with. Beyond Dammerung, I knew the tribesmen and could speak their language.

I mentioned this, and Kendricks looked doubtfully at Kyla. "Can she climb?"

"Can she stay here?" I countered. But I went and sat beside her anyhow:

"How badly are you hurt? Do you think you can travel?"

She said fiercely, "Of course I can climb! I tell you,

I'm no weak girl, I'm a Free Amazon!" She flung off
the blanket somebody had tucked around her legs.
Her lips looked a little pinched, but the long stride
was steady as she walked to the fire and demanded
more soup.

We struck the camp in minutes. The trailmen band
of raiding females had snatched up almost everything
portable, and there was no sense in striking and catching the tent; they'd return and hunt it out. If we came
back with a trailman escort, we wouldn't need it anyway. I ordered them to leave everything but the light-
est gear, and examined each remaining rucksack.
Rations for the night we would spend in the pass, our
few remaining blankets, ropes, sunglasses. Everything else I ruthlessly ordered left behind.

It was harder going now. For one thing, the sun
was lowering, and the evening wind was icy. Nearly
every one of us had some hurt, slight in itself, which
hindered us in climbing. Kyla was white and rigid,
but did not spare herself; Kendricks was suffering
from mountain sickness at this altitude, and I gave
him all the help I could, but with my stiffening
slashed hand I wasn't having too easy a time myself.

There was one expanse that was sheer rock-
climbing, flattened like bugs against a wall, scrabbling for handholds and footholds. I felt it a point of
pride to lead, and I led; but by the time we had
climbed the thirty-foot wall, and scrambled along a
ledge to where we could pick up the trail again, I was
ready to give over. Crowding together on the ledge, I

changed places with the veteran Lerrys, who was better than most professional climbers.

He muttered, "I thought you said this was a *trail!*"

I stretched my mouth in what was supposed to be a grin and didn't quite make it. "For the trailmen, this is a superhighway. And no one else ever comes this way."

Now we climbed slowly over snow; once or twice we had to flounder through drifts, and once a brief bitter snowstorm blotted out sight for twenty minutes, while we hugged each other on the ledge, clinging wildly against wind and icy sleet.

We bivouacked that night in a crevasse blown almost clean of snow, well above the tree-line, where only scrubby unkillable thornbushes clustered. We tore down some of them and piled them up as a windbreak, and bedded beneath it; but we all thought with aching regret of the comfort of the camp gear we'd abandoned.

That night remains in my mind as one of the most miserable in memory. Except for the slight ringing in my ears, the height alone did not bother me, but the others did not fare so well. Most of the men had blinding headaches, Kyla's slashed side must have given her considerable pain, and Kendricks had succumbed to mountain-sickness in its most agonizing form: severe cramps and vomiting. I was desperately uneasy about all of them, but there was nothing I could do; the only cure for mountain-sickness is oxygen or a lower altitude, neither of which was practical.

In the windbreak we doubled up, sharing blankets and body warmth. I took a last look around the close space before crawling in beside Kendricks, and saw the girl bedding down slightly apart from the others. I started to say something, but Kendricks spoke first.

"Better crawl in with us, girl." He nodded, coldly but not unkindly. "You needn't worry about any funny stuff."

Kyla gave me just the flicker of a grin, and I realized she was including me on the Darkovan side of a joke against this big man who was so unaware of Darkovan etiquette. But her voice was cool and curt as she said, "I'm not worrying," and loosened her heavy coat slightly before creeping into the nest of blankets between us.

It was painfully cramped, and chilly in spite of the self-heating blankets; we crowded close together and Kyla's head rested on my shoulder. I felt her snuggle closely to me, half asleep, hunting for a warm place; and I found myself very much aware of her closeness, curiously grateful to her. An ordinary woman would have protested, if only as a matter of form, to sharing blankets with two strange men. I realized that if Kyla had refused to crawl in with us, she would have called attention to her sex much *more* than she did by matter-of-factly behaving as if she were male.

She shivered convulsively, and I whispered, "Side hurting? Are you cold?"

"A little. It's been a long time since I've been at

these altitudes, too. What it really is—I can't get those women out of my head."

Kendricks coughed, moving uncomfortably. "I don't understand—those creatures who attacked us—all women—?"

I explained briefly. "Among the People of the Sky, as everywhere, more females are born than males. But the trailmen's lives are so balanced that they have no room for extra females within the Nests—the cities. So when a girl child of the Sky People reaches woman-hood, the other women drive her out of the city with kicks and blows, and she has to wander in the forest until some male comes after her and claims her and brings her back as his own. Then she can never be driven forth again, although if she bears no children she can be forced to be a servant to his other wives."

Kendricks made a little sound of disgust.

"You think it cruel," Kyla said with sudden passion, "but in the forest they can live and find their own food; they will not starve or die. Many of them prefer the forest life to living in the Nests, and they will fight away any male who comes near them. We who call ourselves human often make less provision for our spare women."

She was silent, sighing as if with pain. Kendricks made no reply except for a noncommittal grunt. I held myself back by main force from touching Kyla, remembering what she was, and finally said, "We'd better quit talking. The others want to sleep, if we don't."

After a time I heard Kendricks snoring, and Kyla's

quiet even breaths. I wondered drowsily how Jay would have felt about this situation—he who hated Darkover and avoided contact with every other human being, crowded between a Darkovan free Amazon and half a dozen assorted roughnecks. I turned the thought off, fearing it might somehow rearouse him in his brain.

But I had to think of something, anything to turn aside this consciousness of the woman's head against my chest, her warm breath coming and going against my bare neck. Only by the severest possible act of will did I keep myself from slipping my hand over her breasts, warm and palpable through the thin sweater. I wondered why Forth had called me undisciplined. I couldn't risk my leadership by making advances to our contracted guide—woman, Amazon, or whatever.

Somehow the girl seemed to be the pivot point of all my thoughts. She was not part of the Terran HQ, she was not part of any world Jay Allison might have known. She belonged wholly to Jason, to *my* world. Between sleep and waking, I lost myself in a dream of skimming flight-wise along the tree-roads, chasing the distant form of a girl driven from the Nest that day with blows and curses. Somewhere in the leaves I would find her—and we would return to the city, her head garlanded with the red leaves of a chosen-one, and the same women who had stoned her forth would crowd about and welcome her when she returned. The fleeing woman looked over her shoulder with Kyla's eyes; and then the woman's form muted and

Dr. Forth was standing between us in the tree-road, with the caduceus emblem on his coat stretched like a red staff between us. Kendricks in his Spaceforce uniform was threatening us with a blaster, and Regis Hastur was suddenly wearing a Space Service uniform too and saying, "Jay Allison, Jay Allison," as the tree-road splintered and cracked beneath our feet and we were tumbling down the waterfall and down and down and down. . . .

"Wake up!" Kyla whispered, and dug an elbow into my side. I opened my eyes on crowded blackness, grasping at the vanishing nightmare. "What's the matter?"

"You were moaning. Touch of altitude sickness?"

I grunted, realized my arm was around her shoulder, and pulled it quickly away. After a while I slept again, fitfully.

Before light we crawled wearily out of the bivouac, cramped and stiff and not rested, but ready to get out of this and go on. The snow was hard, in the dim light, and the trail was not difficult here. After all the trouble on the lower slopes, I think even the amateurs had lost their desire for adventurous climbing; we were all just as well pleased that the actual crossing of Dammerung should be an anticlimax and uneventful.

The sun was just rising when we reached the pass, and we stood for a moment, gathered close together, in the narrow defile between the great summits to either side.

Hjalmar gave the peaks a wistful look.

"Wish we could climb them."

Regis grinned at him companionably. "Someday— and you have the word of a Hastur, you'll be along on that expedition." The big fellow's eyes glowed. Regis turned to me, and said warmly, "What about it, Jason? A bargain? Shall we all climb it together, next year?"

I started to grin back and then some bleak black devil surged up in me, raging. When this was over, I'd suddenly realized, I wouldn't be there. I wouldn't be anywhere. I was a surrogate, a substitute, a splinter of Jay Allison, and when it was over, Forth and his tactics would put me back into what they considered my rightful place—which was nowhere. I'd never climb a mountain except now, when we were racing against time and necessity. I set my mouth in an unaccustomed narrow line and said, "We'll talk about that when we get back—if we ever do. Now I suggest we get going. Some of us would like to get down to lower altitudes."

The trail down from Dammerung inside the ridge, unlike the outside trail, was clear and well marked, and we wound down the slope, walking in easy single file. As the mist thinned and we left the snowline behind, we saw what looked like a great green carpet, interspersed with shining colors which were mere flickers below us. I pointed them out.

"The treetops of the North Forest—and the colors you see—are in the streets of the trailcity."

An hour's walking brought us to the edge of the

forest. We traveled swiftly now, forgetting our weariness, eager to reach the city before nightfall. It was quiet in the forest, almost ominously still. Over our heads somewhere, in the thick branches which in places shut out the sunlight completely, I knew that the tree-roads ran crisscross, and now and again I heard some rustle, a fragment of sound, a voice, a snatch of song.

"It's so dark down here," Rafe muttered, "anyone living in this forest would *have* to live in the treetops, or go totally blind!"

Kendricks whispered to me, "Are we being followed? Are they going to jump us?"

"I don't think so. What you hear are just the inhabitants of the city—going about their daily business up there."

"Queer business it must be," Regis said curiously, and as we walked along the mossy, needly forest floor, I told him something of the trailmen's lives. I had lost my fear. If anyone came at us now, I could speak their language. I could identify myself, tell my business, name my foster parents. Some of my confidence evidently spread to the others.

But as we came into more and more familiar territory, I stopped abruptly and struck my hand against my forehead.

"I knew we had forgotten something!" I said roughly. "I've been away from here too long, that's all. Kyla."

"What about Kyla?"

The girl explained it herself, in her expressionless monotone. "I am an unattached female. Such women are not permitted in the Nests."

"That's easy then," Lerrys said. "She must belong to one of us." He didn't add a syllable. No one could have expected it; Darkovan aristocrats don't bring their women on trips like this, and their women are not like Kyla.

The three brothers broke into a spate of volunteering, and Rafe made an obscene suggestion. Kyla scowled obstinately, her mouth tight with what could have been embarrassment or rage. "If you believe I need your protection—!"

"Kyla," I said tersely, "is under *my* protection. She will be introduced as my woman—and treated as such."

Rafe twisted his mouth in an unfunny smile. "I see the leader keeps all the best for himself?"

My face must have done something I didn't know about, for Rafe backed slowly away. I forced myself to speak slowly. "Kyla is a guide, and indispensable. If anything happens to me, she is the only one who can lead you back. Therefore her safety is my personal affair. Understand?"

As we went along the trail, the vague green light disappeared. "We're right below the trailcity," I whispered, and pointed upward. All around us the Hundred Trees rose, branchless pillars so immense that four men, hands joined, could not have circled one with their arms. They stretched upward for some three hundred feet, before stretching out their inter-weaving branches; above that, nothing was visible but blackness.

Yet the grove was not dark, but lighted with the startlingly brilliant phosphorescence of the fungi growing on the trunks, and trimmed into bizarre ornamental shapes. In cages of transparent fiber, glowing insects as large as a hand hummed softly.

As I watched, a trailman, quite naked except for an ornate hat and a narrow binding around the loins, descended the trunk. He went from cage to cage, feeding the glowworms with bits of shining fungus from a basket on his arm.

I called to him in his own language, and he dropped the basket, with an exclamation, his spidery thin body braced to flee or to raise an alarm.

"But I belong to the Nest," I called to him, and gave him the names of my foster parents. He came toward me, gripping my forearm with warm long fingers in a gesture of greeting.

"Jason? Yes, I hear them speak of you," he said in his gentle twittering voice, "you are at home. But those others—?" He gestured nervously at the strange faces.

"My friends," I assured him, "and we come to beg the Old-One for an audience. For tonight I seek shelter with my parents, if they will receive us."

He raised his head and called softly, and a slim child bounded down the trunk and took the basket. The trailman said, "I am Carrho. Perhaps it would be better if I guided you to your foster parents, so you will not be challenged."

I breathed more freely. I did not personally recognize Carrho, but he looked pleasantly familiar. Guided by him, we climbed one by one up the dark stairway inside the trunk, and emerged into the bright square, shaded by the topmost leaves, into a delicate green twilight. I felt weary and successful.

Kendricks stepped gingerly on the swaying, jiggling floor of the square. It gave slightly at every step, and Kendricks swore morosely in a language that fortunately only Rafe and I understood. Curious trailmen flocked to the street and twittered welcome and surprise.

Rafe and Kendricks betrayed considerable contempt when I greeted my foster parents affectionately. They were already old, and I was saddened to see it; their fur graying, their prehensile toes and fingers crooked with a rheumatic complaint of some sort, their reddish eyes bleared and rheumy. They welcomed me, and made arrangements for the others in my party to be housed in an abandoned house nearby. They had insisted that I must return to their roof, and Kyla, of course, had to stay with me.

"Couldn't we camp on the ground instead?" Kendricks asked, eying the flimsy shelter with distaste.

"It would offend our hosts," I said firmly. I saw nothing wrong with it. Roofed with woven bark, carpeted with moss which was planted on the floor, the place was abandoned, somewhat musty, but weather-tight and seemed comfortable to me.

The first thing to be done was to dispatch a messenger to the Old-One, begging the favor of an audience with him. That done (by one of my foster brothers), we settled down to a meal of buds, honey, insects, and birds' eggs; it tasted good to me, with the familiarity of food eaten in childhood, but among the others, only Kyla ate with appetite and Regis Hastur with interested curiosity.

After the demands of hospitality had been satisfied, my foster parents asked the names of my party, and I introduced them one by one. When I named Regis Hastur, it reduced them to brief silence, and then to an outcry; gently but firmly, they insisted that their home was unworthy to shelter the son of a Hastur, and that he must be fittingly entertained at the Royal Nest of the Old-One.

There was no gracious way for Regis to protest, and when the messenger returned, he prepared to accompany him. But before leaving, he drew me aside:

"I don't much like leaving the rest of you—"

"You'll be safe enough."

"It's not that I'm worried about, Dr. Allison."

"Call me Jason," I corrected angrily. Regis said, with a little tightening of his mouth, "That's it. You'll have to be Dr. Allison tomorrow when you tell the Old-One about your mission. But you have to be the Jason he knows, too."

"So—?"

"I wish I needn't leave here. I wish you were—going to stay with the men who know you only as Jason, instead of being alone—or only with Kyla."

There was something odd in his face, and I wondered at it. Could he—a Hastur—be jealous of Kyla? Jealous of *me*? It had never occurred to me that he might be somehow attracted to Kyla. I tried to pass it off lightly.

"Kyla might divert me."

Regis said without emphasis. "Yet she brought Dr. Allison back once before." Then surprisingly, he laughed. "Or maybe you're right. Maybe Kyla will—scare away Dr. Allison if he shows up."

CHAPTER SIX

The coals of the dying fire laid strange tints of color on Kyla's face and shoulders and the wispy waves of her dark hair. Now that we were alone, I felt constrained.

"Can't you sleep, Jason?"

I shook my head. "Better sleep while you can." I felt that this night of all nights I dared not close my eyes or when I woke I would have vanished into the Jay Allison I hated. For a moment I saw the room with his eyes; to him it would not seem cozy and clean, but—habituated to white sterile tile, Terran rooms and corridors—dirty and unsanitary as any beast's den.

Kyla said broodingly, "You're a strange man, Jason. What sort of man are you—in Terra's world?"

I laughed, but there was no mirth in it. Suddenly I had to tell her the whole truth:

"Kyla, the man you know as me doesn't exist. I was created for this one specific task. Once it's finished, so am I."

She started, her eyes widening. "I've heard tales

of—of the Terrans and their sciences—that they make men who aren't real, men of metal—not bone and flesh—"

Before the dawning of that naïve horror I quickly held out my bandaged hand, took her fingers in mine and ran them over it. "Is this metal? No, no, Kyla. But the man you know as Jason—I won't be he, I'll be someone different—" How could I explain a subsidiary personality to Kyla, when I didn't understand it myself?

She kept my fingers in hers softly and said, "I saw someone else—looking from your eyes at me once. A ghost."

I shook my head savagely. "To the Terrans, I'm the ghost!"

"Poor ghost!" she whispered.

Her pity stung. I didn't want it.

"What I don't remember I can't regret. Probably I won't even remember you." But I lied. I knew that although I forgot everything else, unregretting because unremembered, I could not bear to lose this girl, that my ghost would walk restless forever if I forgot her. I looked across the fire at Kyla, cross-legged in the faint light—only a few coals in the brazier. She had removed her sexless outer clothing, and wore some clinging garment, as simple as a child's smock and curiously appealing. There was still a little ridge of bandage visible beneath it and a random memory, not mine, remarked in the back corners of my brain that with the cut improperly sutured there would be a visible scar. *Visible to whom?*

She reached out an appealing hand. "Jason! Jason—?"

My self-possession deserted me. I felt as if I stood, small and reeling, under a great empty echoing chamber which was Jay Allison's mind, and that the roof was about to fall in on me. Kyla's image flickered in and out of focus, first infinitely gentle and appealing, then—as if seen at the wrong end of a telescope—far away and sharply incised and as remote and undesirable as any bug underneath a lens.

Her hands closed on my shoulders. I put out a groping hand to push her away.

"Jason," she implored, "don't—go away from me like that! Talk to me, tell me!"

But her words reached me through emptiness—I knew important things might hang on tomorrow's meeting, Jason alone could come through that meeting, where the Terrans for some reason put him through this hell and damnation and torture—oh yes—the trailmen's fever—

Jay Allison pushed the girl's hand away and scowled savagely, trying to collect his thoughts and concentrate them on what he must say and do, to convince the trailmen of their duty toward the rest of the planet. As if they—not even humans—could have a sense of duty!

With an unaccustomed surge of emotion, he

wished he were with the others. Kendricks, now. Jay knew, precisely, why Forth had sent the big, reliable spaceman at his back. And that handsome, arrogant Darkovan—where was he? Jay looked at the girl in puzzlement; he didn't want to reveal that he wasn't quite sure of what he was saying or doing, or that he had little memory of what Jason had been up to.

He started to ask, "Where did the Hastur kid go?" before a vagrant logical thought told him that such an important guest would have been lodged with the Old-One. Then a wave of despair hit him; Jay realized he did not even speak the trailmen's language, that it had slipped from his thoughts completely.

"You—" he fished desperately for the girl's name, "Kyla. You don't speak the trailman's language, do you?"

"A few words. No more. Why?" She had withdrawn into a corner of the tiny room—still not far from him—and he wondered remotely what his damned alter ego had been up to. With Jason, there was no telling. Jay raised his eyes with a melancholy smile.

"Sit down, child. You needn't be frightened."

"I'm—I'm trying to understand—" the girl touched him again, evidently trying to conquer her terror. "It isn't easy—when you turn into someone else under my eyes—" Jay saw that she was shaking in real fright.

He said wearily, "I'm not going to—to turn into a bat and fly away. I'm just a poor devil of a doctor who's gotten himself into one unholy mess." There was no reason, he was thinking, to take out his own misery and despair by shouting at this poor kid. God knew what she'd been through with his irresponsible other self—Forth had admitted that that damned "Jason" personality was a blend of all the undesirable traits he'd fought to smother all his life. By an effort of will he kept himself from pulling away from her hand on his shoulder.

"Jason, don't—slip away like that! *Think!* Try to keep hold on *yourself!*"

Jay propped his head in his hands, trying to make sense of that. Certainly in the dim light she could not be too conscious of subtle changes of expression. She evidently thought she was talking to Jason. She didn't seem to be overly intelligent.

"Think about tomorrow, Jason. What are you going to say to him? Think about your parents—"

Jay Allison wondered what they would think when they found a stranger here. He felt like a stranger. Yet he must have come, tonight, into this house and spoken—he rummaged desperately in his mind for some fragments of the trailmen's language. He had spoken it as a child. He must recall enough to speak to the woman who had been a kind foster mother to her alien son. He tried to form his lips to the unfamiliar shapes of words—

Jay covered his face with his hands again. Jason was the part of himself that remembered the trailmen. *That* was what he had to remember—Jason was not a hostile stranger, not an alien intruder in his body. Jason was a lost part of himself and at the moment a damn necessary part. If there were only some way to get back the Jason memories, skills, without losing *himself* . . . He said to the girl, "Let me think. Let me—" To his surprise and horror his voice broke into an alien tongue, "Let me alone, will you?"

Maybe, Jay thought, I could stay myself if I could remember the rest. Dr. Forth said Jason would remember the trailmen with kindness, not dislike.

Jay searched his memory and found nothing but familiar frustration: years spent in an alien land, apart from a human heritage, stranded and abandoned. *My father left me. He crashed the plane and I never saw him again and I hate him for leaving me. . . .*

But his father had not abandoned him. He had crashed the plane trying to save them both. It was no one's fault—

Except my father's. For trying to fly over the Hellers into a country where no man belongs. . . .

He hadn't belonged. And yet the trailmen, whom he considered little better than roaming beasts, had taken the alien child into their city, their homes, their hearts. They had loved him. And he . . .

"And I loved them," I found myself saying half aloud, then realized that Kyla was gripping my arm, looking up imploringly into my face. I shook my head rather groggily. "What's the matter?"

"You frightened me," she said in a shaky little

voice, and I suddenly knew what had happened. I tensed with savage rage against Jay Allison. He couldn't even give me the splinter of life I'd won for myself, but had to come sneaking out of my mind. How he must hate me! Not half as much as I hated him, damn him! Along with everything else, he'd scared Kyla half to death!

She was kneeling very close to me, and I realized that there was one way to fight that cold austere fish of a Jay Allison, send him shrieking down into hell again. He was a man who hated everything except the cold world he'd made his life. Kyla's face was lifted, soft and intent and pleading, and suddenly I reached out and pulled her to me and kissed her, hard.

"Could a ghost do this?" I demanded, "or this?"

She whispered, "No—oh, no," and her arms went up to lock around my neck. As I pulled her down on the sweet-smelling moss that carpeted the chamber, I felt the dark ghost of my other self thin out, vanish, and disappear.

Regis had been right. It had been the only way.

The Old-One was not old at all; the title was purely ceremonial. This one was young—not much older than I—but he had poise and dignity and the same strange indefinable quality I had recognized in Regis Hastur. It was something, I supposed, that the Terran Empire had lost in spreading from star to star—a feeling of knowing one's own place, a dignity that didn't demand recognition because it had never lacked it.

Like all trailmen he had the chinless face and lobe-less ears, the heavy-haired body which looked slightly less than human. He spoke very low—the trailmen have very acute hearing—and I had to strain my ears to listen, and remember to keep my own voice down.

He stretched his hand to me, and I lowered my head over it and murmured, "I make submission, Old-One."

"Never mind that," he said in his gentle twittering voice. "Sit down, my son. You are welcome here, but I feel you have abused our trust in you. We dismissed you to your own kind because we felt you would be happier so. Did we show you anything but kindness, that after so many years you return with armed men?"

The reproof in his red eyes was hardly an auspicious beginning. I said helplessly, "Old-One, the men with me are not armed. A band of those-who-may-not-enter-cities attacked us, and we defended ourselves. I traveled with so many men only because I feared to travel the passes alone."

"But does that explain why you have returned at all?" The reason and reproach in his voice made sense.

Finally I said, "Old-One, we come as supplicants. My people appeal to your people in the hope that you will be—" I started to say, *as human*, stopped and amended "—that you will deal as kindly with them as with me."

His face betrayed nothing. "What do you ask?"

I explained. I told it badly, stumbling, not knowing

the technical terms, knowing they had no equivalents anyway in the trailmen's language. He listened, asking a penetrating question now and again. When I mentioned the Terran Legate's offer to recognize the trailmen as a separate and independent government, he frowned and rebuked me:

"We of the Sky People have no dealings with the Terrans, and care nothing for their recognition—or its lack."

For that I had no answer, and the Old-One continued, kindly but indifferently, "We do not like to think that the fever which is a children's little sickness with us shall kill so many of your kind. But you cannot in all honesty blame us. You cannot say that we spread the disease; we never go beyond the mountains. Are we to blame that the winds change or the moons come together in the sky? When the time has come for men to die, they die." He stretched his hand in dismissal. "I will give your men safe-conduct to the river, Jason. Do not return."

Regis Hastur rose suddenly and faced him. "Will you hear me, Father?" He used the ceremonial title without hesitation, and the Old-One said in distress, "The son of Hastur need never speak as a suppliant to the Sky People!"

"Nevertheless, hear me as a suppliant, Father," Regis said quietly. "It is not the strangers and aliens of Terra who are pleading. We have learned one thing from the strangers of Terra, which you have not yet learned. I am young and it is not fitting that I should teach you, but you have said: 'Are we to blame that the moons come together in the sky?' No. But we have learned from the Terrans not to blame the moons in the sky for our own ignorance of the ways of the Gods—by which I mean the ways of sickness or poverty or misery."

"These are strange words for a Hastur," said the Old-One, displeased.

"These are strange times for a Hastur," said Regis loudly. The Old-One winced, and Regis moderated his tone, but continued vehemently, "You blame the moons in the sky. *I* say the moons are not to blame, nor the winds, nor the Gods. The Gods send these things to man to test their wits and to find if they have the will to master them!"

The Old-One's forehead ridged vertically and he said with stinging contempt, "Is this the breed of king which men call Hastur now?"

"Man or God or Hastur, I am not too proud to plead for my people," retorted Regis, flushing with anger. "Never in all the history of Darkover has a Hastur stood before one of you and begged—"

"—for the men from another world."

"—for all men on our world! Old-One, I could sit and keep state in the House of Hasturs, and even death could not touch me until I grew weary of living! But I preferred to learn new lives from new men. The Terrans have something to teach even the Hasturs, and they can learn a remedy against the trailmen's fever." He looked round at me, turning the discussion over to me again, and I said:

"I am no alien from another world, Old-One. I have been a son in your house. Perhaps I was sent to teach you to fight destiny. I cannot believe you are indifferent to death."

Suddenly, hardly knowing what I was going to do until I found myself on my knees, I knelt and looked up into the quiet, stern, remote face of the nonhuman.

"My father," I said, "you took a dying man, and a dying child from a burning plane. Even those of their own kind might have stripped their corpses and left them to die. You saved the child, fostered him, and treated him as a son. When he reached an age to be unhappy with you, you let a dozen of your people risk their lives to take him to his own. You cannot ask me to believe that you are indifferent to the death of a million of my people, when the fate of one could stir your pity!"

There was a moment's silence. Finally, the Old-One said, "Indifferent—no. But helpless. My people die when they leave the mountains. The air is too rich for them. The food is wrong. The light blinds and tortures them. Can I send them to suffer and die, those people who call me father?"

And a memory, buried all my life, suddenly surfaced. I said urgently, "Father, listen. In the world I live in now, I am called a wise man. You need not believe me, but listen; I know your people, they are my people. I remember when I left you, more than a dozen of my foster parents' friends offered, knowing they risked death, to go with me. I was a child; I did not realize the sacrifice they made. But I watched them suffer, as we went lower in the mountains, and I resolved—I resolved . . ." I spoke with difficulty, forcing the words through a reluctant barricade, ". . . that since others had suffered so for me . . . I would spend my life in curing the sufferings of others. Father, the Terrans call me a wise doctor, a man of healing. Among the Terrans I can see that my people, if they will come to us and help us, have air they can breathe and food which will suit them and that they are guarded from the light. I don't ask you to send anyone, father. I ask only—tell your sons what I have told you. If I know your people—who are my people forever—hundreds of them will offer to return with me. And you may witness what your foster son has sworn here; if one of your sons dies, your alien son will answer for it with his own life."

The words had poured from me in a flood. They were not all mine; some unconscious thing had recalled in me that Jay Allison had power to make these promises. For the first time I began to see what force, what guilt, what dedication working in Jay Allison had turned him aside from me. I remained at the Old-One's feet, kneeling, overcome, ashamed of the thing I had become. Jay Allison was worth ten of me. Irresponsible, Forth had said. Lacking purpose, lacking balance. What right had I to despise my sober self?

At last I felt the Old-One touch my head lightly.

"Get up, my son," he said, "I will answer for my people. And forgive me for my doubts and my delays."

Neither Regis nor I spoke for a minute after we left the audience room; then, almost as one, we turned to each other. Regis spoke first, soberly.

"It was a fine thing you did, Jason. I didn't believe he'd agree to it."

"It was your speech that did it," I denied. The sober mood, the unaccustomed surge of emotion, was still on me—but it was giving way to a sudden upswing of exaltation. Damn it, I'd *done* it! Let Jay Allison try to match *that*.

Regis still looked grave. "He'd have refused, but you appealed to him as one of themselves. And yet it wasn't quite that—it was something more—" Regis put a quick embarrassed arm around my shoulders and suddenly blurted out, "I think the Terran Medical played hell with your life, Jason! And even if it saves a million lives—it's hard to forgive them for that!"

CHAPTER SEVEN

Late the next day the Old-One called us in again, and told us that a hundred men had volunteered to return with us and act as blood donors and experimental subjects for research into the trailmen's disease.

The trip over the mountains, so painfully accomplished, was easier in return. Our escort of a hundred trailmen guaranteed us against attack, and they could choose the easiest paths.

Only as we undertook the long climb downward through the foothills did the trailmen, unused to ground travel at any time, and suffering from the unaccustomed low altitude, begin to weaken. As we grew stronger, more and more of them faltered, and we traveled more and more slowly. Not even Kendricks could be callous about "inhuman animals" by the time we reached the point where we had left the pack horses. And it was Rafe Scott who came to me and said desperately, "Jason, these poor fellows will never make it to Carthon. Lerrys and I know this country. Let us go ahead, as fast as we can travel alone, and arrange at Carthon for transit—maybe we can get pressurized aircraft to fly them from here. We can send a message from Carthon, too, about accommodations for them at the Terran HQ."

I was surprised and a little guilty that I had not thought of this myself. I covered it with a mocking, "I thought you didn't give a damn about 'my friends.'"

Rafe said doggedly, "I guess I was wrong about that. They're going through this out of a sense of duty, so they must be pretty different from the way I thought they were."

Regis, who had overheard Rafe's plan, now broke in quietly, "There's no need for you to travel ahead, Rafe. I can send a quicker message."

I had forgotten that Regis was a trained telepath. He added, "There are some space and distance limitations to such messages, but there is a regular relay net all over Darkover, and one of the relays is a girl who lives at the very edge of the Terran Zone. *If* you'll tell me what will give her access to the Terran HQ—" he flushed slightly and explained, "From what I know of the Terrans, she would not be very fortunate relaying the message if she merely walked to the gate and said she had a relayed telepathic message for someone, would she?"

I had to smile at the picture that conjured up in my mind. "I'm afraid not," I admitted. "Tell her to go to Dr. Forth, and give the message from Dr. Jason Allison."

Regis looked at me curiously—it was the first time

I had spoken my own name in the hearing of the others. But he nodded, without comment. For the next hour or two he seemed somewhat more preoccupied than usual, but after a time he came to me and told me that the message had gone through. Some time later he relayed an answer; that airlift would be waiting for us, not at Carthon, but at a small village near the ford of the Kadarin where we had left our trucks.

When we camped that night there were a dozen practical problems needing attention: the time and exact place of crossing the ford, the reassurance to be given to terrified trailmen who could face leaving their forests but not crossing the final barricade of the river, the small help in our power to be given the sick ones. But after everything had been done that I could do, and after the whole camp had quieted down, I sat before the low-burning fire and stared into it, deep in painful lassitude. Tomorrow we would cross the river and a few hours later we would be back in the Terran HQ. And then . . .

And then—and then nothing. I would vanish, I would utterly cease to exist anywhere, except as a vagrant ghost troubling Jay Allison's unquiet dreams. As he moved through the cold round of his days, I would be no more than a spent wind, a burst bubble, a thinned cloud.

The rose and saffron of the dying fire gave shape to my dreams. Once more, as in the trailcity that night, Kyla slipped through firelight to my side, and I looked up at her and suddenly I knew I could not bear it. I pulled her to me and muttered, "Oh Kyla—Kyla, I won't even remember you!"

She pushed my hands away, kneeling upright, and said urgently, "Jason, listen. We are close to Carthon, the others can lead them the rest of the way. Why go back to them at all? Slip away now and never go back! We can—" she stopped, coloring fiercely, that sudden and terrifying shyness overcoming her again, and at last she said in a whisper, "Darkover is a wide world, Jason. Big enough for us to hide in. I don't believe they would search very far."

They wouldn't. I could leave word with Kendricks— not with Regis, the telepath would see through me immediately—that I had ridden ahead to Carthon, with Kyla. By the time they realized that I had fled, they would be too concerned with getting the trail- men safely to the Terran Zone to spend much time looking for a runaway. As Kyla said, the world was wide. And it was my world. And I would not be alone in it.

"Kyla, Kyla," I said helplessly, and crushed her against me, kissing her. She closed her eyes and I took a long, long look at her face. Not beautiful, no. But womanly and brave and all the other beautiful things. It was a farewell look, and I knew it, if she didn't.

After the briefest time, she pulled a little away, and her flat voice was gentler and more breathless than usual. "We'd better leave before the others waken." She saw that I did not move. "Jason—"

I could not look at her. Muffled behind my hands, I

said, "No, Kyla. I—I promised the Old-One to look after my people in the Terran World."

"You won't be *there* to look after them! You won't be *you!*"

I said bleakly, "I'll write a letter to remind myself. Jay Allison has a very strong sense of duty. He'll look after them for me. He won't like it, but he'll do it, with his last breath. He's a better man than I am, Kyla. You'd better forget about me," I said, wearily. "I never existed."

That wasn't the end. Not nearly. She—begged, and I don't know why I put myself through the hell of stubborn refusal. But in the end she ran away, crying, and I threw myself down by the fire, cursing Forth, cursing my own folly, but most of all cursing Jay Allison, hating my other self with a blistering, sickening rage.

But before dawn I stirred in the light of the dying fire and Kyla's arms were around my neck in the darkness, her body pressed to mine, racked with convulsive crying.

"I can't convince you," she wept, "and I can't change you—and I wouldn't if I could. But while I can—while I can—I'll have you while you're you."

I crushed her to me. And for the moment my fear of tomorrow, my hate and bitterness against the men who had played with my life, were swept away in the sweetness of her mouth, warm and yielding, under mine. There in the light of the fading fire, desperate, knowing I would forget, I took her to me.

Whatever I might be tomorrow, tonight I was hers.

And I knew then how men feel when they love in the shadow of death—worse than death because I would live, a cold ghost of myself, through cold days and colder nights. It was fierce and savage and desperate; we were both trying to crowd a lifetime we could never have into a few stolen hours. But as I looked down at Kyla's wet face in the fading dawn, my bitterness had gone.

I might be swept away forever, a ghost, a nothing, blown away in the winds of one man's memory. But to that last fading spark of memory, I would be forever grateful, and in my limbo I would be grateful, if ghosts know gratitude, to those who had called me from my nowhere to know this: these days of struggle and the love of comrades, the clean wind of the mountains in my face again, a last adventure, the warm lips of a woman in my arms.

I had lived more, in my scant week of life, than Jay Allison would live in all his white and sterile years. I had had my lifetime. I didn't grudge him his, anymore.

Coming through the outskirts of the small village, next afternoon, the village where the airlift would meet us, we noted that the poorer quarter was almost deserted. Not a woman walked in the street, not a man lounged along the curbing, not a child played in the dusty squares.

Regis said bleakly, "It's begun," and dropped out

of line to stand in the doorway of a silent dwelling. After a minute he beckoned to me, and I looked inside.

I wished I hadn't. The sight would haunt me while I lived. An old man, two young women, and half a dozen children between four and fifteen years old lay inside. The old man, one of the children, and one of the young women were laid out neatly in clean death, shrouded, their faces covered with green branches after the Darkovan custom for the dead. The other young woman lay huddled near the fireplace, her coarse dress splattered with the filthy stuff she had vomited, dying. The children—even now I can't think of the children without retching. One, very small, had been in the woman's arms when she collapsed; it had squirmed free—for a little while. The others were in an indescribable condition, and the worst of it was that one of them was still moving, feebly, long past help. Regis turned blindly from the door and leaned against the wall, his shoulders heaving—not, as I first thought, in disgust, but in grief. Tears ran over his hands and spilled down, and when I took him by the arm to lead him away, he reeled and fell against me.

He said in a broken, blurred, choking voice, "Oh, Gods, Jason, those children, those children—if you ever had any doubts about what you're doing, any doubts about what you've done, think about that, think that you've saved a whole world from that, think that you've done something even the Hasturs couldn't do!"

My own throat tightened with something more than embarrassment. "Better wait till we know for sure whether the Terrans can carry through with it, and you'd better get to hell away from this doorway. I'm immune, but damn it, you're not." But I had to take him and lead him away, like a child, from that house. He looked up into my face and said with burning sincerity, "I wonder if you believe I'd give my life, a dozen times over, to have done that?"

It was a curious, austere reward. But vaguely it comforted me. And then, as we rode into the village itself, I lost myself, or tried to lose myself, in reassuring the frightened trailmen who had never seen a city on the ground, never seen or heard of an airplane. I avoided Kyla. I didn't want a final word, a farewell. We had had our farewells already.

Forth had done a marvelous job of preparing quarters for the trailmen, and after they were comfortably installed and reassured, I went down wearily and dressed in Jay Allison's clothing. I looked out the window at the distant mountains and a line from the book on mountaineering, which I had bought as a youngster in an alien world, and Jay had kept as a stray fragment of personality, ran in violent conflict through my mind:

Something hidden—go and find it . . .
Something lost beyond the ranges . . .

I had just begun to live. Surely I deserved better than this, to vanish when I had just discovered life.

Did the man who did not know how to live deserve to live at all? Jay Allison—that cold man who had never looked beyond any ranges—why should I be lost in him?

Something lost beyond the ranges—nothing would be lost but myself. I was beginning to loathe the overblown sense of duty which had brought me back here. Now, when it was too late, I was bitterly regretting—Kyla had offered me life. Surely I would never see Kyla again.

Could I regret what I would never remember? I walked into Forth's office as if I were going to my doom. I *was*—

Forth greeted me warmly.

"Sit down and tell me all about it," he insisted. I would rather not have spoken. Instead, compulsively, I made it a full report—and curious flickers came in and out of my consciousness as I spoke. By the time I realized I was reacting to a post-hypnotic suggestion, that in fact I was going under hypnosis again, it was too late and I could only think that this was worse than death because in a way I would be alive.

Jay Allison sat up and meticulously straightened his cuff before tightening his mouth in what was meant for a smile. "I assume, then, that the experiment was a success?"

"A complete success." Forth's voice was somewhat harsh and annoyed, but Jay was untroubled; he had known for years that most of his subordinates and superiors disliked him, and had long ago stopped worrying about it.

"The trailmen agreed?"

"They agreed," Forth said, surprised. "You don't remember anything at all?"

"Scraps. Like a nightmare." Jay Allison looked down at the back of his hand, flexing the fingers cautiously against pain, touching the partially healed red slash. Forth followed the direction of his eyes and said, not unsympathetically, "Don't worry about your hand. I looked at it pretty carefully. You'll have total use of it."

Jay said rigidly, "It seems to have been a pretty severe risk to take. Did you ever stop to think what it would have meant to me, to lose the use of it."

"It seemed a justifiable risk, even if you had," Forth said dryly. "Jay, I've got the whole story on tape, just as you told it to me. You might not like having a blank spot in your memory. Want to hear what your alter ego did?"

Jay hesitated. Then he unfolded his long legs and stood up. "No, I don't think I care to know." He waited, arrested by a twinge of a sore muscle, and frowned.

What had happened, what would he never know, why did the random ache bring a pain deeper than the pain of a torn nerve? Forth was watching him, and Jay asked irritably, "What is it?"

"You're one hell of a cold fish, Jay."

"I don't understand you, sir."

"You wouldn't," Forth muttered. "Funny. I *liked* your subsidiary personality."

Jay's mouth contracted in a mirthless grin.

"You would," he said, and swung quickly around.

"Come on. If I'm going to work on that serum project I'd better inspect the volunteers and line up the blood donors and look over old whatshisname's papers."

But beyond the window the snowy ridges of the mountain, inscrutable, caught and held his eye; a riddle and a puzzle—

"Ridiculous," he said, and went to his work.

CHAPTER EIGHT

Four months later, Jay Allison and Randall Forth stood together, watching the last of the disappearing planes, carrying the volunteers back toward Carthon and their mountains.

"I should have flown back to Carthon with them," Jay said moodily. Forth watched the tall man stare at the mountain; wondered what lay behind the contained gestures and the brooding.

He said, "You've done enough, Jay. You've worked like the devil. Thurmond, the Legate, sent down to say you'd get an official commendation and a promotion for your part. That's not even mentioning what you did in the trailmen's city." He put a hand on his colleague's shoulder, but Jay shook it off impatiently.

All through the work of isolating and testing the blood fraction, Jay had worked tirelessly and unsparingly; scarcely sleeping, but brooding; silent, prone to fly into sudden savage rages, but painstaking. He had overseen the trailmen with an almost fatherly solicitude—but from a distance. He had left no stone unturned for their comfort—but refused to see them in person except when it was unavoidable.

Forth thought, we played a dangerous game. Jay Allison had made his own adjustment to life, and we disturbed that balance. Have we wrecked the man? He's expendable, but damn it, what a loss! He asked, "Well, why *didn't* you fly back to Carthon with them? Kendricks went along, you know. He expected you to go until the last minute."

Jay did not answer. He had avoided Kendricks, the only witness to his duality. In all his nightmare brooding, the avoidance of anyone who had known him as Jason became a mania. Once, meeting Rafe Scott on the lower floor of the HQ, he had turned frantically and plunged like a madman through halls and corridors, to avoid coming face to face with the man, finally running up four flights of stairs and taking shelter in his rooms, with the pounding heart and bursting veins of a hunted criminal. At last he said, "If you've called me down here to give me hell about not wanting to make another trip into the Hellers—!"

"No, no," Forth said equably, "there's a visitor coming. Regis Hastur sent word he wants to see you. In case you don't remember him, he was on Project Jason—"

"I remember," Jay said grimly. It was nearly his one clear memory—the nightmare of the ledge, his slashed hand, the naked body of the Darkovan woman, —and blurring these things, the too-handsome Darkovan aristocrat who had banished him for Jason again.

"He's a better psychiatrist than you are, Forth. He changed me into Jason in the flicker of an eyelash, and it took you half a dozen hypnotic sessions."

"I've heard about the psi powers of the Hasturs," Forth said, "but I've never been lucky enough to meet one in person. Tell me about it. What did he do?"

Jay made a tight movement of exasperation, too controlled for a shrug. "Ask him, why don't you. Look, Forth, I don't much care to see him. I didn't do it for Darkover. I did it because it was my job. I'd prefer to forget the whole thing. Why don't you talk to him?"

"I rather had the idea that he wanted to see you personally. Jay, you did a tremendous thing, man! Damn it, why don't you strut a little. Be—be normal for once! Why, I'd be damned near bursting with pride if one of the Hasturs insisted on congratulating me personally!"

Jay's lip twitched, and his voice shook with controlled exasperation. "Maybe you would. I don't see it that way."

"Well, I'm afraid you'll have to. On Darkover nobody refuses when the Hasturs make a request—and certainly not a request as reasonable as this one." Forth sat down beside the desk. Jay struck the woodwork with a violent clenched fist and when he lowered his hand there was a tiny smear of blood along his knuckles. After a minute he walked to the couch and sat down, very straight and stiff, saying nothing. Neither of the men spoke again until Forth started at the sound of a buzzer, drew the mouthpiece toward him, and said, "Tell him we are honored—you know the routine for dignitaries, and send him up here."

Jay twisted his fingers together and ran his thumb, in a new gesture, over the ridge of scar tissue along the knuckles. Forth was aware of an entirely new quality in the silence, and started to speak to break it, but before he could do so, the office door slid open on its silent beam, and Regis Hastur stood there.

Forth rose courteously and Jay got to his feet like a mechanical doll jerked on strings. The young Darkovan ruler smiled engagingly at him.

"Don't bother, this visit is informal; that's the reason I came here rather than inviting you both to the Tower. Dr. Forth? It is a pleasure to meet you again, sir. I hope that our gratitude to you will soon take a more tangible form. There has not been a single death from the trailmen's fever since you made the serum available."

Jay, motionless, saw bitterly that the old man had succumbed to the youngster's deliberate charm. The chubby, wrinkled old face seamed up in a pleased smile as Forth said, "The gifts sent to the trailmen in your name, Lord Hastur, were greatly welcomed."

"Do you think that any of us will ever forget what they have done?" Regis replied. He turned toward the window and smiled rather tentatively at the man who stood there motionless since his first conventional gesture of politeness.

"Dr. Allison, do you remember me at all?"

"I remember you," Jay Allison said sullenly.

His voice hung heavily in the room, its sound a miasma in his ears. All his sleepless, nightmare-charged brooding, all his bottled hate for Darkover and the memories he had tried to bury, erupted into overwrought bitterness against this too-ingratiating youngster who was a demigod on this world and who had humiliated him, repudiated him for the hated Jason. For Jay, Regis had suddenly become the symbol of a world that hated him, forced him into a false mold.

A black and rushing wind seemed to blur the room. He said hoarsely, "I remember you all right," and took one savage, hurtling step.

The weight of the unexpected blow spun Regis around, and the next moment Jay Allison, who had never touched another human being except with the remote hands of healing, closed steely, murderous hands around Regis' throat. The world thinned out into a crimson rage. There was shouting, and sudden noises, and a red-hot explosion in his brain . . .

"You'd better drink this," Forth remarked, and I realized I was turning a paper cup in my hands. Forth sat down, a little weakly, as I raised it to my lips and sipped. Regis took his hand away from his throat and said huskily, "I could use some of that, doctor."

I put the whisky down. "You'll do better with water until your throat muscles are healed," I said swiftly, and went to fill a throwaway cup for him, without thinking. Handing it to him, I stopped in sudden dismay and my hand shook, spilling a few drops. I said hoarsely, swallowing, "—but drink it, anyway."

Regis got a few drops down, painfully, and said, "My own fault. The moment I saw—Jay Allison—I knew he was a madman. I'd have stopped him sooner only he took me by surprise."

"But—you say *him*—I'm Jay Allison," I said, and then my knees went weak and I sat down. "What in hell is this? I'm not Jay—but I'm not Jason, either—"

I could remember my entire life, but the focus had shifted. I still felt the old love, the old nostalgia for the trailmen; but I also knew, with a sure sense of identity, that I was Doctor Jason Allison, Jr., who had abandoned mountain climbing and become a specialist in Darkovan parasitology. Not Jay who had rejected the world; not Jason who had been rejected by it. But then who?

Regis said quietly, "I've seen you before—once. When you knelt to the Old-One of the trailmen." With a whimsical smile he said, "As an ignorant superstitious Darkovan, I'd say that you were a man who'd balanced his god and daemon for once."

I looked helplessly at the young Hastur. A few seconds ago my hands had been at his throat. Jay or Jason, maddened by self-hate and jealousy, could disclaim responsibility for the other's acts.

I couldn't.

Regis said, "We could take the easy way out, and arrange it so we'd never have to see each other again. Or we could do it the hard way." He extended his hand, and after a minute, I understood, and we shook hands briefly, like strangers who have just met. He added, "Your work with the trailmen is finished, but we Hasturs committed ourselves to teach some of the Terrans our science—matrix mechanics. Dr. Allison—Jason—you know Darkover, and I think we could work with you. Further, you know something about slipping mental gears. I meant to ask: would you care to be one of them? You'd be ideal."

I looked out the window at the distant mountains. This work—this would be something which would satisfy both halves of myself. The irresistible force, the immovable object—and no ghosts wandering in my brain. "I'll do it," I told Regis. And then, deliberately, I turned my back on him and went up to the quarters, now deserted, which we had readied for the trailmen. With my new doubled—or complete—memories, another ghost had roused up in my brain, and I remembered a woman who had appeared vaguely in Jay Allison's orbit, unnoticed, working with the trailmen, tolerated because she could speak their language. I opened the door, searched briefly through the rooms, and shouted, "Kyla!" and she came. Running. Disheveled. Mine.

At the last moment, she drew back a little from my arms and whispered, "You're Jason—but you're something more. Different—"

"I don't know who I am," I said quietly, "but I'm me. Maybe for the first time. Want to help me find out just who that is?"

I put my arm around her, trying to find a path between memory and tomorrow. All my life, I had walked a strange road toward an unknown horizon. Now, reaching my horizon, I found it marked only the rim of an unknown country.

Kyla and I would explore it together.

THE WORLD WRECKERS

Prologue

WORLDWRECKERS, INC.

They didn't call it that, of course. But that was what it was all the same, and the men knew it as they went up the long series of interlocking escalators which would take them to the isolated penthouse.

There were two of them, one large and one small and both with the sort of highly forgettable faces which make for good policemen, detectives, or secret agents. The miracles of cosmetic surgery were usually reserved to make people striking; but an astute observer might have guessed that some such cosmetic surgery had been used to remove every trace of individuality from the two faces. Subtly done, of course, but very completely. They had become a part of the crowd, any crowd; and that in itself was a triumph, for they were neither light nor dark, and would not have been noticed, in a crowd of exclusively Afro or Nordic types, as belonging obtrusively to one or the other. If any Masai, or pygmies, had survived on Earth in this year, they would have stood out as not being distinctly of that type; but in this era of highly interracial breeding

stock, with the outer extremes of the human pheno-
type gone forever, they would never be noticed.

One of the men, who used the name Stannard, and
had used so many that he did not remember his original name twice in a year, pondered on it as they stepped
onto the final escalator.

Worldwreckers. He'd been almost everywhere and
done almost everything on any planet which would
hold him but he'd never dealt with them before.

Everybody in the Empire knew about them. Mostly it
was something you heard about underground and wondered about vaguely, if your business didn't lead you
into the tremendous ebb and flow of planetary com-
merce. What was worldwrecking anyway, you might
wonder, and why should anybody care to wreck a
world? It sounded like something out of special three-
dim cinedrama, and it was vaguely funny.

But to the people who did come into it—like himself, Stannard reflected—it wasn't funny at all.

Neither was it tragic.

It was just business.

But why had they let their business be known by
such a name?

He shut off the flow of curiosity—it wasn't what he
was paid for—as the last escalator came to a slow halt.
There were quiet gold-colored curtains all around and
an outer reception hall where a girl, almost as unob-
trusive as Stannard and his companion, examined
their identity cards and let them pass through a metallic door into a small and plain office. Whatever Stan-

nard had expected of this secret network and semi-legal business, it wasn't that it would look like a shipping office with the kind of simple computers which kept records of traffic flow, stored information, and gave out instant library service. Nor had he really expected that the central head of this vast network would be a woman.

A woman, quite beautiful and quite young. Or—Stannard amended his thoughts quickly—apparently young. He could detect no scars of cosmetic surgery or molding and he was trained at spotting them, but some tautness around the eyes betrayed that innocent youth had nothing to do with the fair-skinned, unlined face and smooth throat. Her voice was deep and quiet.

"Mr. Stannard and Mr. Bruce. Please sit down. Your principals, as you probably know, have been in communication with me and have paid the advance deposits which we require before negotiations can be made final. My name is Andrea Closson, and I am fully empowered to deal with you."

They took seats and she went on, in the same quiet and dispassionate voice:

"I am prepared to make guarantees, at this point. How much have you been told about this matter of Darkover?"

Stannard said, "We know as much, we were told, as we would need to know for this conference."

"Very well, then. You know, of course, that this is illegal. By the various treaties of the Terran Empire, any planet has a right to a Class D trade agreement, which means, in Darkover's case—" briefly, she consulted the glass plate atop her desk where the computer readout could be seen, a flurry of fast pale lights for trained scan readers to instant-scan, "means construction of a large spaceport for Type Beta traffic flow, services and concessions to cater to spaceport personnel, a Mapping and Exploring division, Medical Exchange services, and clearly defined tradezones, with no Terran infiltration into native areas and vice versa. The Thendara Spaceport on Darkover has been in full operation for—" again she consulted the scan reader, "seventy-eight of their years, consisting of three hundred eighty-nine days each. Trade is well-established in small medicinals, steel tools, and similar Class D artifacts. Under the terms of a Class D agreement there is no mechanized industry, no mining or surface transit, and no continuous input or outflow of exportable or importable goods or services. All efforts to establish negotiations with native Darkovan authorities with a view to opening the planet to colonization and industrialization have failed. Am I right?"

"Not quite failed," Stannard said. "They've been ignored."

Andrea Closson shrugged that off. "Anyway they have not succeeded, so you are willing to send in our services."

"Worldwreckers," said Bruce. It was the first time he had spoken.

"We prefer to call ourselves a planetary investment corporation," Andrea said smoothly, "although if the undercover branches must be called into use, we cannot operate openly as such. In brief, if a planet refuses exploitation—forgive me, I should have said profitable investment—" but the irony in her expression was apparent, "our agents can give its economy the kind of, shall we say, nudge which will in the long run make it worthwhile for that planet to request outside investors to come in."

"In short," Stannard said, "you wreck the economy so that the planet in question has no recourse but to turn to the Terran Empire to pick up the pieces?"

"That's a harsh way of putting it but I suppose true in essence. And the planet in question, I'm told by the investors, usually profits in the long run. I don't ask *who* it profits. That's not my business."

"It's ours," Stannard said. "Can it be done with Darkover? And how soon? And how much?"

Andrea did not answer at once; she was pushing buttons for the desk-top scan reader. She seemed to have found something suddenly that arrested her attention, for the flickers of her eyes—they were odd eyes, Stannard thought, a very pale, pellucid gray, a color he didn't remember seeing before—the swift flickers of a trained scan reader, suddenly slowed down and stopped. She looked, as far as he could tell, both startled and shocked.

She said abruptly, "Have either of you gentlemen ever been to Darkover?"

Stannard shook his head. "I never go that far off my orbit."

"I have," Bruce volunteered unexpectedly. "I went there once for, well, that doesn't matter." He shivered suddenly. "Hell of a place; I've no idea why anyone wants it opened up; they'll have to give extra pay for volunteers. Cold as space and twice as dismal. Completely unspoiled, as tourist books say. It could use a little spoiling."

"Well, that's what we're here for," said Andrea briskly, turning off the desk-top scanner with a decisive gesture. "Gentlemen, I am prepared to offer terms and guarantees. For the agreed upon sum," she mentioned a sum in milli-credit units, which changed so often it represented a minifortune or a maxifortune that week, "we are prepared to guarantee that within three Central Record Type Empire Years, the planet now known as Darkover will be open to Type B exploitation—to prepare it for Type A exploitation would take twenty years and would never be profitable—with full permission to begin mining and export operations by a limited group of investors. Half of the sum must be paid now, in legal titanium-based hard currency paid into a numbered account on Helvetia II. The remainder will fall due within one Standard Month of the day that Darkover is declared a Class B Open world."

Stannard said, "What's your guarantee that our principals will pay the final installment? Not that they've any intention of defaulting, but it takes Empire Senate action to declare a world Open. Once they've made that legal, why can't my principals simply go in, as any other investors would?"

Andrea smiled, and the smile was so much like a steel trap that Stannard revised his opinion of her age upward by thirty years. "The contract, which you must sign with your principals' real identities by number, states that upon default your entire interest in the planet in question reverts to Planetary Investments Unlimited—which, as you have pointed out, is known widely as Worldwreckers, Incorporated. Furthermore, default in this arrangement entirely voids the secrecy clause."

They had thought of everything, Stannard realized. Because worldwrecking arrangements were illegal everywhere, and any planetary investment unit, bent on exploitation, which hired the services of a worldwrecker, was permanently warned off from that planet.

"We're quite legitimate on the surface," Andrea said grimly. "You have legally hired our services for public relations and propaganda. Most of our agents, the ones everybody sees, will never be within a light-year of Darkover itself. They'll be at Empire Center, attempting by perfectly legal means to persuade the legislators that Darkover should be a Class B Open world. A few more will be doing the same with the Darkovan authorities."

"And the rest?"

Andrea said, "The rest—are none of your business." Stannard agreed. He didn't want to know. He had spent a lifetime doing chores of this sort for a thousand principals and he made a good and almost luxurious living by not wanting to know.

They signed papers and produced numbered identity proxies, and then they went away again, and out of Andrea Closson's life, and out of the story of Darkover forever. They were so forgettable that even she forgot them, as individuals, within five seconds of the time they disappeared into her outer office.

But the minute they had gone, she pressed the scan reader button again, setting it to STOP. The words blurred there. But she closed her lids the better to see it inside her eyes, in memory.

High mountains, a familiar skyline, dark against the crimson sky of the lowering sun; a sun like a red and bloody disk. Only the tall buildings of the Trade City, pictured beneath the incredibly familiar mountains and sun, were new and surprising.

So they call it Darkover now.

A murmur of music whispered in her mind, the total recall that she had found intolerable for the first hundred years and had done as much as she could to desensitize; now she could not remember the name of the melody, and spent a few split seconds rummaging in a past she had deliberately put away, before emerging with the name of the melody and the odd, dry sound of reed wood flutes:

"Weary are the hills."

Yes, that was the name. Another of those intolerable

clear pictures came into her mind again, a girl in a brief yellow tunic playing on the flute; then her mouth twisted and she opened her eyes. "A girl," she said grimly aloud, "I wasn't even a girl then. I was—what I was is what I decided not to think about. I've been here, and a woman, for—Evanda and Avarra! How long? It doesn't bear thinking about, how long I've been here!"

But the memory persisted, running along a track it was impossible to stop, and finally, knowing it was pure self-indulgence, but also knowing it was the only way to put an end to this, Andrea pressed a button and pulled the message unit toward her, speaking softly.

"Fix me a scan-and-destruct tape on everything which has been written about Cottman's Star IV, called Darkover, a Class D Closed world. I'll handle this one myself."

The voice on the other end of this line had been extensively trained never to sound surprised, but Andrea, with her sudden supersensitized awareness, heard surprise anyhow:

"You are going in person? What cover?"

She considered that briefly. "I will go as an animal handler, considering the transport of small legal quantities of native fur-bearers to nearby worlds for breeding and development there," she said at last. She had been so many things on so many worlds. She understood and liked animals and she need never be on her guard against their intrusive thoughts.

But when the scan-and-destruct had been absorbed

and discarded, when she was packed and ready to board her transit on the first leg of the impossibly long transgalactic journey to that small planet out on the rim of nowhere, which now bore the name of Darkover, a fear roused again in her. A fear centuries buried, rousing deep in the curious convolutions of a brain which, living as a human, she used only fractionally.

Suppose, after all this time and all the different people I've been, once I stand again under the four moons and the light of the bloody sun strikes me, suppose—suppose the old me, the real me, the self I was before I was Andrea, before I was wanderer, queen, spaceman, courtesan, businesswoman, suppose the old *me* came back? What then?

What then? Then at least I would die where I was born, she thought with weary resignation, and pressed her long hands over her eyes. For the moment, if there had been anybody to see, she looked neither human nor woman.

Narzain-ye kui, she thought in a language long dead; exiled child of the Yellow Forest, where have you not traveled? Return once more, see what the treading feet of the long seasons have made of the world your people could not hold, and then die here; die alone if you must, knowing that not even a memory remains of the footsteps of your folk in the fastnesses of the Mountains of Light. . . .

CHAPTER ONE

He sensed that there were footsteps behind him again.

It was troubling. They were not the familiar steps and presence of his bodyguard Danilo. Those he heard everywhere he went and because he loved Danilo and had taken the young man as his paxman and esquire, he neither resented them nor changed his steps a fraction for them. Dani would not intrude on his thoughts or his consciousness unless he wanted companionship.

Regis Hastur thought, *I'm too sensitive*, and tried to tune out the footsteps. They probably had nothing to do with him; if he sensed their impact on his consciousness it was only perhaps that the owner of feet and steps was startled to see a young Hastur of Comyn Council abroad and afoot at this early hour. He moved along steadily, a slender man in his middle twenties, with the great personal beauty which marked all the Hasturs and Elhalyns of the Comyn; a striking face made more noteworthy in that the page-trimmed hair above the narrow face was not flame red, as with all the Comyn, but snow white.

If Dani had his way I'd never go out without armed escort. What kind of life is that?

Yet he knew remotely and with grief that it was true. The old days of Darkover, when the Comyn walked unhurt through war, armed insurrection, and street riots, were gone forever. He walked now to pay his last respects to another of his caste, dead at an assassin's hand in his thirty-seventh year; Edric Ridenow of Serrais. *I never liked Edric. But must we all die, when so many of us are dead or in exile?* The houses of the Seven Domains are laid waste. All the Altons gone; Valdir dying a hundred years past; Kennard dead on a distant world; Marius dead in psychic battle with the forces of Sharra; Lew and his last child, Marja, in exile on a distant world. The Hasturs, the Ridenows, the Ardais—decimated, gone. *I should go too.* But my people need me here, a Hastur of Hasturs, so they will not feel wholly abandoned to the Terran Empire.

Blast fire is silent. Regis did not hear it but felt the heat, whirled, heard another cry, then silence of a shocking kind; then someone called his name and he saw Danilo come running up to him, drawn weapon in hand. The younger man stopped a little way off, lowering his weapon.

He said, stubbornly and with concealed anger, "Now maybe you'll listen, Lord Regis. If you go out again without a proper escort I swear by all of Zandru's hells that I will not be responsible; I will ask my oath back and return to Syrtis. If the Council doesn't have me flayed alive first for letting you be killed under my very eyes!"

Regis felt weak and sick; the dead man lying in the street had no ordinary weapon but a nervegun which would have made him—no, not a corpse but a vegetable, all his neural circuits paralyzed; he might live, spoon-fed and incommunicado, forty years. He said through suddenly trembling lips, "They're getting rougher. That's the seventh assassin in eleven moons. Must I become a prisoner in the Hidden City, Dani?"

"At least they don't send dagger men against you anymore."

"I wish they did," Regis said. "I can hold my own with any dagger man on this world; so can you." He looked at Dani sharply; "You're not hurt?"

"A graze. My arms feel dipped in molten lead, but the nerves will heal." He brushed off Regis' concerned queries, his offers of help. "The only help I need, Lord Regis, is your promise not to walk alone in the city again."

Regis said, "I promise." But his eyes were hard. "Where did you get the weapon, Dani? A Compact-forbidden weapon? Give it to me."

The younger man surrendered the blaster. He said, "It isn't illegal, *vai dom*. I went into the Terran Trade City and applied for a permit to carry it here. And when they knew whose body I guarded they gave it to me with a good will—and so they should."

Regis looked troubled. He said, "Call a guardsman to bury that," he pointed to the charred corpse of the assassin. "No point in examining the body, I'm afraid; it will be like all the others, a nameless man, no trace of his whereabouts known. But he needn't lie in the street, either."

He stood by, distressed and aloof, while Danilo summoned a green-and-black uniformed City Guard, and gave orders. Then he turned to Danilo and his eyes were hard.

"You know the Compact." For generations on Darkover war and combat had been unknown; mostly due to the Compact, the law forbidding any weapon which can go beyond the hand's reach of the user; a law which allowed dueling and raiding but wholly prohibited the wide spread of battle or carnage. The question, addressed to Danilo, was purely rhetorical— every six-year-old child knew of the Compact—and the youth did not answer. But even before Regis' angry gaze—and the anger of a Hastur could kill—Danilo Syrtis did not drop his eyes.

He said, "You're alive and unharmed. That's all I care about, Lord."

"But what, in the name of any god you like, are we living *for*, Dani?"

"I, to keep you alive."

"And what are we living about? We are living, among other things, so that the Compact be kept on Darkover and the years of chaos and cowardly killing never come back to our people!" Regis sounded half

wild with rage and despair, but Danilo did not quail
from his angry stare. He said, "The Compact would
be much worse kept with you dead, Lord Regis. I am
your most loyal—" the boy's voice suddenly shook,
"you know my life is yours to keep or spend, *vai dom
cario*; but do you really know what would become of
this world or your people with you dead?"

"*Bredú.*" Regis used the word which meant not
only friend but sworn brother and reached out with
both hands for Danilo's; a rare touch in a telepath
caste. He said, "If this is true, my dearest brother, why
should seven assassins want me dead?"

He didn't expect an answer and didn't get one.
Danilo said, his face drawn, "I don't think they come
from our people at all."

"Is that—" Regis pointed to where the corpse had
lain, "a Terran? Not as I know them."

"Nor I. But face facts, Lord Regis. Seven assassins
to you alone; and Lord Edric dead from a strange dirk;
Lord Jerome of the Elhalyns dead in his own study
and no man's footprints in the snow; three of the Aillard women dead in mishandled childbirth and the
midwives dying of poison before they could be ques-
tioned; and—the gods deal with me for speaking of
it—your two children."

Regis' face, hard before, was bleak now, for although he had fathered the children without any love
for their mothers, as a sworn duty to his caste, he had
cared deeply for the two sons found dead in their
cribs—from sudden illness, they said—not three months

ago. He said, and the terrible control in his voice was worse than tears, "What can I do, Dani? Must I see a murderer's hand or the hand of conspiracy in every blow of fate?"

"It will be worse for you if you don't than if you do, Lord Regis," said Danilo, but the deep compassion in his voice belied the harshness of the words. He added, still harshly, "You've had a shock. You'd better get along home. Your mourning at Lord Edric's funeral, such mourning as anyone could summon up for such as he, won't do his memory half as much good as you guarding your life to look after his womenfolk and people!"

Regis' mouth thinned. "I doubt if they have spare murderers in reserve on one day," was all he said. But he went with Danilo, not protesting further.

So it was a war, then, a complex conspiracy against the telepath caste.

But who was the enemy, and why?

Isolated incidents like this had never been uncommon on Darkover, although it was more common for an assassin to file what was known as an intent-to-murder; this placed it nominally under the age-old duello code of Darkover and the slayer enjoyed immunity; a slaying in fair duel was no murder.

His lip curled faintly. He had carefully avoided embroiling himself in any of the warring alignments and factions on Darkover ever since he knew that Derik Elhalyn, nearest heir to the rulership of Comyn Council, was mad and could not take office.

Thus, no living man on Darkover could justly claim that Regis Hastur of Hastur had wronged him. Furthermore, as Danilo had reminded him, there were few who could match him in the use of any legal dueling weapons.

Who, then? Some of their own people who wanted the Comyn, with its complex hierarchy of telepaths and psi talents, out of the way?

Or, the Terrans?

Well, that he could verify at once.

Shortly after he had assumed the position as chief liaison man between the Terrans and his own people, he had come to live in a house near the edge of the Terran Zone. It was a compromise and he hated it; neither a Terran residence, which, although boxy and cramped, had at least comfort and convenience, nor a Darkovan one, with space and air and the absence of separating walls, though essentially comfortless. It was further still from anything like the feel of Castle Hastur where he had spent most of his childhood.

He detested, with a loathing so completely culture bound that it was almost inborn, almost all of the artifacts of Terran Empire technology and using them daily was one of the most suffocating handicaps of his liaison position. Making an average visiphone call was a process made lengthier by the need for overcoming his revulsion and he made it as brief as he could.

"Trade City Headquarters; Section Eight, Medical Research."

When the screen had cleared he requested, "Department of Alien Anthropology," and when that went through he asked for Doctor Jason Allison, and finally the face of a young man, restrained but pleasant, took form before him.

"Lord Regis. An unexpected pleasure. What can I do for you?"

"Forget the formalities, for one thing," Regis said. "You've known me too long for that. But can you come and see me here?"

He could have asked his question easily enough on the screen and been answered. But Regis was a telepath and had learned young to rely, not on the words of an answer or the face of the speaker, but on the "feel" of the answer. He did not think Jason Allison would lie to him. Insofar as he could like or trust anyone not of his own caste, he liked and trusted the Darkover-born Jason. But without lying, Jason might evade or shade the truth to avoid hurting him or talk around what he did not know.

So, when Jason had joined him there, and the first few words of formal courtesy and inquiries had passed, he looked the young Terran straight in the eye and said:

"You've known me a long time; you know I'm no fool. Level with me, Jason; is there some sort of feeling around the Terran Empire that telepaths are more trouble than they're worth, and that—even though the Empire may not issue a price on our heads—that no tears would be officially shed if we were picked off, one by one?"

Jason said, "Good God, no!" but Regis did not even hear the words. What he heard was the perfectly honest shock, denial, and outrage in the young Terran scientist's mind.

Not the Terrans, then.

He probed further, just to satisfy his own conscience.

"Maybe something you hadn't heard about? Not your section. I know that Alien Anthropology has been trying to work with some of us."

"Not the other sections, either," said Jason firmly. "Spaceport authority couldn't care less, of course. The science division—well, they're still exploring your various sciences and they realize that Darkover is unique, a reservoir of psi talents unequaled anywhere in the galaxy so far as we know. They'd be more likely to try to round you all up and put you in—well, not in cages, but in protective custody until they could study you to their hearts' content." He laughed.

"Maybe that wouldn't be such a bad idea," Regis said without humor. "If it goes on like this, there won't be a telepath with *laran* power left alive on Darkover!"

Jason's grin faded. "I heard a rumor months ago that someone had tried to assassinate you and failed," he said. "With all the duels going on, I didn't take it seriously. Was it true, then? Has there been another?"

"You don't know, then," Regis said, and told him.

Gradually the color faded from the young Terran's face. "This is frightening. I can only say that nobody official among the Terrans is doing it. And who else would have reason?"

That, of course, was the question, Regis thought. He said, "The most powerful mind in the universe, the greatest psi talents on Darkover, are still vulnerable to knife, bullet, or gun. I could name a dozen, beginning with the Keeper Cleindori and running down to my cousin Marius Alton, two or three years ago."

"And without the telepaths," Jason said slowly, "we have no key to the matrix sciences of Darkover and no hope of ever finding a key to them."

"And also without the telepaths," Regis said, "our world and our economy falls apart. Who profits by that?"

"I don't know. There are plenty of interests who would like to see your planet open to commercial export and import. But that battle's been going on for three or four generations, and the Terran Empire has always held that a planet has the right to decide for itself in the long run. They're not even lobbying on Darkover any more. After all, there are other planets."

But Regis heard the unspoken part of that sentence, too; *There are other planets,* but not with a big spaceport and a sizable Terran Zone and colony. Darkover was a crossroad between the upper and lower Galactic Arm and had a spaceport twice as big as most planets its size, five times as big as the ordinary Class B, to handle the traffic. A pivot planet—and it was getting in the way of those who hated to see such a plum unpicked.

Just the same, Jason said, "I don't honestly think it's anyone in the Empire or the Zone, Regis; they'd go about it differently. If you have a bulldozer, you don't need a snow shovel. This is something undercover and uncommonly nasty."

"I'm inclined to agree. I'll have to see if there are any more straws in the wind," Regis said. "Picking off the telepaths wouldn't change our stand on the Empire. We don't want to be part of it; and we don't want to become just one more link in the chain; and we don't want your technology to swamp us. And most of the common people agree. If someone's trying to change their minds, I should be able to find it out. Meanwhile—"

"Meanwhile, it's part of my responsibility to see that there aren't any more of you murdered. Protective custody might not work. Not with you people—" Jason smiled, adding, "You damned thick-headed isolationists of whom I happen to be one. But it would help if we had something to offer in return for the extra services it may take to keep you from disappearing."

"I can offer one thing," Regis said grimly, "and it isn't anything we want to give. But it's for everybody's good to keep the matrix sciences from dying out just from lack of telepaths to work them. I'll give ourselves, Jason. There are telepaths out there," his gesture swept the night sky and the infinite stars.

"Not so many as on Darkover, perhaps, or with so many talents. Remember; before the Ages of Chaos, we bred for *laran* gifts. We went too far; we're inbred. Find us some more, Jason. Find out how the Darkover telepaths differ—if they do—from those on Terra or Vainwal or the fourteenth planet of Bibbledygook. If we can survive as a caste, or if what we have can be trained into others—well, maybe this thing can be stopped. Because if we're all that's keeping Darkover out of the stream of entropy—and whether you like it or not, the Empire *is* a process of entropy, and I won't argue ethics with you again—well, we've got to keep standing in that door. We *had* our time of Chaos," he added, "I can show you radioactive craters in the Forbidden City. What's left of us isn't primitive, Jason, or barbarian; it's what left after we've been to the limits of so-called Progress; and the few who survived it have learned what not to do with it. Find us more telepaths, Jason, and you have the word of a Hastur that you'll learn what and why we are!"

CHAPTER TWO

Department of Alien Anthropology:
Cottman Four (Darkover)

To all Empire Medical Services on Open and Closed planets: You are directed to seek out any humans bearing telepathic or psi talents, preferably those latent and undeveloped. This offer does not extend to those who are using clairvoyant gifts for profit, as those can be stimulated by advanced technology. You are empowered to offer them Class A medical contracts. . . .

When you sweep a wide net to the ends of the known universe, some curious things are caught up in the meshes. . . .

Rondo was a little, wizened man of no particular age, and he was very badly scared. He could feel the fear like a cold taste in his mouth, and he tried to shut it off, knowing it interfered with the control so necessary for what he was trying to do.

He was only one of the fifty-odd pairs of eyes

following the helical path of a ball, spinning through an increasingly eccentric orbit inside the great crystal gambling machine. As it hit other randomly spinning specks of matter, the orbit altered, changed, drifted, as it spun down, down through weightlessness, to fall— to fall into one—into one of the cups—

Here, *here.* The *thing* in his mind—he had no other word for the gift that had always been with him— reached out and touched, delicately, the ball. Like another fleck of drifting dust, it moved the unpredictable orbit, ever so lightly, toward the mouths of the continuously spinning row of cups at the bottom of the machine. *Slower, faster—wait, wait, mine's not here yet . . . now, NOW!*

The ball spun down faster, as if magnetized; down it went *click* into a cup. There was the sigh of released tension from all the fifty-odd waiting throats, mouths. Then, inarticulate, a sigh of disappointment, of frustration.

The croupier droned, "Number eight-four-two wins, six to one."

Rondo was shaking so hard he could hardly reach out to rake in his winnings. The eyes of the croupier belied the passionless drone. They said, "Wait, you bastard. They're coming. You've pushed your luck too far this time, you little bastard. . . ."

This was his thought while he was droning, "Place all bets for next round. All money down," and his hand tripped the punch which sent the little ball up for another round of the long-orbit game.

Rondo fumbled in his winnings and, as if compelled, started to shove them all toward the cup which yawned—two inches across to every eye, a waiting chasm to his—just before him. He should have quit before; he knew this and yet in the grip of the compulsion that was like a disease, he saw one cup shining, gleaming, brimming with gold that could be his. . . .

He shoved them toward the cup, which opened up like a vast mouth in his imagination, gripped with the sight of a flow of gold. . . .

It was a sickness. He knew it as he watched the ball spin; a sickness, perhaps born of that uncanny skill of his. Again, helplessly, now that the bets were placed, he sought the spinning ball with his eyes and berated himself in self-castigation so rough it seemed that the men beside him in the gambling parlor must hear:

Damn fool—no sense—take winnings and get out— they're on to you, they're on to you, take winnings and run, RUN, RUN, they're COMING, COMING NOW . . .

But he stood quite still, paralyzed, until the hand fell on his shoulder and a quiet voice arrested the upward spin of the little gold ball, with:

"All bets off, ladies and gentlemen. The next game will commence in three megaseconds. We have reason to believe—"

Ronda squealed, not hearing what came next, "You say yourself your machines are cheat proof, you dirty welshers! Did anybody see me touch a finger to the machine?"

The voice was quiet, but rang like a bell inside the gambling parlor. "No machine is proof against an esper. You've been winning too damned often." The hand on his arm tightened and Rondo went without another word. He knew protest was useless, and his fright ran counterpoint, *my own damned fault . . . no restraint . . . no proof, no PROOF. . . .*

Outside the hall, the gripping hand relaxed a little, then tightened. The man towering over the little gambler said, "We have no legal proof and there's no law against esping a machine to win. If you'd been a little cleverer—we can't touch you legally. But get the hell out and if we catch you in here again you won't live long enough to enjoy your winnings."

A rough hand turned his pocket inside out. "You've made enough already," the man said, "forget about today's harvest. Now get!" A well-placed kick and Rondo stumbled out of the building into the street, under the great, brilliant artificial moon of the pleasure planet of Keef.

He stood there, shaking like a whipped dog, numbly fingering his empty pockets. He had done it again. He had been banned, by now, from every gambling hall on Keef, just as he'd eventually worn out his welcome on four or five worlds just like it. Sooner or later they spotted him. It was the sickness of the compulsive gambler that kept him going back and back, that would not let him make a small killing, normal winnings, and get out, to play again some other day or week.

He stood under the huge fake moon, with its rose-colored light, and hated, and hated. But mostly he hated himself. He had done this to himself; he knew it in his saner moments. The reason why was buried deep in a life where the strange thing which made him able to predict, to control the fall, was also buried—and had made him hated everywhere, even when he had used it (for a little while, long, long years ago) to warn, to help, to heal. And now the sickness he could never control kept him going back and back, to wipe out everything in the fever of the fall of a card, a ball.

What could he do now? Hidden in his lodgings was less than his necessary getaway money. He was stranded here on Keef, and Spaceforce at this end of the Empire was far from the gentle with the indigent. On a planet of the affluent, the stranded, sick, or impoverished were herded out of sight. He could perhaps find work as a bath attendant in the great pleasure houses euphemistically called the baths; he was neither young enough nor handsome enough for anything else there, even if the thing in his mind had allowed him to be that close to the average pleasure seeker on such a world as this. He could keep from sickening only by using all his forces on gambling. . . .

And now he was shut away even from that.

His jaw tightened and his face was very ugly indeed. They had thrown him out because he won too often. Very well, let them see what they had done when they incurred his anger! The red overpowering rage of the poorly controlled psychotic began to flow across him. No matter what had done it to him. That was ages ago now. Now he only knew that he was barred from the one thing on the whole pleasure planet that held pleasure for him, the fall and spin and drift of a long-orbit ball, and he hurt, and he wanted revenge.

He stood there motionless, his mind gripped on the one thing that made sense to him; the falling ball, the falling ball. . . .

Around him the world faltered, came to a stop. The thing in the telepath's semi-psychotic mind was paralyzing him and paralyzing, too, the one thing which made sense. . . .

Inside the gambling parlor, seventy puzzled gamblers and a croupier and a manager stared in dismayed incomprehension as the spinning, falling gilt fleck inside the machine hung suspended in midair, not moving.

After half an hour of this, as the angry patrons began to drift into the night again in quest of other pleasures, Rondo came to himself and remembered to run. By then it was too late.

They left him finally, bloody, bleeding, and more than nine-tenths dead, lying in the gutter of a darkened alley, to be found moaning there an hour later by two Spaceforce men who didn't know who he was, gave him the benefit of the doubt, and took him to a hospital. And there he stayed for a long, long time. . . .

When the world began to go round again under him, he had two visitors.

"Darkover," Rondo said, not believing, "why in the name of all that's unholy would I want to go there? All I know about Darkover is that it's a cold hell of a world off on the edge of the universe, and not even decently part of the Empire. Other telepaths? Hell, it's bad enough being a freak myself. I'm supposed to like the idea of other freaks?"

"Nevertheless, think it over," said the man beside his hospital bed. "I don't want to put pressure on you, Mr. Rondo, but where else would you go? You certainly can't stay here. And forgive me for mentioning it, you don't look as if you have much chance for any other employment."

He shrugged. "I'll find something," he said, and meant it. There were always suckers coming in on the big ships. He wasn't a marked man all over the planet. He'd get a stake somehow and get away; and there were still planets he hadn't tried.

It wasn't until the second visitor came along that he changed his mind. The plan sounded tempting enough. All gambling machines were equipped, by the stiff Empire law which couldn't be bribed or bought off, with tamperproof fields—but, the visitor told him beguilingly, a tamperproof field couldn't keep out esp. They'd provide disguises, and a liberal cut of the winnings. . . .

And through their persuasions he caught the

unmistakable feel of the gangster. One such group had beaten him within an inch of his life. Now he was supposed to get involved with another?

Rondo was a loner, had been one all his life, didn't intend to change now. Bad enough to be at the mercy of one gang. The thought of being caught between two made even his self-destructive gambling instinct flinch.

Anyway, even though Darkover didn't sound like his kind of place at all, they couldn't make him stay there. There must be a big spaceport, and where there was a spaceport there was gambling, and where there was gambling he could make a stake—and then there was a whole big galaxy waiting for him again.

He called the number his first visitor had left.

Conner was ready to die.

He found himself floating again, as he had floated so many times since the accident a year ago: weightless, sick, disoriented. Dying, and death wouldn't come. *Not this again. Overdosed, I was ready to die. I thought it would cut this off. Now here again, is this my hell?*

Time disappeared, as it always did, a few minutes, an hour, fifty years, floating across the cosmos, and a voice said clear and loud in his brain, not in words, *Maybe we can help, but you must come to us. Such pain, such terror, there is no reason. . . .*

Where, where? His whole world, his whole being, one silent scream, *where can I turn this off?*

Darkover. Be patient, they'll find you.

Where are you who speak to me? Where is this place? Conner tried to focus in the endless spinning.

The voice drifted away. *Nowhere. Not in the body. No time, no space here.*

The invisible cord of contact thinned, leaving him alone in his weightless hell, and Conner screamed inside his mind, *Don't go, don't go, you were with me Out There, don't ever go, don't go. . . .*

"He's coming to," remarked an all too solid voice, and Conner felt despair and loneliness and anguish all disappear under a sudden sharply physical ache of sickness. He opened his eyes to the too brisk, all but accusing eyes of Doctor Rimini, who made reassuring sounds which Conner disregarded, having heard them all too often before. He listened without speaking, promised blandly not to do it again, and sank into the lifeless apathy from which he had emerged only twice, both times for a futile attempt at suicide.

"I don't understand you," Rimini remarked. He sounded friendly and interested but Conner knew now how empty the words were. No, Rimini didn't give a damn, although they regarded him as a stubborn and still interesting case. Not a person, of course, with a unique and horrible way of suffering. Just a case. He opened a crack in his mind to hear the doctor chattering on, "You displayed so much will to live after the accident, Mr. Conner, and after surviving that ordeal it seems all wrong that you should give up now. . . ."

But what Conner heard with a shout that drowned Rimini's words were the doctor's own fear of death which now struck Conner as a sickening, small, petty thing, and the doctor's fear of what Conner had become—can he read my mind, does he know that I . . . and the stream trailed off into a wilderness of the small obscenities which were at least part of the reason for his will to suicide, not the doctor's alone; too many were like him, so that Conner had found even the hospital, with its animal shudderings of minds and bodies in agony, more endurable than the outside with men preoccupied with their own hungers and lusts and greed. He had crawled into a hole in the hospital and pulled the hole in after him, emerging only to try dying as a change, and never succeeding.

When Rimini had babbled himself away again, Conner lay looking at the ceiling. He felt like laughing. Not with amusement, though.

They spoke of the will to live he had demonstrated after the accident. It had been a bad one, one of the big ships exploding in space, and the personnel hardly having time to crowd into lifeboats; four of them, instead, had made it into the experimental plastic emergency bubblesuits and had fallen into space in those.

The others had never been recovered. Conner wondered sometimes what had happened to them; had the life-support system mercifully failed, so that they died quickly and sane? Had they gone mad and raved mindlessly down to death? Were they still drifting out there in the endless night? He quailed from the thought. His own hell was bad enough.

The bubbles had been meant for protection for minutes, until pickup could be made by lifeboat, not for days or weeks. The life-support system was fail-safe, and hadn't failed. It had worked too well. Conner, breathing endlessly recycled oxygen, fed by intravenous dribbles of nutrient, had lived. And lived. Lived for days, weeks, months, spinning endlessly in free-fall in an invisible bubblefield, with nothing else between himself and the trillions upon trillions of stars.

He had no measure of time. He had no means of knowing up from down, no means of orientation. He had nothing to look at but distant flaming points of star that spun and wheeled round him in his tiny days of rotation on his own center.

Five hours in a sensory deprivation tank, back in the prehistory of psychology, had sent men insane.

Conner spent the first ten days or so—he later figured—in a desperate hope, clinging to sanity and the hope of rescue.

Then, in his own endlessly prisoning universe, he went insane. Contemplating his own center, he spun like a god and emerged knowing there was no protection or death, even in madness. There was not even hunger upon which to orient himself.

There was only his own mind, and the universe. And so he began spinning, ranging through the universe, his body left behind, his mind wholly free. He visited a thousand, thousand worlds, touched a thousand, thousand minds, never knowing dream from reality.

They picked him up—chance, the merest fluke—some four months after the crash. And Conner was insane, but in a strange way. His brain, left alone with itself too long, had learned to reach beyond, and now he was something he could not name, or others guess. Fixed firmly in a body chained to hunger, thirst, gravity, and stress, he could not leave himself behind again; nor could he endure the life he had resigned himself to lose.

"Mr. Conner," a voice interrupted his thoughts, "you have a visitor."

He heard the man, incurious, wishing he would go away until he heard the name of Darkover, and then he didn't believe it.

He accepted only to escape any further contact with the hospital whose shelter had become a blind alley, a mousetrap for his soul. And because, on a world of telepaths, there might be some who could help him to handle this thing, to turn off the nightmare he had become without desiring it and without knowing why.

And, perhaps, a little, to find the voice in his dream. . . .

David Hamilton wiped the sweat from his face as he came blindly through the door, leaning briefly against the light paneled wall.

He'd made it this time, but God! The blind terror when the anesthetic began to blot out light—

No, it was going to be too much. He'd have to quit. Around him the hospital, crammed with humans and non-humans, breathed and sweated pain and misery at every crack in the walls; and although David, from years of practice, could shut most of it out, his defenses were lowered from the strain of the operation just past and it began to wear in on him again from every direction.

Is the whole world groaning in pain? His sharpened nerves gave him an absurd and frightening visual commentary, a planet splitting like a fractured skull, a globe of a world with a bandage round its equator; he started to giggle and cut it off just that fraction before it became hysteria.

No good. I'll have to quit.

I'm not insane. The doctors went all over that when I was nineteen and just beginning Medic training.

I made it through Medical school on nerve and guts; and whatever else it did or didn't do, it gave me an uncanny knack for diagnosis. But here in the hospital it's too much. Too many symptoms, too many people in fear and terror. Too much pain, and I have to feel it all. I can't help them by sharing it.

Dr. Lakshman, dark and grave, his eyes full of compassion beneath the white surgical plastic cap, put a brief hand on David's shoulder as he passed through the hall. David, fresh from horror, shrank from the touch as he had learned to do, then relaxed; Lakshman, as always, was clean sympathy and all kindness, a restful spot in a world grown full of horror. He said: "Pretty bad, Hamilton? Is it getting worse?"

David managed a smile, wrung out like a used mop, and said, "With all of medical science these days you'd think they'd manage a cure for my particular type of lunacy."

"Not lunacy," said Lakshman, "but unfortunately no cure. Not here. You happen to be a freak of a very rare kind, David, and I've watched it killing you for over a year now. But maybe there is an answer."

"You didn't—" David shrank; Lakshman of all people to violate his confidence? Who could he trust? The older man seemed to follow his thought; "No, I haven't discussed this with anyone, but when they sent out the message I thought of you right away. David, do you know where Cottman's Star is?"

"Not a clue," David said, "or care."

"There's a planet—Darkover they call it," Lakshman said. "There are telepaths there and they're looking for—no, listen," he added firmly, feeling David tense under his hands. "Maybe they can help you find out about this thing. Control it. If you try to go on here at the hospital—well, they can't let you go on much more, David. Sooner or later it will distract you at a crucial moment. Your work is all right, so far. But you'd better look into this; or else forget all about medicine and find a job in the forest service on some uninhabited world. *Very* uninhabited."

David sighed. He had known this was coming, and if nine years of study and work was to be thrown away, it didn't much matter where he went.

"Where is Darkover?" he asked. "Do they have a good medical service there?"

CHAPTER THREE

They saw the guards lockstepped around him as he came through the crowd to the airstrip. It was icy, cold, near evening, only a few red clouds lingering where the red sun had been, and a bitter wind eating down from the sharp-toothed crags behind Thendara. Normally there would have been very few people on the streets at this hour; Darkovan night sets in early and is as cold as their own legendary ninth hell, and most people seek the comfort of heated rooms and light, leaving the streets to the snow and the occasional unlucky Terran from the Trade City.

But this was something new, and Darkovans in the streets put off minding their own business to watch it; to follow and murmur that singular and ugly murmur which is, perhaps, the first thing a Terran on a hostile world learns to identify.

One of the four Terran guards, hearing the movement, tensed and moved his hand closer to his weapon. It wasn't a threatening movement, just an automatic one, just close enough that he felt reassured that the weapon was there if he needed it. But the prisoner said, "No." The Terran shrugged and said, "Your neck, sir," and let his hand fall.

Walking at the center of the close drawn guard, Regis listened to the muttering and knew it was directed as much at him as the Terrans guarding him. He thought wryly, do these people think I like this? Do they think I enjoy it? I've made myself virtually a prisoner in my own house just to avoid this kind of display, the shame of our world; a Hastur of Hastur no longer dares to walk free in his own streets. It's *my* life I'm giving up, *my* freedom, not theirs. It's my children, not theirs, growing up with Terran armed guards standing around their nurseries. I am so constantly reminded that a bullet, a knife, a silk cord, or a single poison berry in their supper can mean the end of the Hastur line forever.

And what will they say when they hear that Melora, bearing my child, is being sent to the Terran Medical for her confinement? I can hear it now. I've tried to keep it secret, but I had enough trouble persuading her family, and these things leak out. Even if there had been much between us, this would have ended it. Melora wouldn't even speak to me when I visited her last, and the trouble is, I don't blame her. She just stared coldly over my head and told me that she and all her family were obedient as always to the will of Hastur. And I knew that such little love or kindness as there had been between us, for a few months, was gone forever.

It would be so easy to damn all women, but I must remember that the ones who love me are under an infernal strain—and that's been true of the women unlucky enough to love a Hastur, all the way back to the legend of the Blessed Cassilda herself, my hundred times great-grandmother—or so the story says.

And not the least of the strain they're under is this damn self-pity!

He sighed and tried to grin and said to Danilo, walking beside him, "Well, now we know how the freak at Festival Fair must feel."

"Except that we don't get our porridge and meat from having to listen," Danilo muttered.

The crowd was parting to let him through. As they stepped toward the special transit plane, Regis felt, deep inside the crowd, someone with a hand raised. A stone thrown? At him, at his Terran guard? He could hear the angry thoughts:

"Our lord, a Hastur, prisoner of the Terrans?"

"Has he asked them to cut him off from his people this way?"

"Slave!"

"Prisoner!"

"Hastur!"

It was a tumult in his mind. The stone flew. He groaned and covered his face with his hands. The stone burst into flame in mid-air and disappeared in a shower of sparks. There was a little despairing "Ahhhh!" of horror and wonder from the crowd. In its backlash and before it could die away, Regis let his bodyguard hustle him up the steps of the special transit plane, dropped into a seat inside, and remarked to nobody in particular, "Damn it, I could sit down and howl."

But he knew it would be repeated all over again; guards, mutterings, crowds, resentments, maybe even thrown stones on the airstrip at Arilinn.

And there wasn't a thing he could do about it.

Far to the east of Trade Cities and Terrans, the Kilghard Hills rise high, and beyond them the Hyades and the Hellers; layer on layer of mountain ridges, where men and nonmen live in the deep wooded slopes. A man afoot could travel for months or live a lifetime, and never come to the end of the woods or the ranges.

A gray and rainy dawn was breaking over a morning of disaster as a group of men, wrapped in tattered, cut, and smoke-scorched furs, dragged themselves downhill toward the ruins of a village. The walls of a stone house still stood, rain-drenched and stark white, the blackened remnants of a dozen flattened wooden houses around it. Toward this still-standing shelter they made their way.

Behind them, three miles of forest lay, a blackened horror with wisps of smoke still rising in the rain and sleet. As they came under the roof, sighing and staggering with exhaustion, one of the men lowered the half-burnt carcass of a deer to the floor. He motioned with his head and a worn-looking woman in a smoke-damaged fur smock and cape came to heft it. He said wearily, "Better cook what's left of it before it spoils. Little enough meat we'll taste this winter now."

The woman nodded. She looked too tired to speak. On the floor at the far end of the stone-walled room, a dozen young children were sleeping on furs and an odd assortment of cushions and old clothes. Some of them raised their heads curiously as the men came in and carefully shut out the drafts, but none of them cried out. They had all seen too much in the past two weeks.

The woman asked, "Was anything saved?"

"Half a dozen houses at the edge of Greyleaf Town. We'll be living four families to the house, but we won't freeze. There isn't a roof standing in the Naderling Forest, though."

The woman shut her eyes spasmodically and turned away. One of the men said to another, "Our grandsire is dead, Marilla. No, he wasn't caught by fire; he *would* take a pick with the rest on the fire lines, even though I begged him not; said I'd do his share and mine. But his heart gave out and he fell dead as he ate his supper."

The woman, hardly more than a girl, began to cry quietly. She went and picked up one of the smallest children and automatically put it to her breast, her silent tears dropping on the small fuzzy head.

An older woman, long gray hair straggling in wisps around her face, looking as if she had been roused from sleep three days ago and had not had a moment since to wash or comb her hair, as was in fact the case, came and took a long spoon from a rack by the fireplace. She began ladling a rough nut porridge into wooden bowls and handing it to the men, who dropped down and began to eat quietly. There was no sound in the room except the sobs of the young woman and the sighs of exhausted men. A child whimpered, sleeping, and murmured for its mother. Outside the sleet battered the wooden shutters with an incessant hissing sound.

It was like an explosion in the quiet room when someone began to hammer on the door, with blows like gunfire, and shouting outside. Two of the smallest children woke and began to wail with terror.

One of the men, older than the rest and with an indefinite air of command, went to the door and flung it part way open. He demanded, "In the name of all the gods, what is this racket? After eight days of fire fighting, haven't we earned a breakfast's worth of rest?"

"You'll be glad to leave your breakfast when you hear what we have here," said the man rattling the door. His face was grim and smoke stained, eyebrows burnt away and one hand in a bandage. He jerked a head over his shoulder. "Bring the *bre'suin* here."

Two men behind him thrust forward a struggling man in nondescript clothing, much burnt, cut, scratched, and bleeding from a dozen wounds that looked like thorn scratches. The man holding the door open glanced quickly back at the women and children inside and thrust the door shut, but some of the men eating breakfast put down their bowls and came crowding out. They were mostly silent, waiting grimly to know what this was all about.

One of the men holding the stranger said, "Father, we caught him setting light to a pile of resin-branches at the edge of the Greyleaf Forest, not four miles away. He had piled the thing like a beacon, to blaze and catch living wood. We had an hour's work to put it out, but we stopped it—and brought *this* here to you!"

"But in the name of Sharra and all the gods at once," said the older man, staring in disbelief and horror at their prisoner. "Is the man mad? Is he crackbrained? You—what's your name?"

The prisoner did not answer, simply increased his struggles. One of his captors said roughly, "You hold still or I'll kick your ribs clear through your backbone," but he seemed not to understand, and went on madly struggling until the two men holding him kicked him quietly and methodically into unconsciousness.

The Darkovans stared at the man on the ground, almost without believing what they had seen and heard. In the mountains of Darkover, the only threat which will unite the fiercely anarchistic little tribes and families, riddled with blood-feud and independence, is the universal threat of forest fire. The man who breaks the fire-truce is outlawed even from his own fireside and his mother's table. The story of Narsin, who a hundred years ago in the Kilghard Hills met his father's blood-foe on the fire line and slew him, and was in turn hacked apart by his own brothers for breaking the fire-truce, exists in a dozen ballad versions. The idea that a man would deliberately set a living tree ablaze was as inconceivable as the thought of serving a festival feast of children's flesh. They stared at him and some of them made surreptitious signs against ill-luck or madness.

The older man, an elder in the burnt-out village, said in an undertone, "The women mustn't see this. They've been through enough. Somebody get a rope."

Someone asked, "Shouldn't we try to ask him a few questions; find out why he did this?"

"Asking questions of a madman—what for? Ask the river why it floods, or the snow why it hides the sun," one of them said; and another, "A man mad enough to set a blaze would be too mad to tell us why."

The village elder said quietly, "Any chance this is a Terran? I've heard that they do mad things."

One of the young men, the one who had told the girl Marilla of their grandfather's death, said, "I've been in the Trade City, Father, and seen the Terrans when they were on Alton lands, years ago. Mad they may be, but not like that. They have given us farseeing eye lenses, and news of new things, *chemicals*," he used the Terran Empire word, "to smother fires. They would not set a forest to burn."

"That's true," murmured one; and, "Yes. Remember when the lower Carrial Ridge burned and men came from the Trade City to help us put it out, flew here in an airship to help us."

"Not the Terrans, then," the older man said. He repeated, "Get a rope—and don't say a word to the women."

By the time the sun broke over the lower ridge, red and dripping with cloud and fog like a weeping cyclops' eye, the man had ceased to struggle and hung limp like a black flag above the dead forest.

The villagers, breathing easier and thinking that now, perhaps, the rash of terrifying fires would cease, had no way of knowing, in the widely scattered and wild mountains, that in the thousands of miles of forests this scene, or something very like it, had been repeated at least a dozen times in the last year.

No one knew that except the woman who called herself Andrea Closson.

"Darkover. It's a damned funny place, you know. We hold scraps of it, by compact, for trade, just as we do with planets all over the galaxy. You know the routine. We leave the governments alone. Usually, after the people of the various worlds have seen our technologies, they start to get tired of living under hierarchies or monarchies and demand to come into the Empire of their own accord. It's almost a mathematical formula. You can predict the thing. But Darkover doesn't. We don't quite know why, but they say we just don't have a thing they want. . . ."

Disgruntled Terran Empire Legate, repeating a common complaint of politicians on Darkover.

"You are to house and feed them with the best and treat them well," Danilo Syrtis repeated to the small crowd of swart mountain Darkovans. He indicated the four Terrans, uniformed with the dress of Space-force. He ignored the protest he could sense and added, "It is the will of Hastur, and—" he made a ritualistic gesture, seizing the handle of his small dagger, and said, "I am authorized to say to you: an insult to one of these men will be avenged as an insult to Regis Hastur's own self."

"*Vai dom*, Syrtis; need we see the Compact outraged at our own fireside?" asked one man, and Danilo flushed and said, "No." He told the Terrans, "You won't need your weapons. Better give them to me."

One after another, reluctantly, the men surrendered their regulation shockers and Danilo turned them over to a green and black Darkovan City Guard official, saying, "Keep them in bond until we return."

He walked, head lowered, back toward the Arilinn Tower which rose at the edge of the small airstrip. Regis was waiting for him there, with their cousin, Lerrys Ridenow—tall, red-headed, saturnine, a man in his early forties, long-faced and looking cynical. Lerrys gave Danilo a casual cousinly greeting, kissed Regis on the cheek, and said, "So you made it here. I thought you'd stay in your snug nest in the Terran Zone, like a worm in a bale of silk."

"More like a rabbit trapped by a weasel in his own hole," Regis said, and followed Lerrys into the Tower. He thought he had never felt such relief in his life. Inside here, at least, nothing could touch him, and he need not fear what would happen to his world or his family if an assassin's knife or bullet found his heart. Lerrys asked, "Is it true, then? That they hold you prisoner in the Terran Zone? We heard that rumor and I told them even the Terrans could not keep you, even by force, against your own will. Have they some new weapon against you, then?"

"No, I asked for the guard," Regis said, and took a drink from Danilo's hand. "Thanks, this is welcome. What, not going to taste it for poison?"

Danilo looked stricken and grabbed it from Regis' hand with a look of horror. Regis struck his arm down, laughing. "I was joking, pudding brain. Dani, I must laugh at all this or I'd curl up my toes and play dead!"

"It doesn't seem much to laugh at," said a man from the corner of the room, "that you have to treat your captors as honored guests, just to save your miserable life a little longer, Regis."

"Let him alone," Lerrys said, "and a truce to all this, Rannirl. He's had enough trouble, and he's out there on the firing line. Your neck is so worthless no one cares to set a price on it. I'm sorry, Regis, I started all this, and I only meant to ask: is it that bad in Thendara now?"

Danilo answered for him: "It's worse than you can imagine, but it isn't the Terrans doing it."

"But Spaceforce men *here?* In uniform, with shockers?"

"They're not bad people," said Regis wearily. "Think how easy it would be for them, to sit back and let someone murder us all, one by one? And it must take a special kind of heroism. They volunteered, all four, to come here, even though they knew they'd be mocked, insulted, and reviled for guarding someone whose life doesn't matter a straw to them, personally. I can admire them sometimes."

"We all know that," Lerrys said, "I can too; I wanted to make compact with Terra years ago, myself. But I thought it was the Hasturs who were against it."

"We were and are," said Regis patiently. "And you know it as well as I do, all of you." He looked around the room: a large old room, hung with draperies in the ancient style of Darkover, paneled with translucent lights. He let his eyes move in brief greeting to the half dozen young men, and as many more women, gathered there, most of them red-headed, Darkovan aristocrats of the telepath caste; minor nobles all. "I came at your bidding, but why did you send for me?"

"I did that," said Danvan of Hastur, rising from where he sat and coming toward Regis, who rose and went down on one knee in the old formal gesture. The old man put his hands on his grandson's shoulders, where they lingered a moment in deep affection. He said, "I wouldn't let them make any decision without calling you in, Regis."

Regis met his grandfather's eyes and felt a little shock of dread. The old man looked so tired now, and so frail. He thought: *from childhood I leaned on his strength, we all did; now he is failing day by day and I must be the rock on which my people can lean—and I myself stand on quicksand!*

"Is it something new, Grandfather?" He rose, and the old man said, "Not very new; the same old thing; I dealt with it myself, with the help of Kennard and a Comyn Council, twenty years ago. The same old thing—a clamor for Terran mining, manufacturing, investments, you name it. The usual people who see only profit and forget the side effects of an industrialized world. But now there is something new, and I swear by Cassilda that I don't know what to say to them. We can deal with greed. But this—we may have no choice but to ask for help from the Empire, Regis."

This from his grandfather, who had been the prime mover in the long struggle to keep Darkover clear of the Terran Empire, struck a surge of ice to the young man's heart. But he tried to speak with calm.

"Let's go down, then, and listen to what they have to say to us."

As the group made their way toward the door

leading into the reception hall, a young girl came to Regis' side. She said, with a quiet self-possession, "Lord Regis, you may not remember me."

"I don't," he said, and looked down into the lovely face. The girl was young and had the heart-shaped face and dark russet hair of their caste, and she had an air of calm and self-mastery quite at odds with her youth. He said, "That will be remedied when next we meet, *dumisela*. You lend me grace; how may I serve you?"

"I am Linnea of Arilinn," she said, "born in High Windward, and I have worked in the relays here for seven years, Lord."

Regis flushed faintly. "Then must I have touched your mind many times unknowing; forgive me, I have lived long among offworlders and I keep my barriers up without realizing it."

"Nevertheless, I know what is going on in Thendara," she said, "and I know you are looking for telepaths to work in this project with the Terrans."

Regis' eyes rested with a sort of relief on the sweet young face and he thought, *I wish she were going to be with us there. She would understand.* Nevertheless, putting temptation aside, he said, "Child, we have too few Keepers to work the few telepath relays and circles we can command now. You are of more worth at your post in Arilinn, working in the matrix screens."

"I know that, Regis," she said. "I wasn't speaking of myself, and anyway I'm not that good a telepath. I meant—my grandmother was trained as a matrix

Keeper when she was a young girl. She gave up her post and married when she was in her early teens, but she would remember the old way they were trained back in the mountains."

"I don't know your family, forgive me. Who was your grandmother?"

"She was Desideria Leynier; she married Storn of Storn, and my mother was their third daughter, Rafaela Storn-Lanart."

Regis shook his head. "She must have been Keeper years and years before I was born," he said. "I seem to have heard the name, but she must be older than— I hadn't believed any of them were still living, that group trained by the Aldarans. Was she—" suddenly his face went white as his hair, "was she one of those who raised Sharra in the hills, seventy years ago? Long before their rebellions, of course—"

"Our family have always honored the forge-goddess," said Linnea quietly, "and we had nothing to do with the abuse of that power later."

"I know that, or you would have died when Sharra's matrix was broken," Regis said. Normal color began to flow back into his face. "Then, if your grandmother is not too old to make the journey from the hills—"

"She is too old, Lord Regis, but she will make it just the same," Linnea said, and her gray eyes glinted with mischief. "You will find her a surprising person, my grandmother."

Acting on sudden impulse, Regis drew the girl's

hand through his arm as they went into the lower Council room. Suddenly, he felt less lonely.

As Old Hastur had said, much of what happened in the Council room was more of the same. Regis had been hearing it for seven of his twenty-four years and it had had a familiar sound long before that. There had been, for almost a hundred years, one or another party on Darkover fascinated by Terran technology and the hypothetical benefits of joining their interplanetary civilization. They were in the smallest of minorities and seldom listened to. Once every few years the Council, or such a council as there was in these days, gave them a formal hearing, thanked them for their opinions, solemnly voted to ignore their recommendations, and it was all over for a few more years. This was no exception. Regis sat in the seat marked with the insignia of the Hastur, the silver fir on the blue ground and the Hastur slogan, *Permanedó* (Here we remain), and looked around the ancient highseats, filled now with the merest remnant of the old *laran* caste; with minor nobility, younger sons, anyone who could or would take responsibility for one of the Domains.

He could ignore the first delegation, that group of smug businessmen who called themselves the Pan-Darkovan League. They looked sleek and firm. Despite their complaints, they weren't hurting, even though, he was willing to admit, there were fat profits to be had from an expanding civilization and it hurt them to miss out.

But when the delegation from the lower foothills of the Hellers was ushered in, Regis sat up and suddenly began to take notice.

He knew some of the mountain men. He'd climbed with them, in the days when he could manage to get away on such trips. He'd lived at the edge of the mountains all his life. He liked them, in many ways, better than the complacent lowland people of the Domains.

These were mountain men of the old style: booted and wrapped in thick fur shirt-cloaks, swarthy and long-haired, and although some of them were young, their faces were lined with rough weather and their eyes wrinkled with seeing into the far distances. They looked up at Regis with the old kind of respect for the Comyn caste, a direct and simple awareness; but they were wild-eyed with fatigue and grief which had been sustained much longer than men are meant to bear such things. And even though they tried to speak with stoical calm, some hint of this showed.

Their leader was an old man, grayed and grizzled with a profile something like one of the sharp-toothed crags behind the city. He addressed himself to Old Hastur, even though Regis sat in the seat of the head of council. "I am Daniskar of the Darriel Forst," he said briefly. "I swore thirty years ago that I'd starve to death and all my family with me before we crawled down into the lowlands to ask help of the Comyn, let alone the accursed *Terrans*." He looked about to spit, evidently remembered in time where he was and didn't. "But we're *dying*, Lord. Our children are starving. Dying."

Mine too, thought Regis, *not starving but dying*, and leaned forward, speaking in the mountain tongue. "*Com'ii*, I am to blame that we have heard nothing of crop failure or famine in your hills."

Daniskar shook his head. He said, "You don't get crops back there, Lord, there's no plowed land for crops. We live off the forests. And that's the problem; we're being burned out. *Vui dom*, do you know how many forest fires we've had just this season? You wouldn't more than half believe me if I told you. And nothing we can do stops them. Forest fires are nothing new; I fought them before my beard was grown. I know as much as any man from the Kadarin to the Wall Around the World about forest fires. But these—nothing we can do stops them. It's as if resin fuel had been poured on them. Our beacons fail. I'd say they were being set by human hands, only what living man could be so evil? Men can kill men if they hate them, but to harm a forest so that men who never harmed them would suffer, friend and foe alike?"

Regis listened in shock and horror, seeing his own horror mirrored in other faces around the Council room, and his mind, trained to think on many levels at once, ran counterpoint to Daniskar's words. Darkover is a wooded world, and without our forests we die. No cover for beasts means no meat for those who eat it, no nuts for bread where grains do not grow, no furs for warmth, no fuel where the lack of fire means freezing and death. The death of the forest means no resin or phosphorescents for light, no fruits for wine, it means no soil, for only our forests hold the soil on the mountains with so much rain and snow to wash it down to the lowlands. Without forests, over half of Darkover would quickly become a frozen lump of dust, starving and dying.

"You people talk fine about keeping us free of the Terran Empire," said one of the businessmen, looking up belligerently at the council members and especially, it seemed to Regis, at the two Hasturs. "And you have a right to your own politics, though I notice you're quick enough to take advantage of Terran things when you're rich enough to afford them. Like coming here by plane, under guard, instead of packing over the mountains on horse and by snow sled as I did! I don't even say you're all wrong; anyone who takes a helping hand must turn to his helper's path! But how far are you going to make us go for this thing you call freedom, *vai dom'ym?* Must all our mountain men die before you ask the Terrans to pull us out of quicksand? We have given them a spaceport and a crossroad in their Empire. We could be a pivot in that Empire, an important one. Why don't we make them give us more?"

"We don't care about that," Daniskar said. "We don't want the Terrans here half so much as you do, Lords. But we need more help than you can give us. They have flying machines, chemicals, quick communications, they could put a real effort to it."

"Do you want roads, factories, machinery in your world? Do you want another Trade City in the Hellers, Daniskar?" Old Hastur asked.

"Not me, Lord. I saw the edge of a Trade City once and they stink. But it's better than seeing all our people die. We need help from somewhere, and fast—or there won't be enough of us left to care whether we get it or not!"

And the Terrans, Regis knew, would be only too glad to help. World after world had fallen into the Empire in just such a way. A bad season, or an epidemic, or a few too many deaths from famine, and the proudest world, knowing that now there were alternatives to the hard laws of survival of the strongest, were no longer willing to submit themselves to those hard laws.

It's as if the gods themselves were against us.

First the telepaths go. One by one, in fratricidal blood-feud, or sterile from inbreeding, or by assassination and mischance. Our old science goes from lack of telepath minds to make the matrices work.

Now our forests.

Soon we will have no choice.

But why? Who?

It was like the flashing of light; this was no blow of the gods. It was too deliberate. Darkover was being murdered; not dying of natural causes, being murdered.

But who would possibly want to wreck a world? Who could profit?

When the delegation from the mountains had finished, they all waited expectantly for Regis to speak. Even his grandfather turned his eyes on Regis, to see what he would say.

And what could he say? "You must have help with the fire problem," he said at last, "all the help you can get, whether it comes from the Terran Empire or elsewhere. But I'm not prepared yet to ask them to reclassify our world for Open status, just for this. So far, we can pay for the help we ask for. As far as needed, I can pledge my own private resources for this." He did not need to look at his grandfather for approval of the rather reckless commitment he had made; it was the only thing to do. "We can also make demands of the chiefs in the lowlands, assess a part of the payment from them."

One of the men from the Pan-Darkovan League said, "Are you expecting us to bankrupt ourselves? If we had Open status as an Empire world we could demand this sort of help as a right, and there would be outside investors coming in to help us exploit our unused resources to pay for it."

Regis said dryly, "My thanks for the lesson in elementary economics, monsieur. Nevertheless, although I'm sure you have made a study of the problem, I'm not sure I agree with you about what would be exploited." His eyes, hard and piercing gray, and angry, met the lowlander's and it was the other man who dropped his gaze.

It was a delaying action, Regis knew, not a victory.

Forest fires, if this were simply an unlucky season or a series of natural catastrophes, could be coped with. But in combination with the attack on telepaths—*my children*, he thought again with the familiar anguish, and tried to shut off the vivid, almost visible memory-picture of the two small fair faces in their coffins—or if some unknown force were actually working to upset the delicate balance of forces on Darkover, then it was probably hopeless. The Darkovans could cling to their own patterns and die—or change so radically that it would be a form of death for most of those who knew it.

Is there any hope at all? Are we all doomed?

He had delayed a decision, but as they broke up and moved out of the room, he knew that it would descend on him personally, more heavily than ever. He stopped to say a few gracious words to Daniskar of the Darriel Forst. The other nobles would give adequate courtesies to the Pan-Darkovans, but the sensitive and proud mountain men must not be neglected. When he took leave of the chief, he realized that the girl Linnea was still close at his side, no longer touching him (physical contact was rare in a telepath caste except in direct sexual or emotional encounters) but well within the range of his perception. He turned and smiled at her, tiredly, and said, "This wouldn't be your first council, but I dare say it's the worst yet."

She nodded, gravely. "Those poor men," she whispered. "They are my own people, Lord Regis, men from our own villages, and I had no idea, I've been away in the lowlands so long. How terrible for them. And for you—Regis, Regis, I had heard nothing about your children—" She raised her eyes to his. As their glances locked they were suddenly in deep rapport. She blurted out, abruptly, "Let me give you others."

He raised his hands slowly, and laid them on either side of her face. Like the girl, he was too deeply moved for speech. For an instant time stopped and they stood together outside it, more deeply joined than in any act of love.

It was a new thing to Regis, although women had been attracted to him all his life. Mostly for the wrong reasons, of course. And a telepath could never be ignorant of the reasons. Many had been attracted to him because of his position and power; still more had ben strongly drawn to him because of his extraordinary good looks, because of his vitality, even—and he knew it—because of his own strongly sensual personality. He had grown cynical about women, even while he took what was offered. Especially during the last few years, promiscuity was expected, even strongly urged, among the young telepaths of his caste.

The offer itself was nothing new. He knew, completely without vanity, that he could have virtually any woman he wanted, and as a result there were not many he wanted.

But this was the first time that a girl of his own

caste—and Linnea, he began to realize, was an extra-ordinary telepath—had come to him in such complete simplicity. It wasn't pity, it was a sudden, deep sharing of his own emotion. There had been no hint of the status which she, of a minor house, might gain by bearing a *laran* heir to Hastur. There was not even any sense, except perhaps at the deepest level, of wanting him sensually; like most extravagantly handsome men he had grown very tired of that, and it repelled him rather than otherwise.

None of that. Linnea had simply sensed how difficult his life had become, and through a sudden deep sharing had wanted to make it easier for him, and had offered what she had to give.

They had stood locked together only a few seconds; but both of them knew how the world had changed for them. Then, the wheels of the universe began to go around again, they fell back into the elaborate games of ordinary life; and Regis sighed, let his hands fall from her cheeks, leaned forward and kissed her lips gently. He said, with infinite regret, "Not now, my darling. Although, if we are later blessed—but just now we need you where you are. There are so few of you girls, now, who can work the matrix relays. How can I put out more of the lights on our world?"

She nodded, in a serious and infinitely tender understanding. She said: "I know. If too many of us are taken away at once we will be what the Terrans call us, a world of barbarians."

Their clasped hands fell apart. They did not need pledges or promises for what was so deep a part of them. Yet Regis reached out again and drew her within the curve of his arm, suddenly struck with a spasm of fear.

A child of Linnea's would be too precious to risk to fate. . . .

Must I fear for her too? Will she be the next target?

The chieri came out of the forest, dazed and wild-eyed, staring about like some feral thing from the deepest woods. Even on Darkover, where human and half-human had lived side by side since the depths of their world's prehistory, this was something to collect a crowd; and it did. Murmurs of awe, astonishment, and wonder were hushed in the streets as the tall and strange being moved, with slow, deliberate purposefulness along the cobblestoned walkway where none of his kind had ever trodden before.

The chieri were a legend; most people had never more than half believed in them; and as soon as the rumor spread that a chieri, alive and in the flesh, was walking the streets of Arilinn, people came quietly out of their houses and watched, edging back with little silent whispers of astonishment as the non-human moved—slowly and deliberately, as if dragging a reluctant way—toward the tall loom of the Arilinn Tower.

It moved more and more slowly and finally its slow footsteps came to a halt. It turned toward the crowd and said something, in appeal. The voice was clear and light and beautiful, as legend said, but the words completely incomprehensible, and the people simply stared without understanding until finally an old man in a scholar's robe said, "Let me through; I believe he is speaking in a very old mode of the *casta*. I have seen it written in old books, though I never attempted to speak it. I will try." The crowd made room for the old man, and he made a deep bow to the non-human and said, "You lend us grace, Noble One. How may we serve you?"

The chieri said, slowly as if the words were long rusty with nonuse, "I am— very stranger here to this place. I have been—" a word none of them could comprehend. "There is a Hastur here. Can you direct me to that place where he is?"

The old scholar said, "If you will follow, Noble One," and led the way toward the Tower. He told his friends later: "It looked at me, and I realized it was *afraid*, afraid in a way that none of us has ever been afraid. I still shake all over when I think about anything like *that*, being as frightened as all that. I wonder what it wanted?"

Regis Hastur was at breakfast in his rooms in the Arilinn Tower, making ready for the departure of the plane that had brought him here, when one of the young matrix workers of the Tower, a boy of seventeen or eighteen, came to his door.

"*Vai dom*—"

Regis turned and said courteously, "How may I serve you, Marton?"

"Lord, there is a chieri at the gates below, asking to meet with you, with the Hastur."

"A chieri?" Suddenly Regis laughed. "This language of Arilinn still defeats me at times; I misheard you; a kyrri we would say in Thendara, one of your nonhuman servants here. Can you find out what it wants for me?"

"No, my lord, not a kyrri," Marton looked scandalized. "As if any of them would so presume! No, Lord Regis, a chieri, one of the old Beautiful Folk of the Forest."

Startled, Regis said, "If this is a jest I find it illtimed," but another look at the boy convinced him that the youngster was as surprised and disbelieving as he was himself. He rose without further delay and went down to the foot of the Tower.

A chieri! Even in his grandfather's day it was rumored that few or none of that oldest race on Darkover still survived, deep in the deepest woods. Never in living memory had one come out of the forest; at most there were strange tales of folk lost or hurt or benighted in the forest, who found themselves succored by strange hands, gentle voices, and kindliness, and promptly guided on their way again, and no more than this.

He came out of the dark corridors at the foot of the Tower, and into the pale light of the rising sun, and there, standing in a little awed circle of the servitors, the furred kyrri and the uniformed City Guard and a few bystanders, he had his first sight of the chieri.

It stood on the cobblestones, seeming to stand apart from the others, looking very much like a tall young man, or even a tall young girl, except that the features seemed a little too thin, too pale, too delicate to be human. It was taller than tall Regis, by almost a full head. It had quantities of pale hair that glinted silver gilt. It turned slowly to Regis, moving with a grace and beauty alien and unknown to humankind; and then Regis raised his eyes and met those of the chieri.

The chieri had pale gray eyes, very pale gray with silvery lights deep in them, and as Regis looked into the nonhuman's eyes, he suddenly stopped thinking in terms of awe and wonder and reverence and old legends. He suddenly realized that this chieri was only a young creature, very confused by the strange sights of the city, very young, very wild, and very frightened. He put out his hands with a sudden spontaneous sympathy and said, in *casta*, the archaic and little used tongue of the Comyn Domains, "Why, you poor thing, how did you come here? I am Regis Hastur, grandson of Hastur; and I am at your service. Will you not come in out of the cold—and away from all these eyes," he added suddenly.

"I thank you, young Hastur," the chieri said in that slow, halting speech. Regis stepped back in courtesy to allow his strange guest to pass inside. With a wave of his hand he dismissed the guards and the others.

Danilo followed them as Regis led the chieri into one of the small reception rooms on the lowest floor, a room of white translucent stone hung with pale luminescent hangings. Regis motioned the chieri to a seat, but the nonhuman remained standing, seeming to misunderstand the gesture, and said in his hesitant, slow, archaic speech, "It has come to us in the Yellow Forest, Hastur, that you are searching for those with the old powers: to study these powers, to know more of them, whence they came, and what manner of folk have them."

"Why, that's true," Regis said. He realized that the chieri was already imitating his own accent and speech and that he could understand it perfectly well. "But how did you come to know it in the Yellow Forest, Noble One?"

"We chieri—such as we are in these days—know things, Lord of Hastur. It seemed well to us that one of our kind should come and be with you in your search, if you will have us. And since I was the youngest and they felt I could—adjust myself—most easily to leaving the Forest and to changing myself to live among mankind, I was told to come to you and do as you would have me do."

"How far have you come, then?" asked Regis in wonder.

"Many, many days journey, Regis Hastur. I went first to Armida, for my people knew some young folk from there a generation ago; but they were gone, all the Altons, and so I came here."

Danilo stepped forward and motioned to Regis. He did not speak aloud, but linking directly with Regis asked, "Are you sure you can trust this non-human? Are you sure it's not a trap?"

"It is not," said the chieri aloud, turning to face Danilo and smiling at him. "I have no contact with the enemies of your friend; before this day I have never had speech with a man of your people, Danilo."

"You know my name?"

"Forgive me—I do not know your ways—is it a rudeness to speak the name?"

"No," said Danilo, baffled. "I just didn't know how you knew it, but you must have uncanny good telepathic power; more than I'm used to dealing with in nonhumans."

The chieri's light gray eyes met Danilo's for a minute; then the chieri smiled and said to Regis, "You are fortunate in your friend; he loves you well and would protect you with his own life. Nevertheless, reassure him that I will never harm you or your kind. I could not if I would."

"I know," Regis said. He felt suddenly warm and at ease. He had heard old tales of the chieri, of their beauty and kindliness, and although this one seemed young and frightened by the strangeness, Regis knew that there was no threat here.

Danilo was about to speak; then he looked from the chieri to Regis, struck at once by something strange. The nonhuman was taller, by about a head, and more slender, his face narrow, the pale, narrow, six-fingered hands inhumanly long and graceful; yet the resemblance, like a shadow, was there, accentuated by Regis' prematurely white hair; the curious cast of feature which marked off the old Comyn type on Darkover.

Some of those old families, they used to say, were akin to the chieri. *I can well believe it.*

Regis said, "Are you willing to go back with us, then, to Thendara?"

"I came here for that," said the chieri, but he looked around him in an appeal that was like panic. "I am not accustomed to being—within walls."

Poor thing, what will he do on the plane? "I'll look after you," Regis said. "You mustn't be afraid."

"I am afraid because it is very strange and I have never been out of the shadow of my forests before this," said the chieri, and somehow the confession of his fear had a deep dignity which added to Regis' respect and sympathy. "But I am not afraid otherwise and I am at your disposal."

Regis asked, "What is your name? What can we call you?"

"My name is very long and would be hard to say in your speech," said the chieri. "But when I was very small, I called myself s'Keral. You may call me Keral, if you like."

Regis called a servant and asked him to have the plane made ready at once. His brain was spinning.

It had not been more than a few months since the project to study telepath powers had been set up by the Terran Empire's medical facility. Not more than a scant half-dozen Darkovans had been willing to give themselves to this project. And now a chieri, oldest and least known of the nonhuman races of Darkover, traditionally most alien to mankind (despite old stories, never more than legends, of chieri and mortal), had come unasked and unsought to them, volunteering—when they had hidden for centuries even from the Comyn, except for legends as impalpable as leaves blown on the wind.

How had this happened, and what would come of it?

He suddenly realized that he could not even decide adequately whether this strange being out of the woods was male or female. In its positiveness and strength and in the prompt manner it had reassured Danilo, it seemed like a man; yet the delicate voice and hands, the flowing hair and light garments, the timidity and the way in which, as they passed the doors, it clung to Regis' hand in a renewal of panic, was altogether feminine. *Do they have gender at all, anyhow?* There was an old joke about the nonhuman *cralmacs* which had become a proverb on Darkover: *the sex of a* cralmac *is of interest to nobody but another* cralmac. He supposed the apparent sexlessness of the chieri was some such thing.

I'll have to remember that Keral isn't human. From the minute it went into rapport with me, it seemed that Keral was all too human, one of my own kind, more than most of the people I'd known. . . .

Small wonder the legends speak of men who died of love, having seen a chieri in the woods . . . and pined away for a voice, a beauty more than mortal. . . . Regis was shocked, startled at the turn his own thoughts were taking. He said to Keral, not looking at the chieri, "We will go soon," and went to take leave of his grandfather.

CHAPTER FOUR

A hospital was a hospital, even at the far end of the galaxy. Waking early and not yet sure where he was, before opening his eyes David felt the familiar ambiance around him, the years-long texture of the life which had become second nature: the preoccupation of busy doctors, the subliminal feel of pain kept under, and, at a distance, the hurried pace of healing.

Then he opened his eyes and remembered that he was on Darkover, uncounted light-years away from his own home, and that if they had quartered him in a hospital it was not because of the M.D. that he could still write after his name but because of the generally medical nature of this project.

Freaks and telepaths—and I'm going to be one of them! What kind of a planet have they landed me on?

All he remembered of disembarking last night— spaceports were all alike—was a glimpse of a great, luminous, pale purple moon, and another, smaller and crescent, floating low in a strangely colored night sky.

The light in here was Earth-normal yellow, but when he went to the window he saw high, craggy, dark mountains and a great, inflamed, red sun, already high in the sky. He'd come in late; they'd let him sleep, but probably someone would be coming for him sooner or later. Try as he would—and he had tried on the ship that brought him here—he couldn't work up much enthusiasm for the project. Hell, he didn't want to know more about the freak talent that had swept away his chosen career; he wanted to be rid of it!

Oh, well, he thought, turning away from the strange sun and mountains and going toward the bathroom, maybe this will help, and if not maybe it will help somebody else. Treat it like research—a chance to research a rare and freakish disease. Like Madame Curie studying her own radiation burns, or Lanach on Vega Nine doing work on *space rot* when he was literally rotting away with it.

Anyhow, there was no point to a long face. If his fellow members on the project were telepaths, a cheerful one wouldn't fool them, but it might raise his own morale. By the time he had finished his bath and dressed, he was singing under his breath. He was young and, against his own will, curious.

The hospital cafeteria, where they had told him last night to go for meals, was crowded at this hour. David hated crowds, always had—it took too much work to shut out the sense of people jostling him even when they weren't—but at least it was a familiar crowd, even though there were racial and ethnic types he'd never seen before. Doctors and nurses, mostly in the caduceus-adorned uniform of Terran Empire Medical, but they all had the unmistakable stamp of the profession. Many of the younger ones were a single unfamiliar type he supposed must be Darkovan, swart-skinned with dark crisp-curling hair, ridged foreheads, short broad six-fingered hands, and gray eyes.

He was finishing his breakfast when a young man, not in medical uniform but in green tunic and high, soft leather boots with short-cut red hair, came up to him and said, "Doctor Hamilton? I recognized you at once. Will you come and join us, please? My name is Danilo. I hope the food is to your liking; that is one thing we can never predict. I know that here in the Terran HQ building they can adjust the lights and even the gravity to the planet of your origin, but cultural preferences about what is and what isn't good to eat—" he shrugged. "All they can do here, I guess, is offer a sort of inoffensive lowest common denominator and hope it won't offend anyone too much."

David chuckled. "In hospitals that's standard, I guess. As a matter of fact, I've gotten used to eating whatever they put in front of me and hoping I'll have time to finish it before somebody yells for me. If you were to ask me what I just ate, I probably couldn't tell you under oath." He looked curiously at Danilo. "Are you on the hospital staff?" The kid didn't look old enough to be a doctor but you never could tell with some planetary types.

Danilo, however, offered no explanation of his status beyond a negative gesture. "Come along and meet the others on the project."

"Are—they—all here already?"

"Most of them. The Darkovan ones are lodged in the city, but at least at first, they felt that the facilities here might be more helpful. Jason—" Danilo raised his voice and a young doctor, hurrying past through the halls, came toward them. He was sturdy and dark-haired. David liked his looks at once. He said, "Dr. Hamilton? How was the trip? I've never been off Darkover myself—born here. I'm Jason Allison." He offered his hand and David shook it, realizing suddenly that this was what had been lacking in Danilo's greeting. Darkovan custom? "I see Danilo's introduced himself. I'm a liaison man between Darkovan medical staff and trainees and Empire medical people. Incidentally, I'm a doctor myself, though I don't have time to practice much."

He led the way along the corridor, Danilo easily keeping pace. Now that the meeting with the others on the project was imminent, David's unease became palpable again. *A crew of freaks—and he was one of them.*

"Dr. Allison—"

Jason Allison grinned. "Jason will do. And I'll call you David, if you don't mind. Darkovans don't use honorifics unless they're way up at the top of the caste hierarchy; any title below *Lord* simply doesn't exist. No misters, ma'ams, doctor, this or that. It simplifies things, anyhow."

Swept away. Even that gone. "David's okay," he said listlessly. "I—I've never met another telepath—"

Danilo laughed. "Now you have," he said, and grinned. "We don't bite. Or go around casually reading minds. And you aren't a telepath anyhow as far as I can tell. You're an empath and probably have some other psi talents."

David stared at the kid and shook his head slightly, abruptly revising a lot of preconceived notions. Danilo said, "I'm sorry. I was brought up around Darkovans with *laran* and I spot it automatically. I take you for granted because I feel comfortable around you, that's all; you feel like one of us."

David felt bewildered. Jason said, "Slow down, Dani. David, believe it or not, I know how you feel; remind me to tell you sometime about my first clash—and it was really a clash—with the Hasturs. Here we are."

It was a long room, filled with light and hung about with translucent draperies in pale and lightly varying rainbow colors. David took it in at a glance, the talent he had never recognized because he took it so much for granted that he believed everyone had it and didn't consider it worth mentioning:

—impact of fear/ brilliance/ fear from a tall girl at the far end, tall girl/ no, boy/ no, girl, with masses of long, loose, fair hair, slender, sexless figure—human?

—slight, authoritative young man with white hair and young gray eyes

—wizened small man in his forties, Earth-type, tanned, shifty-looking

—dark-skinned nonentity, trembling, spaceman's uniform

—tall, commanding old woman, old to decrepitude but with the same air of command and dominance as if she were young and queenly

—slight, sensual-looking, sullen girl slouched in a deep chair with her eyes moving, in little quick glances like a mouse's, all round the room and among the men—

—and yet again: fear/brilliance/fear from the tall girl/boy with the light hair, in the long tunic. . . .

Is this all?

"You are David Hamilton," said the slight young man with the hair which David somehow knew to be prematurely white. "I am Regis Hastur. I'm very glad you are with us, Dr. Hamilton. Nothing of this sort's been done before; ordinary medical men may be all at sea. The people who know about telepaths don't seem to develop medical sciences; for all I know, don't need them. We didn't, especially. And the Terran medics aren't even sure we exist. They've had to admit it but they don't like it—present company excepted," he added, with a friendly look at Jason Allison.

"I'm being brought here as a doctor?"

"Oh, yes. Once you get this thing, this talent of yours, in hand, it should make you an especially good one, you know," Regis said; "and it won't take you long to learn how to shut out contacts you don't want; every Comyn teenager manages to learn it within a few weeks. You will too, being around other telepaths.

That was your problem, you know; no one to help you handle it. Lucky we found you young enough. A lot of isolated telepaths in non-telepath cultures go psychotic and are no use to anyone. We found that out when the HQ was hunting for them for this project. So, as you can see, having one who's also a well-qualified doctor—well, we were ready to fall on your neck and hug you!"

It was like the sudden lifting of a black cloud. David never wondered how Regis had known of his deep encompassing fear. He didn't even try to hide the smile of wondering delight that replaced his strain and fear. It may have been this which made him, for the first time in his life, relax and accept the flow of sensations which came now, unstressed, across the level of his heightened perception as Jason said, "Didn't they tell you this, David? Come on; meet the rest of us; you're the last from offworld in this group; there may be another shipment later but this was the sum of what the Empire could find in nonpsychotic telepaths; Rondo—"

The small, weathered-looking man met David's eyes with a flash of steel blue stare, then almost visibly shrugged. *He's a straight one; no interest.* David, without experience in Rondo's type of underworld, was baffled by the hostile indifference.

The man in spaceman's uniform seemed sunk in apathy, but he got up politely enough and offered David a hand. "A pleasure, Dr. Hamilton. My name is David Conner."

"Then we're namesakes," David said with a smile.

His thought, quickly guarded: *nonpsychotic? What's the matter with him?* Conner's type was at least familiar; he was tall, thin, slightly balding, skin between brown and black, dark, gleaming eyes, now dulled with apathy and the barest pretense of civility. He wasn't hostile, but David felt, with a crawling of his skin, that if all of them dropped dead Conner wouldn't even blink. He would shrug and envy them.

Jason led him on. "Keral."

The tall boy/girl, almost two or three inches taller than David himself, turned with a swift grace. David met a fluid impact of clear eyes, deep as running water, and a light, lovely, girlish voice which murmured in a soft unaccented tone: "You have done us a kindness to come here, David Hamilton."

Who and what—!

Jason murmured in his ear, "A chieri; a Darkovan tribe; most of us didn't believe they existed until he came and asked to join us."

"He—?"

Jason caught his confusion. Then and later David was to wonder, never to know or prove but to suspect, whether Jason Allison, perhaps without knowing it himself, was near enough a telepath to pick up thoughts. "He or she, you mean? I don't know either; you can't exactly ask an I.B.—pardon me; Empire Medic slang for *Intelligent Being,* sapient nonhuman— what sex he, she, or it is. Not when you're unsure how they'll react. Maybe Regis knows."

David's eyes went back to the chieri, and Keral

looked up again and for the first time smiled, a lovely thing that transfigured the fair, frightened face. It was a gleam of brightness which made the chieri like a light in the room and David wondered how the others could take their eyes off her—him? *Damn!*

Conner looked up and came after them. He chuckled low-voiced in David's ear. "After you've been on a dozen planets and seen a dozen cultures you get used to that. You haven't lived until you've made attempts to pick up what you thought was a charming girl and had a nasty surprise or two when you found the delightful creature was one of the local swordsmen. Cultures are peculiar things."

David shared the laughter and felt a little relieved. Conner's psychotic apathy wasn't a constant thing then, for at this moment the spaceman seemed normal and good natured.

Conner went on, still in that friendly intimate tone, "Never made a mistake about this one, though. Missy—?"

The sullen-faced girl looked up at David with deliberate and practiced charm. She had thick, light hair, gathered into an elaborate coiffure, and David thought her dress, for anyone who had been warned of the icy and stormy Darkovan climate, was courting death from exposure; but as Conner had said, cultures on different planets set impregnable standards for feminine behavior, and there was evidently some reason for this one to flaunt her femaleness in this exact way.

She smiled with that quick-eyed radiance and murmured, "Hello, David."

"Which David?" Conner demanded; and David Hamilton thought swiftly, *he's jealous*, as the girl Missy murmured, "Why, both of you, of course." She held David's hand an extra moment, but the hand was cool and soft and belied the look of sensuous beguilement the girl turned on them both. She said in her lovely murmur, "I'm a little bewildered here." *A lie*, something in David said, cold and precise. "I thought it would be exciting to meet all of you. An adventure." *Another lie. What does she want?*

Jason urged him on and Conner sank into the seat beside Missy. That was evidently what he had wanted.

"Leaving me till last, as usual," said a sprightly voice. It was the old woman, and she was even older than David had thought: wrinkled, her face shrunken, but erect and slender as ever in a long graceful robe of thick, dark blue woven wool, over it a slight shawl of knitted fur. Her hands, knotted and gnarled with age, were still graceful in motion, and the voice clear and high. Her eyes rested on Missy, not with the condemnation of age for youth but with an echo of David's own curiosity. Then she came back to David. "You must be weary of running this gauntlet. I am Desideria of Storn, and if I am rude, forgive me; I have never met Terrans in this number. But no one, as they say in the mountains, is so young he cannot teach or so old he cannot learn. So let us see what we have to learn from one another, all of us. It's likely to be more than any of us expect. I am too old to waste time in preliminaries. Jason?"

Dr. Allison said, "Regis, you're the expert. You take charge."

"But that's exactly what I am not," Regis Hastur said.

David admired the way that without moving, without raising his voice, he gathered all their eyes to him. For the first time David thought, at the back of his mind, that perhaps being a developed telepath who could use all the latent powers of his own mind might not be such a bad thing.

Regis went on: "As most of you know, telepaths were once abundant on this planet. They are now growing scarce, and their old powers are to a large degree lost, bred out or diminished for lack of knowledge on how to use them. To some extent I know what I can do with my powers, such as they are. I don't know exactly what they are or how I use them. I gather most of you are in the same situation. Hence this project, which at the moment is only a small pilot project to find out what powers, exactly, each of us has; how we got them and why; exactly what they are good for; whether training plays any part in their development; and so forth. In short, to find out what telepaths are made of. But as to where we start—I have no idea. Each of us has some experience. Each one of you is welcome to contribute ideas and questions and we'll follow up as many of them as seem to have the slightest bearing on the case. Meanwhile—" and he made a courteous gesture, "please consider yourselves my guests, and if there is anything any of you require, you have only to ask."

"Then as the only nontelepath in the group," Jason Allison said, "I'm going to suggest that we start in a peculiarly Terran way. There is a lot of superstitious rubbish talked about psi powers. The first thing we Terrans usually do if we run across something we don't understand is to *measure* it. So, if all of you will cooperate, I am going to start—with David Hamilton's help—by giving each one of you a physical examination to see if you have any physical features in common. This will mean, among other things, a full reading of detectable brain electricity and radiation. After that I am going to try and measure your psi abilities, although I'm prepared to find out that we don't have the right measuring sticks. You can't measure anything until you develop the right scales. But maybe some of you can help me find a scale for measuring. David, suppose I start with you, and then you can help me with the others. The laboratories they've given us are just a few doors from here; I'm sorry to keep the rest of you waiting, but it won't be long."

As they went into a small examination room—it was marked *SPECIAL PROJECT, A, Allison*—David said to Jason, "What's the idea? You have Medical HQ records on me on the big computer, covering everything from measles vaccine at six months to the time I broke my little toe as a fourth year Medic student playing tennis; I know these kinds of records followed me to Darkover! You need to examine me like you need two heads!"

"Guilty as charged," said Jason. He went to the desktop scanner and punched out David's name and Terran Empire contract number. "Did they tell you you're on salary to Empire Medic, by the way? No, I wanted to start with a chance to talk to you. I do want your EEG; the ones they take for Terran Medic are only checking for epilepsy or overt brain damage, and if you had any of those I'd know. I want readings from all of you—" he was moving around, attaching the narrow electrodes to David's skull as he spoke, "and later I'll want them while you people are trying out your telepathic talents, to see if there's a measurable energy discharge. But we can skip your heart and lungs and digestion for the moment. Here, lie back." He connected the machine. "Just breathe for a few minutes."

"The one I'm dying to get my hands on," he continued a few minutes later, removing the taped EEG record from the reader, "is the chieri."

"Are they human?"

"Nobody knows, even on Darkover. I doubt if any Terran has ever spoken to one. If they have, they aren't telling. Fortunately I have permission to keep this project entirely under wraps, or the Terran Medical HQ would be all over the poor creature, just out of simple curiosity, of course. A new specimen."

"I can see why. I admit I'm curious too." David did not say that his interest was not medical.

"I lived with nonhumans—the trailmen—for a few years when I was a kid," Jason said, "and worked with Terran Medical during a bad epidemic a few years ago." He sounded vaguely bitter "Oh, the Terran HQ was very nice to the trailmen. Did everything they could to make them feel at home here, but still—specimens in a zoo. Maybe you have to be Darkovan and live with nonhuman races long enough to take them for granted, before you start thinking of them as *people*."

"Are there so many nonhuman races on Darkover?"

"At least four that I know about," said Jason, "and more that I don't, I'm sure."

David thought about that for a moment. He said, "Could that be why there are so many natural telepaths here? Telepathy might be the only way of really communicating with nonhuman races."

Jason said, vaguely startled, "That's a viewpoint that hadn't occurred to me. Nobody but a telepath would be likely to know—how did Regis put it?— what telepaths are made of. Well, shall we start on the physicals for the others?"

Much of the morning was routine work after that, a reassuringly humdrum beginning to a project David had feared would be terrifyingly outré. They discovered little that they did not already know, and that afternoon, during a brief break for meals, sat looking over the results. Routine physical examinations of Conner had disclosed abnormal EEG patterns akin to, but different from, those associated with hereditary migraine and some psychomotor epilepsy; David showed these also, although in a subclinical degree. So, to some small degree, did Rondo and Danilo. Confusingly, Regis Hastur did not, and they had not finished with Desideria or begun with Missy or Kerul.

"I wonder if this is going to be the one common factor?" Jason asked.

"I doubt it, or why doesn't Regis have it? I gather he's something extraordinary in the way of telepaths," David said, *and extraordinary in every other way*, he thought.

"He certainly has extraordinary charm," Jason agreed, and David laughed aloud. They were already, it seemed to him, close friends. "Jason, do me a favor. Let me take a reading from you."

The older man looked at him in momentary surprise, then laughed and shrugged. "Suit yourself. Eventually I'm going to feed all these records through the big Medic computer and find out if there is *any* common factor—minor blood fraction, whatever?"

"I can give you two common factors right now," David said. "They *all* have gray or blue eyes—all the Darkovans, that is, and all the offworlders except Conner. And his obviously isn't hereditary, but—with that history—post-traumatic."

Jason was thinking that over. He said, "Years ago, a group of Terrans worked for a while with a group of the Comyn, investigating telepathy and matrix mechanics—you know what that is?"

"I've read about the Darkovan matrices—aren't they jewels which transform brain waves directly into energy without fission or fusion by-products?"

"That's right. The simpler ones can be used by anyone, even those with no telepathic talents. The more complex ones demand a high degree of telepathic talent to use them all, which is why the trade in them died out; not enough telepaths around to handle them; and for obvious reasons, telepathy is dangerous to the ordinary politician. So there have been subtle pressures against any publicity about the Darkovan telepaths. But as I started to say, over the last hundred years there have been sporadic efforts to work with Darkovan telepaths. The Darkovans haven't usually wanted to cooperate, until now, when it may be too late. We found out one thing; at least on Darkover, telepathy is linked to red hair. If you see a red-headed Darkovan, he's a telepath."

"That would suggest that telepathy may be linked to the function of the adrenal glands," said David. "I can tell you another thing they all have in common. They're all ectomorphs."

"Ecto—come again?"

"Body types—ectomorphs are tall and thin, mesomorphs run to muscle, endomorphs run to fat and gut."

"So far that's true," Jason said, pushing away his

plate. "Let's get back and see if it holds true with the others."

It was true of Desideria, at least. The old lady was exquisitely cooperative, although she smiled her delightful wry smile when they punctiliously summoned a nurse to be present to assist her in disrobing:

"At my age, this is the nicest compliment you could have given me!"

Even the nurse had trouble keeping her professional face on at that one, and David had to turn away to hide a grin. *God, what a charmer she must have been forty years ago.* "How old are you—for the record?" he asked.

She told him, but Jason, long acquainted with the Darkovan numeral system, had to work it out for David and convert it into standard Empire years. It worked out at ninety-two. Following the clue they had had, David asked her: "It's true that Darkovan telepaths all have red hair?"

"True," Desideria said. "When I was a girl mine was as red as fire. The tradition is that the redder the hair the more talent for matrix work and the stronger the *laran* gift, and in general we found that this was true. I was one of a small group of girls at Castle Aldaran being trained for matrix work with some of the Terrans. Let me see if I can remember the technical names. I used to have total recall," she mused, "but remember how old I am." She was silent for a moment. "I have—or had—clairvoyance, a high degree of clairaudience, a small degree of precognition not exceeding three months, and limited psychokinesis, manipulating objects not exceeding fourteen grains in weight without the aid of a matrix," she said finally. "Perhaps the records have been kept at Castle Aldaran, if they weren't destroyed during one of the mountain wars. I can try to find out, if you like."

"We like," Jason assured her eagerly. "Did any of you ever run to fat? Or were you all tall and thin?"

"Tall and thin or small and thin," she said, "but again, they used to say: the taller they are for a girl, the stronger the *laran* talent. There's an old story that some of the mountain Comyn telepaths had chieri blood, and looking at Keral I can believe it."

Jason and David both caught the implications of that long before Desideria realized she had said anything unusual. They stared at each other in a wild surmise: "If humans and chieri could crossbreed—"

"That means the chieri are not nonhuman but a human subspecies," David finished.

"This is only a legend," Desideria cautioned, "from prehistory almost."

"Find us some of those legends, will you," Jason requested, trying to hide his eagerness, and turned back to the EEG machine. He began meticulously explaining how it worked before attaching the electrodes to her scalp, but Desideria waved him away. "Enough, enough. You Terrans have your technology and I'm too old to be curious about it. As long as it won't give me a shock, that's all I care about." She lay back, smiling, on the table.

David was calibrating the switches prior to turning on the recording needle when he felt it, completely out of context, like an electrifying shock wave and without any prior warning:

—Deep in his body, sharp, intense, almost painful surge of physical desire; sexual waking; intense, exquisite sensation—

Shocked and abashed, he straightened with an indrawn breath. Jason, frowning vaguely, had stopped what he was doing, but seemed oblivious. The physical upsurge went on; David realized that without any direct stimulus he had a strong erection. *What? How—*

—*Gentle woman's fingers, caressing him. Soft words, murmured almost too low to hear, in a language he could not understand. The softness of a warm, womanly body, under him, around him—*

Where the hell was this coming from? In all his experience of involuntary telepathy in his home hospital, David had never picked up anything like this, and it was shocking and somehow shaming; he felt like a voyeur. He looked at Desideria, wondering. Her eyes were closed, but he sensed quickly that she was equally baffled. *Was she feeling it too?* For an instant, the thin and frail gray form of the old woman seemed to shift and blur, and a young and lovely girl in a cloud of luminous copper gold hair lay there, smiling up at him, her eyes closed, in soft, sweet, feminine awareness. David felt his very guts wrenched with the agony of desire.

It spread like a sparkling net, a thin spiderweb of

physical awareness. It was not in the room at all. Conner's anguished, deathly, aching loneliness, reaching out, clawing deep for contact—David suddenly knew: it was Missy he held in his arms, pinned down with his own naked body, thrusting deeper and deeper until the violent explosion came. . . .

In the aftermath, while his breathing returned to normal—*had he himself exploded in orgasm? No, not physically at least*—David felt on the fringes of the thinning net of spiderweb contact, Regis' puzzlement, Rondo's satirical, sated laughter, a flare of luminous brilliance which he already associated with Keral; it reached out, wrapped him in a sudden twist of closeness. . . .

David? It was almost a voice, and David felt a soft surge of content, of gentle reassurance; *I'm here, Keral. I don't understand it either, but I suppose it's nothing to be frightened about.*

David was still bewildered. Desideria, still lying motionless, looked to his confused mind—*were his eyes open? Under oath he could not be sure*—like a double-exposure, an exquisite young girl/an old woman, curled softly and sweetly in love. As if compelled, David reached out and touched her hand, raised it lovingly to his lips. She opened her eyes and was the old woman again, and her gray eyes were brimming with tears. She put her hand against his cheek and David realized that his own eyes were brimming. Abruptly the room was normal again, the overflowing waves of sexuality dimming, dying away. They were alone with the oblivious Terran nurse, still moving around quietly picking up scraps of gauze and assembling the paraphernalia of routine examinations.

"No," Desideria whispered, "No." He thought she was going to sob aloud, but she didn't. She drew a deep breath and mastered herself. "No, David. I'm an old, old woman. It wouldn't—oh, damn her. Damn her, that consummate little bitch. No, that's not fair. She's young, she may not even know, and she's not under any vows."

They both heard Regis, like a mental flash;—*I'd stop her, but I hate to start exercising authority so soon. They aren't even Darkovan and I'm not their overlord.*

Desideria said quietly, "Damn that fool of a girl for starting this so early in the game. Loose sex in a random crew of assorted telepaths is like putting a bitch in heat down into a wolf pack; it starts all sorts of odd explosions—David, had I better tell her a few of the facts of life?"

Regis dropped in, from outside: *Do, Desideria. We can't have this. You've got to remember, though, she may never have met another functioning telepath in her whole life. She probably did it in all innocence. Why shouldn't she and Conner go off for a bit of pillow pounding if they want to? But they've got to learn how not to broadcast it all over the scenery. I wish to hell it hadn't happened. You talk to her and David can talk to Conner, if you like—*

—*Thanks—I think*—David said ironically to himself, and was astonished to hear clearly, like Regis' voice;

—I would talk to him myself, but you're at least a Terran. He wouldn't listen to me.

Abruptly David returned to normal consciousness. Jason was vaguely red around the ears, but he shook his head. "I can tell that something's going on," he said, "but I don't know what."

David said, with an embarrassed glance at Desideria, "I think I'd better explain later. You wouldn't believe."

"Living on Darkover," Jason said, "you learn to believe at least six impossible things before breakfast every day. I picked up a little, that's all. But why did she choose Conner?"

"Who else?" Desideria said. "Exclude Regis as too high in the scale of authority for her and Danilo not interested, you and David too busy, Rondo too old and too psychotic, Keral too uncanny—and too ambiguous in outward gender. And it's normal for her immediately to establish an instant sexual rapport with someone; it's her means of survival. Conner is young, male, and virile. But damn her for starting this so early."

David felt as if a thunderstorm had subsided. He knew, in a strange unconscious knowledge, that he had shared something very strange, particularly with Desideria and with Keral, but the very strangeness of it blurred it. He was relieved, and ashamed of himself at his relief, when Desideria said, "If you don't need any more records just now, can I claim the privilege of my gray hairs and ask to rest? You can get the rest of your data later."

"Of course; nurse," Jason said, "take Lady Storn to her quarters. Then come back and bring us Keral."

Neither of them spoke until the chieri entered. David looked up, astonished and a little abashed at how eager he was to see again that luminous brilliance and luster of Keral's smile.

Keral came in and sat obediently where they suggested. Jason hardly knew how to begin, but the chieri took it out of their hands.

"I am very young and very ignorant of your ways here," Keral said, "and I am slow to learn your language, and have few words to describe the things I can do. Maybe you will help me learn. Regis has told me that you want to examine my physical structure; I am completely willing. I am also curious about your kind of beings, and would like to learn. We shall share knowledge, then."

Jason turned on the Darkovan nurse and said fiercely: "Tanya, if one word about this gets out of the project before I give my signed okay, you can pack for space and you'll find yourself doing routine physicals in the mines of Wolf 814."

"I know the rules, doctor," she said stiffly.

"Make damn sure you keep 'em, then."

The chieri stripped without hesitation and stood before them, calmly, as if nakedness were no more unusual than being clothed. *No nudity taboos in his culture, then.* Yes, *his,* for Keral was male. So much for that question. Oddly, David felt a little saddened. The routine data were simple, though he punctiliously explained to Keral what he was doing. Blood pressure: slightly below human norm. Heart action: somewhat faster, and his heart was slightly to the right rather than to the left; there were also slight abnormalities, by human standards, in the shape of the aorta, the inner ear, and the retina of the eyes. But the big surprise was still to come.

"You realize," said Jason, low-voiced, as they hooked up the electrodes.

"Yes. But is Keral a sport—" he could not say freak—"or is this normal for a chieri?"

"It's not clearly normal for a human," Jason said, "and it's not normal for the trailmen, either, though I have heard it's not uncommon. You realize, of course, what it is. Keral is at least theoretically a functional hermaphrodite—dual-sexed, with perhaps a faint balance toward maleness."

David said, looking at Keral and meeting that unexpectedly close look again—*just what had they shared?*—"I suggest we just ask him. I doubt if it's a particularly taboo subject. Cultures without nudity taboos don't have many sexual taboos either."

But, although Keral seemed willing enough to answer their questions, he was unusually dense about that one, and David could not make him understand. His people? No, of course they were not all like him, every being alive was different from every other. No, he had never fathered a child. No, he had never borne a child. (The questions seemed to distress him; David thought for a moment that Keral was going to cry and felt again that almost anguished need to comfort him.) Finally they abandoned the questioning. As Keral learned their language he would learn what was meant. Perhaps as he grew into rapport with David he could put the question directly without the need of a language barrier. David realized that he had come a long way in a single day, for he was already quite willing to contemplate this as a reasonable solution to a question.

Keral was dismissed, with a gentle look backward at David. David sighed. He was tired. "Only Missy left," he said. "Tanya, bring her in." He thought, amusedly, that they both took it for granted it was safer to have the nurse around.

She looked up at him with a faintly provocative smile, but made no comment while he took her history. Name? Melissa Gentry, usually known as Missy. Planet of origin? Vainwal VI. *Lie*, thought David. Age? Twenty-four. *Another lie*. Why is she lying so persistently? How does she think she can get away with it, in a crew of telepaths? Doesn't she *know*?

He realized, suddenly, that she was beaming a direct seductiveness at him; a provocative smile, a deliberate little sensual wriggle, a spark of awareness. Is she an exhibitionist? Or a nymphomaniac? Or very stupid? He was cold and professional as he directed her to disrobe. "Tanya, give her a sheet," he said, and turned away while she was carefully draped.

Height: five feet ten. Taller than she looks. Weight: ninety-nine pounds. Blood pressure: 70 over 48. Dangerously low, but I don't know the gravity she's used to. Heart rate: 131. Dextrocardiac. Appendix: can't find the damn thing by fluoroscope. X-ray—hm, what's this? Female—oh, unquestionably, after that performance earlier, but there are certain structural abnormalities. . . .

Confusing. He hooked up the electrodes for the EEG, reassured her, asked her to lie still, watched as the slow spikes, strange, unmistakable, exactly like—

He stared, in wild surmise, at Jason.

Once before, not more than a few minutes earlier, they had seen that identical pattern, and never before.

Never before in any human.

Missy, the liar, the nymphomaniac, was a chieri.

And from way-the-hell off at the other end of the galaxy.

He disconnected the electrodes, trying to keep his voice normal, bored. "That will do for now," he said, and when she had dressed and gone, the two doctors looked at one another.

"Well," David said at last, "we've made a good start at finding out what telepaths are made of. And I'm more bewildered than I was this morning."

Jason's answer was instant and heartfelt. "You and me both!"

CHAPTER FIVE

A small caravan of pack animals wound slowly over the hills, through a heavy, drizzling rain. At the head of the caravan rode the two Darkovan guides who had been engaged in the city near the spaceport; both were members of the Guild of Free Amazons, and wore the customary Free Amazon dress: low boots of soft leather, undyed, fur-lined riding trousers, a fur smock, brief enough for riding, and heavy embroidered leather jackets and hoods. One had pale red, braided hair, coiled low on her neck and tucked into her hood; the other, close-cropped dark curls. They both had the somewhat hard, boyish look which women wear when they choose, against all the sanctions of a patriarchal society, to do a man's work and take a man's freedom. In addition, the one with braided hair had the flat body and hardened jawline of a woman artificially neutered. This was still illegal on Darkover but could be obtained, like most contraband, for a price.

"The coldest damn spring in forty seasons," the

one with braided hair complained to her comrade, hugging her cloak to her. "What prompts this wretched offworlder to travel in the hills at this season?"

"She *says* she is surveying fur-bearing animals to consider exporting them," the younger girl said with a skeptical shrug. "She must come from a cold world; at least, the climate seems not to bother her; I offered to supply her with fur cloaks and blankets and she told me not to bother. Also she rides in the rain without a waterproof, but if she wishes to end her days bent like a cripple from dampness it's her lookout. Offworlders are all mad, if you ask me, madder than the *Terrans* themselves. But what's wrong with the climate, Darilyn? I was reared in these hills. There is too little rain for this season—drizzles where we should have downpours—and it's far too cold."

Darilyn moved her head grimly toward the distant hills. Where a familiar skyline should have risen grayed green and blue with the thick evergreens, the hills lay ragged and black. "Forest fire," she said, "what else? Remember those wretched children in the last three or four villages, lining the road? Beggars— in the mountains!" she spoke with disgust and fury. "There was a time when our people would have starved rather than suffer such shame, Menella."

"Maybe too many of them did," Menella said slowly, and as they topped a small rise, she looked down, her mouth contracted with bitterness, at the gray, dirty gullies where mud was washing down the side of the hills. "Even with this little rain, look at that. If a Ghost Wind blows this summer nothing will be left in these hills but bare rock."

Riding several hundred feet behind them, Andrea Closson watched the Darkovan women without interest. Her mind was on her own plans, and she was observing carefully every sign of erosion and change.

This world might as well be a spaceport town. There's not much here worth keeping, she thought without sentiment. *The forests I knew—they must have vanished long ago, with those who dwelt there.*

A fool's errand, to come so far. What was I hoping to find, to see?

She drew up her horse and waited for the pair of her assistants to come even with her. Both were shivering, wrapped in furs and heat-suits, and she looked at them with dispassionate contempt, wondering how the other agents spread out and filtering around the planet were faring. She herself found the climate damp but tolerable in her ordinary riding dress. She said, "We won't go much farther. Have you enough specimens to make it seem credible?"

One of the men nodded. He said, indicating a pack animal laden with small cages, "Half a dozen, mixed male and female, of at least a dozen small fur bearers. I understand they are the kinds most used by the natives for clothing and ornament. Some are right pretty, too."

"We'll do a full-scale analysis of their breeding strength, likelihood to prosper in various other climates, and the like, when we return to the Trade City," Andrea said. "The girls have done a good job as trappers as well as guides. Meanwhile it might be a good idea to collect soil and food samples from their natural habitats. We'll camp here for the night, do that, and turn back in the morning."

Before long, the clearing they had reached was bustling with the activity of setting up small tents: one for the two Amazons, one for Andrea, one for her assistants. One of the assistants wrote in a locked record book. The Amazon girl Menella went off with her snares to fetch meat for supper. Andrea stood under the trees, silent, her eyes fixed on the distant skyline, the black and jagged stumps rising lonely to the rain. *Not a pleasant sight for any lover of trees,* she thought dispassionately; *but I've seen lovelier worlds than this die in a good cause. In my own way I'm dying in a good cause, helping man to spread further, have more progress. I have no child, nor shall I ever have, but some of these great spaceports, the giant steps mankind takes between stars, are perhaps my children. And if a world stands in the way of technology, who is to judge the fittest to survive? One race dies; another is born. Who should know that better than I? A race without the strength to survive dies like the better races which have come and gone before it.*

They told me in the spaceport that Free Amazons were better guides and woodsmen than most men, and so far they are right. Yet it is a strange sight to me; women who might bear children, electing of their own free will not to do so. A sign, perhaps, of a sickness between men and women, in any world. I do not understand men. How could I? I do not understand women, either.

Does anyone ever understand anyone? I'd better sick to my own job. I understand planets and ecologies and I've got a job to do on this one.

She returned to her tent and unlocked a metal box with a heavy combination lock. She did not turn the lock, but touched one finger lightly to her temple and laid a finger of her other hand against the lock. After a moment it whirred and dropped open. From inside she took a small sealed packet, which she thrust into her pocket, and went off into the woods.

Under the trees she knelt, dug up with her own strong hands unaided by any tool a small hole in the ground. She picked up a handful of the soil. It was moist, soft, rain-drenched, and sweet-smelling, and alive with small invisible creeping things.

Andrea wrapped the small package from its protective coating of impervious plastic. It looked like a grayish dust with black flecks. It too is alive, she thought. Well, that is the way of life. New times—and new predators.

Which will survive? Can I load the dice strongly enough? *This*—she fingered the living soil of Darkover—*or this.*

She emptied the grayish black, evil-smelling dust into the soil; covered it; fastidiously brushed the dust from her long fingers. She walked back toward the camp.

A picture rose in her mind; the crystal black virus working under the ground, against all the creeping things, worms, nematodes, all the things that make a soil live; spreading, growing, reseeding itself to make a dying soil even more barren.

What would I have done to those who poisoned my forests?

Why should I have done anything? We no longer had need of our forests. But on the other hand I need shed no tears for those who came after us. If it is their turn to be swept away—well, they will go as we went.

She checked off a mental list.

Telepaths.

Forests.

Soil.

Ocean? No. The population which remains must be fed somehow. Leave the ocean alone. In any case it is not much used now, and as food supplies decline, the movement of men from the forests to the oceans will cause enough social disruption in itself. So the very existence of an untapped ocean resource will work for me; it's only necessary to make the people demand the technology which will open up the ocean to exploring and mining.

She moved slowly back toward the camp. A whiff of sweet-smelling familiar smoke from the campfire came to her, with a smell of cooking food. She saw Menella moving around the fire with her companion, her own assistants watching the girls; but oddly without desire, she realized. The Free Amazons puzzled her a little. They seemed to have the trick of coexisting with men without arousing either desire or resentment, as if at will they could become men. . . .

—*Dangerous ground. Don't think along those lines!*

The effort to turn off a recurrent, dangerous train of thought blanked her face almost to automatism. She reached up, not thinking, and brought down a handful of leaves and buds which, in the springtime rains, were expanding into down-filled pods. Her hands moving slowly, by old habit, she stripped the pods to their soft fibers and her long fingers twisted, gently, relentlessly, to a soft thread.

Still spinning the soft fiber between her hands, she walked into the camp; suddenly, realizing what she was doing, she crumpled the thread and threw it away and walked to the fire.

She asked, deliberately jolly, "Whatever's cooking smells good. When do we eat?"

CHAPTER SIX

They had issued a hospital uniform—the white synthetic smock with the red and blue caduceus of Terran Medic and two small stars on the sleeve, indicating service on two planets—to David Hamilton, and he was surprised at how much better it made him feel. Among other things, it meant that he melted into nearly complete anonymity anywhere on the spaceport or in the HQ or hospital buildings; just another Medic on the staff. It also gave him unquestioned access to any testing equipment he might want, without the need to route his requisition through Jason Allison.

He hadn't yet been outside the hospital building, even though Regis Hastur had offered, most cordially, to show them the city and he knew that Missy and Conner and Rondo had all taken advantage of the invitation.

Because of this, he had not seen any of his fellow members of the project that day, and had spent the day going over the data from the physical examinations, with the final startling revelation that Missy was a chieri. Was she too a functional hermaphrodite? He realized that without being aware of it he had from the beginning thought of Missy as "she," although his early confusion about Keral's gender had been only partially resolved. Now, at a table apart in the cafeteria, he still held the comparison charts up beside one another. Missy displayed all the marks of the chieri, the anomalies of inner structure and the unmistakable brain wave development. Genitally, although major structures of both sexes appeared to be present in rudimentary form (as they are, of course, in embryonic humans) the male structures appeared in a state of near-atrophy. So there must be at least minimal gender differences among the chieri. Missy lied to every question we asked her; why? If she's not accustomed to being among telepaths, does she even know we knew she was lying? Maybe when she trusts us more, she'll "come clean." She looks younger than twenty-four; I'd have guessed her about fourteen. Teeth—well, she has twenty-two, which may or may not mean anything, and four still unerupted, compared with twenty-four for Keral. Does this mean she is younger?

Keral's chart. Similar structural features. *I wish I knew his own language! I gather even Regis can't talk to him freely because of the language barrier. That would be a really meaningful use for telepathy!*

He shut off the feeling of warmth he got from thinking about Keral ever since that instant of rapport, and returned to scientific objectivity. Externally Keral appeared rather more male than female; fluoroscopy showed undeveloped although present and potentially serviceable female organs, but on superficial inspection naked, both Jason and David had taken him for male until the fluoroscope showed otherwise. Why did our questions about sexuality disturb him? With his intelligence, and the lack of nudity taboos, it doesn't seem to make sense.

He put the two charts back into the folder as he saw Conner approaching him across the cafeteria, carrying a laden tray. The dark face looked sad, abstracted, and lonely, but brightened a little as he stopped at David's table:

"Join you?"

"Glad to have you." David made room. "Back from the city? What's it like?"

"Fascinating, though I've seen stranger around the galaxy."

"Did you all come back? Rondo, Missy—"

"No, they chose to stay," Conner said. "They evidently have more tolerance of crowds than I do. Regis told me I could learn to barricade my—esp sensors, I think he said—and learn to get along in crowds. He admitted, though, that I'll probably never feel happy about 'em. I gather it's just one of the drawbacks of being—what we are."

"How did you find out what you were?" David asked; but Conner's flinch was so perceptible that he said quickly, "Skip it. Forget I asked."

"Some day. When I'm more—detached," Conner said. "It's pleasant, not being the only telepath around, but it's going to take some getting used to."

They ate in a companionable silence, but David felt vaguely uneasy, remembering that he had an unpleasant and intrusive duty ahead. How in the hell did you tell a near stranger that you had unwittingly played voyeur on an emotional experience that had evidently meant a good deal to that stranger? *Damn Regis for shoving this off on me!* It would be simpler if I could either like or trust Missy, but considering that everything she said to me or Jason was a flat-out lie, I feel uneasy about her.

And the closer I am to Conner the more uneasy I feel. She can't care about him. He's too—too straightforward. Too nice. Or must have been before whatever it was that threw him into a tailspin.

Conner looked up from his plate, piled with an odd-tasting mixture—fruit and beans?—into David's eyes. His grin was laced with irony. "I gathered from something Regis said today that there's a fairly elaborate etiquette of the privacies and the decencies in a telepath society to rub off the raw edges," he said. "Obviously none of us has had a chance to develop it, but there must be something indicating that it's rude to think about a man in his presence, Dr. Hamilton."

David wished his face was as dark as Conner's; he knew he was blushing. "I'm sorry; I haven't learned the code, either, if there is one, Conner. And won't you call me David?"

Conner, still piling food into his mouth, said, "I didn't get it all, but let's level with each other. Why am I on your mind? I was thinking it was good to have a doctor on the project who realized I was more than just a case; what were you thinking about me?"

"First, that you were a David too, and wondering what to call you," the younger man temporized. "The rest—well, not here. Why not come up to my quarters and we can talk?"

"Pleasure. Have you noticed these?" On his way out, Conner stopped at a machine which dispensed small packs of a mixed fruit-nut-candy snack. He said, apologetically, "I seem to be always hungry. I think it's the air here."

David picked up a handful of the bars. He had tasted them earlier; they were evidently, like most of the food in the HQ building, a local product. He said, "One thing everybody on the project seems to have in common is abnormally high metabolisms, which suggests telepathy demands a high energy output. Although I understand it appears in a trance state too." He noticed a package under Conner's arm. "Been souvenir hunting already?"

"No. Danilo gave it to me and suggested I put it up in my room, and that maybe I'd find it an interesting piece of machinery. It goes without saying that I'm going to check it out carefully; I'm inclined to trust Danilo—but I wouldn't put it past them to use us for some experiments, either, just to see how we react."

They moved in silence up the long elevators toward David's small room in the HQ. Inside, David busied himself putting the chairs neatly on the built-in desk while Conner unwrapped the small machine. He moved a lever and a dull vibration began in the room. David felt it jarring his brain, cutting off sight and hearing—

No. He could see and hear as well as ever. What was cut off was the sudden sense of an extra sight and hearing; not cut off, exactly, scrambled. Like the blind spots of a migraine headache, interfering with vision without actually stopping it. . . .

"Well, I'll be damned," Conner said quietly, moving the levers to a null position that cut off the vibration. David felt himself extended to normal again. "And they say, around this end of the galaxy, that the Darkovans have no technology?"

David said, not knowing exactly how he knew, but as sure as if he was reading it off a printed page, "None that the Terran Empire can understand, they mean. I want to study that thing too, Conner. When we learn how a gadget will shut off telepathy, we will have gone a long way toward knowing what telepathy is. But I'd bet good money that they themselves don't know exactly why these things work, just how to build them. That's typical of societies with a low level of technology. Think how long the Terrans used electricity without understanding its structure, back in the early days of space."

"Might be." Conner was examining the structure

with slender competent fingers. "I'll bet this dingus is what they call a telepathic damper. I heard the phrase used when I was in the city. Wonder why they gave it to me?"

David raised his eyes, suddenly grinning. He had the perfect opening, and he used it. "Well, for one thing—to give you and Missy a spot of that privacy you were talking about, I should imagine."

The next minute, David found his head striking the wall. Dazed, he picked himself up, angry and protesting—he had meant no harm, damn it; Conner might have warned him if he was angry enough for a fight, rather than striking unaware—then, slowly and dazedly he heard Conner's cry of amazement and contrition and discovered that the older man was helping him tenderly to his feet.

"David, I swear I didn't move! I only *thought* about punching you in the face. I realized right away that you hadn't meant any offense, only by then you were flying through the air! Good God, *what am I*—oh, God, God—" Conner was trembling, about to cry. "*I ought to be dead. . . .*"

David felt a rushing need to reassure the man. He had suffered so much himself, only in such a different way. "Conner—Dave!" he said, urgently, "take it easy, I'm not hurt. This is just part of whatever it is we've got."

Conner nodded, slowly. His face had the gray pallor of a black man gone bloodless and sick. He said, "I read something about poltergeists back in the hospital on Capella IX. They seem to be linked with—well, with sexuality, disturbed sexuality, in some people. I guess we've just had a demonstration."

"Sure. Tomorrow we'll see how well you can control it," David said. "We were going to level with each other, remember. Didn't you know that you and Missy were—broadcasting it to all of us?"

"I knew while it was happening. I could feel all of you," Conner said. "It didn't seem to matter. It was the first time since the accident that I—that I hadn't been alone." He lowered his eyes. "Now, I'm embarrassed. I wasn't, then."

David said, with more gentleness than he had ever guessed that he could summon, "We may all have to learn not to be embarrassed, then, Conner. Until we learn more of the mores of living among telepaths. I'm damn sure of one thing, though; we're all going to have to give up a good many of our own preconceived notions, and I don't only mean about sex. Being here has already changed us both."

The tension slackened. They were both, to some degree, barricaded against each other again. Shortly afterward, Conner said good night and went off to his own room, and David sat, without any desire to pick up the charts again, chewing on the Darkovan sweetmeats without really being aware that he was doing it.

What's going to happen when he finds out Missy isn't human?

He felt desperately uneasy for Conner, without

clearly knowing why. He thought, I'm changing too, I'm learning about this thing I am.

What will it do to me?

He had fallen asleep without turning out the light, when suddenly he came awake, all his senses screaming with violent panic. *Lights! People! Strange faces, critical eyes, they're coming to find me, David, David, help me. . . .*

The cry had faded, he wondered if Keral had even known he made it, but he was out of his chair in a bound, running down the corridor, impatient with the slow movement of the escalator, taking the moving staircase down three or four paces at a time. Vaguely and in the back of his mind, as something not very important, he realized that he had no doubt about exactly which way to go, that pinpoint shriek of panic led him like a homing beam, although he had never been outside the building here before. . . .

Outside it was getting dark with no sign of the sun and the night sky starless against the lights of the spaceport. *Confusion . . . no moons . . . nothing to find my way . . .* the air was icy, wind gusting up in little ripples, cutting through David's thin smock like a knife, but he ran on, heedless. Keral's panic was wordless now, a whirling frightening thing. David rounded a building, came out into the glare of lights before a little plaza. There was a crowd there, murmuring, muttering; their tone: wonder, extreme surprise, a sort of staring gawking hostile curiosity which

David associated with the crowds that gathered around freaks and extreme disaster. *Oh, God, if he's hurt—*

David shoved through the crowd, saying with the crisp authority he had learned the first week in his hospital, "All right, let me through here—let me through, I'm a doctor, let me through—" thanking his lucky stars for the uniform he wore. In the hospital it made him anonymous, a nobody, just another person with a right to be there; outside the hospital, though, it gave authority. They sidled back before him and David thrust through, using his elbows and broad shoulders without mercy.

He saw Keral and for a moment his heart stopped. The chieri was crouched over, huddled, arms wrapped around his head, so pale and white that for a moment of horror David wondered if he had literally been frightened to death. A delicate high-strung creature, unaccustomed to the society of people at all; what had brought him out into these crowds? Then his eyelids flickered, and David went up to him and put his hand on Keral's shoulder and said in a soft voice: "It's all right; I'll have these people out of here in a few seconds."

He turned to the crowd. "All right, just move along, there's nothing to see. Or shall I radio for Spaceforce to come and move you on?"

Most of the crowd were Terrans and he realized that they had meant no harm, they were simply staring idly at a strange thing. David felt suddenly ashamed and abashed at being human. Slowly, they began to drift along, and David put his hand under Keral's elbow and raised him to his feet. He said, "They're gone, but you'd better come inside with me for a little while."

Keral's breathing was rapid, his face white. He said, "I was coming to see you, I was sure I could find my way. Only, inside the spaceport I lost my way, and they began to follow me and stare. And when I began to run it was worse, I think some people did not know what the crowd was, they thought they were hunting down a—a fugitive."

"Well, they are gone." David led him back the way he had come. His bump of direction had deserted him now that he was no longer following the signals of Keral's panic and he had to inquire the way twice. It was icy cold, the wind growing in intensity with every minute, and David realized he was chilled through. The chieri reached out with a quick gesture and flipped a corner of his own long cloak around David's shoulders.

The warmth of the HQ building closed around them and David relaxed thankfully. He felt, from Keral's direction, a faint surge of renewed panic, and turned to him in anxious solicitude, but Keral only said faintly, "I am not used to being within walls. Never mind, it is better than the crowds."

A picture, swift, strange, and beautiful flashed in and out of his mind, multidimensional, multisensed:

—soft wind, blowing leaves; a thousand fragrances

each known, accepted, cherished; a roof overhead that smelled of leaves and gave softly to the wind, yet gave warm security from slashing rain; water, splashing, softness underfoot—

"Your home?"

He did not need an answer, and he felt oddly apologetic as he drew the chieri onto the first of the maze of intertwining escalators he took for granted in a large building; *Damn it, David,* he berated himself, *quit being romantic. Living in a forest may sound and smell great, but you're here and there's work to be done.*

Nevertheless, the contrast nagged at him as he drew Keral into his own bleak, depersonalized quarters. Had he really lived for years in surroundings as grim as a jail cell, absorbed in his work? He fussed around, finding his strange guest a place to sit, and felt the shivering tension in the chieri slowly relax.

"You said you were coming to see me, Keral, when you panicked in the crowd. Not that you aren't welcome, even at this hour. But what did you want?"

"It seemed," Keral said in that light strange voice, "that while your people learned of me, I could also learn of you, and I could do this better among you here than in isolation. I am not yet fluent enough in your language; it is easier if I touch you—" he reached for David's hand, clasped it lightly, and the flow of images reached the Terran:

. . . . *a civilization new and strange and yet not so different from those my people knew millennia ago. Perhaps we have been selfish, withdrawing into our forests and (knowing we die, alas, singing our lamentation alone) wait-ing here and silently living in beauty and memory; perhaps those who come after us may profit from what we are/what we know. Let us go among them and learn from them, see what people will live in our world when we are gone. . . .*

The strange, forlorn sadness of the flow of thought brought an almost anguished feeling of loneliness to David. Feeling that he might burst out crying if he didn't, he pulled his hands away from Keral and swallowed hard. Keral looked at him, curious and not offended.

"Is it not mannerly, in your culture, to touch? For-give me. I could not do it with everyone, but you are—I *can* touch you and it does not—frighten me," he fumbled for words, and David, moved again, reached out and reclasped the thin, cool hands in his. He said softly, "Why are your people dying, Keral? Regis told me they were only a legend now."

. . . . Infinite sadness, like a song of farewell borne from distant shores . . . leaves fall, buds wither unborn, our peo-ple grow old and die with no children to renew their songs . . . and I, loneliest of all because I die here in exile . . . hands of a stranger clasped in mine, a loving stranger but stranger still. . . .

David: *Willing exile is exile nonetheless.*

. . . . who will reconcile me to the paths I must walk alone. . . .

David: *Mountains divide us and a world of seas . . . and we in dreams behold. . . .*

The wave crested; broke; splashed in soft surf on a

silent shore of pain. David swallowed hard and their hands fell apart. They had come briefly closer than even their growing ease with one another could tolerate, and they drew apart again. Keral said, "I came here for that; that you could learn about my people. Many of the others are too old; they would die away from their forests. I am willing to give you what I can; but I too am curious to know. Let me be part of your researches, David. Let me know what you find out; share with me what you learn. I can pick up your language quickly; my people have a gift for this."

"You certainly have," David said, suddenly struck by this; yesterday when they were introduced Keral had fumbled in speaking even a few words of Regis' rather scholarly *casta* language, and yet now he was speaking in easy, fluent phrases, the *cahuenga* or lingua franca spoken all over Darkover by Terran and Darkovan alike, which David had learned by educator tapes on the ship coming here. He said, "I have no objection; I am sure that Jason and the authorities would be happy to give you this privilege if you want it. And if you want to stay here, I'll do what I can to help you feel less—hemmed in. Although I have no authority on my own, and you ought to take it up with Regis, of course. If you want to know what we're learning, you're welcome to share what I've found out myself. But will you answer a few questions, too? You were so confused yesterday, and it was so hard to get through to you and make you understand. For instance: how old are you?"

—He looks about seventeen, though he must be older—

"I am a stripling of my own people," Keral said, "almost the latest-born among them. But you would know how many sun-circlings I have lived, and I cannot tell you. I think perhaps your people count time differently than we do. To us, many turns of the sun go by and it is as a sleep and a sleep, the beginning and ending of a song. I must try and think in different ways when I talk to your kind of people, and that is why the elders among us cannot any longer tolerate to come among you. The days and leaf fallings seem to— to regulate your thoughts and your words and your inner processes. I was born—how can I mark it in ways you can understand?—in the time before the great star over the polar ice shifted to its latest place. Does that mean anything to you?"

"No," David said, "I'm no astronomer but I'll bet someone can pinpoint it in time." He felt stunned. *Are you trying to tell me you're maybe hundreds of years old? Legends of immortal races!* "And yet, long-lived as your people are, you say your people are dying? I don't want to give you pain, Keral. But we must know."

"We have been dying since many centuries before the Terrans came to Darkover for the first time," said the chieri. His voice was quiet and positive. "We were never a plentiful or prolific race—is this the right word?—and although during our high years we grew and multiplied as with a tree in bud, all things run down and perish. As time meant less and less to us, we did not realize. Perhaps some change, the cooling of the sun, made this change in our innermost cells. The times when we can bear children are spaced apart—many, many sun-circlings apart. I think as the sun cooled they grew further apart. It often happened that when one of our people was ripened for mating, there would be none other ready to mate with her. And although we did not die of ourselves, we could be killed by accident, beasts, weather, or mischance. More died than were born. This process was slow, so slow that even we did not know, until our elders saw that no children at all had been born, until some of the youngest were past mating at all; and inevitably, some day, not soon but not in the unforeseen times either, we must die and be gone." His voice was flat, unemotional, and clinical. "We sought many remedies; as you learn to understand our words I will tell you what I have heard from my elders—of the shifts we sought to preserve our people. Yet there was no help and we will vanish and be as if we had never been, like the leaves of the last springtime."

The very quietness of Keral's words tugged at David's heart with their bleak, forlorn acceptance. He could not bear that quiet; he could not bear to see the luminous brilliance he had first touched in Keral extinguished in this misery; yet what could he do?

"Well, my people have a proverb: *never say die*," he said. "Regis believes that the Darkovan telepaths are all dying out, but he's doing something about it, not singing sad songs of sorrow. Maybe it's not as late as you think, Keral; and even if it's true, we are going to do our damnedest to learn everything we can and be grateful for the chance to get it from you."

Keral's luminous smile lit up again. "It does me good to hear this; as I told you, my people have sat too long in our forests singing songs of sorrow and waiting for the leaves to cover us up. So that—here I am."

David took up the folders he had been studying at supper. He said, "You are convinced there is no other race like you?"

Keral's silent affirmative.

David dropped his bombshell, gently, almost without emphasis: "Did you know that Missy is a chieri?"

He was not prepared for Keral's surge of violent revulsion, disgust, and shock.

"Impossible! That—female animal? No, David; believe me, my friend, our people are not like that. David, I *touched* her; as I touched you a few moments ago. Do you honestly believe I could be mistaken?"

"Not by your own standards," David said, puzzled but prepared to defend the findings of his own science until Keral could give better grounds than physical revulsion. "In that case there is a race like enough to yours to be twin. Let me show you what I mean."

He spread out the physiological data. Keral betrayed more knowledge of anatomy than David would have believed; evidently, the language barrier once surmounted, he had a very good grasp of these things. David had to explain the instrument readings and diagrams to him; but once Keral grasped them, he examined them with a frown and a growing disquiet.

"David, I cannot understand it but my instinct tells me you are wrong, while my intelligence tells me you must be right! How shall we resolve this?"

"Missy lied to every question we asked her. Every question, without exception; compulsively. If she is a wide-open telepath, and she is—we both know that from what happened with Conner—why did she do it? How did she believe she could get away with it?" Almost too late he remembered that a touch on the question of sexuality had made Keral freeze and draw away, earlier. Yet Keral had spoken clearly and clinically, though regretfully, just now, about his own people and their declining reproductive powers. A puzzle. . . .

Keral said: "I know of only one way to be sure, and it could even be dangerous, but let us take it. Can we bring Missy here without alarming her, David? I might know of a way to question and find out her truths. Why does any being lie? Only out of fear or a wish for profit, and what profit could she have in lying? Perhaps we can find the fear behind her lies and soothe it."

"I'll try," David said, and went off down the hospital corridor, having left Keral (curled on David's bed, curiously nibbling the fruit-and-nut candy) to wait. He remembered that all of them except the Darkovans had been quartered in rooms in this wing; he felt briefly embarrassed. Suppose he interrupted Conner and Missy in bed again? Oh, hell, who cares? At home on Earth if I found two acquaintances in bed, I'd excuse myself and ask them to come along when they were finished. It's the damned voyeur taboo and after all, telepaths would have to get used to that, I guess. It didn't seem to bother Regis, he was just afraid it would disrupt the rest of us who didn't expect to be overhearing such things.

Yet if Missy's not human, but can and does have sex freely and openly with humans, can the chieri be said to be nonhuman at all? And if they *do* interbreed with humans, why are they dying out? Hell, here I am looking for answers even before I have the right questions. I'd better get some facts.

Missy opened the door of her room and he saw that she was alone.

David? What does he want? I felt him coming.

It's idiotic to go through all these motions when we can pick up each other's minds and emotions. I guess none of us is used to it yet.

Aloud, to ease off the odd disquiet both in himself and her, he said, "Missy, if you're not busy, would you come down to my room for a little while? We'd like to ask you a couple of questions."

Curiosity flickered in her pale gray eyes. She said, "Why not?" and came along. He noted again the slender height and grace, not as outré as Keral's odd beauty, but still enough to mark her anywhere on any world. She reacted with mild surprise to the sight of Keral, but made no comment. David felt a strange wariness in her as she accepted some of the candies he had brought from downstairs, curled up on a corner of his bed beside Keral.

Habits of movement, speech, all are culture bound. Missy walks and acts like a lovely woman, sure of her own desirability, confident in it—

Or does the confidence go so deep? There's something forlorn about her. She looks lost, that's it; she's not like anyone else. . . .

He tried to make it an ordinary social occasion. "Sorry I've nothing to offer you; when we've been here longer it may be more organized. There must be a place to get something to drink somewhere around here. At least if there isn't it will be the first Empire planet I've heard about where there wasn't. Missy, I've forgotten; what world did they find you on?"

—wariness, wariness. A blur of fear like a small animal scooting to ground in its hole.

. . . . there have been so many. . . .

"It's one of those with an unpronounceable name," she said.

Keral raised his pale eyes to hers. A faint spark flew. "I'm good at languages," he said lightly. "Try me."

Panic. Retreat. Terror. She jerked her hands violently away.

She did not. She did not move. "I was born on Lanach, so I suppose you'd call me a Lanchy."

David did not get the warning flicker of earlier lies, and sensed she was telling the truth, or believed she was. He said: "I've seen Lanach on star maps, but I believed it had been colonized mostly by the darker races and ethnic groups."

"It was," Missy said, "I always felt a bit of a freak." She drew a shaky breath. "That's why I left it and I've never been back."

"Were you a foundling?"

wariness, wariness . . . careful . . . what do they want. . . .

She said, "I suppose so, although I'm not sure. I don't remember my parents." Again she lifted her eyes to Keral's; again the curious, puzzled spark flew between them, and then Keral quickly turned his face away. David could feel his unease, his revulsion like an almost tangible thing, and the sense of undercover pressure built up again. Damn it, how could a girl who looked fifteen put him at a loss? And was it simply the awareness of her earlier sexual exploits which had upset Keral? That was evidently an area where all of them might have to be careful with the chieri—an odd sexual code? Declining racial fertility meaning sexual hangups and taboos. . . .

Keral commanded himself. He said, in a flat quiet voice, "Why did you lie to us, Missy? How old are you?"

Panic. Violence . . . break/run/disappear/flight/a twisting trapped thing gnawing desperately. . . .

That image blurred. Other waves of magnetic awareness damped it out. Missy moved with a soft little seductive wriggle on the bed, stretching out with her hands behind her head. David wondered why it was he had thought she looked immature. Her smile was slow and luminous. She said softly, "It's a girl's privilege to keep her age to herself. But I'm over the age of consent."

She did not move, but for a blurred instant it seemed to David that she stretched out her arms, that there was a deep movement in his groin, that in another instant he must reach for her—

Keral made a strangled sound of disgust and revulsion.

One of ours? And like this? Madness, and yet I feel . . . it is true, yet how . . . a foundling? Yet maddened, a bitch ravening . . . all manner of men on all worlds. . . .

David, brought to quick sanity by Keral's recoil, drew back from Missy. He said coldly, "You worked that trick on Conner, but it won't work on us, Missy, not now anyway. You're overwhelmingly beautiful, but that isn't what we came here for. All we want from you is the truth, Missy. Why lie to us? What harm could the truth do you? Where did you come from? How old are you?"

Panic. Fear. Disquiet and an agonizing, chattering loss of self-sureness; if they won't want me what am I good for, how shall I hide . . . hide, hide. . . .

Without warning the room exploded. David's brushes, lying on the top of the built-in counter, flew across the room and into the mirror. Missy, like a madly spinning cat, whirled within a vortex which picked up chairs, wastebasket, pens on the desk, flinging them madly about; Keral flinched and covered his face, but the blankets crawled up snakelike and wrapped with strangling force around him. A flicker of fire crawled up the wall. . . .

David heard screams of rage and terror, and yet at another level the room was wholly silent, in a sort of cushioned, timeless instant of dead silence.

Abruptly, Missy froze as if suddenly turned to stone. She writhed and struggled in an invisible grip, without actually moving, caught as if held in strong hands.

Behave yourself! It was like an actual voice, cold, imperative, and angry, and it held the very note of Desideria's presence. *I know you have neither manners nor training, but it is time you learned control. A natural gift like yours left to run wild is dangerous, my girl, and the sooner you learn it the better.*

Missy fell to the floor as if the invisible grip had physically dropped her. Around her the flying, spinning furniture slowly settled down. The sense of Desideria's presence withdrew, like an ironic flick of apology. Keral and David gasped and stared at each other.

Missy, breathing heavily and sobbing, scrambled to her feet and fled.

David let his breath go in a long, "Whew! What in ninety galaxies brought *that* on?"

"We scared her," Keral said without irony. "I asked the wrong question; how old she was."

David saw abruptly, without words, the picture in Keral's mind, contrasted with Keral's own quiet, unaging timelessness:

. . . . fleeing from world to world when they saw

she never changed, never aged; instantly seeking a
new protector; deserting him as he grew old and died;
a new world always rising to be conquered, to be hidden from; at the lowest level, her gift good only to
seek out and conquer, put a man under her instant
spell with bondage to her body. . . .

Keral said shakily, "I am sorry. I felt sick, that is all.
That one of our race—oh, yes, she is, she must be, although I still do not know how. We, our people *cannot*, that is all. The—the change must be a thing of
deep involvement; no, I know you do not understand." He seemed frightened, wild as he had been at
their first meeting, in a half maddened retreat.

"Keral, Keral—don't—" David reached for his
hands again, hoping to quiet him as he had done before, but Keral shrank again in a spasmodic rejection.
Don't touch me!

But as David drew back, distressed and hurt, Keral
forced himself to calm. He said, "There is so much to
tell, and I cannot tell it all. My elders must know
about this. But we have failed with Missy, and this
much I can tell you. Earlier I told you our race has
been dying since before your people came first to this
world you call Darkover. We were not always a forest
people. We had cities, worlds, ships which could tread
the stars, and when we knew we were dying we left
this world and for many, many years, we ranged
among the other worlds of all kinds of men, seeking a
remedy, trying to find a way to live and not to die . . .
and there was no remedy; and at last we returned here

and left our ships to rust into the bottom of time and our cities to fall into the very dust of eternity; and we withdrew into the unending forests, waiting to die and be no more. . . .

"But on some of those worlds some of our people must have remained. Unknown. Unguessed. Warped out of knowledge by what they had been through with other races who could not know them or understand.

"I guess that Missy is one of these, but I do not know. . . ."

He dropped his face into his hands and fell silent. He said faintly, "I am weary. Let me sleep."

The hospital quarters rooms were arranged so that extra beds could be pulled out from the furniture; David, realizing that Keral was at the end of his endurance, silently drew one out for him and watched the chieri fall swiftly into a stunned, unconscious sleep that was like trance. He, himself, sat staring at his notes for hours, his mind in turmoil with all he had discovered.

The next morning they found that Missy had disappeared.

CHAPTER SEVEN

Linnea, Keeper and *leronis* of the Arilinn Tower, had
few hours of leisure, and when they came she tried to
keep them inviolate. The work of a Keeper, a worker
in the matrix screens which provided such small technology as was accessible on Darkover, was arduous
and brain grating. Trained since early childhood in
difficult telepathic work, like all the Keepers she
shrouded herself from all casual contacts with those
who were not telepaths, conserving her energies with
every means at her command.

So that when one of the few servants in the Tower
brought her word that two Free Amazons from the
mountains sought to see her, she was both incredu-
lous and offended.

"I do not see guests or travelers. I am not a freak to
be seen by paying a penny. Send them on their way."
A few years ago, she thought, no one would have
dared to suggest such an insolence.

The servant seemed almost equally embarrassed:
"Do you think I did not tell them that, *vai leronis*? Yet

when I said as much, and rudely too, the one said that she was from your own village, one of your own, and that now your grandmother had gone from the mountains there was no soul within a thousand miles who could help her. She claimed that she would wait all night and all day for an hour of your convenience."

Linnea said, startled, "Then I suppose I must see them." *But what is a woman of my hills doing in Arilinn, so far from the Kilghards, so far from the mountains of Storn. . . .*

She went down the long stairs slowly, rather than exert her wearied body and brain to control the elevator shaft. Passing through the blue force field that shielded the Keepers at work from intrusive outside thoughts, she braced herself for an interview with outsiders, nontelepaths. It was so incredibly difficult, after months and weeks of seeing only those who could blend into your inner moods and senses, to mingle with and touch outsiders; minds and bodies cold, barricaded, alien. . . .

She touched rudimentary sensitivity at once from the tall Free Amazon with braided red hair (a telepath? neutered? Linnea, celibate by harsh necessity like all Keepers, felt the faint shock of revulsion for the sexless being) and it made her voice cold:

"What urgent necessity brings you here to the world's end, my countrywoman?"

It was the younger woman who looked up and spoke, a quietly pretty, plumpish girl wrapped in the furs of the hill people. She said, "Lady Linnea, I knew you as a child at High Windward. I am Menella of the Naderling Forst. This is my freemate Darilyn, and we are here because—" shyness overcame her, and she looked up in open appeal at the taller, red-haired Amazon. Darilyn said in a flat, abrupt, cold voice, "We should not have disturbed you, *leronis*, but there was no other person who would understand or believe us. You know what I am." She raised her gray eyes briefly, almost in defiance, to Linnea's, and the quickly-barricaded touch of recognition passed between them.

Like you, I live shielded, Sorceress. Because of what I am, guarded against man's touch: vulnerable, like all our fast-fading kind.

Linnea lowered her eyes; the condemnation in them was gone. Linnea had been born into a noble family; had she chosen not to work in the Towers as a telepath Keeper, she would have been given in marriage to a man of her own kind; one who could equal her own sensitivity, a fellow telepath. Darilyn, born into a village, growing up surrounded (a freak; a throwback) by those who could neither understand nor respect what she was, had chosen to have her womanhood destroyed by the neutering operation rather than subject it to a man who would be, to her, only a dumb beast.

Linnea's voice was gentle as she said, "Be welcome, countrywomen. My discourtesy was born of weariness, no more. Has refreshment been offered you? Is it well in the hills of our homeland, Menella?"

"It is as evil as can be, *vai leronis*," Menella said, "But we did not come to tell you a twice-told tale. You know that fire and hunger have ravaged us. Darilyn, tell her what you saw."

Darilyn, outwardly composed, was wretchedly nervous. She stated, "My freemate and I recently traveled with an outworld woman, not a Free Amazon, though she behaved much like one of us. She had contracted for our service as guides and hunters through the mountains. She was strange, like a Keeper who had lost her powers, but outworlders are all mad and we were not surprised at that. I could read her thoughts a little; she did not trouble to hide them and so I thought she had nothing to hide." Suddenly, Darilyn began to tremble.

"She was *evil*," she said with utter conviction. "She passed the blighted forests, and she looked at them as if her own hand had set them to flaming. She looked on me, and I knew that with her will all of our kind would die. And once I saw her from far off, burying a charm in the woods, and I knew that by her will, the soil would be blighted and die. I know this is madness, Linnea. I learned before my breasts grew that there were no witches and that evil will harmed no one any more than good intentions helped. Yet I cannot help it; I know that this woman's evil will would kill our world. It is a riddle I cannot read, *vai leronis*, and none in our world can read it if a Keeper cannot."

Linnea said, "This is superstition and folly." And yet her voice weakened and died.

A plot against our world?

What had Regis said?

The work of a witch? Impossible. Yet were these girls saying, in the light of their limited understanding, a truth? Truth, or at least that they believed it implicitly, was in every line of their stubborn, boyish faces. In any case, no Darkovan would lie to a Keeper. This conviction made her voice gentle as she said, "I do not see how what you say can be, and yet you must have seen something to make for such a belief. Have you left this woman's service?"

"Not yet, Lady. As we passed near Arilinn we told her we must pay you our respects and she thought nothing of it."

Linnea spoke decisively. "I will look into it. You know I must have something belonging to her."

"I cut a piece from her garments without being seen," said Menella, and Linnea could have laughed at the odd contrast of superstitious fear and practicality. Everyone knew that without something belonging to a person or at least in contact with that person, it was difficult to pick up the vibration of the person's thoughts. Yet they had thought the stranger a witch?

She dismissed further talk of the stranger, offered them refreshment, talked the amenities of their shared childhood for a further half hour before sending them away. Yet all during that time, while she listened to the disturbing news from their homeland, a coldness was growing at her heart.

Regis Hastur had seen this.

A plot. But why? From whom? Had these girls seen to the core of it?

She must somehow find out.

But at her heart there was a single-minded hunger. Regis knew so much more about these things. Was she only making excuses for herself to see him again? For she knew she must take this to him.

Regis. . . .

Linnea! My dear one, where are you (so far from me, so near)—

At Arilinn, but I must come there, even if it means closing all the relays; it's that important.

Beloved, what is it? (You are frightened. Can I share your fears?)

Not this way, where anyone open to us can overhear. (Not only frightened but in terror for our world and all our people.)

Linnea, I can send a Terran aircraft for you if you are not afraid to ride in it, and if you can face the anger of the others. (I long for you here; I could see you this very night, but for myself I would never ask it.)

I am not afraid (to see you again I would face more than anger but not for my own sake) and I must tell you what I have learned.

Regis let the contact drop away and sighed, feeling his many fears and problems overwhelm him again after the brief respite. He was eager to see Linnea again, but the fear he had sensed in her thoughts came near to pulling the switch on his panic. Furthermore, he was exhausted with the terrible hunger and depletion from maintaining contact over such distances. This was something they should study in the Terran project, he thought, the physical depletion which came after prolonged contact or contact over longer distances. At the back of his mind, too, was another thought; direct contact all the way from Arilinn, more than a thousand miles, would hardly be possible for most of the telepaths on this world; Linnea must, indeed, have more extraordinary powers than he had believed. Most of the Keepers in these days, when powers were depleted and ill-trained. would have gone through the two intermediate relays between here and Arilinn, not even trying to come through to him in person. It was a mark of Linnea's panic that she had attempted the long distance contact without intermediates, and a mark of her power that she had succeeded even for these few seconds.

He knew there would be no questions asked if he requested the Terran authorities to dispatch a plane to Arilinn; and there were not, but he worried nevertheless while he was making the arrangements. This would mean criticism again, for himself and for Linnea; not from the Terrans (*they* were eager to put the Hasturs under obligations, damn them!) but from their own people. Damned by the one party for having anything at all to do with the Terrans; damned by the others for not having more to do with them. Just damned.

He had, at this minute, another appalling problem and was facing an uncomfortable interview. He shrank from going toward the Terran HQ hospital, even though he knew that most of what he would meet there would be good-natured. There was the problem of Missy. Where had she gone? Darkover spaceport was a big one, the Trade City enormous; and it had closed over her head as if she had never been there at all. He knew rationally that she would seek anonymity, not trouble, but still the fear nagged at him.

And then there was the more personal problem. He lingered in the hospital corridors, braving the curious glances of the passing nurses and doctors who wondered (some of them; the others knew all too well) what a man in the dress of Darkovan nobility was doing there.

He finally knocked at the door of the Project A Telepath offices, hoping it would put off the other visit a bit longer. Jason and David were both there; and Keral, who had taken to spending much of his time around the hospital, picking up much of what they were doing; Regis had been astonished at the swiftness with which the chieri had absorbed the technical knowledge he apparently desired.

Jason's hearty smile, friendly though it was, made Regis wince a little as the Terran said, "Regis! A pleasure to see you, though I didn't think you'd have time for us this morning! Dr. Shield told me congratulations are in order. A fine boy, I understand, six pounds and perfectly healthy."

Regis said, "I was going to visit Melora and the child now—if she will see me. She must be very angry; she sent me no message."

"You couldn't have done anything here," David said, "why should you lose your sleep? She was perfectly well looked after; I've met Marian Shield, and she seems to be as good an O.B. as is working on this world."

"I'm sure she was taken care of, and I'm grateful to all of you," Regis said. "But the very fact that she did not have me told—"

He caught David's eyes and saw a flash of quick understanding in them.

—A woman who loves the man who has fathered her child wants him near her at such a time.

"I must go and see Melora, at least," Regis said. "Has there been any word of Missy?"

"Not a syllable, Regis," Jason answered. "They'll stop her if she tries to leave the planet, of course, but short of that—well, you have a damn big world out there and evidently she's used to running and hiding."

One of my people; fugitive!

Keral's thoughts were almost palpable, and Regis felt the obscure wish to offer some comfort, without knowing how. He saw David reach out, without a word, for Keral's hand, and their clasped hands filled him with curious half-sorrow; as if he had, somehow, lost something precious without ever realizing that he had it until it was forever beyond his reach.

He shook his head, dismissing the thought. Absurdities! Then a flicker of comfort struck him; Linnea would soon be here, and even though this might complicate matters still further with Melora (she was sure to decide that Linnea was here at Regis' personal wish) he simply did not care.

Keral said unexpectedly, "I have never seen a newborn human child. May I come and see your son, Regis?"

"Of course; I'm always glad to show off my children," Regis said. David decided to come too, and they went up through the hospital corridors, the tall slight chieri provoking curious glances; but here in the hospital HQ the curiosity was friendly; many of them had seen and spoken to Keral now, and he was simply another alien, not an unheard-of curiosity.

Melora had been put in a private room in a corner wing with a window looking on the mountains, a room often kept for important Darkovan guest-patients, and a Darkovan midwife and a nurse from her own estates had been permitted to attend her. She was sitting up in a chair, wearing a long, fleecy blue robe, her cheeks faintly flushed. She was a pretty girl, auburn-haired, gray-eyed, tall and dignified; and at the moment, with her long hair braided and falling over her shoulders, she looked hardly more than a child herself. Regis' eyes went swiftly, with the old fear, to the small, screened crib where the baby was lying (no more than a small red face asleep in a white hospital blanket) but he quickly brought his attention back to Melora, gesturing to her not to rise, bending and kissing her cheek. "He is lovely, Melora. Thank you. If I had known I would have been here with you."

"There was nothing you could have done, and I was very well cared for," answered the girl coolly, turning her cheek away from the kiss. The tension in the room was palpable; the three facing her, all telepaths of greater or lesser power, could all feel her anger. Regis knew suddenly that he had been cowardly to let the others come in the hope that Melora would not make a scene before outsiders; she had been distressed at the need to bear her child in this strange place; she did not understand why Regis had demanded it of her; and she was (Regis realized) entitled to make a scene if she wanted to, unhampered by outsiders.

Keral created a small diversion by going to the baby; Melora gave a small cry as the stranger bent over her child; then as Keral's beautiful eyes turned to her, she relaxed. She actually smiled at the chieri, saying, "Yes, take him if you like, Noble One; you lend us grace."

Keral picked up the infant. His long hands slipped competently around the little swaddled body, as if he were quite accustomed to handling children, although David, watching him, knew without knowing how that Keral had never seen or touched a young baby before. Keral's smile was curiously distant, fascinated.

"His thoughts are so strange and formless. And yet how different it feels from touching a small animal."

David privately thought the baby looked like any other newborn thing, small and nondescript, but he knew that this was born of the cultivated cynicism of the medical student. He tried for an instant to see the child through Keral's eyes, a small wonder, a miracle of newness. It was too intense; he dropped away from the contact and said to Regis, "What will you call him?"

"That will be for Melora to say," said Regis, smiling at the young mother, "unless she asks me to give him a name."

Melora's face softened and she laid her hand in Regis'. "You may if you like," she said, and David touched Keral's shoulder. Keral put the baby down quietly and they went out, leaving the young parents alone with their child.

David thought, later, that it was this moment of contact with the child and with Regis which sensitized him; but at the time he let it drop from consciousness and spent the day with the remaining members of the project. Rondo was sullen and uncooperative to attempts to measure his control of small objects, unwilling to discuss his gambling career or how he had managed it, unwilling to attempt manipulation of the test objects Jason and David showed him. Desideria was snappish and seemed apprehensive. Conner had sunk into apathy again and would not even talk, let alone cooperate. David could sense, like a tangible thing, his grief and sense of desertion now that Missy was gone.

Regis was not with them at all, and Danilo, who turned up briefly, made Regis' excuses, on the grounds of urgent private affairs, and took himself off again as well.

In the end, after Rondo had sullenly pleaded fatigue and headache (and David felt that Conner would have done the same if he'd cared even that much about what happened to him) David simply asked Desideria to tell them something about the training of a telepath Keeper, and he sat listening and making listless notes—pure waste motion, he knew, as it was all being put on tape anyhow.

"We were trained at first with games, like manipulating this stuff—when we were young, that is," Desideria told them, moving her head at the assembled dice, feathers, and other small objects with which David had been trying to arouse Rondo's cooperation. "There were also games where sweets and other things were hidden and we had to find them, and later much more elaborate games where there was fairly strenuous physical training of the nerve currents; breathing, concentration, hours and hours spent in breath control and meditation, learning to work both in and out of the physical body. All this before we ever saw a matrix, of course. When we could control all our natural talents, then we began to work with the matrix jewels, the small ones first—"

David reflected that much of this sounded like the

old traditional yoga training, still used by some groups of Terrans for religious or health reasons. He put away curiosity until all this could be evaluated at leisure.

All during that evening the same sense of dullness, of everything hanging fire, pervaded all of David's senses. Keral was edgily quiet and uncommunicative. He had been assigned to a room in the hospital HQ near David's, and, as they had fallen into a habit of doing, they went to supper together in the cafeteria, but he did not speak a dozen words nor did he offer to come to David's room and talk as usual. Conner, too, seemed not to be speaking to anyone, and while Keral's silence did not worry David, Conner's did. If this apathy continued, would it trigger another suicidal phase in the spaceman? He had come back to life for Missy. If she was gone, would it take away his interest in living? Damn Missy anyhow! But David hardened his heart. He couldn't, and wouldn't, take on responsibility for the mental and physical wellbeing of the whole blasted project! That was Jason's baby and he could rock it.

Nevertheless, it was a long time before David could sleep; he kept having the curious illusion of voices just at the edge of consciousness, in the same way that distant cries or sobs, even after they have ceased, seem to be going on just below the level of hearing, keeping the listener's ears and senses strained and his nerves on edge with the fear of hearing them again.

Nevertheless, he did fall asleep at last, the sort of

light sleep where the sleeper knows he is sleeping and is conscious of shuttling back and forth, half aware, from true sleep and dreams into light half-awake drowsing and back again. Two or three times he startled upright with the brief sharp shock of falling, weightless horror, and knew his dreams wove into Conner's; Missy's face, nightmarish and contorted with crying, swam in and out of his dreams; and Keral, his alien hands cradling the small pink form of the baby and a weird croon of song weaving into the dream.

Abruptly, with a sharper sense of spinning awareness cutting through the dream, he was upright and on his feet, half-dressed, running. . . .

Bare corridors. Keral's flying feet matching his own. The startled white face, eye pupils dilated, voice dulled; *you can't go in there!*

Door flung wide, crashing. The dark form of an intruder, menacing; Melora's breathing slowed, slack, dilated, discolored pupils. . . .

Keral bending, heaving, upraised dark form, a terrible scream and the shape of the intruder flying against the wall, the crunch, crack, shriek of bones breaking and snapping—and something died. Melora's white slack face; press up one eyeball with practiced fingers, shouting for help.

The room filled with doctors, nurses; nurse crying dazedly, drugged. Bending, mouth to the girl's mouth, breathing, breathing, breathing—

"Here, Dr. Hamilton. I'll take over."

Stand aside, breath quieting to normal. Keral, stark white. The baby in his hands; Keral's voice, ragged and unreal:

"He will need help breathing; his chest is not crushed but I think ribs are broken"—the tiny brittle feel of minute ribs under his hands, the fitful choking crying of a half-smothered baby slowly coming to life again. . . .

Crowding forms bending over the dead man in the corner. Keral's shaking hands, white face just a wedge of terror; questions, voices, uniforms. An official voice, cutting through the others:

"In his pocket here; ampules of the same drug he gave the girl. He must have drugged Nurse Conniston, too. Dr. Hamilton, what brought you here? It looks as if you were just in time to prevent two murders."

David heard his own voice, but it sounded unreal to him. "I'm not sure. Possibly I heard Keral—did you call out, Keral? All I know is that I woke up with this sense of terrible urgency. I don't know how I knew that Melora and the—the baby were in danger."

"Who is he?" Officials crowded around the dead man.

"Same old story, he could be anything. Some drifter from the spaceports—surgically altered fingerprints, even."

"Damn good thing, too. Imagine what would have happened; Regis Hastur confides his son to us for safekeeping and the child and the girl murdered right

here in the Terran HQ? Just imagine the political capital they could make out of that!"

Vaguely, still in the blur, David wondered who *they*
were and just what political capital could be made out
of the death of a child, and what kind of monsters
could imagine such a move. He had to tell his story
twice more, feeling more and more disoriented and
disbelieving every time. The baby was in no danger,
but the HQ officials tripled the security guards
around the nursery. David stood by, not needed by the
team working over Melora (it was more than an hour
before she began to breathe again normally, unaided;
she had been almost fatally drugged). Jason Allison
turned up and drew away the Spaceforce men who
were questioning David (Keral; where was Keral?
David could no longer feel his presence, and felt cold
and bereft—) and the Spaceforce men, listening to
Jason, stood staring at David as if he were some kind
of alien.

Somewhere in that hour, Regis turned up, white as
a bleached skeleton. He tried to say something to
David, couldn't manage it, his face working; and finally, wordlessly, he threw his arms around David
and embraced him, pressing his cheek against the
Terran's.

With the touch, David's world cleared suddenly into
bright colors and reality again, like fog suddenly clearing away. He knew suddenly that he was awake and
that this was all real, not a wild, confusing nightmare.

He came up to reality with Regis' hands clasped hard over his own, and said, coming back to himself:

"It's all right, Regis; they're both going to live and nothing more will happen now that everyone's warned. But—Good God! Where is Keral; what's happened to him?"

He had a sudden, stark déjà-vu of Keral's face, stark with horror, standing over the man he had killed.

No chieri has ever killed any living thing. He doesn't even eat meat!

David went back to his own room, knowing without knowing how that he would find Keral there, and he did. The chieri was curled up, hiding his face, only a wordless ball of misery and rejection, and his breathing was so slack and silent that for a heart-stopping instant David thought the shock had killed him. The pale, alien face held no recognition, even when David spoke to him. David turned him gently over. He was struck again, poignantly, at the almost feminine beauty of the chieri; his own dream came back to him with its curious overtones, and David felt an instant of startled shock and shame. Then, in sudden anger at himself, he drove the thought out of his mind.

Keral needs you and you can't judge him in human terms or in terms of your own private sexual hangups!

Keral was icy cold, almost as rigid as death. David knelt beside him on the bed and gathered him close, holding him with blind instinct, speaking his name in a soft, repeated murmur.

"Keral, Keral. It's me, it's David. Come back. I'm here. It's all right; it's going to be all right. Keral, Keral, don't die." The words were only a meaningless croon, but they were a way of focusing his whole mind, his whole personality on a deeper call, a deeper search:

Keral. Where have you gone? Come back, come back and be with me. I call you back, with all of myself, searching through the nowhere into which you have gone, seeking you out in the silences of fear. . . .

He felt it first, the black and formless horror in which Keral had gone down and almost drowned:

Death. I brought death on a living thing. He had the child between his hands; he was killing him. How can anyone kill a child? How can anyone bring death? My own hands and they brought death . . . I am dying in his death, drowning in that darkness. . . .

"God help me," said David, half aloud, "how can I reach him?" He filled his mind with the picture of life slowly coming back into the baby's blued, choking face, the surge of gratitude and love that had flowed into him from Regis' touch. Slowly, like the faltering beat of a heart under the reviving touch of a pacemaker, he felt Keral's awareness beginning to come back to life, coming up slowly through the darkness. He kept on holding Keral and murmuring to him (like a child; like a woman!) until at last the chieri's gray and luminous eyes blinked open, and he looked into David's face with a reviving, desolate grief.

"I did not want to kill him, even such an evil one. But I did not realize how weak he was and how strong my own arms when I was angry." He was trembling. "I'm so cold. So cold."

"That's shock," said David very gently. "You'll be better soon. There was nothing else you could have done, Keral."

"The child—"

"He's fine," David said, and marveled again. Keral's race, by Keral's own statement, was dying. Keral had never seen a child of his own people. How could the alien become so deeply involved with a child of another kind? Such a deep sense of identity—

He realized that Keral was slowly warming, the rigid, deathlike shock in the alien's body dissolving, and became, belatedly and with some bashfulness, aware that he was still lying close to Keral, holding the other in his arms like a lover. He let him go, rather quickly, and drew away, the practical trained self taking over as he rose. He said, "Are you still cold? Let me get you something hot to drink. And wrap up in the blankets." He had an excruciating sense that he had missed something, that the clue to Keral had just somehow eluded him, the clue to the whole mystery; but he had no way to solve it.

Keral sat up. "I want to find out—"

"Stay where you are," David commanded. "Doctor's orders. I'll go and find out how Melora and the baby are when I get something for you." He didn't trust sedatives with the alien physiology of the chieri, but certainly a hot drink wouldn't hurt him: coffee which was always on tap somewhere in the HQ or the bitter-chocolate tasting stuff which seemed the Darkovan equivalent.

It had been a damned exhausting night. He wasn't at all surprised, as he glanced through the window, to find that it was sunrise.

Nor was he especially surprised, later that morning, to find that Conner knew all about what had happened. He was, David reflected, getting used to being a telepath, and it had its uses.

He was also, although slowly, formulating the questions he knew he must put to Keral. Scientific inquiry about the chieri seemed to be getting them nowhere. He was going to trust his own intuitions and follow them wherever they led.

Regis Hastur emerged into the reddening morning, wrapped in fog, and stared at the sky almost without comprehension. Melora was out of danger and, thanks to Keral's quick action, the child had never been in any real danger. Both were sleeping now, and Regis had left them in good hands. But he was deathly weary and terrified again with the long struggle.

Perhaps more than any living person he could see all the ramifications of this. Had it been done by some Darkovan of the rabid anti-Terran party to discredit the Terrans—a Hastur child murdered under their very noses? Was it part of the plot to destroy all telepaths which he had sensed earlier? How would he face Melora's parents, after the struggle he had had to get them to permit this unheard-of thing—a Darkovan noblewoman to bear her child under the auspices of the Empire?

If it was one of our people who plotted this, we aren't worth saving! he thought with the bleakness of despair, and drew his perceptions inward so that he need not sense the Terran guards who followed his steps, trying not to intrude on the strange man they guarded.

He knew, with the perceptions of the trained telepath, that there were strangers in his own house, and stood in the half-lit hallway, trying to sort out if there was any menace. He felt upstairs, where the two older children slept with their nurses in the guarded nursery. They were peaceful and undisturbed. He had sent the youngest surviving child to Castle Hastur, under guard, with his mother. The sense of a stranger present persisted—

Linnea! I had forgotten, on this dreadful night—have you come so soon?

He did not look up as he felt her running down the stairs to him; looked up just to clasp her in his arms. He held her, hungrily, with an almost anguished need, feeling her slight body melting into his as if the barriers between flesh could physically fade out and he could somehow absorb her into himself. (Far away in the HQ building, at that moment, David released Keral with a sudden abashed awareness. Far out in the Trade City, Missy stirred uneasily in her sodden sleep and whimpered.) Then he put her down, and drew away, sighed, and smiled.

"It's selfish of me, *preciosa*, and I should send you away again. But I'm glad you've come."

"My great-grandame was glad to see me too, although she pretended to be shocked that I had left my post at Arilinn and wondered aloud what sort of girls they were training these days," Linnea said, laughing. "I am glad Melora and the child are safe. I will visit Melora if the Terrans will allow it and not think me a clever assassin."

"The worst of it is that I must listen to them all saying that they told me so," Regis said. "Although I am ashamed to think of that when they have both been in danger of death."

"You're too tired to think sensibly," Linnea said. "Let me call someone to bring you food. And then— Regis, I hate to pile more fear and responsibility on your shoulders, but I must tell you what I have seen."

Private Notebook of Andrea Closson; kept in code:

The level of forest fire has served its purpose and no further effort need be made in that direction, as crop cover has been reduced below the critical level in at least three widespread areas. The normal lightning set fires during this season should be sufficient, considering the demoralization of fire fighters in the mountains.

With the beginning of the spring rains in sectors IV and VII, erosion should begin in the Hellers and spread into the foothills. Reduction in the water table due to excessive runoff in the burned areas should soon become critical. With the expected start of the dry season near Carthon there should be dust storms, reducing crops to a critical level.

Some food supply relief can be expected from the well-watered towns in the lowlands, but this will not be enough. Demands made on the Terran Empire may spark some political decisions favorable to the desired agreement. (N.B.; the Empire has submitted a request for enlargement of the spaceport facilities which was turned down in Council last year. The question is to be raised again in five months. This will be a watershed decision.)

Expected agricultural disasters will begin this summer although they will not be crucial, and true famine will not exist, except among isolated, forest-dwelling, nonhuman cultures, until three years from now. Nevertheless, some small amount of panic can be expected.

Agents should be dispatched to begin work among the nonhumans, stirring up panic and rebellion. If an attack on human towns can be engineered, this would be worth a great deal toward the ultimate solution, as war between human and nonhuman at this time, although not conclusive, might drain resources which would otherwise be turned to salvage work in agricultural areas.

Efforts should be redoubled to eliminate interference from any of the Hasturs. The telepath relay towers are probably impregnable, but the relatively low level of sophistication in interplanetary politics should keep anyone from awareness and coordination until too late. Fortunately, the highly individualized social order on this world precludes coordinated effort.

If my calculations are correct, the point of no return could be reached within a matter of months. After that time, efforts need no longer be kept secret, as the process will be irreversible and Darkover, for bare survival, will be forced to negotiate with technological experts in planetary repair. It is possible that this point has already been reached, since the apparent level of Darkovan technology would not make it possible to reclaim the world for the old style of life without expert help. For this help they would be forced to make political concessions which would achieve the desired objective of planetary opening equally well. It is possible I may have underestimated the Hasturs, but at this moment they seem to be preoccupied with minimal government facilities. In effect, there is no central government. This world is wide open.

CHAPTER EIGHT

"This planet is wide open," Regis repeated slowly, his eyes fixed on Linnea. "I should have guessed before. I've read enough Empire history—did I never tell you, when I was a boy, I wanted to go offworld, into space?—to know what worldwrecking is. I don't know why I thought Darkover would be immune."

Danilo Syrtis said, "I never trusted those Empire bastards." His tense, young face was implacable. "Some of the mountain men had the right idea. Rise up and throw every one of the accursed Terrans right off our world, tear down the spaceport, and sow the ground there with salt."

"You're a fool, *bredú*," Regis said gently. "It's not the Empire. They have played honestly with us and they have honored their commitments. If they wanted to open this world by force they could and would have done so three hundred years ago."

"But who, then, Regis? If not the Terrans?" Linnea asked.

"All I can say to that is that it's a big galaxy and

there are I forget how many inhabited worlds," Regis answered. "Talk about hunting for a nut in a forest! Even on one world, looking for one specific person— the facts of the matter are, Linnea, we don't have the kind of *centralized organization*—" he spoke in lingua franca, as the old Darkovan language had no such concepts or words—"to deal with this sort of thing. It's war; and we've done away with war long since. Fights, yes. Feuds, yes. Raids, yes. I fought my first raid-battle before my beard sprouted, when Kennard Alton led us against Kadarin and his crew. But we do our fighting and our hating by ones and twos and tens. It just isn't *reasonable* to hate large groups of people who have never harmed us personally, just because they're *there*. It's why we never really fought the idea of the Empire, although I don't think most people really wanted a spaceport on Darkover. It's a big world and there's always room enough for every kind of idea; that was what we thought. We've learned a lot from the Terrans, and they've given us a great deal. And in return we've made our own impression on the Empire. But while that kind of thinking is the only sane kind in the long run, we're looking at the short run now. And it's conditioned us against thinking in terms of war. We're a peaceful people, by and large, and we're wide open to this kind of sabotage."

"Do you mean there's no way to stop it, then?" Linnea asked; and Danilo, clenching his fists, said, "We can fight if we have to."

"I don't mean that," Regis said, "but we aren't set

up to handle it now. We have one hope, and that's dying out."

"And that is?"

"The old telepath technology of Darkover," Regis said. "But we're inbred, our fertility is going downhill, and we're being killed at an appalling rate, as witness the attack tonight. There aren't enough of us alive on Darkover for the kind of coordinated effort we'd need to stop this. Oh, we've had warnings enough. For the last hundred years, the Terrans have been trying to work with us, to develop our old sciences, learn how to work with the matrices, encourage the training of more matrix technicians and telepaths. If we had several hundred functioning telepaths, with Towers and relay circles in full function, we could survey the planet, find out just what's being done, and reverse it. As it is, we have to rely on alien technologies, and our whole way of life is opposed to them."

He closed his eyes and considered. The first few weeks of Project Telepath had come up with only a few isolated telepaths, untrained; and the study had so far been unprofitable. True, David had saved Melora's life; they had some new and fascinating knowledge of the legendary chieri, but this was a drop in the bucket. A dozen or so telepaths discovered on other worlds were on their way to Darkover, but how many of them would turn out to be psychotics like Rondo, or, like Missy, unable to endure questioning?

Danilo asked, "How many telepaths *are* alive on Darkover?"

Regis said wearily. "Aldones! Do you think I am a god's self, that I know such things?" Then he was suddenly electrified:

But I can know!

Fool I am; I have studied everyone's powers but our own.

He said, with a controlled quiet that belied his own sudden excitement:

"Let's think about this. How many working Towers are there in function, Linnea?"

"Nine," she said, "widely scattered. At Arilinn there are eight of us; in the other towers, anywhere from seven to twelve or fourteen."

Regis said, "In the Trade City we have forty licensed matrix mechanics. I happen to know that there are other telepaths born into the various old families—throwbacks, and some of them not even trained, who have some of the old *laran* powers. No one has ever bothered to count them or to demand that they use their powers. But if we all worked together—"

"It's fantastic," Linnea said, "and probably impossible. You know what a Tower circle has to go through before we can work in concert, as a group, and accomplish anything. Every time a new member joins us, it takes weeks for us to tolerate his presence easily enough so that we can work with him touching our minds. Seven or eight seems to be the tolerable maximum."

Regis said, half aloud. "Three of us, linked in

depth, destroyed the Sharra matrix. What could five hundred of us do?"

Linnea flinched. "All of the old matrix screens above ninth level were destroyed years ago. They were adjudicated to be illegal weapons, and too dangerous for human beings to handle, Regis." Her eyes went slowly to his bleached-white hair. "An hour with one of them did—that—to you."

He nodded, slowly. "Yes. It's too dangerous, in human terms. But if the alternative is the destruction of a planet?"

"The question is academic in any case," Linnea said, "since the matrices no longer exist and no one alive knows how to build them. And a good thing, too."

"Still, it's the only hope we have," Regis said, "the one thing Darkover has which the Empire cannot duplicate from outside. For this, the Empire might help us without demanding political concessions which would destroy Darkover as we know it. It's going to be a race; a race against time. But I'm going to do it." His face was bleak. "I didn't ask to be placed at the head of the Council," he said. "I never wanted anything of the sort. But I have that power and for better or worse I've got to use it."

"I don't understand," Linnea said. "Why should the Empire *want* telepaths? From what *I* hear, they just barely believe we exist!"

"Look," said Regis violently, "use your head, Linnea. A matrix, with a sufficiently trained telepath, can produce energy—right? What little mining we have on Darkover is done with a matrix circle to locate and teleport the minerals to the surface—right? We make do with small use of metals because we do not want factories and manufacturing industry, but for the small amount we use, we have technology sufficient to our needs, or did, until recently."

"Yes, but the human expenditure—"

"Can be compensated. A matrix, operated by a trained telepath, can substitute for conventional aircraft. And so we have use of aircraft only in emergency; we do not use it wastefully. And there is communication: we on Darkover have no need of long range mechanical communications equipment."

"Right—" The main function of the relays on Darkover, especially now, was the long distance transmission of messages.

"The Empire has long since realized what telepaths would be good for," Regis said: "in space, for communication. For the controlling of mechanical equipment when ordinary machinery fails, through levitation or energon-control; any child with a matrix can see into the structure of matter enough to reverse oxidation or metal fatigue, for instance. The bottleneck is the small supply of telepaths—and the general unwillingness of Darkovans to collaborate with the Empire. None of us has been available for study. We don't know ourselves how we use these old sciences. The few efforts made to study these things have lost out to human failures. But there must be a way, and now is the time to try it."

"What are you going to do?" Linnea shrank from trying to read his thoughts directly.

"I am going to demand that the relays send out a call to every telepath on Darkover," Regis said, "with all the authority of Hastur, *with all that means*."

Linnea met his eyes briefly and shrank from the contact. Regis seemed, at that moment, almost superhuman, and she thought of the old legends of the Son of Hastur, who was more than human—and Regis had once wielded the Sword of Aldones, forged for the hand of a god. Which was another way of saying that he had somehow managed to tame and use forces of the human mind which were incomprehensible to the ordinary person.

She seized on a minor aspect of this;

"Can we shut down the relay towers and pull them all in here? Can we afford to do away with what little technology we do have? We'd be barbarians, Regis."

"Yes," Danilo said unexpectedly, "Darkover takes the telepaths, the work of the relays, entirely too much for granted. Shut down the towers for a few months or years and let our world see what it would be like without the telepath powers. Within a month they'll rise up and stop letting us be killed off one by one. There was a time when a man who laid a rude hand on a Keeper would have been tortured to death. Now they can slaughter women and children without anyone even caring."

"Are you saying that we could stop what they're

doing to our world just by telepath powers?" Linnea asked.

"No, I don't think so," Regis replied. "There is too much physical damage to the planet, I suspect. But we can find out who is doing it, and stop them. And we can, perhaps, trade on even terms with the Empire, for the help we need now. In any case, it's time to stop playing and take the telepath project seriously. Otherwise we are going to go the way of the chieri; and there are plenty of people in the Empire who wouldn't regret us at all. That would leave Darkover wide open for the kind of exploitation they want. We're standing in the door," Regis repeated, "and we've got to stay there."

It was a commonplace room, dull and dark and evil-smelling, and Missy lay huddled and quiet for long periods at a time, hardly knowing what was going on either within or without her. Time had ceased to have meaning, although she had long slowed her perceptions to see the world at least partly as those others did; the ones she must perforce live with.

So many changes, so many strangenesses. And the strange touch now. For the first time, someone who had returned the seeking touch, the thing she had never understood in herself. Always before, men had been merely a means of survival. She had known herself alien, freak, unable to find anyone who was able to meet her, join with her. Her body she had given

freely to whoever wanted it. After the first few times
(even now she flinched from remembering that old
horror, the discovery that what meant much to her
was beast-nothingness to them) it had meant nothing.
But now:

Conner. Emotions long deadened, reaching and
touching her (she could feel what had gone on within
him, the strange fears and loneliness that had shaped
him) in a way she hardly understood. She knew little
of her own emotions. She had never dared to be in-
trospective, but she sensed that if she looked within
herself she would see and feel some such whirling
horror as had shaped Conner's madness. And now,
far from him, she still felt the helpless loneliness of his
need (how could she hold herself from running, flying
back—).

*Missy, I need you. Missy, come back, without you I am
maddened and lost again. . . .*

And the blind outpouring of her name, the name
which meant nothing to her (she had borne it only a
few years) but the ache of Conner's far-off crying for
her. He had touched her innerness, and she could not
forget, she knew she could never forget. But she could
get out of range. . . .

She could have stayed with Conner indefinitely,
she knew, in what happiness was possible to the
strange thing she was. (Ah, but could she have borne
to see him grow old, die?)

But the touch of *that other*—

Keral had reached right inside her, as if he had

physically put out his hand and thrust it through her and inside her body and twisted something. He hated her. He feared her. And yet there had been something between them, though he wasn't even a man. What was Keral and what had he *done* to her? And the other, David, had been indifferent to her, to Missy, (for the first time the spell had failed) when she knew that no man alive could normally resist.

From that instant of grabbing rapport Missy had felt a weird flowing, twisting, changing in her; deep in her body, deep in the forever unplumbed and umplumbable depths of her mind. She had known, then, that no planet could hold them both, and she had no taste for killing. She had killed twice: once to protect her life and once to protect her secret; but she loathed what it had done to her and would not kill again except in extremity.

Better to run again.

"Let me go," Conner said. "Look, I'm a spaceman; I know my way around the quarter. Darkover is a port like any other; if you've seen one, you've seen them all. I can hear the gossip of the quarter, and anything that's going on, I'd find out about."

He looked so lost and miserable that David felt wrenched with pity, in spite of his tendency to feel that he could, personally, survive Missy's absence from their midst. It was Rondo who said roughly, "Face it, Conner; good riddance to bad rubbish. The girl's a whore, and psychotic at that."

288 Marion Zimmer Bradley

David said, "Conner, it's true. And there's something else; if it hadn't been for Desideria, she might very well have killed Keral. She's dangerous."

Jason Allison contributed: "We'll be alerted if she tries to leave the planet; there's a stop order at the spaceport. But I'm afraid that without her own cooperation we have no authority—"

"I'll keep her from hurting anyone else," Conner said miserably, "but I must find her. I *must!*"

It was Desideria who came, unexpectedly, to Conner's aid. "I think Conner is right," she said. "A psychotic whore with full *laran*, psychokinesis and poltergeist factor running around loose on Darkover and hating the whole human race isn't anything I can contemplate without at least a dozen shudders. Go ahead, Dave—and if I can help you, call on me."

The dim light in the room had faded to a dying glow and the dark sun was a drooping red coal in the sky when Missy rose and smoothed her long hair, made herself beautiful with gestures so automatic that she hardly needed to glance in the poor and cracked mirror in the room. She drew her light robe around her and went out into the muddy street, picking her way carefully in her light shoes.

The "Red" sector of the spaceport city was the same on all planets; cheap bars and amusement centers, restaurants and pleasure houses, gambling halls and wineshops, of all kinds and status levels. Missy had known them under a couple of dozen suns. Darkover was a little colder than most, a little more brilliantly lit. She moved from bar to bar, slowly, calculating and assessing each place the moment she stepped inside. Usually she could sum up the clientele, their average salary and the tone of the place within four or five minutes, and in most of them she kept her loose hooded cloak flung over her hair and behaved with modest detachment, so that few noticed her at all; and those who did saw only a small, slight girl, perhaps a spaceman's or port official's young daughter, possibly waiting for someone and quite unaware of her unrespectable surroundings. Even in the others she kept her appeal muted and gently rebuffed all advances until she spotted her desired prey.

He looked prosperous. His uniform told Missy at once that he was the second officer of an Empire-sponsored passenger ship—in short, he had authority and position, as well as wealth.

The officer raised his eyes from his drink to see a young girl, exquisitely pretty, with masses of loose, copper-toned hair falling like a cloud around her slender face, eyeing him with deep and luminous gray eyes. The impact of the eyes was such that afterward he felt confused and could never explain why he moved toward her, like a man under a spell. He was no novice with women—no ship's officer would be, certainly not one who wore on his stripes the seven small jewels indicating service on seven planets—but words almost deserted him; he could only say, like a confused youngster, "Aren't you cold? In that light dress, on a planet like this?"

Missy's smile was gently enigmatic. "I'm never cold," she said, "but I'm sure we could find somewhere warmer than this."

He wondered, afterward, why an approach so obvious had seemed, in the enchantment of glamour that seemed to fall around her, new and strangely fascinating. He had stayed under the spell all during the next hour, of which he remembered very little; he was still under the spell when he followed her through the dimmed and darkening streets to the mean little room. She had asked nothing of him. Long experience had taught her that afterward men were even more eager, more generous. She did not know why; she put it down to the curious glamour she could throw over herself at such times. She had no real doubt that afterward she could persuade him to smuggle her aboard his ship. Not less than ten times before this, a ship's officer or captain had risked his career to do so and then thanked her for the privilege. It was balm and reassurance to feel, within herself, the pressure of his driving need and hunger—after her failure with David (was that Keral's doing?) she had needed that assurance desperately, to ward off the terrible sensation of change, of not knowing herself.

His hands, his touch, his mouth on hers had become desperate, insistent. She lay back, allowing him to undress her. Her eyes were enormous, brilliant, and the ship's officer moved like a man in a dream, fumbling, excited fingers stripping away the light silken garments—

And then his rough hands struck her, knocking Missy half across the room, and his harsh, suddenly enraged voice, sick wit disillusion and fury:

"Damned, filthy, stinking pervert! Lousy bastard of an *obrédin*—I heard Darkover was full of you goddamn lice but I never saw one—"

Cold claws of icy terror closed around Missy's heart. In the cracked, blurred mirror she had barely seen her own face, but now with a merciless clarity it gave back the naked body, the unbelievable and insane alterations there. She stared from the naked, raging man, advancing on her with fists upraised, and still unbelieving, cowered away.

This couldn't be happening! This was impossible! And in a fit of mad illogic: *somehow Keral did this to me ...* as she stared down, her enormous eyes dilated to blackness, at her own body, as if she were trapped in an insane amusement park mirror which gave back not her own familiar body, but a pale, undeveloped and yet unmistakable reflection of the furious man's own conformations; her breasts still there but shrunken, and below them, unmistakable, small but there, the pink protrusion of a male genital. . . .

Missy screamed, less from the pain of the blow than from panic, horror. She screamed again as the man's fist found her face; fumblingly, she put up her slender hands to shield her face. She did not even understand the mad abuse he was pouring on her. She was beyond hearing, making only the faintest movement to ward off the savage and brutal blows. She felt blood break from her lip, felt a rib crunching under his kick.

And then Missy went mad.

She had always known, in a general way, that she was stronger than any woman. It was part of her physical freakishness; she had never had the faintest fear of physical abuse, and had defended herself with skill and strength from unwanted advances on various occasions in her long and rough life. Here she had been taken off guard; but the smell of her own blood, and general panic, turned her berserk. She came up off the floor like a spitting, enraged tiger. A blow from unbelievably strong arms knocked the man across the room. She *reached* for him, with that inner force which had sent the furniture in David's room spinning, and he howled and clutched his groin, bawling like a wounded bull. A bench rose and flung itself across the room, striking him in the head with a blow that would have felled an ordinary man. But he was no ordinary man, and the sight of flying furniture only sent him further into the berserker fury. Outside in the street, clouds of whirling dust gathered and spun and spat. Rocks hurled themselves against the doors. Missy warded off kicks and blows, but when the officer seized the flying bench in mid-air and struck her on the head with it, she collapsed and lay still.

Then there was a hammering at the door and a stern shout, and four men in the black leather of

Spaceforce kicked in the lock and took in the scene—the naked man, the unconscious and bleeding thing that looked at first glance like a naked girl—and hauled them both off, with prompt efficiency, to the spaceport prison and hospital.

And there they made discoveries which threw them into the same bewildered panic as the ship's officer.

The face on the visionscreen was bewildered after being passed along from official to official.

"You're Doctor Jason Allison? You're in charge of a special project in Medic, with some outworlders?"

"I'm Allison, yes."

"Well, we have something down here. Are you missing one of your people? We don't know what it is and we can't handle it; will you please come down here and take her or him or it away before it sets the whole goddamn spaceport on fire or something?"

Jason said to himself, "Oh, oh," and wished he had a panic button to push.

He knew without asking that they'd found Missy.

My kinfolk. . . .

Keral. It is well with you among the aliens, Beloved?

It is not well, although one among them is dear to me as born blood-kin. And I have learned much, much of our own people and this world. But I am alone and desolate; I cannot long endure the life within walls. And what shall I do if the Change comes upon me, or the madness of which you warned me? There is so much strangeness that I am always in fear. Already once I have wounded and once I have killed, both times without intention. And there is a strange one here who has put me in fear. I do not want to die. I do not want to die. . . .

CHAPTER NINE

Jason had brought along a sedative capable of calming down a couple of rogue elephants, but Missy, lying numb and shocked, her face a bleached blob above the blankets wrapped confiningly around her, made not the slightest protest. She neither spoke to him nor opened her eyes as he had her carefully loaded on a stretcher and carried to a waiting ambulance. During the short ride back to the HQ, he sat quietly at her side, not touching her, his face grim as he considered what the spaceport police had told him. He had seen with his own eyes the wreckage of the cell, including the charred patch where blankets had been set ablaze.

"I've seen an almighty damned strange batch of telepaths and psi talents on Darkover," he said to himself, grimly, "but an uncontrolled poltergeist is a new one on me and damned if I know how to handle it. Regis is going to have to help me out on this one. It's his field of competence, after all. I'm a Medic, not a warlock."

The change in Missy, even on superficial inspection, appalled him. Although the curious and compelling beauty was still there, the fair skin seemed to have roughened, with a blotched look. Her eyes were lusterless—shock, of course, could account for that— but the most curious change was an intangible. Jason had been far from indifferent to the flaunting, exotic sexuality which Missy seemed to project from every pore—and now that had vanished, without a trace.

Well, shock and a brutal beating could account for that, too. She had evidently been very thoroughly mauled and maltreated; and evidently the doctors in the spaceport jail had been afraid to touch her. *Not that he blamed them.*

Fortunately, Missy had never shown any hostility to him. When he had examined her before, she had cooperated, even been—to a certain limited degree— friendly. It was David and Keral to whom she had reacted with hostility.

He had hoped to bring her into the Medic infirmary unnoticed, but—perhaps this was something he'd just have to get used to, working with telepaths— they were all there, waiting for him. He motioned to the men guiding the stretcher to wait, beckoned to David—at least David was a medical colleague—and said, in a low voice:

"You others will have to wait. She's been very badly hurt; she may have concussion, or internal injuries. David, come with me; and the rest of you, wait here." His eyes moved quickly over their faces; Regis,

strained and frightened—why? Conner, gray with
anguish and despair, moved him to brief pity, and he
laid his hand on the man's shoulder. "I know how
you feel," he said, "I'll let you in to see her the minute
I can, believe me. She'll need someone who cares
about her, after being roughed up like that."

Conner let himself be moved back, but David,
tuned to sensitivity, could feel the man's helpless
anger and protest:

*There's no one else to care about her . . . she needs me,
to them she's just a case . . . as I was in the hospital after
the accident in space. . . .*

and his thoughts trailing off into incoherent rage, despair and desire, so entangled that Conner himself
did not know which was which. David wondered, *how
can he care so much for her?* and closed the door, glad
to shut away the dark and far too expressive face.

Missy's face on the pillow was white and bruised-
looking, one eye swollen shut with great purple
bruises, her fair hair matted and tangled. David felt a
choked sense of misery as he looked at her and wondered vaguely if he were sensing the girl's own emotions; or Conner's; or empathizing that strange,
elusive and painful sense of resemblance to Keral.
There would be scars on that fair and untouched face,
that cheek where a fist or some blunt instrument had
ripped away skin. . . .

He moved toward her and began to draw away the
blankets.

Missy's eyes blinked open, cold and brilliant as

steel. "No," she whispered, shaping her bloodied lips painfully, "don't touch me. *Don't touch me!*"

Poor kid, Jason thought, after what she's been through I don't blame her. "It's all right, Missy," he said quietly, "no one is going to hurt you, now. I've got to look at those cuts on your face, and see what other injuries you have. I think we can fix you up without too many scars. Tell me, have you any pain? Let me see—"

He grasped the blanket firmly, trying to pry loose her fingers that huddled it round her.

The next minute, in a shower of flaming sparks, Jason flew through the air, shouting, struck the opposite wall and fell, awkwardly, landing in a collapsed heap. Missy spat out the words:

"Don't touch me!"

"Hey, now—" Jason protested, picking himself up in astonished consternation, "I won't hurt you."

But Missy's eyes were blank and unseeing; a metallic, cold glare. David, standing beside her bed, picked up a whirling snowstorm of thoughts, a tornado of terror and shame too frightening to be untangled—

"Wait, Jason," he said, and bent over Missy.

"Child, it's all over; no one will hurt you. It's only the doctor, he wants to see how badly that man hurt you. Please try to tell us; did he rape you? We can't tell you how sorry we are—" David was trying, desperately, for the first time in his medical career, to reach out through that blind barricade of terror and touch the terrified girl within. He was unconscious now of Missy's strangeness, he spoke as he would have spoken to a frightened child. The specifically sexual content of the terror, wordless but clearly identifiable, led David to an entirely wrong conclusion. "Missy, if you're afraid of us would you like to have one of the women here, Doctor Shield perhaps, come and be with you?"

An even more violent explosion of rage, tension and terror, like a palpable storm in the room. Missy's eyes were a glassy glare of panic, and when David tried to touch the blankets she had hauled around her body, his hand jumped back in a numb tingling paralysis like an electric shock.

Jason said, still trying to be reasonable, "Miss Gentry, this is ridiculous. How can we help you, or even dress those wounds of yours—look, your face is still bleeding—unless you let us?"

"It's no good to try and reason with her," David said in a low voice. "I don't think she even hears what we're saying, Jason."

The door opened and Keral said in his low, diffident voice, "Dr. Allison, I think I know what has happened to Missy. Remember, she is one of my own people, one of my race. This is something you cannot understand. Let me try to reach her mind. . . ."

He looked drawn and frightened, and David could sense, like static in the room, his fear that was like Missy's: *it is the madness of the Change . . . and if she has been reared on another world, not knowing that this may happen, if it has come upon her unknowing. . . .*

"Hear me," he whispered. "Be with me. Missy, I am not your enemy. I am of your own people. . . ."

She lay back, her eyes still glazed but lax and motionless, her breath coming in a harsh and deathly rattle. David knew that she heard Keral, but the glassy eyes did not flicker. Keral's voice trembled, and David sensed his own rigid self-control, but there was a tenderness in the tones which made both listeners achingly aware of the strange aloneness of the chieri.

"Missy. Open your mind and heart to me. I can help you; you need not fear me, strayed nestling from our world, little sister, little brother, little lost bird. . . ."

Missy's staring eyes flickered with live knowledge, she drew a harsh, sobbing breath—

And then the room exploded. Keral screamed in anguish and beat wildly at the flames that burst out under his hands; a tornado wind whirled wildly in the center of the room, tipping over the medical trolley with its array of bandages and instruments; it fell with a noise of metal, shattering glass. David dodged flying glass fragments; Jason shouted in rage and consternation—

Keral backed away, his face white, gripping his seared hands together in voiceless agony. He whispered, harshly, "I can't reach her, she's insane . . . get Desideria, she can handle Missy. . . ."

In the corridor outside, slamming the door on the chaos of the room, they looked at each other in terror and rising dismay. The others crowded around, with concerned questions; Jason beckoned to Desideria, and said briefly, "How do you handle a crazy poltergeist? Regis, you're the expert; what do you do when your people go berserk?"

"I've never had to handle one before," Regis said. "David, you look after Keral, he's hurt—Desideria, can you quiet her?"

Linnea, standing quietly at the outskirts of the group, said, "If you can't alone, Grandmother, let me try—if two Keepers cannot handle one madwoman, what are we here for?"

Jason stood aside for them to step into the room. David, drawing Keral after them—after all, this was the emergency room and this was the only place he could find bandages and medicines for the burns on Keral's hands—watched with detached curiosity as the two women moved toward Missy. A few steps away, they stopped, close together, clasping hands. Desideria's snow-white crown of hair and Linnea's flaming copper one were close together, and the elusive, strong likeness between the women gave a curious sense of power. Their two pairs of gray eyes, so like Missy's, focused like a visible beam of light. . . .

David bent and picked up the trolley, shoving the scattered instruments out of the way, pushed Keral into a chair, and rummaged in a cupboard for burn remedies—*thank God for Universal Medical Labels, I*

couldn't cope with Darkovan script just now, he thought
at random as his eyes found the familiar flame emblem
on a packet of anesthetic spray—and gently uncoiled
Keral's fingers, drawing a breath of consternation at
the cruelly blistered palms. Behind him he could sense
the tension in the room, as Missy struggled wordlessly, trembling, under the focused pressure of the
two women. . . .

Desideria said, in a cold voice, "Do what you have
to, Jason. She'll be quiet."

Linnea drew a deep, sobbing breath. She said, "Oh,
Grandmother, no . . . oh, Evanda have mercy! Poor
thing. . . ."

David drew the bandages tight on Keral's hands.
He said, wetting his lips, "That will heal in a day or
two, Keral. There won't be any permanent harm. Are
you all right? Do you feel faint?" The chieri looked
deathlike, his mouth trembling. David felt a terrifying rage against Missy, which he controlled with an
intense effort, and when Jason said, "David, if you've
finished, give me a hand here," he moved toward
Missy's inert body, trying for a professional calm to
drop over his own fear and rage like a cloak.

Jason drew away the blankets, visibly controlling a
shrinking as he touched them, but this time Missy lay
quiet, looking shocked and half unconscious. Jason
bared the slender, rounded upper arm, slid a needle
into the inert flesh. After a tense moment, Missy's
eyes closed and she began to breathe in long, drowsy
breaths.

Jason said to the women, "Relax; that will hold her. Thanks; she could probably have killed all three of us." He looked at them in bafflement, the conflict between medical ethics—you don't examine a patient in front of outsiders, if you can help it—and an obvious dislike of being alone with the dangerous patient, fighting a very clear-cut battle in his face.

David said, "Let them stay, Jason. They know more about telepaths—or aliens—than we do."

He watched, with a curiously detached lack of surprise, as Jason finished undressing Missy. He felt a strange and frightening pity; no wonder the change had driven her mad; her own body became an alien and terrifying thing . . . but he quenched this entirely subjective empathy (*Keral! What had this done to Keral?*) and tried to examine the changes with a totally scientific detachment.

The breasts had definitely altered in size and contour. Not that they had ever been large, of course, not much larger than those of a girl of twelve. But still, the change was perceptible. The skin texture, although he was not sure, seemed somehow to have altered, lost its luminous quality. He handled it with some curiosity as he helped Jason cleanse the cuts and abrasions. The genital changes were somewhat more marked; he had been aware of certain minor structural anomalies before, enough to classify Missy as a slightly abnormal female; now, on first inspection she would have struck anyone as a male. A somewhat underdeveloped male, it was true, but nevertheless unquestionably male in gender. *Poor kid, what a frightening thing to have happen to her!* Her? By habit he was still thinking of Missy as a girl, and when he thought about Conner his face burned with vicarious shock. *Here I am sorry for Missy; how am I going to explain to Conner that his girlfriend isn't even a girl?*

"Well, we've certainly opened one hell of a can of worms," Jason said hours later. Missy still slept, drugged and still. David flicked the pages of the medical report in his hands. Massive hormone changes, still continuing and probably unstable, shifting back and forth between androgens and female hormones—no wonder the emotional instability had resulted! "Are all the chieri like that, I wonder? You're Keral's buddy; maybe you can get him to tell you the whole story. Didn't he say that thousands of years ago the chieri went into space, looking for some way to save their race and then came home to die? Evidently Missy is one of those who got lost, somehow or somewhere. Probably never knew what she was—what the hell, if she was a foundling, as she said, someone decided at first look that she was a girl, and who's going to question the evidence of her own eyes? But are we going to have to cope with something like that happening to Keral? What was the phase he used—*the madness of the Change?* Oh hell," he burst out, "I can't cope with it. What good is this whole project anyway?"

David, sensing a sudden despair which had nothing to do with his patient, asked quickly, "Jay, what's wrong?"

Jason shook his head. "Personal problems. I've just had word my own people are dying like flies—you didn't know—I was brought up with nonhumans myself; the trailmen. You don't realize—you haven't been on Darkover long enough—but there have been forest fires, and the people of the forest are dying. . . . What's the good of saving a project, or a few people, if this world is going down the drain?"

David felt powerless to comfort him. He said, at last, awkwardly, "I guess we just have to do what we can, Jason. I'll talk to Keral and see what I can do."

He delayed the talk until later, not knowing why it was hard to face the chieri. Night had fallen, and the view of the great spaceport towers was a twinkling glow through the rainy darkness, when he returned to his own quarters and found Keral there, silent, withdrawn and paler than ever. He hardly greeted David, and it seemed to the young doctor that the whole gestalt of friendships and rapports formed since he had come to Darkover, the first real human contacts of his life, were falling into fragments around him. Conner sick with wretchedness over Missy—David had still shirked telling him what was wrong—Regis, withdrawn and filled with fears; Jason, cracking up with fear for his friends; a world groaning in agony as it split apart, ruined and broken . . . and his own deep empathy for Keral, now guarded and afraid. He remembered Missy's white terrified face, and it seemed to him that the echo of that terror and madness was in Keral's pale eyes; and then, with a start, he remembered that morning which now seemed far away. Had it only been a few weeks ago? He had first seen Keral in the office room downstairs and now he remembered his own original uncertainty; Keral had seemed to him first a boy, then a delicate girl, and until he had first examined him the uncertainty had remained.

"How are your hands, Keral?"

"They're well enough. Missy?"

"Still doped. I hope she comes out of it sane. We could probably help with hormones, but I don't know."

"I feel responsible," Keral said slowly. "It was contact with me which touched this off."

"Keral, you were only trying to help her, and if she'd been sane she'd have known it."

"No. I think it was—contact with me—which made her go into the Change."

"I don't understand. . . ."

"Nor I, and I am afraid," Keral said painfully, "because it could have been myself."

David stared in wonderment but dared not interrupt, sensing that Keral's tight reticence had broken; and after a moment Keral said, still in that hard, controlled voice:

"Understand. All the long seasons of my life, I have known myself the only and last child of my folk.

All the others of our race are old, old past—not past mating, but past bearing. Past—engendering. And I reared among them, young, young. . . . Now, for the first time, I am among other young people, people who are, allowing for the differences in the way we experience time, near to my own age. For the first time in my life I am among—" he stopped and choked over it, and David could only vaguely envision the tremendous emotional charge of the concept, "—among potential mates. And so I know that, at any time, I may become unstable and change, as Missy did."

And, although David had seen fear in Keral before, now what he saw was terror.

David said quietly, trying to be detached, "Is it that you think it's Missy to whom you'd react? Biologically, you mean; the very fact that you're in the presence, for the first time, of a nubile member of your own race?" It would be, it occurred to him with a strange, stricken sense, a perfect and simple solution. That these two, last of their alien kind, should be a renewal of their line. . . .

"No," said Keral, and there was a sick sort of revulsion in his voice. "I *could* not. I know this is one of the reasons why our people died away, and yet . . . our kind was shaped wrong in the beginning of the world; I know this. I've heard the story often enough; the sexual drives too low, the—the sensitivity too high. I have no right to judge Missy, knowing what her life has been. I pity her. I pity her until it makes me almost sick with it, knowing how terrible it must have been for her, driven to this to survive, to use her gifts only to fascinate and enslave alien men with her body. But she is, she is what she has been in contact with, and I cannot—I cannot come so close to it."

David, remembering something Regis had said, and with a faint bitter memory of his own early adolescence, said wryly, "I gather this is common enough among telepaths. It's rare for them to have much to do—sexually—with anyone who can't return that—awareness, in intimacy. I had a hell of a time, as a result—" he laughed a little, "my own experiences with women have been, let's say, minimal. A few experiments, and—I more or less swore off. I gather it was even worse for Conner—until he found Missy. He couldn't stand to be around people at all, and she was the first one whom he could stand to touch."

"It must have been hard for you," Keral said, with that immediate awareness of emotion which was so new, and so welcome a thing to David.

"I must admit it's crossed my mind lately; that if there are telepaths on Darkover, there may be women who will be able to—" David flushed slightly. "Not that I've had all that much time to think about it, but seeing Regis with that girl who had his child a little while ago—and now with Linnea, it's so obvious how very much they're in love—" he laughed a little. "Living among telepaths must demand some peculiar changes in attitude, I mean sex becomes such an open, aboveboard thing. Keral, does it bother you to talk about this? God help me, I'm not even sure whether you're a man or a woman!"

Keral met his eyes with a quiet, level gaze. "Like all my people. Either, or both. We—change, as occasion warrants. And, as I say, when we—come together—the emotions must be very deeply involved, or else—I'm still not sure about your language, but I've learned something of your technology—otherwise, fertilization cannot take place. Oh, we tried all the obvious things, David, our people. Artificial insemination. Our women, or rather, those of us in female phase, under sedative drugs which dulled their minds, mating with members of other races, in a desperate hope—"

"And you could not interbreed with other races?"

"Not—deliberately," Keral said, "although there are legends, here on Darkover; yes, the Comyn telepaths are said to be of chieri blood. There is a legend—a woman of our people . . . you saw Missy. . . ."

"Yes. She changed, but you say it was contact with you. She was in—female phase, you say? And yet you—"

"I think contact with Conner sparked the change," Keral said. "After all this time with those alien to her, so that they were beasts, animals, the first touch of someone who could reach her mind and her emotions, roused her out of the phase we call *emmasca*, neuter. In the neuter phase, she could have sexual contact with anyone—passively—but Conner reached her emotions and—endocrines? So that the mating with Conner was a real thing, something which stirred her deeply, more deeply, perhaps, than any experience of her life."

David said, "I think I understand. But according to computer analysis, her male and female hormones are almost identical with the human ones. I should think, if it's a question of chemistry, Conner's maleness would have pushed her further into female phase."

"I don't know," Keral said. "I have only meaningless theories. One is this; that when the change first takes place, it is a—a fluctuating thing, until the hormones stabilize. I had been warned by my elders that if the change came upon me, there is sometimes madness."

"I'm a doctor, Keral. I can be detached if anyone can."

"Can you, David?" Keral smiled faintly. "I told you, we have interbred with other races, now and again . . . by chance. It happens at times, that one of our people, when the season of change comes, if there is no other of our kind ready to mate with her, drunken with moonlight and the madness of the changes in her body and mind, will run mad in the forest and lie down, mindless, with any man who comes to her arms. It is—it is a thing we do not speak of. Some have killed themselves, after. But a few bore alien children. It is said that a few such children, cast out from us and fostered among humans, here on Darkover, brought the *laran* gifts, the telepath powers, into the Comyn line. This is such a terror and a thing of shame among our people that it is spoken only in whispers. And in no other way—in no other way—" Keral, shaking and white, broke down and began to sob.

David knew that knowledge, scientific detachment, were worse than useless here. Blindly, in the grip of intense emotion, he reached out for the chieri and drew him close; Keral, in a convulsion of terror, wrenched free of his arms.

David quickly let him go; and they stood staring at one another, Keral still sobbing. David in a wild and frightened surmise. Keral said at last, through a painful smile, "You see? It's you that I'm afraid to touch."

David tried helplessly to get hold of himself. He reminded himself that Keral, coming from a hermaphroditic race and totally isolated from ordinary human culture, would know nothing of human taboos or perversions, or even the very concept. The fact that they were both males would mean nothing to Keral. Both males, hell! He himself hadn't been sure Keral wasn't a girl, at first. But it still took some getting used to. Finally, mastering his first shock and outrage, he said in a low voice, "Keral, I don't understand. Are you saying that you and I could be—mates?"

"I don't know." Keral sounded, and looked, wretched. "Have I hurt or—or offended against you, David?"

David found himself struggling against a blind impulse to take Keral in his arms again. It wasn't desire, certainly not sexual desire—although, he realized tardily, that was there too, muted and deeply buried but still there in his consciousness—but it was an overwhelming impulse of closeness, a sudden blind ache for contact, a sort of desperate merging. He fought to control it and keep his detachment, but the surge of overpowering emotion went so deep that it was all he could do to be calm. He reached out his hands to Keral. He had to touch him somehow. He said, in a low voice, "I don't understand what's happened, Keral. I'm frightened, too. But—Keral—" he raised his eyes and as he met the level gray gaze of the chieri, a great and blind happiness surged over him. "I don't care what it is. I love you, you know I do. I'd do anything for you, you know that, but don't be afraid of me. I won't touch you, unless you want me to. And if you do—" he said at last, very simply, "we're friends. And friends can be lovers, too."

Keral did not move. His slender bandaged fingers closed slightly on David's but he remained very still. His face moved, convulsively, and at last he said, "I *am* afraid. It's like being a stranger to myself. And I can't help wondering if my people sent me here for this. I don't have to tell you what it could mean to our race, life rather than death . . . and yet. I wonder, simply, if I have gone mad."

David dared not laugh. He said, still holding

Keral's hand, "We must wait and be sure. We must find out—"

"Don't tell anyone," Keral begged suddenly.

"I won't, but I wouldn't give much for our chances of keeping it a secret. Remember Conner and Missy? But before anything else, Keral, before we take any chances, let us find out—" his voice collapsed. Suddenly he could not help incongruous laughter. "I'm not laughing at *you*, Keral, but—it *is* funny—oh, God, suppose you had a child by me—"

Keral's beautiful eyes met David's with unflinching honesty. "Like any of my people, I would risk anything for that," he said. "Even madness. Even my own death, several times over. But I trust you, David, and I love you. And I think it is possible."

And then, through the gravity, a flicker of mad merriment broke forth:

"Oh, what fools we both are, David, to be together and so grave and sad and somber; I can read your thoughts so clearly sometimes, *a cold-blooded experiment!* How much of this have you understood? I thought I made it clear—that unless my own emotions were so very much involved—what are you afraid of?"

They stood clinging together, laughing into each other's eyes like children, and then Keral gently pushed him away.

"You're right," he said almost in a whisper, still laughing. "We have all the time we need. And we must find out everything we can about each other;

and first of all, we must find out about Missy. I—" he laughed, and it sounded rueful, self-directed:

"I want to find out what might be in store for me! But David, it's a promise."

Their clasped hands clung together; and suddenly David realized that, more deeply than any spoken pledge of love, it was a promise and a commitment.

It was for this that he had come to Darkover.

It could well have been for this that he was born.

CHAPTER TEN

The hard, bitter Darkovan winter had settled down over the hills of Thendara. The spaceport lay buried under snow six feet deep, just barely kept in control on the landing areas by constant working crews with all the resources of Terran Empire machinery. The days were short and bitter, the red sun grayed with storm clouds or snow.

The woman who called herself Andrea, knowing her work completed, had intended to take ship and leave Darkover as soon as possible. With the mountains lying deep in snow, nothing further was possible; the torrential spring thaws and rains on barren soil would complete the process beyond repair, unless certain highly technical and drastic steps were taken, demanding enormous financial and engineering resources.

It wasn't that these resources were unavailable on Darkover, even now, Andrea thought. It was that no one now living here could spot the ongoing entropy and apply them in the right places with the right kind of concentrated effort.

She knew she should book her passage on one of the big ships, and go. *Go where?* she thought, with a sort of fierce, worn weariness.

Anywhere. Anywhere in the galaxy. You have everything you could desire, or the means to purchase it.

Yet she lingered, delaying, slowly realizing that there was nothing in a thousand worlds which could tempt her to move on. *I am old, too old to care.* So that she lingered on from day to day, letting each departing ship leave without her, not even clearly aware that she was reluctant to leave the dim red sun, the high, jagged, and achingly familiar skyline which she could see, when the snow cleared, from the window of her room. *If I do not go soon I will die here,* she told herself; for she had seen others of her kind die, simply because there was no longer anything to hold them to life.

Cast out, abandoned, forgotten by everyone. As I cast out and abandoned my poor changeling. . . .

The memory, hundreds of years sealed, burst through, a nightmare peeping through a dark curtain, and was instantly covered over again under layers of other memories. Shame, terror, anguish, the compelling memory of madness, buried under deliberate mind-sealing; hardness; rage against those spawning races who lived and would die. Even guilt and shame a hundred years forgotten.

I do not deserve to die beneath my own sun. . . .

She had dismissed her assistants, paying them off and paying them well to get lost and stay lost in distant parts of the galaxy. One of the high technical perfections of the trade of worldwrecking, which she had brought to a fine art, was that by the time the damage could be assessed and identified, all of the hands which had done it were scattered on a hundred planets across uncountable lightyears and could never be traced or identified or made to testify. Well, they were gone and no one but herself could identify the damage; and there was no way to connect her with it. The one link, the Free Amazons who had seen her burying the sterilization virus, she dismissed with contempt. Simple women who knew nothing!

So she lingered on from day to day and week to week, telling herself that when the spring thaw came, she would go. The old love for her own sun, her own sky, on a ruined world, could not tempt her to stay and see the planet die.

Don't be sentimental. It won't die; it will enter a new period of life as a flourishing Empire marketplace. Just another planet with nothing unusual about it.

It had become deep-rooted habit with her to find, and pay well, spies wherever she went. About three weeks into the winter snow, one of them came to her with vaguely disquieting news.

"There's little travel at this season," he told her, "but there's movement, all through the mountains, of caravans. And each of them holds two, three, five of the telepath caste. They seem to be converging on

Thendara, on the old Comyn Castle which has been abandoned since the old Comyn Council broke up, five or ten years ago. I don't know what it means, or why, but you asked to know everything concerning the telepath caste."

Andrea paused to consider this. Elsewhere she had heard another rumor, that the Terran HQ had sent out a call for functioning telepaths, all over the galaxy. She had even toyed with the cynical thought of going and offering herself for their study. They'd get some surprises, she told herself, that they never expected. But the deep-rooted habit, so deep as to be instinct, to keep their race's very existence secret from other beings, had made this idea the briefest, most surface, mental game. In any case, all others of her kind were long dead, long vanished; why tantalize them?

However, if anyone could find out what was being done to Darkover it would be these telepaths. She thought with a curious, almost personal rage of Regis Hastur. How had this young man managed to evade fourteen assassins in a row? Was it possible she had underestimated Comyn telepaths?

Well, one thing was certain. If they were all gathering together in one location, for whatever reason, they would be a convenient target.

She might as well make a good job of it; wait until they were all assembled, and with one final stroke, free Darkover of the last barrier from becoming another planet in the chain of Empire.

Even with all the resources of Worldwreckers, Incorporated, at her fingertips, a mass murder on this scale would take time and planning. Well, she had all the long and bitter Darkovan winter to plan it.

Hour after hour she sat at her window watching the snowstorm and the distant mountains. And beyond those mountains, more mountains, and more forests, and in those forests. . . .

Nothing. No one. Death and ruin. Not one left alive. Except only me, and that not for long.

The isolation sign was still on Missy's room, and the guarding nurses and hospital personnel had grown tired of repeating to Conner: "I'm sorry. No visitors for this patient."

Conner was at his wit's end. On the seventh day, he bullied his way through to Jason and David, demanding: "Why are you keeping her drugged and isolated? You promised I could see her! You've told me she was recovering, and no matter how badly she was hurt, she must be healing up by now! She'll be wanting me. I've got to see her!"

"Conner," Jason said gently, "don't you realize, she won't be wanting *anyone*. She isn't responding to people at all—she just isn't in contact. Missy is *insane*."

"So am I, according to Terran Empire official directives," Conner said. "Or didn't you read my record? Maybe it takes one lunatic to help another."

Jason put out his hand. "Sit down, man—don't stand over me like that! I'm on your side. But don't you realize? This—this creature nearly killed Keral;

his hands are just now healing. She tore up a space-force jail and our emergency room."

"Yes," David said, "and she nearly killed *you*, Jason; if your head had struck the doorjamb instead of the wall, it would have smashed like an eggshell. It was all Desideria and Linnea, together, could do to hold her long enough to get her under drugs. Quite frankly, we don't dare let her regain consciousness."

Conner said stubbornly, "She won't hurt me. She needs me. And I love her."

David felt the shock and upheaval of his own deep ambivalence, like a disrupting blow. Conner was wide open to him, with all the misery of a desperately lonely man who has at long last found something and had it snatched away again. Between pity and dismay, David burst out, "Conner—we've been trying to keep this from you just because you *do* love her, but haven't we told you what happened to—to Missy? She's changed; she's not even a woman now!"

"I don't understand—"

David said, "I'll spare you the technical report. I knew how you reacted to Missy; we all knew, remember? But how about some nice, sexy nude photos?" Pity and rage made him ruthless of how he hurt the older man. He took the pictures of Missy, lying in drugged sleep, from a folder and handed them over.

"Here's your—girlfriend. Love? Look, Conner, she couldn't even react to you as a woman—"

Conner took the pictures. His face drained slowly of color, turning the grayish green sick tint of a black skin gone pale. He wet his lips, swallowing hard, and laid them down. Then he said, his voice strained and harsh, "I don't know how this happened. Maybe you can help her. But—with this happening—she'll need me more than ever. She'll need me to care for her."

"You don't understand," David almost shouted, "you still speak of *her*, she isn't a girl, she isn't a—or maybe you have a secret yen for men?"

Conner's face congested with rage and for a moment, as they faced each other, David felt it like a tangible, beating thing which would reach out, strike and kill. He faced Conner, not flinching, and then Conner drew a deep breath, controlling his fury.

"Listen, you bastard," he said evenly, "it's Missy I love, care about, need. Not the fact that she has a body I happened to enjoy going to bed with. I don't discount that, but I could get that almost anywhere, if I needed it that much. I happen to love Missy—*love* her. Or him. Or *it*, if you prefer. Which means that I care what happens to her, whether I can bang her or not. Which is something you evidently have never felt for anyone, and I'm sorry for you, you bastard. But if you keep me away from her any longer, damn you, the wingding she threw is going to look like a little girl crying for her doll, compared to the one I'll throw!"

The words echoed in the room, tangible, vibrating, as if they had been written in lines of fire in the air. David said, and had the sense that it was an enormous and somehow personal capitulation, "Dave. I didn't understand. I'm—I'm sorry. Forgive me. Jason—"

he turned to the other doctor, "I think we'll have to let
Missy see him. If he can get through to her, if he can
make her understand this, maybe we won't have any
more trouble with her."

"It's a risk we've got to take. But suppose she kills
you before you can get through?"

"That's a risk *I'll* take," Conner said. "You don't realize. Missy brought me up alive out of hell; and do
you think I'm going to stop at trying to bring her out
of her own hell, whatever it may be?"

The room was white with the reflected light from
the falling snow beyond the windows. Missy lay
huddled beneath a sheet, pale and motionless, her
colorless hair spread on the pillow. Her face
seemed narrow, pale, and inhuman, features bony
and protruding.

No, Conner thought with a curious pang, she was
no longer beautiful. Had she ever been beautiful or
was it only the strange glamour she cast about him?

Jason had told him that the drugs were being allowed to wear off; that she would waken naturally
soon. Conner went quietly to her side and sat down to
wait. She slept still, breathing quietly and moaning a
little under her breath, and even through her disturbed dreams Conner sensed grief, shock, and a
frightening shame. He reached for her limp white
hand and took it between his own. The skin felt rough
and harsh, faintly discolored. Conner had the sketchy
medical training given to all ship's officers who may

have to be responsible for passengers and crew in the absence of trained men, and he could follow, to some slight extent, the briefing Jason had given him. Extreme hormone imbalance; recession of female hormones and overbalance of androgens, pituitary and thyroid imbalance out of control; this created the skin troubles. Recession of breast tissue, partial atrophy of female genital structures, all accelerated. . . .

"The instability is hormone induced, of course," Jason had said, "but the emotional shock is considerable, too; I gather she wasn't aware this could happen."

Conner could reach her frightened mind, feel her fear and shock at the failure of the one stable thing in her world, her fascination over anyone she sought to fascinate. (Had her failure to attract David touched off the first uncertainty?) Conner set himself to reach out, in the old way he had learned. . . .

. . . spinning in space, a point of nothingness, he left his body behind, reaching out with the inner self which had nothing to do with his body:

Missy, Missy. I am here. I am with you. Bodies are little to us: we can use them or leave them, enjoy them or forget them; but we are more together than we would be, locked in love, when we can reach one another this way. . . .

He came back slowly to awareness. Missy had opened her great gray eyes and lay staring up at him.

"Dave?" she said, in an accepting whisper, and smiled. His dark hand clasped hard on her pallid one. There was no need for words, but he whispered them anyway, his face bending over hers:

"I don't care what you are, Missy. I love you, and I need you. Maybe they can help you, but whether or not they can, we belong together and we'll come through this together, one way or the other. Now we've found someone to belong to, nothing else matters."

She was too weak to move, but she turned her face and pressed her lips to his palm. Then she fell asleep, her hand still clasped in Conner's.

CHAPTER ELEVEN

Day by day, they streamed into the city, in caravans and alone, red-headed Darkovan telepaths: Comyn and commoner, city dweller and rustic, noble and peasant, with only one thing in common; the flaming red hair which had been, from time immemorial on Darkover, linked indissolubly with the telepath genes and the *laran* powers of the ancient world.

No; more than one thing in common. Each one, as he came, through snow-clogged passes or dust-choked dry plains, had another story to tell of a world lying in ruin, near death.

"For the fall plowing, the earth has turned to black choking dust," said a quiet bitter man from the lowlands. "Even the weeds will not grow. The soil is barren as a woman of ninety years."

"We die from the blazing sun," said a tall, wild-faced mountain lord, dressed in the embroidered leather cloaks which had been abandoned in the cities for more than a hundred years; "there is no fog on the hills, no rain. The fumes of the resin trees poison our beasts in the sun."

"The trees are leafless, turned to yellow brown and spreading no seeds this autumn," said a quiet aristocrat with the face of a Hastur and the gray eyes of the forest people. "The trailmen are dying in their villages; they come to the edge of their forests with their red eyes seared almost to white, standing there, no longer afraid of mankind. We spare them what food we can, but we too are facing hunger and privation."

"There is no Ghost Wind, and yet the Ya-men are coming from the hills," said a sad-faced girl with braided hair, her dress caught with silver butterflies and the blue starstone of a Keeper like a pendant jewel at her throat. "No living human has seen them before, and now we see only their dead bodies lying at the edge of the deep woods. We have feared that always, because when the Ghost Wind brought them from the hills they came in a cannibal rage, to pillage and tear and raven, but it is terrible to know that they are dying away and there will be no more."

"The very land is washing away where there has been fire. . . ."

"The trees bear no fruit, no nuts, no oil. . . ."

"The voices even of the catmen are stilled in the ranges. . . ."

"We are dying. . . ."

"We are dying. . . ."

"Dying. . . ."

The Terrans set up food programs; but with the

lack of transportation on Darkover, there was little help available for the more remote districts. Regis had thrown his own personal fortune into the gap, but it was necessary to prove, first, what was happening and how. As more and more of his kinsmen streamed into the city—kinsmen and others, kin by virtue of the curious genetic quality they bore—he grew silent and desperate. How could he find a way to draw them together, in some fashion that would save their world? Could even all the resources and wealth of Darkover do it?

He had left Project Telepath to David and Jason. There was no time for it, now. If it could be of help, Jason would know, and tell him. His own personal life was in abeyance, held to the one agonizing preoccupation of safeguarding his surviving children.

Linnea had not returned to Arilinn; she remained at his side, and her presence was both comfort and torture; the torture of longing and need; and yet he would not expose her to the danger that had struck at Melora and her child within the very walls of the Terran HQ. If an assassin could strike there, then the very Tower of Ashara or the sanctuaries of Hali could provide no surety for the woman who bore the seed of Hastur. And he would not expose Linnea to that.

With Regis withdrawn, much of the onus of the project fell on David, but it seemed meaningless, and he had abandoned routine tests. What good would it do to discover that Desideria could manipulate small objects up to but not including eighteen grams gross weight? He occupied himself, feeling faintly guilty, with the records of the curious changes in Missy. He and Keral were together in his quarters late one afternoon going over them with interest.

"I found it had to believe what you told me, about emotional factors initiating the changes," he said; "but it seems to be contact with Conner which is having some effect on Missy. Evidently the shift back to female phase is reasonably complete, although it's true we've used some hormones. It was a matter of desperation; she was terribly ill; there was a partial failure of the adrenals and thyroid. We had to try."

He studied Keral and did not have to say the next thought in his mind: that the increasing delicacy of Keral's skin color, something in his growing passivity, made him suspect a slow, beginning change in the chieri. It was a faintly frightening thing to contemplate. Keral, following his thoughts with that bewildering accuracy, said, "David, could you bring on that change in me? You said the hormones were similar."

"With Missy, it was life and death," David said. "I wouldn't risk it for anything less, Keral. Even with humans, hormone treatment is risky and inexact, and we've been studying it for three thousand years! The quantities needed for changes are so minute, and a mistake can mean madness and death. We've simply got to wait and see . . . how long does the shift usually take?"

"Under the proper stimulus," Keral said, "not long.

As you know, we chieri are not so tied to clocks and sun cycles as you; but perhaps, for a full phase shift, a night and a day . . . at a rough guess."

"What usually touches off the shift, Keral? Is it the seasons? The phases of the moons?" There were four, David remembered, on Darkover, and keeping track of their eclipses and phases would have been a task to drive an astrologer wild.

"I am not certain what brings on the change to a fertile state," Keral said. "How could I be sure? I have been told by my elders that I am of an age for bearing—no, I don't mind talking of it now; earlier I did not know you, or your language, well enough to make myself understood. In the ordinary way, many things which we find hard to—analyze in your way—can bring on the changes for mating. The most common is—well, the preliminaries of love, the very stimulus of contact. I don't know how it works, myself."

David said, with some wryness, "I never thought I'd be part of an investigation into the sex life of your people. It might be easier if I, if I hadn't involved myself in it!"

Keral said, "Do you wish you hadn't?"

"No, I'm committed." He laughed suddenly, stirred by a sudden and imaginary picture of Keral as a woman. It was hard to imagine, harder to believe. His picture of the chieri as a female was ineradicably colored by his memory of Missy as he had first known her, and her somewhat crude seductiveness.

"I know," said Keral in a low voice, "I'm afraid of

that, too. And perhaps that very fear is—is inhibiting the changes."

The knock at the door which interrupted them was welcome, at least to David; but Keral flinched as he saw Missy standing in the door.

The only remaining trace of the acute psychotic episode was a certain scarring and discoloration of her skin; and she had wholly ceased to project the blatant female sexuality, although she had a faintly feminine appeal which David was glad, for Conner's sake, to see. She was still, obviously, in the neuter state, and David had no idea whether she and Conner had resumed any sort of sexual relationship, though he supposed, if they had, he would probably know. He was quite aware of the tension of abstinence between Linnea and Regis, and it was very wearing. What had Regis said, that sex let loose in a group of strange telepaths was disruptive? That was an understatement if there'd ever been one. There were times when, looking at Desideria, he still saw the vague and disturbing image of the exquisitely sensual young girl which she had once been, and could not control a flare of desire quite incongruous when he looked at the present Desideria, with her great age and sexless dignity. Well, she was one hell of a personality and she'd be a woman until she died! He wouldn't have touched her—good God, she could have been his great-grandmother—but it was there, and they both knew it, and it made them gentle and warm with one another, and strangely like lovers. . . .

He came back quickly to Missy; taking refuge in the commonplaces of courtesy.

"Did you want something?"

Keral had gone white with fear, and Missy looked past David to say quickly, "I won't hurt you, either of you." Her eyes rested on Keral with a curious, veiled contempt as she said, "You've lived a sheltered life, haven't you?"

Keral said, "I've no right to judge you, Missy."

Her face softened slightly. "I know what you were trying to do, Keral. I'm sorry I couldn't—respond. I wasn't sane. But I do thank you, and I've come to ask you to do something else for me."

Keral bent his head. "I'll do what I can to help, you know that."

"You tell me that I belong to your own race, your kind. I know nothing, nothing of my people. I was a foundling, literally a castaway, abandoned with my birth wounds still bleeding, thrown out to die like some abortion." Her face was bitter with an old anguish and Keral shook his head in bewilderment.

"I cannot understand it, either. To our people, children are precious beyond words, beloved, welcome, cause for incredible rejoicing and joy. That a woman of the chieri should cast her own child out to die . . . unless she herself was dead or mad—"

"You've had proof that we can go mad, all right," said Missy with a wry smile. "Oh, I believe what you say; I saw you with the child in your arms, the child of Regis Hastur's woman, and it evidently did something strange to you, too. But I want to know more of your people."

"You shall know everything I know myself," Keral promised, and David said, "There are also legends of the chieri among men. Desideria knows those, and she has promised to tell what she knows—for Keral and me. Why not come with us, Missy? I'm sure she'd be glad to have you. . . ."

Missy flinched slightly, then laughed a little. Like Keral, she had a magical laugh, light and clear as the chiming of a bell. "I'm still afraid of her," she confessed, "but she didn't mean to hurt me, either. And I must learn not to be afraid."

"That's true," David said gravely. He knew that somehow a strong bond was being woven, and that all resentments must vanish . . . and he was not sure why, but it was a part of what he must someday become.

It felt incredible now, to realize that he had not wanted to come to Darkover at all.

Before he came here, he had been only half alive. The thing he had regarded as a freakish deformity was now the major part of his life; and as he reached out to Keral for the familiar touch, he knew that being without it now would be worse than blinding.

CHAPTER TWELVE

"This is a legend told in the heyday of the Comyn, years before the Terrans came with their ships and their Empire. I heard it when I was a young girl, Desideria Leynier, being trained in Castle Aldaran as a matrix Keeper and technician. But it stems from the days before the Terrans ever came to our world, with their ships and their Empire.

"In the ancient days when the valley lords held court at Thendara, and rode forth from Arilinn to Carthon, there dwelt a lord of the Old People in Carthon, king over those who dwelt there. There were no Seven Domains in those days, and none of the Comyn.

"There was a maiden of the Fair People of the Wood, Kierestelli by name, which is to say *Crystal* in the valley speech. The legends say much of her beauty, but beauty dwells in the eyes of love and not in any single feature. In those days there was an evil queen in the forest, and she drove out Kierestelli to wander long in the woods alone, to flee into the lands

of the valley people, and there she met with the Lord
of Carthon, by the wells of Reuel. He took her home
to his castle in the ancient city that now lies drowned
in the Bay of Dreams, beyond the isle of Mormallor,
and there she dwelt in happiness; but word came that
she was held prisoner there, and the chieri lords sent
a great treasure in gold and jewels—for they knew
that the People of the Valley valued these things,
which are nothing to the chieri folk—for her ransom.
But Kierestelli chose to remain with the Lord of
Carthon, because she loved him; so the Lord of
Carthon sent back all the treasure but a single gold
ring, which was long a treasure in the house of Hastur.

"The treasure of the forest folk is a legend in the
Venza Mountains, for when the Lord of Carthon sent
it back, the caravan was waylaid and came never to
the Yellow Forest. So the sire of Kierestelli said, 'These
people would keep both gold and woman,' and gathered his people for the last battle to rescue her; but before the first arrow flew, Kierestelli came from the
besieged castle, in her shift and barefoot, her hair
hanging loose about her face, walking through the assembled defenders and besiegers alike, and knelt before her father, laying her hand in her lord's, and
begging them to be reconciled.

" 'I will not bear a child in war and terror,' she told
him, and when the chieri lord saw that her body was
heavy with the child of Carthon, he laid down his
spear and wept, and then he called his men back into
the forest; after, they pledged friendship eternal, and

there a great feast was held—they still say, in the mountains, when someone shows great honor, 'They feasted him like the Lords of Carthon.'

"In the end the friendship was broken, and the chieri withdrew again across the Kadarin and into the hills beyond Carthon; but from the sons of Carthon was born Cassilda, who was the bride of Hastur, and from whom were descended the sons of the Seven Domains."

Desideria ended her story, and her listeners sat silent for a moment. Then David, seizing on a salient point, said:

"They speak of a *woman* of the chieri. . . ."

"That is the way she appeared to your people," Keral said quietly. "To me what seems important about this tale—and it may well be true—is that a child was born between human and chieri, without madness or fear. I have known long that the Comyn people here on Darkover bore the blood of my people in your veins. We chieri think of you as our far grand-children. And so, although we die, some part of our folk survives, even at far remove."

David asked, "But where does the red hair come from?"

"I'm not sure," Jason said, "but I've studied Dark-ovan history; there's a theory, you know, that Dark-over was originally colonized by one of the 'lost ships'—ships from the twenty-first and twenty-second centuries, before the Terran Empire, before the hyperdrives, when so many ships vanished and were never heard of again. Red hair—adrenal function—is commonplace in one or two old Earth strains, particularly the highland Celts who were said to be psychic—second sight. Possibly this became fixed in the telepath line."

Desideria said, "I think I mentioned the belief among matrix workers—the redder the hair, the stronger the gift. But there was also the theory that very intense psychic work would make a Keeper go gray early. My own hair turned white almost overnight after the Sharra contacts."

"So did mine," said Regis in a low voice.

"Partial adrenal exhaustion?" Jason theorized.

"In the mountains where I had my home," Desideria said, "I heard many tales of the chieri, how fair they were. There is an old song. I cannot recall it now," her brow furrowed in a strange, inward-turned attempt at recall, "which tells of a chieri woman seeking for her mortal lover, not knowing—so long they live—that in the years between, her lover had grown old and died. . . ."

Missy said, not looking up, her voice almost a whisper, "Before I knew what I was . . . only once did I ever think I loved; I remained young, a child in looks and years, and he grew old, old. . . ."

Her voice died. Keral reached out quietly, across Conner, and touched her hand. She smiled, a brief sad glint of a smile, and was silent. Regis reached for Linnea's hand, drew her fingers under his arm.

"Always—a *woman* of the chieri," David murmured, hardly aware that he spoke aloud.

Linnea raised her eyes and looked at Keral. She said, "I am not idly curious, believe me. But I have heard strange things, in legend. Legends lie; *to lie like an old song,* is a proverb with us. Tell me this, then. Is it true that your people take a mate but once, and if death or misfortune part you, seek never for another?"

"Not entirely true," said Keral, "although it is true that once our hearts and emotions are set on one, we seldom seek elsewhere. I am speaking from the long memory of my people, not from my own experience, you understand, Lady. Rare is the chieri who comes not to his lover untouched—as she to him. It is not that we demand this, it is simply that all things come in season; and we do not, as we say, seek fruit in spring, or blossom from a winter bough...." He sighed. "It is not only that we desire no other; we can endure no other, as a common thing. And this is why we died, our people.... Perhaps it is Evanda's way to cancel the gift of long life she gave us when the world was shaped. Our women are able to bear for only—I know not your words—*cuere*—one turn of the seasons? A year? Yes; maybe one year in a hundred, and sometimes for many *cueru* at a time, those of us in male phase can sow only barren seed. So rarely does it happen, as you can see, that both would come together, *raiva*—ripened for mating: one to engender, and his mate to conceive, in a single season. So fewer and fewer children were born to us. There are exceptions. There are times when one of us, desperate to bear, would seek another mate. Yet, it has ever been a bitter, hard thing, and seldom can any one of our people bring herself to this. Something in our blood will not allow it, as I have told you."

Linnea said: "Is it true then, what else they say—that your people lie down together—" she used the courtly and evasive casta word, *accandir*, but spoke calmly and without embarrassment, "only when they desire children?"

Keral laughed aloud. "*That* tale, at least, is false—or else it would make us a strange folk indeed! No, Linnea, I suppose we come together like any other people in this world, or any other world, for consolation in loneliness, for pleasure, for heart's ease. But—except in the madness of the Change—it is not a drive, a compulsion. Not a need, but a pleasantness, as with music, or dancing."

David said slowly, "A people without divided sexes, then, without an overwhelming sex drive—"

"Would have a low survival factor," Jason said; and Regis added, "Something of this has come down in our blood from you. I've known for many years that among telepaths the sexual drive is lower than in ordinary men."

Conner, who had not spoken aloud yet, said quietly from where he sat in shadow, "This makes sense. Those with 'closed minds' have no way to reach one another except in the blind touching of bodies in sex. . . ."

"And sex can be a deep contact," said Linnea gravely, "or it can—if you're doing intense telepathic work—act as a kind of static, so disruptive that it was believed, for a long time, that a Keeper must be a virgin. Most of them aren't, these days—I'm not—but some care is needed. Men doing heavy telepath work in the matrix screens are impotent a good deal of the time."

Desideria nodded. "When I was a girl, it was believed a Keeper must be a virgin," she said. "I was banned from my place with my first love; I found soon that I had not lost my powers, but it was years before I had the courage to use them again."

"Another thing," said Linnea, looking straight at David, "among the Comyn telepaths men and women are not regarded as so different, and it is common enough for young girls to fall in love, first, with other girls, and young boys with their playmates."

"It's not unknown among Terrans either," said Jason, "but the taboo is very strong."

Regis said, holding Linnea's hand, "For me, this was a frightful conflict. I was brought so young to know that I was the last male Hastur; my father died so young, my grandfather so old. From my earliest childhood I came to feel they regarded me only as *seed.* I came to hate women, for a time. I felt at ease only with other men, my kinsmen and cousins. . . ." He looked quickly, smiling, at Danilo.

David laughed. "They could have solved that in the Empire," he said; "they'd have had you contributing to a sperm bank." He chuckled at Regis' look of noncomprehension and explained, and had the surprising experience of seeing Regis Hastur blushing. Evidently sex wasn't quite the no-taboo thing among telepaths that he had been led to believe. Silently he reflected that despite the strong taboo on overt homosexual behavior in Terran cultures, he had often felt closer rapport with his male friends in the hospital than with most women.

—*You establish rapport quickly*, from Regis.

I'm not homosexual!

Would it matter so much if you were? Regis caught them all up quickly in the swift net of rapport. Conner and Missy, their fingers lightly intertwined, fair and dark, dropped a curious bittersweet note into the contact; a swift touch of warmth from Desideria, *I love you all, although none of you has ever touched me or will*; a strange tense reaching from Keral, still hesitant and filled with fear. . . .

—*the preliminaries of love play . . . how break this deadlock. . . .*

There was a long silence. Outside the glass, soft snow beat on the panes and a silent wind whirled, white against the darkness. In Keral's mind was a picture of a forest, lying quiet under snow, light forms moving in a snowflake dance through the bare trees and groves . . . a moment they all felt the soft blowing through the chieri grove as it lay silent in the winter twilight.

Then Regis said softly, aloud:

"Among my people they say that when men come together with men, or women with women, as lovers—we call it the *donas amizu,* the gift of friends— it is recognition of a deeper truth. That within every woman is a hidden man; within every man, a hidden woman. And it is to this inner self, the polar opposite of your own, that you give your love."

"The *animus* and the *anima*," Jason murmured.

"And in the chieri," Missy said softly, "the inner side is not hidden, and lies nearer to the surface. This is new to me, too. . . ."

"—but not a thing of shame."

And once again the intense awareness caught them all up, Regis, Linnea, Desideria holding them all together in a close bond. David suddenly knew that he had found his own truth. Man or woman? He touched Conner for a moment and sensed a like sense of homecoming; felt Linnea nestling like a flower in his consciousness, reached out briefly with his hands, drew her close and kissed her lips; felt himself embraced quickly by Jason; dropped in and out of swift awareness; Missy flaring like a comet across his senses; the swift stir of warmth and love that was Desideria; returning to Keral with a sense of homecoming.

He knew, now, that although they would be afraid of each other again, the deadlock of shame and fear had been broken, and he and Keral would somehow find a way to one another.

The rapport slid apart, and they were separated. But David knew he would never be alone again.

Even as they drew apart, an undertone of mirth ran through their minds, still lightly linked, with Linnea's laughing protest:

"I love your kinsman, Regis; but must he go wherever we go? Will Danilo sleep at our feet? Can we never be alone?"

And the quick, sobering answer: "Would you meet Melora's fate? Alone?"

And as the contact fell apart into its last disappearing shreds, a scrap of thought that there were some things even a bodyguard could not do.

CHAPTER THIRTEEN

When they separated, quietly and without leave-takings (what for? They knew they would always be together), David and Keral walked home quietly across the city, guided by the lights of the Terran HQ like a vast white tower in the clearing dark. They clung lightly to each other's hands as they walked, but neither spoke much until, as they passed through the spaceport gates, Keral said, as if answering David's words, "I don't care, now, if they know."

"No."

"Contact with Conner brought Missy back from the worst madness of the Change."

They did not speak again, but went quietly up to the rooms assigned to David. It had the familiarity, now, of home.

Taking advantage of privilege, David had supper sent to their rooms, and they ate together in a growing sense of closeness and isolation, deepened by awareness of the falling, insulating snow, all around them. Keral was in the merriest of moods, and it was infectious;

everything either of them said seemed witty, and they kept going off into gales of mad laughter, from a dim awareness that somehow their very presence was funny in a solemn way. What had they been afraid of? David suddenly became aware that he was moving perilously close to the edge of drunkenness and pushed aside a third glass of the sweet, pale wine from the Darkovan mountains, Keral followed the gesture and said gravely, "I wasn't trying to get you drunk, but does it matter if we are?"

"Only that I'm not sure of the effects of alcohol on your metabolism—and too damn sure of its effect on mine!" David laughed and put it firmly aside. "Anyhow, I don't want to spoil anything by being out of focus."

"It means so much to you, to have everything clear and defined? Maybe things aren't meant to be quite that clear. It might be a good thing if the edges were a little blurred." Keral came over, bent and took David's head between his hands; a strange gesture and David sensed at once, an unusual and intimate one. He said, almost whispering, "After all, it's only safe to look at the sun through smoked glasses."

"It's too serious for that."

"And you think it isn't serious for me?" Keral turned David's face upward by main force and their eyes met; and something inside David turned over. He had been living with this for weeks, but suddenly it was there crystal clear and without the merciful blurring: desire and tenderness, too entangled to be sure which was which. Keral said, "If I didn't take it more seriously than you can possibly know—I wouldn't be here."

Keral dropped to the floor and laid his head on David's knees. His long hair felt soft and fine; David felt a faint shivering run through Keral, and wanted to seize him in his arms, but he knew, rationally, that he must wait. For Keral this would be a slow-rising, slow-culminating thing, and any shock might arrest or damage the whole process.

Keral looked up, and David, aware now of his subtler expressions, knew he was on the edge of tears.

"I'm afraid, David. Missy was actually in a man's arms when the change came on her, and it went the wrong way. How can we be sure?"

David almost panicked at that. Keral had been sure that all would be well. If he lost confidence, what lay ahead?

But; perhaps this was inevitable. As polarity ebbed and flowed, male to female, passive to active, there must be—David found it quieted him to think clinically—some fairly drastic hormone changes, and this would make Keral's emotions volatile, uncertain, labile. The very knowledge of the inevitability of the process may be what's making Keral panic, as if he's started something he can't change or control . . . as inevitable and drastic as birth. . . .

David thought, *using a male pronoun is part of what's probably bothering me, too.* No good; however hard he tried, he could not think of Keral as a woman; any more than he could sense, psychologically, Missy as a male though he had actually seen her as one.

Yet there was woman in Keral. . . .

The hidden woman. . . .

He must accept it; help it to emerge.

David bent over Keral, repeating Keral's gesture, hands at either side of the delicate pale face. "Don't be afraid. I'll try not to—go faster than you can follow."

Keral smiled but did not speak. David, finding that clinical thoughts calmed him, ran deliberately over his knowledge of the alien physiology. Keral's present neuter phase, with a slight balance to maleness, would, if the stimulus was adequate—and this was a big if—if the psychological and physiological stimuli were all in balance, gradually tip the balance toward the female: hormones, genitals, psychology.

From a strictly physical point of view, actual intercourse should be possible; even now, it should be possible. That was all they knew; that theoretically, with their knowledge of anatomy, there was no reason it should *not* be possible.

But there was a hell of a long gap between the theoretical and the practical! He thought, *I've never had hypothetical sex before,* and realized he must still be on the very edge of being drunk. He wondered how long the shift to female phase took.

"I don't know," Keral said, and David never knew if he had put the question aloud, "we're not as tied down to clocks as you people. I've never timed it. To guess—with one of my own—perhaps two or three hours or less. But with you—I'm not trying to be vague; I don't *know!*"

"It doesn't matter," David said quickly, recognizing near hysteria. *The hormones are identical. Theoretically he should react to me exactly as to one of his own people. But the psychic factor means a hell of a lot too.*

David felt a sort of fierce tenderness. Difficult and frightening as this was for him, for Keral it must be almost unbelievably so. David only broke a superficial taboo against sex with someone with similar organs. *A damn silly taboo anyhow.* David would at least remain in his own familiar gender and role. Keral, after unimaginable years as a male—how old was he? Three or four hundred or even more?—must change. And—this distressed David even more—it was Keral as a male he had learned to love. Would Keral as a female seem so strange that love would vanish in the strangeness? Would he be less beloved?

Keral was still shivering violently; David held him, wondering with a curious, distracted curiosity if some more directly sexual stimulus would help or hinder the psychic, or even the physical changes. It might ease the sense of strain, or heighten it. He didn't know. He could only guess. Tentatively, he kissed Keral; Keral accepted the kiss passively, neither refusing nor responding, and David began to draw away; but Keral's hands tightened and he kept David close.

Damn it. It seems so cold-blooded, to psych him out like this. Like an experiment.

David finally found his voice. "Keral, I'm afraid

too. I don't know how you respond, or what to expect at any given moment, or even how you feel about this. If this is going to work at all, there's one thing we don't dare do, and that's to assume the other one *knows*. I've found out that this mind reading business tends to come unstuck at the damnedest times! If this is even going to be physically possible, let alone the way we want it, we've got to be completely frank with each other. Completely. If I go too fast, or do anything you aren't ready for, you're going to have to stop me; and don't be upset if I do the same with you. Because we can't take the chance of blundering down blind alleys."

He said, with a faint, fey smile, "We'll have to keep our minds open about—blind alleys, and give ourselves a chance to recover, if we hit them. I can't imagine anything you could do that would turn me against you. It would be only a mistake, not a catastrophe."

"Was it a mistake to kiss you? Some Terran groups don't—"

"Not a mistake. A little before I was ready, maybe."

David felt the effort it was costing Keral to put this all into words, not even in his own language, during this tremendous emotional and physical upheaval. He felt cruel for forcing this alien game of total frankness on Keral, but he saw no other way to come through this without hurting each other deeply, inflicting emotional wounds which could drive a deep wedge between them.

What diversion, then, while Keral moved at his

own pace toward some unimaginable goal? It struck David that they had seen each other unclothed only under the most ordinary of circumstances; it might be wise to get used to each other and not risk being surprised by strangeness later. Keral was completely matter-of-fact when David suggested it, saying quietly that his people went clothed only against the bitterest weather or among strangers. He drew off his clothes without a hint of shyness or erotic awareness. David felt slightly less matter-of-fact; nakedness, to him, *was* a furthering of intimacy and did have sexual overtones. It heightened his awareness of Keral, and of himself. He was glad that they had grown used to each other's bodies under more impersonal conditions, but he seemed to be seeing Keral for the first time. Keral was tall, inches taller than he, although David was tall, and his frail, fine-boned body was pale and almost hairless except for a faint silvery shadow across the loins. Despite the smallness of the breasts, it was not too hard to think of it as feminine even now. Next to Keral, David himself felt gross, rough, almost apishly masculine.

They stood looking at each other for a time, trying to recapture their old selves to fit this new time and place; then, with a small shiver, Keral held out his arms and they stood embraced, carefully, not too close. David found himself laughing, and cut it off, aware of the dangers of hysteria. Instead he tried kissing Keral again, and this time there was a hesitant, infinitely shy response. When they drew apart Keral said timidly, "I don't even know—what forms of love play are—customary or permitted with you."

David felt an almost dizzying, sudden wave of desire and fought an impulse to crush Keral against him, roughly, forcing some sort of response . . . the slow pace was torture, advance and retreat, tantalus . . . but he mastered it, knowing this was the blindest of blind alleys. He suspected rape would be physically impossible, and even if it were possible, what could it possibly accomplish but alienation and anguish? He said, very gently, "My dear, does it matter what's customary? This isn't a customary situation. You said nothing I could do could turn you against me. I feel the same way, but we'll simply have to take our time and see what happens." And David realized this was something of a crucial breakthrough. As the infinitely delicate polarity tipped, male to female, Keral would become more shy, more passive. It was David's turn to take the lead.

An experienced woman can take the lead with a young or shy male. But he didn't even know how much experience, among his own kind, Keral might have had, and in any case it would now be irrelevant. David must now initiate; lead; and still be aware of response or refusal.

He drew Keral down beside him and they lay embraced, full length, kissing gently, then moving with a growing response. David said at last, huskily, coming up for air, "This isn't too fast for me—but it might be for you, Keral." He took Keral's hand gently in his own and guided it, but Keral jerked violently away.

For an instant David felt a spasm of anger. Nothing in Keral had prepared him for what seemed like prudery. Then, coming back to sanity (*he had to think. Violent erection, desire, or not, he couldn't let his body do the thinking here*), he realized that Keral was afraid. Physically afraid, and if that fear began to spiral upward, out of control, they were finished. Keral's whole body was shaking with the effort to conceal his fear, but it was like a scent. David sat up, moving away.

"See? I'm still in control, Keral. I promised; nothing you're not ready for. But I wish you'd told me before it got so bad. I can't read your mind now; your emotions sort of blur everything. So you'll have to tell me."

"It's not; I wanted you to touch me, but—"

David said, on sudden intuition:

"Am I so different from one of your people in male phase? Different enough to frighten you?"

"Not really, although—I think you're stronger than I believed. I'm always—it's hard to say this—I'm always a little afraid in the early stages. But it isn't just that. Among us there is more, more continuing change, and if you are already like this, I am afraid that later, when I am ready—"

He was shaking terribly now, very near tears, and David suddenly understood. He almost laughed, it was too much like some stupid dirty joke, but he cradled Keral gently in his arms and held him tight. He said quietly, "No. No, Keral. you forget. We reach the full stage of arousal quickly. As I am now—that is what I will be when you are ready. No more."

Of course. If Keral was used to a slow and gradual sexual change, a growth which lasted over a period of hours, and if at this early stage David had already reached maximum size and intensity, how could Keral know that? They were, after all, David realized, more alien than civilized man and savage; and even among men of a single breed and single planet, there were endless misunderstandings and alien taboos.

Keral was calmer now. He said, "Of course; it was foolish to be afraid. I wish I were ready for you."

"I can wait."

"You're trying so hard to meet me halfway. I'm ashamed."

"Don't be, Keral."

He felt pliant, almost brittle in David's arms; David felt gross and rough and almost unsure of the kind and type of physical change he would see in Keral. David said, at last, "I'm still in unfamiliar country, without a map. I want to be sure—"

Keral said immediately, "Yes. This at least is so. We must know completely what the other is . . . even if we were two of a kind, it would be wise, and now there's no other way."

David was glad to be detached and almost clinical again as Keral slowly explored his body with his hands. The touch was exciting, but not dangerously so, and mutual curiosity relaxed the tension. *To hell*

*with theoretical specimens and anatomical generalities, I
want to be sure about this one, individual one!* As he
touched Keral curiously, he wondered, embarrassment and unsureness mingled, would the strangeness
be enough to repel him? Could anything about Keral
make him feel revulsion? The textbook drawings he
had made from the first medical examinations of both
Keral and Missy were in the back of his mind. When
he made them had he guessed this? He touched the
folded genital slit, thinking randomly that it was a
more sensible arrangement than the exposed one of
his own kind of human. "Promise to stop me if I hurt
you."

Keral laughed. "I don't think you will. I'm not
really that fragile. I didn't hurt you, touching you, did
I?" David realized that they had come a long way;
Keral could touch him now, easily and without hesitation or fear. The change must be far advanced, and
he took courage from that.

There was no great strangeness and nothing repel-
lent. At the front of the slit, retracted now like a small
folded bud, the male organ, smaller now than a
human baby's, although when David, telling himself
that he must somehow come to terms with the male in
Keral, touched it gently, Keral murmured softly with
pleasure. Behind it, deepening in color and faintly
swelling, was the female organ, and David, losing his
detachment, trembled slightly as he felt the slow
throb under his hand. He closed his eyes and moved

away, afraid again to hurry anything. Keral broke into violent shuddering and pulled him closer.

"I'm not sure; it's not the same—I can't stand this," he said fiercely, "not knowing, something's got to change, it's killing me—"

We should have expected this, David thought bleakly. *Deadlock.* So far and no further, and the cultural taboos so strong neither of us can break through them. The attempt had to be made before he lost his nerve, and yet the fear of what a premature attempt could mean held him paralyzed. He moved carefully above Keral, and the chieri's eyes closed, as he clutched David's shoulders, still trembling. He said, "I don't know— I'm afraid—"

David himself was so frightened that it nearly unmanned him. *Oh God, why did we try, we had so much. . . .* He found himself sobbing, limp, lying across Keral's breast and crying helplessly. He had never known such terror. Keral was crying, too; they held each other, clinging in a sort of blind panic. David finally managed to gasp, "What shall we do? What shall we do?"

Slowly, Keral quieted. He held David close, his lips against David's hair, and for the first time tonight, David was aware of the softness of his skin, the feminine lightness of his touch, as Keral whispered softly in his own language, words David could not understand, although he knew them for endearments. At last he murmured, "David, my dear, we should have expected this. We were both too—too tense, too aware. Maybe love needs a little madness. Remember what you said about blind alleys?"

"It's hopeless, then?"

"No. No. A mistake, not a catastrophe. We were frightened, and—well, self-conscious." He raised himself and kissed David, brushing the hair out of his eyes. "Lie here close to me, David. We were both in a hurry. As if we had to make sure of each other right away."

"I'm ashamed—" David muttered.

"I was before, but it's easier for me if I know that you're frightened too," Keral said simply. "You seemed so sure of yourself, I wondered if you had any idea how hard it was for me—"

"I was pretending," David muttered against his throat, "I wanted to give you confidence, too."

Slowly they quieted, lying close together, feeling the rhythm of each other's hearts. They had been like this before, David remembered, but not so honest with each other. Warmth and security had done their work. David found himself erect again, throbbingly aware of Keral warm and trustful against him. Keral smiled and pulled him close.

"Don't be afraid. We can try."

At first David could not find the entrance and Keral had to help him. He. She. *Damn, Damn.* Fear again, and momentary awkwardness; a drawn breath from Keral; tension that nearly undid David again. Then he realized that he had actually entered. He felt dizzily strange, resisting the instinct to move, and whispered, controlling himself:

"Keral?"

"It's all right—" but the voice was a threadlike gasp.

"Not—afraid?"

"A little, but—go on, I want you to—"

It was hard and awkward, and for a moment they struggled helplessly toward each other, in a renewed spasmodic fear and anger; and Keral sobbed again, in a last flare of panic trying to fight him away. And then, suddenly, they found that they fitted together, and David felt a relief so enormous that he could have burst into tears again. He rested a minute, leaning down to kiss the wet face beneath his, then hunger and desire quickly overcame him again, surging up at the lessening of the seemingly endless tension and fear.

They clung together, moving almost savagely, learning each other's rhythms and movements. Keral was still sobbing, but not, now, with fear. And then, swiftly, it was over for David, in an exploding, blackout burst of light.

When he got his breath again he leaned down and kissed Keral; then, in swift compunction for his tears, gathered him close:

"Don't, there's nothing to cry about—is there? Did I hurt you so much? I tried—"

"No, no, you didn't hurt me, I was so afraid something would go wrong again and now—now I want to cry, to laugh, to fly. . . ."

They fell together into silence, still aware of the soft snow whispering against the window. David had not realized how wholly the strangeness had gone, and yet; this was still Keral. He still did not think of Keral as a woman; and yet—oh, hell! Why struggle for labels? Keral was Keral; and he loved him; and he didn't care; and he fell asleep in Keral's arms not caring.

CHAPTER FOURTEEN

On a day late in the winter, Jason stopped by the laboratory and said, "David? Regis Hastur just sent me a message; he wants us all to come up to the castle. He didn't say why. Will you walk there with me?"

David got his heaviest coat—a Darkovan one; the ones he had owned on other planets would have been summer-weight here—and came along. Jason asked, "How is it going?"

"Busy, as usual. I was right, by the way; all of the other telepaths in the new group have gray eyes, and all of the Comyn and Darkovans have the typical brain wave readings; not as pronounced as in the chieri, but the same thing on a lesser scale."

Jason chuckled, "Did you ever see so many redheads?"

"No, I read an old story once—from prehistory—called "The Red-headed League," a foolish tale about something that was a crime then; I can't remember, but one paragraph in it—I thought of it this morning: 'I never hope to see such a sight as that again. From north, south, east and west, every man who had a shade of red in his hair had tramped in. I should not have thought there were so many in the whole country. Every shade of red they were: straw, lemon, orange, brick, liver, clay and the real flame-haired tint.'"

"Well, you look as if you belong," Jason said, and David laughed. "Coincidence; when I was a kid on Terra, red hair wasn't associated with anything except bad temper. I had that too; that was before I realized that everybody around me couldn't tell what I was thinking as easily as I could tell it about them. But where in hell did *you* get it, Jason? You're not red-headed."

"I was as a kid, but I'd forgotten. My mother was," Jason said; "she was Darkovan, but she died before I was old enough to remember. As for being a telepath, I never suspected I was until being around all of you I started picking things up. Where's Keral?"

They had gone down to the spaceport gates now and passed through, climbing the steep old streets toward the old castle on the cliffs high above them. David said, "He went out for a walk in the fields; I think the streets and buildings stifle him."

"Alone?"

"No; Conner was with him, and some guards—I had work I wanted to finish."

"Keral doesn't look nearly as—well, as girlish—as Missy. I notice you still say *he*."

David shrugged. "I still think of him that way. Maybe Missy changed so much only because she was mimicking humans; a lot of behavior we think of as sex linked is really just culture linked; I don't know."

Jason said, "I loved a Free Amazon once; in many ways it was like loving a man, and more so toward the end than at first."

"I've heard Linnea speak of the Free Amazons but somehow I thought they only loved other women."

"Oh, no! But they do as they please, and no man holds one of them for long. Kyla stayed with me for three years and that was a long time, for a woman with no child; then she grew weary of the city, but my work was here and I decided to stay. I'm not sure if I was right or wrong, but I'm a doctor, and for better or worse—" Jason fell silent, and David said, "I understand."

"The work we're doing now, a reliable study of telepaths and their powers, is going to make all the difference to Darkover," Jason said; "it's been tried before, but nothing ever came of it; the Darkovans wouldn't cooperate. Now they are doing it of their free will."

"Not entirely of their free will," David said, "but of necessity. I think seeing Keral and hearing about his people has frightened them; they see themselves. Their birth rate is falling too, you know. Appallingly. Not one of the women here has had more than one child, and the men—" he shrugged. "A few, like Regis, felt it their duty to make sure they had children; the others never thought of it."

Jason asked, "A case of nature breeding back to the norm?"

"I think not. It's a case of—sensitivity," David said. "Once you get habituated to that kind of contact, nothing less seems real. And there aren't so many potential mates either; marriages are made for political reasons, too, and the girls are brought up in isolation, seeing only their own blood kin. No one ever thought of trying to breed deliberately for the telepath genes, and as a result, half of the telepath families are diluted until the gift hardly shows, and the others so inbred that some awfully freaky recessives are coming out."

"True enough," Jason said. "Well, perhaps something will come of this gathering." As he spoke, they passed under the high gates of the old castle. The guards on duty there looked faintly askance at the two Terran Medics, in their white uniforms, but let them pass, and inside the corridors, which were, like most Darkovan buildings, of pale translucent stone with colored lights behind the panels, one of the servants told them that the Lord Hastur had given orders to bring them to the Council Chamber.

David already knew that the orders sent out by Regis to bring every known telepath on Darkover to Thendara had resulted in two hundred and thirty adult men and women—which on Darkover meant over fifteen years old. About a hundred more were accounted for as unable to come because of inaccessible weather and climate, extreme old age or illness, and a few because of advanced pregnancy. This was not a great number for a population which numbered somewhere in the low millions—a census of Darkover had never been made. David had heard the old estimates; in the old days, roughly one in a hundred of the population had displayed measurable telepathic gifts.

Regis did not long leave them in doubt about why he had called them together. After rehearsing a few of the known problems, and begging them to cooperate in the Terran-sponsored program to measure their gifts and train those which were latent, he broke off the formal speech and stepped down from the high platform from which he had spoken.

David had been in contact with him often enough to sense his complete dedication, but he had never before thought of Regis as much of a leader. Always before Regis had seemed to him a quiet, rather diffident youngster, pushed reluctantly into a position of power and not enjoying it. Regis was not especially tall, even for a Darkovan—they were not a particularly tall race. He was about five-foot-nine, and although his features were fine, the snow-white hair lending them a steel-toned distinction, he would not of himself have drawn all eyes. But now, as he spoke, David sensed that he was drawing on some force which seemed above and beyond his own personality.

"Our world is in the hands of wreckers," he said, "and I cannot even urge you to seek help from the Terrans. It might be better to die our own way than to live in theirs. But I do not believe these are our only alternatives. We are something quite unusual among the hundred thousands of inhabited worlds; and we must keep what we have.

"Our traditional ways and governments have been broken up, and nothing has emerged to take their place. The Terran Empire is all too ready to step into this vacuum.

"The Comyn and the Comyn Council, our old hierarchy, are gone. I am going to ask you all to join with me in forming a new council; a council which will not rule Darkover, but which will lead it and work to restore it.

"For hundreds of years, those of you who, like myself, were born into telepath families and castes have had the tradition of spending your gifts for the good of our world as a whole. You have sacrificed yourselves and lived in isolation, working with the screens and matrices to give us such small technology as we have. And those of you born into other families and castes have been considered outcasts, freaks, strange and uncanny, both revered and feared.

"I ask you to join together: Comyn and commoner, peasant and lord, Free Amazon and stranger, valley man and mountain man. I ask you to spend yourselves further for our people. And for the time being, I ask you to lend your gifts to the Terrans in return for the help we need to rebuild our world. But in return I guarantee that we will never become just another of the lockstep worlds of the Empire. Maybe we can be the leaven in their dough. Maybe, when they find that they cannot remake us in their image, they will find that they remake themselves more like us.

"Will you give me all your help?"

He stood silent, and for a moment there was no answer.

It was not needed. It was like a visible storm in the room, as every man and woman there rose physically to his feet—and David found himself locked into the sudden and incredible joining.

There were superficial differences; there would even be hostilities. But at this moment they were all united; and David knew that never in the history of the known universe had anyone led such a united group with such a single mind.

He didn't know how they would meet the problems their world faced. But he'd bet on them to solve them—and he knew in that blinding moment of revelation that he would be a part of the answer.

The winter wore away, day by slow day, while Andrea Closson studied her plans, listened to her spies, and cogitated the final act which would leave this planet defenseless. Once or twice she thought that she could hardly have planned it better, all the remaining telepaths coming together into the Comyn Castle; it was as if, in some lemming rush, they hastened to put themselves into her hands.

The few who remained, old, insignificant, ill, or trapped in isolated districts, they did not count; even the few young pregnant women who remained away.

Nevertheless, without realizing it she was relieved, for she had an irrational prejudice against killing a woman with child, and this eliminated the need. Regis Hastur, who, when her assassins were still on this planet, had been her prime target, was rumored in the city to have another mistress. Andrea had never seen Regis Hastur, but she felt a vague admiration for him; he had thwarted so many attacks. Well, let him enjoy such time as was left to him and his people, in peace. The few who remained after her last act would be too few and too feeble to rebuild their kind; in another generation they would be no more than a memory and a few isolated throwbacks.

Working through a few agents (like most Trade Cities, you can buy anything in the main spaceport of Darkover if you have the price) she had managed to secure the materials she wanted.

One night toward spring, she heard the news she was waiting for:

"It's one of their special Festivals," the man told her, "and all of them, including the telepaths they've brought in from offworld on this special HQ Medic project—ten or fifteen of them by now—will be up in the castle that night. It's some kind of dance—to celebrate the spring thaw, or the first green leaves, or something like that. I don't know why they're taking time off to hold a dance at this time of year with all they've got on their minds, but I guess I'll never understand Darkovans."

"How reliable is this information?" Andrea asked.

"It's as straight as a computer readout," the man assured her. "One of the chaps in the telepath project is a great gambler. I can get his tongue loose if he wins—and I make sure he wins."

"Fool," Andrea said dispassionately, "if he's a telepath he probably knows you're picking his brains."

"Whether he knows or not, he doesn't give a damn," the spy retorted. "I don't know what you're plotting, or planning, if anything, so he couldn't read much. So what if he knows I don't mean them any good. I'm no telepath, but I don't need to know that this cat Rondo means them no good either. He's probably delighted to know that I'm reporting back to somebody who doesn't love them."

Well, the harm was done; but Andrea doubted if anyone, now, would trouble to track down who was behind a single spy. In any case she doubted if anyone born human could read her thoughts. Certainly not after all these years. (Once, in the forest, when a copper-haired Free Amazon had watched her burying the black virus, she had felt a trace of contact and dismissed it with contempt. And after all, nothing had been done, although a brief check had told her that the Free Amazon had run to some local seeress for a counter-charm. So much for Darkovan telepaths!)

And if they read her mind too late—well, it *would* be too late. She never let it come up to the surface of her mind that after this final act she had not bothered to plan her own escape. (What for?)

Her excuse was simple. There was no one else she could trust to know her plans, or the telepaths would pick up the knowledge from his mind.

So that it would be her own act and another race would die. Like her own.

Without knowing it, David echoed the very words of Andrea's spy:

"I don't know why, with all they have on their minds, they're taking time off for a dance tonight!"

Jason chuckled. "When you've been on Darkover a few years longer, you'll understand it." It was taken for granted by them both now, David thought, that he was committed for life to this world. "Dancing is a big thing here. Get three Darkovans together anywhere and they hold a dance."

Regis said, "It's a primary study. I think it goes back into prehistory; perhaps rising out of old folk festivals at the eclipses; I don't know. It's the one exclusively human activity; there is a parallel for every other human thing in some lower animal, even music—the birds sing, and even some insects make artistic patterns. But there is an old poem which states it: only men laugh, only men weep, and only men dance." He was resplendent in a jeweled costume of blue and silver; Linnea, at his side, was covered with pink flowers, some real and some artificial. He smiled kindly at David and asked Keral, beside him, "Do the chieri dance?"

"They do," said Keral softly, "in the forests—in the sun or moonlight—in ecstasy."

David, as always, sensitive to Keral's moods, thought that Keral was near the edge of ecstasy himself. Although he normally avoided crowds, tonight he had dressed himself in his own garments—a curious long tunic of shimmery fabric which he said was woven of spider's silk—and joined them. The Change was complete in Keral now, and to David he seemed lovelier than Missy had ever been; but tonight there seemed a positive glow, a visible light and shimmer around the chieri.

Behind them, the lighted ballroom was aglow with a thousand sparkles, crowded with men and women in brilliant costumes, hair of every shade of red. There was soft music with quiet, well-marked rhythm, but Regis turned his back on it all and walked across the dark garden. He looked up into the sky at the four floating moons. He looked round again, at the pale gleam of Keral's moonlit hair; at Conner's face, a mere blur against the dark.

Conner said, "You know I have one of those 'out of focus' time things. Watch it, Regis; something's going to go wrong tonight. I was just *there* for a minute and felt it, but I can't control it."

Regis said slowly, "I don't sense anything, but precognition isn't a Hastur talent. What was it like, Conner?"

He ridged his brow with effort. "I can't completely control it," he said. "I'm not sure. Like—like fireworks."

"Maybe it's the past you sense and not the future. This castle has a long and sometimes a bloody history, my dear friend."

"Maybe." Conner looked troubled though and reached in the darkness for Missy's hand. Regis watched as they moved away. Missy's fantastic beauty had never come back, but from what Keral said about the chieri in general, there was time for that. Much more time than Conner had. Lifetimes. But Conner was content with her as she was.

David, returning to the lighted ballroom, stood at the side—dancing was something he knew little about—watching the intricate patterns: couples, groups, long chains of people, an occasional sudden solo dancer emerging from the group. It was like watching the flight of brilliantly colored birds. Regis and Linnea briefly emerged from the group, dancing entwined, and the love between them was like a palpable awareness. Not that the dance held any note of eroticism, and yet an essence of sexuality wove like a line of light between them, and he sensed that in some curious way they were actually flaunting it. He thought, with some amusement, that since he had come to Darkover he had spent an inordinate amount of time thinking about other people's sex lives. Well, sex was pretty basic. After all, most people spent a lot of time thinking about it. On Darkover—or at least among telepaths—it simply wasn't possible to keep it out of casual conversations and encounters. It made little sense to treat a girl as if you were uninterested when she was just as conscious of your undercover feelings as of her own. He wondered if that was why the telepaths had created what seemed a very elaborate code of almost ritual politeness—for instance, never staring deliberately at a young girl; perhaps a way of emphasizing, "I am a sexual creature and I respond to you, but I emphasize that I await your response and consent." It had evidently, from what he knew of Darkovan manners in general, filtered down to groups which were not telepathic at all, and he wondered what rationalizations they had developed to account for it. He knew that dueling was common on Darkover—to compensate for the inability to conceal hostility? A backlash against painful empathy? Or a way of asserting cock-of-the-walk masculinity?

Keral reached for David's hand, and David clasped it in his own, with the never-failing awareness of response, empathy. Keral seemed even more joyous than usual tonight, the gray eyes seeming mad with merriment, his color higher than David had ever seen it, a positive radiance of glow and joyousness. His silky hair, very long, shoulder length and more, seemed to catch the light breezes and blow in an invisible current no greater than that which made the lights dance and sway. David said, "You look happy, Keral," and realized that the words were inadequate.

"I am. Do you remember what I said to you, the first time we were together—*I want to laugh, to sing, to fly?*"

"I remember; how could I forget?"

"I am even more happy now. Don't ask me why, not now, not here. I will tell you very soon. But now—here—" He threw back his head and stood there in an attitude of intent, close listening intensity. It seemed that he heard some sound, some voice from nowhere; rapt, ecstatic. Then he raised his arms, stood swaying for a moment like a tall flower stem swayed by the invisible breeze of the music, and began to dance.

David, watching, felt the music drop away into silence, or perhaps he no longer heard it. He was only conscious of Keral, first like a drifting leaf borne on the currents, then whirling into a mad dance of ecstasy. It was the frail and sensitive Linnea who caught the contagion first, breaking away and whirling across the floor behind him; and after her, first by twos and threes and then by tens and dozens, like some mad flight of birds wheeling, dipping, circling and rising. David, his whole awareness swept up into the dance, saw, at the edge of his consciousness, Conner flinging himself into the flooding movement, saw Desideria moving lightly, drifting with her delicate draperies afloat; then his own separate awareness drifted away in a rising tide that broke over his head and swept him out into the moving flood of his own people.

Rise and fall, drift and circle and whirl on the invisible tides of the world the force of flooding spring in the heart and soul. The currents of moonlight, an invisible magnet that drew them, whirling and surging, through the great doors and out into the cool misty garden. David, his feet treading the measure in rhythm with the others, felt the cool air on his face, and in a split second of brief, amazed, sane self-awareness, wondered, *what are we all doing;* and then the thought was swept away again in the pull of flooding moonlight, shared consciousness, dizzy motion of sheer joy for its own sake. It was vaguely like swimming underwater, with a blind unfocused pressure pulling him along on its own swift current, and he surrendered to it, seeing with scraps of awareness little instantaneous fragments of beauty; Keral's hair silvered by moonlight, his rapt face upturned and almost wholly human; Missy, blown like a circling leaf; Conner, drawn volitionless on a blind tide; Regis, moving slowly with his eyes closed and yet somehow resembling an arrow in flight. And then David was swept away from his friends and into the center of the spinning ecstasy, whirled faster and faster into the rising vortex of awareness. He moved in a dream, but his body was wholly alive and aware of the joyous freedom of motion, the pull of the tides of moons and sea, each separate moon a different living tingle in his nerves. Each star in the luminous sky seemed a separate living thing, exerting its own pull on his brain; and each of the separate dancers in the crowd was a different force, a separate feel. With infinitely extended senses, like long streamers of cobweb brilliance, almost palpable in the thin and scented air, he touched each individual one of them, feeling their uniqueness, their own special joy.

And more. And more. The spring leaves bursting bravely and unseen throughout the ruined land. The mosses unfolding under the snow. The quiet and secret life of birds here in the garden and far away in the hills and forests; the fierce prowling of the nonhuman catmen on the hills, driven by hunger and fear; the rising sap in the blood of beasts driven by tides and currents to race fiercely in mating; everywhere, everywhere, all things reawakening, rising, flooding into spring and rebirth and a new world. Far away in the forests, without knowing how, in a vividness past picturing, David saw *them;* the old kindred, tall and still and old and wise beyond knowing, with their grave gray beautiful eyes like Keral's, and their long flowing hair, and the ageless sureness in their hearts, resigned to the long slow fall of their last autumn, suddenly sensing the new spring and rebirth and knew that they, too, wheeled and danced in the overwhelming awareness of returning life and spring and a world reborn.

(And somewhere in a high hidden vantage point above the garden, Andrea too saw the madness of the dance whirl through the red-headed ones and even through senses blunted for centuries, felt the old madness of surging life and renewal, and stood paralyzed, caught up, anguished, with old throbbings beating through her life and battering at closed and agonizing doors. Caught in an anguish beyond endurance, clamped in fearful agony of remembrance and grief, she stood frozen, her eyes burning in silent and out-flooding fury. . . .)

The surging, flooding beat of the invisible music, the very life of the planet, the magnetic currents of the spring itself, beat in them all, wakening them to the total ecstasy of the world. Even the dying felt the call, life struggling and surging to reestablish itself through the prevalence of death and ruin on a planet struggling helplessly for survival. It was Regis in whom the surge of renewed life first reached explosive force of need; sudden, dark and mindless, it surged through him and he reached out, still blinded with the surging life of the gathering dance, and drew the girl at his side into his arms. Together, they sank down into the soft grass.

And then, spun away one by one from the wheeling dance of life, they moved together, sinking down in twos and threes. David, feeling the waves crest within him, breaking over his head, blind and dizzied with the madness of life, felt hands on his body, a whisper, was blindly conscious of an exquisite girl's face surrounded by masses of flaming hair. He felt himself drop out of the dance, sink into her arms. He was almost wholly unaware of movements or how it happened, but within what seemed seconds they were lying close together, naked on the warm moon-flooded grass. It was like madness, with the damp scent of flowers all around them both, and all around them in the night the sounds of love; kisses, murmurs, the final dropping down of the last dancers into silent groups, hot plunging fierceness, cries of supplication, hunger, content. He was caught up unknowing, moving in a blind and deaf need with the delicate strength of the girl's body in his arms.

And yet—blind? deaf? Or more aware than with all of his ordinary senses because he no longer used them? *Not me alone,* he knew, as for a timelessly brief and yet unending instant he blended into the familiar and intense sweetness of Keral transfigured by love (*Again, again, I am here with you, beloved*—); and then, as if the last garment had been swept away, leaving him wholly naked for the first time in his life, he found himself blending, swiftly and intensely, into the overwhelming life around him.

He felt, as he had never felt any touch before (although he knew beyond sight that she was at the far end of the garden, lying in Danilo's arms) Linnea's soft lips touch his face; felt yet again the wild sweetness of Keral, so well-known and eternally unfamiliar; sank into a momentary rapport with Jason, as his friend's hands closed violently over the breasts of an unknown girl; and then sank into fierce rapport with Regis (images, blurring even as he sensed them: of crossed swords; the meshing of wrists in the flying grip of aerialists; the violent and intensely sensuous struggle of wrestlers gripped in a hold more ardent than lovers). For an overwhelming and releasing moment, he sensed what it would be to let his own awareness of manhood disappear—had Keral had to face this mingling of grief, joy, and humiliation?—as his mind and body melted into that of an unknown girl, and he looked up into Regis' eyes at the very instant of surrender and consummation. Then David was back in his own body, the girl under him soft, pliant, demanding. And there was nothing else . . . and everything else . . . for a blind instant . . . forever . . . heat . . . explosion . . . slow subsiding waves . . . stars that spun and whirled inside and outside, and a world slowly darkening into silence.

Three seconds, or three hours later—none of them ever knew—David surfaced slowly, like coming up from a very deep dive. The girl's soft body was still cradled in his arms, her silken hair blinding his eyes. He stroked it softly and kissed it before brushing it away from his face, raised himself on his elbow, and looked into the startled and smiling face of Desideria. There was a moment of shock and amazement and instantaneous rearrangement of awareness, and then the memory of what had brought them together came back and David laughed. What did it matter? Age, or even sex, were at this moment, and to what they were, irrelevant. He saw the backlash of doubt and regret sweep the old woman's face; he laughed and kissed her and saw the fear dissolve. She said softly, in a whisper, "I have heard it said in old stories; what is done under the four joining moons is the will of the gods and outside what men would wish or desire. But

I have never known until this moment what was meant."

He smiled at her and clasped her hands. All around them, the garden was quiet with the soft murmurs of returning, separate, ordinary awareness. David reached about for his clothes, for it was chilly even in the spring, and felt like a dog who cocks his ears at a sound no man can hear. It was quiet and peaceful in the garden, but a nag of fright and sudden awareness kept jerking on an invisible nerve. He looked around with sudden apprehension, reached out for Conner.

David? I don't know, I don't like it—fireworks . . . for the first time in my life healed and happy . . . never again to drift alone, but even here, here . . .

Keral screamed suddenly, a wild cry of mingled terror and joy, as a faint burst of light moved in the garden, and eight or ten tall forms appeared out of the tingling air, tall and pale with silvery floating hair and great grave eyes that seemed to gleam of their own light. He ran toward them, moving sure-footed through the conjoined couples still lying in the grass, and was caught up in embrace after embrace, while David, staring in amazement, recognized and knew who they must be; the surviving chieri, appeared—as legend told man that they could appear—out of nothingness, come to see their youngest and their beloved in his moment of happiness and returning of life and hope. All around them, the workings of the ordinary world of night were beginning to return, and stirrings of wonder, of joy and amusement, and laughing chagrin, and a shared purpose too deep and real for ordinary words were returning. David knew, at too deep a level for speech (was it Regis who had cast the thought into the invisible net?), that nothing would ever again wholly separate the telepaths of Darkover; they might have separate purposes on the surface, but a potential lost or mislaid for years had returned; and as the chieri had been before them, they were a people at one with themselves and each other.

Keral was still laughing and murmuring with the joyousness of reunion. And yet beneath it all, an undercurrent of fear was beginning to run, like a palpable smell of danger. David felt the hairs on his body bristle. Danilo, putting Linnea gently aside, reached like a cat for his sword; no visible danger, pure instinct. Conner sprang to his feet.

And then, unmistakable, it was Rondo who yelled— or were there words?—a great cry of outrage and anguish:

No! I told you their plans because I wanted to get free of this world, but they have never harmed me, and I want no part in murder—

And a running figure which suddenly froze and rose upward, upward, physically upward through the thickening air, like a flying demon, surrounded with a glare of growing light. He seized something with a strange twisting gesture, in mid-air, and body and glowing thing rocketed upward, upward. . . .

In mid-air, thousands of feet above the castle, it burst like a great shower of fireworks; there was a silent scream of unbelievable pain and dying anguish and there was a ripped out silence, a great gaping toothache hole in the world where Rondo's thoughts and voice and mind had been. And then came the sound of the explosion, muffled by distance, far out in space and harmless, but still it rocked the castle, reverberated—and died away.

And then, in the midst of the chieri and surrounded by their light, stood a woman, wearing drab Empire clothes, struggling against the invisible force that had thrust her out of concealment and into the light; the look of sated and triumphant rage on her face giving way to fear, amazement, and disbelief.

I thought you were all dead. I did not know any of you had survived to return to this world, even to die.

"No." The voice of the eldest of the chieri, a tall and beautiful woman, ageless and beyond everything in man, was like a reverberation in the world. "We live, although not for long. But we cannot give death; we must give life for death—"

"Her name is Andrea," said the young, red-haired Free Amazon, rising from the garden darkness, "and I knew she would have destroyed us if she could, but I did not know—"

"No," said the old chieri again, with infinite grief and gentleness, speaking directly to Andrea. "We know you, even over these many, many turns of the years, Narzain-ye kui, child of the Yellow Forest, who abandoned us in despair during the years of our search. We mourned you as one long, long dead, beloved. . . ."

The face of the woman was drawn with agony and grief. "And I bore a child on one of the outer worlds, to a stranger whose name I never knew, or face I never saw—a child conceived in madness and thrown out to die, in madness, thinking you all dead and gone—"

"The long, long years of madness," Keral whispered, and took Andrea's face between his hands in infinite tenderness. She opened her spasmodically closed eyes and looked up at him, seeing the glow of heightened beauty, the infinite power which lay within Keral, the height of potential life. Keral said quietly:

"All is not ended. I live—and you see what has happened to me. Perhaps even the child you bore lives somewhere; we are hard to kill—" and his eyes briefly sought for Missy in the crowd, in speculation which could be read on the clear features. "But our race lives, Andrea, in these people; I knew even as a babe that our blood survived in them. And as you see—"

Keral's unearthly beauty seemed to shimmer, and for the first (and only) time, David perceived Keral for an instant as the exquisite girl he had at first thought Keral and in instantaneous recognition knew the truth; that the chieri showed the height of the Change, and full feminine awareness (Missy had only mimicked it) in pregnancy. And now he understood Keral's madness of joy, which had swept them all away—and saved them all; and probably saved a world as well.

And then, with trained medical awareness, forgetting that he was still half-naked, he leaped forward, catching Andrea in his arms as the aging chieri woman crumpled senseless to the ground.

Epilogue

The woman who for centuries had called herself Andrea Closson sat on a high balcony in the Comyn Castle at Thendara, looking out over green and faraway hills. The point of no return had been very nearly reached; and yet, as she told herself before, the world could be saved, but it had demanded resources which were not available on Darkover:

Except for herself.

She had not spared herself. Every scrap of talent which she had used, for two hundred years, in learning how to wreck worlds, had been thrown into the struggle to save one; and every cent of the enormous fortune it had made her had been placed at the disposal of those who were struggling on every front to return Darkover to itself. This world was her own, and had been miraculously returned to her when she knew that a handful of her people survived and that their blood survived in the very Darkovan telepaths she had despised. And now, as they awaited the birth of Keral's child, she knew it would remain, even though not a pure line.

The chieri might not survive. This alone could not return her race to strength and survival. They had, indeed, reached the point of no return. It was certain that Missy would never bear a child; she had been too deeply damaged and blunted in the hundreds of years of struggle for survival, abandoned. Andrea faced her own guilt, but it was as if it had happened to someone else; what is done in madness cannot be remembered in sanity without worse madness. Still, Keral lived, and Keral's child would live, bringing new vigor and new powers to the telepath race.

"And that's not all," said David, coming out on the balcony. He had a strange ability to follow Andrea's thoughts, and she had grown to love him in her own strange and hidden way. Jason, Regis, and Linnea were with him, and David said, "The telepaths here, at least, will not die out. Do you realize that—how many is it, Jason?"

"One hundred and one," Jason said, "that's women of the Telepath Council—pregnant. And at least nineteen of them with twins and three with triplets. That at least ensures a flourishing younger generation." He looked at Linnea, who laughed and took Regis' hand. She was very near her own time now, heavily pregnant but as beautiful as ever.

"We are going to work with the Empire," Regis said; "It was decided in council; Darkovans cannot cut themselves entirely off from a galactic civilization.

We will train telepaths for spaceship communication. We know, now, that contact with telepaths will arouse latent telepathy in those who don't seem to have it. I expect, from Darkover, it will spread out all through the known galaxy. And those who are born with it won't go insane, so that in a few more generations there will be a sizable leaven of telepaths on all planets; and we will bring them here, and train them to use their powers in sanity and happiness. And in return for this we have a pledge that Darkover will remain always the world we know, and love, and need for our continuing sanity and nourishment; never just another world in a chain of identical worlds."

David listened a moment, as if to an invisible voice; went away. Linnea, seeming to listen also, smiled and pressed Regis' hand. "It won't be long for me, either, now," she said.

Regis came and sat beside Andrea. She had aged greatly in the long months of struggle in the woods and mountains, working with close directions to save the ruined world; explicit instructions on how to restore soil to life, which trees to plant for the swiftest ground cover against erosion, what to do in every niche of the complex ecology. But her lined face was peaceful and gentle, and again she looked like a chieri, inspiring the old awe and love. He said: "What will you do now—" He hesitated, then called her by her chieri name, and she smiled:

"I await only the birth of Keral's child; then I will return to my own forest with my people, for the few last *cuere* allotted to me. But I will lay down my years content, knowing that if my own leaves fall, there will be new buds in the spring I will never see."

Regis reached out to touch her hand, and she clasped it, quietly. They sat there, looking out over the mists on the hills.

Linnea said, "You have given so much—"

Andrea smiled. "I do not need a fortune now."

"I wish you had come back before," Regis said, wrung with honest grief.

"Perhaps it would have been too soon," Andrea's calm voice was speculative. "In any case, I knew no longer where my own world lay. . . ."

"Those who hired you—what will they do? When Darkover does not fall ripe to their hands—"

"What can they do? To trap me, or even to claim my bond, they would have to admit they hired me, and worldwrecking is illegal. I think they will just admit their defeat. But now the Terran Empire knows exactly how they work; they will have a harder time wrecking other worlds."

There was a stir behind them, and Keral, pale and lovely, with David just behind, came out on the balcony. They came straight to Andrea, and Keral turned, took a small squirming thing from David's arms, and laid it in Andrea's.

Keral murmured, "Not for love, but because it means more to you than any other; look here and see a world reborn."

Andrea reached out and touched Keral's soft hair. "Yes," she said in a whisper, "for love."

David drew Keral away, and they stood clasped close, looking into the green world. They were both still bemused, not needing to look to see: still, the tiny, infinitely strange and beautiful scrap of a baby, with red-headed fuzz; the first of a second chain of telepaths with chieri blood. And it was their own stake in a newborn world. This had begun with a child in Keral's arms, the complex train of emotions and experiences, and David thought they would always have a debt to Melora and her child. Over Keral's shoulder he met Regis' eyes and smiled.

Andrea lay back, closing her eyes and yet seeing, without sight, a green and growing world, with life springing up from the soil, leaves falling from the trees and returning in endless cycle, rivers, valleys, mountains, surging with life, and beyond them the endless life of the silent forests of Darkover under the moon. Far away, like a distant song, she heard the music of her people in the forests of falling leaves, where they awaited her coming. Time would pass over them, and they would not return, but fall like leaves; but while Darkover lived they would never wholly die, and after them the very Empire would be seasoned with their memory, with their beauty and the eternal gift of bridging the gap between man and mankind; the gift that was love.

She smiled with her eyes closed, feeling the strong life and already budding sensitivity of the child in her arms; hearing the distant music, which rose and fell like wind in the leaves, and faded quietly into silence, like a falling breeze in the forest.

Not until Keral's child began to stir and fret and kick in her cold arms did any of the others realize that Andrea Closson, chieri, child of the Yellow Forest, worldwrecker and redeemer, had come home only to die.

THE WATERFALL

The lady Sybil-Mhari, fifteen years old and as frail as a branch of willow, stood at the edge of an enclosed courtyard, staring with pensive gray eyes into the valley, flooded with the strange moonlight of the four moons. A low wall of stone, barely knee-high, was the only thing dividing the court where she stood from a steep, sheer, and hazardous cliff that dropped away sharply to a raging, foaming torrent of white water that fell, nearly a thousand feet, into the valley. The muffled roar of water beneath her, and the cold moon-flooded night, cut through her with the dampness that rose from the waterfall far below, seemed to tremble hotly in her young body, twisting a thick lump in her throat, a feeling that was like hunger or thirst—or something else. . . . Something she could not even guess; a hunger, a loneliness, for something she had never known

Love? No. Her waiting-women chattered and squealed of love continually, whispering together, giggling confidences of stolen kisses and furtive touches, of seeking hands in the darkness, of courtly verses and songs. And for a little while Sybil had believed it was, indeed, love for which she hungered; but as confidences had grown more definite, they had evoked neither excitement nor longing, but only a shudder of disgust. What—she, Sybil-Mhari Aillard, *comynara,* the delicate and queenly little sister of the Lord Ludovic, lonely and perfect as a single star, to surrender herself to these hungry indecencies? She, born into the castle of Comyn, apart and above, bearing—so the common folk said—the blood of Gods, *she* to swoon in the arms of some clumsy esquire, to lend herself to secret kissings, fumbling fingers, whispered words of love, in corridor or hall or chapel? No. And no. The hunger that was in her was surely for something other than this; it was as a burning fire seeking fuel, and these huggings and clutchings were damp and commonplace, smothering instead of feeding the flame.

She looked down at the white water that coursed and plunged and raced, throwing up silvery spray so far beneath her that the water seemed all one whiteness in the moonlight, and suddenly imagined herself flying, falling through that vast space, into the race and torrent; whirled, battered, drowned—or would she, as some old legends said that the Comyn folk could do, put forth sudden wings, fly wingless far above the world, wheeling on hawk-pinions, looking down from far above. . . . But that was legend. Or dream. She hugged herself with thin bare arms and clutched dizzily at the wall, almost hypnotized by the tumult and sound of the distant waterfall. To fly, borne on invisible wings, or the secret powers of the Comyn, aloft, above everyone who sought to pin her down and keep her earthbound . . . but that was long ago. Legend.

Now the Comyn held only the powers of the mind, and even those she had been denied. The *leronis*, the great sorceress of Hastur blood, had called Sybil to her but this year, had made her look into the starstone, so that Sybil felt she stood more naked than if the woman had stripped from her the last garment, feeling the touch of the *leronis* on her mind. Sybil had stood unflinching, not daring to show fear; but inside her something cowered and wept and could not raise its eyes, and at last the *leronis* had sighed and put away the stone. "You have *laran*, my child; you bear the Gift of our clan. And yet . . ." the woman sighed again, and shook her head. "There is a power in you, Sybil, that I do not understand; and yet I had thought I knew all the Gifts of Comyn. You are telepath—not greatly, but enough. You could be trained in a Tower; could wield all the power of a *leronis*, perhaps a Keeper. Yet something in me—something I have come to trust—says . . . *no*."

Sybil had protested, "Why, lady?" There was a sullen anger in her. The women of the Towers wielded power and force, they used the trained powers of the mind—all other women of the Comyn were powerless, given in marriage and forced to bear children for their clan, but wielding no power of their own . . . and the *leronis* would deny her this! Rage had surged in her, but she made her voice sweet and docile as she had been taught, and murmured, in the voice that her brother Ludovic, lord of the clan, had said was like the gentle murmuring of a green rainbird, "Why, lady? I am *comynara*, I have *laran*, you yourself have said it . . . why?"

But the Hastur sorceress only shook her head, meeting Sybil's eyes with a flash that told the girl that the older woman knew, and did not fear, all of her hidden rage. She said, "Because your mind is not the mind of a woman, Sybil; it holds something other than *laran*. I do not know what it is, but I fear it; and I fear you; and I will not have you in a Tower. If you are to master the craft of the starstones, if you are to wield all the ancient powers of the Comyn, I must know, absolutely, that you are to be trusted. So I say no."

And then Sybil had raised her eyes and glared at the woman and had thrust forth a power she did not know was in her, to seize the woman, to compel her will upon her—*I will have this power.* The woman had pushed her mind away easily, and had shaken her head with a sad laugh. "You see, my poor child? I do not fear you as you are now; but I fear what you might be, wielding the craft of the starstones." And she had gone away, taking with her Sybil's young foster-sister Rohana, to be brought to the Tower and trained in the craft of the starstones, and Sybil had been left here to loneliness, and hunger, and melancholy, and the aching need of something . . . something, she could not guess what it might be. . . .

After a long time, aware that she was cramped and chilled to the bone, she straightened and slowly turned away. Behind her lay the Comyn Castle, a great and sprawling mass of stone and echoing silence; the empty courtyards gave resonant sighs as her silk-shod feet whispered on the flagstones, and even her own breathing seemed to stir an echoing murmur. The icy cold of the stones crept up her stiffened legs and throbbed in her breasts. From very far away Sybil heard a halt, a clash, a challenge, the echo of ringing steps and silence; the Guardsmen were making their nightly rounds. Hurrying her steps a little, she slipped shadowlike under an archway, sheltering against the chilly night breeze; then she started, catching her hands to her throat with a little squeak of surprise as a light, thrust abruptly forward, rayed harshly across her face.

Half blinded, she pressed her fingers over her eyes; then as her pupils slowly adjusted to the light, she lowered her hands to see a man's face above the crude flare of the lantern.

"Well, now! Look what I found!"

Sybil shrank back as the unfamiliar face spread into a wide grin. The voice was deep and harsh, almost hoarse, but it sounded good-natured. "What are you doing here, you?"

The spreading light was less painful to Sybil's eyes now. She could distinguish black leather straps on a green cloak; one of the Guardsmen who came from their homes, at Council season, to guard the Comyn lords and ladies. She had seen them from time to time; they bowed deeply as she passed, and lowered their eyes in humility when, as sometimes happened, she spoke some condescending word or gave some minor command. But this was one she had never seen before—and never before had one of them dared to address her uninvited, by so much as a word.

She said coldly, "Go about your business, fellow."

"Easy there, wench," the man chuckled. "My business is right here, see; finding out who goes in and out of this court. What's yours?"

Sybil's small white teeth clamped in her lip. It would be too humiliating to identify herself to this . . . this roughneck! She saw that he was a thickset man, with a heavy neck and burly broad shoulders, and his grin, through the untidily sprouting whiskers, showed very long, strong white teeth like a horse's!

"I live here," she said shortly.

The man laughed. "And so do a dozen other women, but I'll take your word for it. Come, give us a kiss, *chiya*, and I'll let you go." He bent and deliberately set the lantern on the ground, then deliberately stepped toward her, and Sybil—too frozen in astonishment to move—felt his rough hands on her bare arms. The hoarse, chuckling voice was very close to her ear.

"Who were you looking for, girl; won't I do instead?"

Paralyzed, a horrid sick emptiness clawing inside her belly, Sybil felt the rough arms around her waist, felt her feet leave the ground as he caught her up bodily against his chest, and the stubbled face scraped hard against her soft cheek. For a moment she hung limp, unable to move a muscle—this *couldn't* be happening! Then, in a convulsion of terror, she exploded like a frantic cat, arching backward, silently clawing at her captor. She opened her mouth to scream, but her dry throat would give voice only to a little whimper of terror.

"Take it easy, hell-cat!" the strange voice muttered in the half-dark. She felt rough and weathered fingers searching the silks and ribbons that confined her breast, and her voice came back in a choking scream.

"Put me down! How dare you? You'll be flayed alive for this!"

Something in her imperious command, even through the shrillness of hysteria, came through to the man, and he set her abruptly on her feet, snatching up the lantern. "Zandru's hells," he swore, "*Who are you?*"

She swayed as he released her, dizziness blurring her eyes, and caught for support at the rough stonework, steadying herself with a hand flattened against the wall. Her voice sounded high and strange in her own ears.

"I am Sybil-Mhari Aillard," she said hoarsely, "and the Lord Ludovic will have the skin stripped from your body in ribbons an inch wide!"

"Domna!" The man's voice was husky and disbelieving. He said protestingly, "But . . ." and he sagged
and leaned back. A curious little stab, like a cramp in
her belly, sharp but somehow not unpleasant, suddenly weakened Sybil's knees again as she contem-
plated his whitening face. He stared, gulped audibly
once or twice. After a moment he managed to collect
himself somewhat, the hoarse voice was puzzled and
apologetic, but if Sybil had expected him to cringe—
and she had—she was oddly disappointed.

"My lady, I must beg your forgiveness. I took you
for a serving-girl—and what in the name of the
Blessed Cassilda," he finished rationally, "are you
doing, my lady, out here in the courtyard in the night
air, in your smock like any wench from the kitchens?"

Sybil blinked, put oddly on the defensive. She
started to say, I wanted to look at the waterfall, but
then she realized she need not explain herself to a
common Guardsman! The doings of a Comyn lady
were no concern of his! He was holding the lantern
close to her face, and his own features emerged more
clearly—rough-cut and bronzed, an old scar seaming
his cheek, but with twinkling eyes that even now
looked good-humored. His breath was none too
steady as he said, "Well, my little lady, it's perfectly
sure I'd be buzzard meat if you wanted to make trouble for me, but you wouldn't do a thing like that,
would you? I meant no harm, you know, and after all,
who'd expect the Lady Sybil-Mhari to be roaming
about the courtyard after moonrise?" His smile was

coaxing, almost intimate. "I can only say I'm sorry—
or maybe I'm not," he finished suddenly. "If you'd not
told me who you were, maybe I'd have wanted more
than a kiss, and taken it too!"

Sybil swayed slightly, feeling—as she had felt
when she looked into the starstone—the strange alien
touch against her mind . . . *Desire* . . . *Fear*. . . . His hot
eyes were still fastened on her, searching through the
untied ribbons at her bosom, but hesitant, somehow
held back . . . *fear*. She could feel his fear . . . and the
desire, burning into her, burning *through* her . . . he
dared not touch her now. . . .

She swayed slightly, and, this time without apology, he put his arms behind her shoulders, bent to
support her light weight.

She whispered, "I feel . . . faint . . ." and let herself
fall limp against him, her head dropping pliantly into
the hollow of his shoulder; she could feel the slow
pounding of his heart through her jerkin, she could
feel . . . she buried her forehead still more closely into
the heat of him. *There is a power in you*, the *leronis* had
said. Now, feeling its surge, she knew what lay behind
his fear and desire; her hands felt icy cold, and, shivering, she caught one of his warm ones and pressed it
to her throat.

"I . . . I can't breathe," she whispered, making her
voice soft, beguiling. She made sure, before releasing
his hand, that he would not be able to let her go again.
She closed her eyes, as he lifted her; hung suspended,
it seemed, swaying between air and fire, and felt

again the strange ecstatic sensation of hurling, tumbling, flying, falling—the waterfall roaring beneath.

When she opened her eyes, he had laid her down in a sheltered grass-plot opening from one of the courtyards and was kneeling beside her, his rough hands working, with deft blunt motions, on the ribbons imprisoning her breast. She breathed deeply and whispered, "Now I feel better—I don't know what happened to me. . . ." But when he would have drawn his hands hesitantly away again, she captured and held them.

"No, no . . . don't let me go," she begged, feeling the cold, emptiness surge back again. She was frightened, sick with the fear she felt in him, and yet compelled by something more powerful still, something building. . . . She did not know what it was, was it only this? Then his arms were around her again, disbelieving, hungry, gentle, and his mouth forcing her lips apart.

It was strange, shaking and strange, the surge and tremble that overwhelmed her. Never before had she known any touch like this; the fumbling and sweatily respectful hand-kiss of her cousins, the cold fatherly hand of the Lord of the Domain on her brow, the giggling embrace of her girl-companions—nothing like this rough hunger, so tender for all its fierceness. "My little lady," he whispered huskily, against her throat. "You don't even know what it is you want, do you?"

No. But I will know, I will. . . . The memory spun in her, *there is a power in you, and I fear it . . .* but could it be only this, only this? She fastened her mouth to his, biting savagely at his stiff lips, struggling furiously—not in protest, but in eagerness, against the gentle pressure of his hands. There was a writhing, a straining, a moment of agony; she felt the dew damp on her back, icy cold through the thin silk of her dress, his heavy rough hairiness drowning her silken breasts. She twisted and fought, not with any desire to escape, but rather in the same savage determination with which she fought to grip an untamed horse with her thin thighs, the same grim conflict with which she struggled to hood an unruly falcon. She knew what was happening to him, she knew what was happening to her, but it was not what she thought, it was only a beginning, as she felt all his fear, respect, hesitation, sink down and die beneath the growing urgency, need, hunger. . . .

She pushed away his hot kisses as the man's spent breathing hissed past his parted teeth, and sat up, re-tying her shoulder-ribbons with flying fingers. Was this the final ineffable joy, the delight immeasurable, about which the other maidens squealed and whispered? She pushed his hand away when he would have assisted her, her whole body flinching in revulsion. She felt bruised and shaken, and she clenched her teeth tight to keep them from chattering. She broke into his whispered stream of endearments with a quick, shaken, "Take me back—they will be looking for me."

He raised her gently, as he might pick up a child

who has stumbled, and she drew a deep breath, something . . . she hardly knew what . . . growing to swift birth inside her tight, throbbing breasts, her bruised and aching body. She forced herself to conceal her shaking, and to smile up at him, then leaned her head hard against his encircling arm and murmured with deliberate pathos, "You must take me back—I am almost a prisoner, you know."

He supported her faltering steps, half carrying her, whispering, "Yes, yes, my little silken bird, my little flower." He paused at the edge of the archway, retrieving his lantern from its hiding-place, and looked at her, saying hesitantly, "Little lady, you cannot return like this!"

In the crude light Sybil looked down at her crushed and torn ribbons, her crumpled and stained dress, tasting the blood on her lips with a slow satisfaction. She touched her tangled coppery curls with exploring fingers as he persuaded, "Come, little one, smooth your dress, let me fasten your sash. No one must see you like this!" There was fear in him again, and she could feel it like a taste in her mouth. Sybil tilted her head to one side, then heard the sound for which, without knowing it until this moment, she had been waiting. The clash of pikes, the ringing step and the challenge. She clenched her small fists, feeling her breath roughen and catch in her throat, smiling up at him.

"Must they not?" she murmured, then suddenly

whirled, breaking away from him, and cried out imperiously, "Guard! Guard, to me!"

"What . . ." the man took a backward step; booted feet, running, echoed in harsh sequence on the flagstones and an explosion of lights burst in their faces; the face of a steel-capped Guard—*Blessed Cassilda be thanked! It's a Guard who knows me by sight!*—thrust through the archway and a startled voice gasped, "Lady Sybil-Mhari!"

She pointed, with a dramatic gesture, feeling the frightening power surge up inside her. "Kill him!" she commanded, and heard her voice breaking on what she herself would have taken for a wild sob of shame and fright, if she had heard it from another throat. She could almost see herself reflected in the Guard's eyes, in his mind, swollen lips oozing a trace of bitten blood, the loosened ribbons falling to show her bruised breast, the skirt torn to show a hint of narrow thighs. The Guard spat out a cry of dismay and horror, shouting to his confederates; Sybil turned away, modestly mantling her face with her hair, as a second Guard appeared behind the first and his face echoed all the changes she had seen in the first. A tiny smile of contempt trembled on Sybil's lips, but she made it into a piteous grimace, widening her eyes as she looked down at the man in whose arms she had lain only a few minutes ago. She whispered pathetically, "The Lord Ludovic must never know—my honor is in your hands—but how can it be? But if he were . . . somehow . . . to fall into the waterfall. . . ."

And now she saw the blanching of terror, the whitening of nostril and jaw, as the man's eyes sought hers in wild entreaty.

"Lady . . . little lady . . ." he gasped helplessly, and his hoarse and husky voice, as when he had whispered endearments, sent a thrill of warmth through her.

There is a power in you . . . and I fear it . . . oh, she thought ecstatically, *if the Hastur sorceress could only know . . . she would have robbed me of this. . . .*

She watched the Guards seize the man, expertly pinion his arms; followed like a shadow, hugging herself with her thin arms, on the crest of rising excitement, as they hustled him rudely toward the cliff. He was shouting now, hoarse indecencies, until one of the Guards shoved a hand over his mouth. They struggled briefly at the wall, and suddenly Sybil felt a wild thrill surging through her body. It knifed hotly through her breasts, overwhelming as a kiss; stabbed fluid warmth all through her, gripped her thighs in a vise of pleasure. She gasped, her breath jolting out on the cresting heat of it, and cried aloud in unbearable delight as the man's figure tottered on the ledge, clawed wildly at the air, flailed, and disappeared. Sybil sank down in the grass, breathing in heavy sobs, knowing now what was the true power, the joy of love—vaguely, in her overwhelming surge of emotion, she wondered what his name had been, how she could discover his name. She would remember it always in her prayers for the dead, the name of the one who had released the power within her, had brought her to fulfillment. She became aware that one of the Guards was bending solicitously over her. She was too spent to rise; she let him lift her, leaning heavily on his arm, swaying helplessly.

"Lady Sybil," he said gently, "your honor, and your secret, are forever safe with me. I will conduct you safe to the women's quarters; see you only that your maids do not gossip, and this night's work shall never be known." He guided her tottering steps with reverent hands. "Poor little lady, if I had been at hand, that beast, that disgrace to the Guards and their honor, had never dared lay his hands on you . . ."

She lowered her long lashes. "What is your name? I would thank my . . . my preserver in my prayers, before I sleep."

"Reuel, my lady."

"Reuel. I shall . . . remember," she whispered. She would not make that mistake again. "You will not find me . . . ungrateful." Again the unendurable pleasure gusted up through her as she saw his thin swarthy face go foolish and soft with a sudden, incredible hope. She murmured, "I often walk in the courtyard here. Will you protect me?"

"With . . . with my very life, Lady," he stammered, and she looked at him and smiled. With him the terror need not strike till she had fed on the desire for a day or two, and the fear, and the hope . . . till she had fed herself full. Now that she knew her power, she could wait for her pleasure.

She smiled, with the drunken joy of a woman who has discovered true love, and ran lightly up the stairway toward her chamber.

Marion Zimmer Bradley
& Deborah Ross

A Flame in Hali
A Novel of Darkover

On Darkover, it is the era of the Hundred Kingdoms—a time of nearly continuous war and bloody disputes, a time when Towers are conscripted to produce terrifying laran weapons—weapons which kill from afar, poisoning the very land itself for decades to come. In this terrifying time of greed and imperialism, two powerful men have devoted their lives to changing their world and eliminating these terrible weapons. For years King Carolin of Hastur and his close friend, Keeper Varzil Ridenow, have dreamed of a world without war. But another man, Eduin Deslucido, hides in the alleys of Thendara, tormented by a spell so powerful it haunts Eduin's every waking moment—a spell of destruction against Carolin Hastur... and all of his clan.

To Order Call: 1-800-788-6262
www.dawbooks.com

DARKOVER

Marion Zimmer Bradley's Classic Series

Now Collected in New Omnibus Editions!

Heritage and Exile
0-7564-0065-1
The Heritage of Hastur & Sharra's Exile

The Ages of Chaos
0-7564-0072-4
Stormqueen! & Hawkmistress!

The Saga of the Renunciates
0-7564-0092-9
The Shattered Chain, Thendara House
& City of Sorcery

The Forbidden Circle
0-7564-0094-5
The Spell Sword & The Forbidden Tower

A World Divided
0-7564-0167-4
The Bloody Sun, The Winds of Darkover
& Star of Danger

To Order Call: 1-800-788-6262

www.dawbooks.com